demiGod

JA Laflin

Agnec Press
P.O. Box 1875
Beaverton, OR 97075
www.jalaflin.com/agnec-press

demiGod is a work of fiction. Names, characters, places, and incidents are either the product of the author's imagination or are used fictitiously. Any resemblance to actual persons, living or dead, events, or locations is entirely coincidental.

ISBN: 0692381058

ISBN-13: 978-0692381052

LOCCN: 2015901868

First Edition

10 9 8 7 6 5 4 3 2 1

To Elias,
whose imagination is insatiable and whose creativity knows no
bounds.

CONTENTS

ACKNOWLEDGMENTS

With so much time and effort that has gone into making this book a reality, it is hard to thank and acknowledge everyone that truly should be. But I will start by thanking Brittany, whose patience and support I may have completely pushed to a breaking point, but nonetheless, without her I would not have finished the book.

A special thanks: To those who supported my funding efforts on IndieGoGo.com, especially Matthew Hickey, whose donation went to good use; To Brenda Errichiello, my awesome editor, for her invaluable input and work; To Ryan Spencer and Joel Lux, for their input and support; To Brian Matekovich and fam; To the Hypertrophic Cardiomyopathy Association, for allowing me to contribute to their cause with my work; Last, but never least, to Aaron Loften and Tiffany Gilman, for believing in my story back when it was a lowly webcomic (it's come a long way since then!). To everyone else, thank you!

Part I

Prologue:
The Burning

Aiden stared into the flames and could not believe that this had happened again. The fire ate away at the hanging tapestry, while dark smoke cascaded into the ceiling of the auditorium. The palms of Aiden's hands were still warm from producing the fire.

John stammered in disbelief, looking rapidly back and forth between Aiden and the flames. Aiden already knew what John was thinking. John had been threatening to pummel Aiden just moments before, but now the tall boy was speechless and wide-eyed. He finally managed to utter something unintelligible, clasping his closely-shaven head and looking wildly around.

John raced from the room, his sneakers squeaking and echoing chaotically on the flooring. Aiden felt glued to the spot. He released a sigh of exasperation and blinked uncontrollably for a moment. When the blinking had subsided, he realized that people were rushing into the room and gasping at the fire.

Shouts filled the expanse and bounced off the walls. Someone told the others to remain calm, but Aiden heard a handful of feminine shrieks from somewhere behind him. The flames had crawled to the top of the hanging by now and were sprawling along the fabric connecting the other tapestries. What once had been a symbol of school pride now hung as a smoldering hodgepodge of threads and charred materials.

A firm hand landed on Aiden's shoulder. It was Principal Sevalis.

Aiden said nothing, especially in light of the man's firm demand that Aiden follow him. The principal was a rotund man who always wore striped jackets, and when his mustache twitched—as it did now—students knew the man was serious. Aiden trailed the principal out of the auditorium and into the hall, keeping his own small frame in the large man's shadow even as crowds began to gather around the fire. Principal Sevalis' eyes were furious, and he reached around to grab Aiden by the collar. They were now side by side. They continued on in silence, and the man only stopped to bark commands to teachers passing by. He was letting the others deal with the emergency, and Aiden prepared himself for what he knew would come next.

In moments, Aiden found himself in a seat against the wall, just across from the school receptionist. After his face had grown a shade of red, the principal told Aiden to wait. After a moment, Aiden heard the principal talking to someone inside his office, then came the clack of the receiver, abruptly ending with a small ding.

All was quiet behind the Principal's closed door, so all Aiden could do was wait.

Aiden might have been more upset or even scared, if this sort of thing hadn't already happened at two other schools within the last couple of years.

He observed the scene just outside the large office windows. Firemen rushed through the hall, followed by teachers. Finally a handful of police followed. A whirlwind of energy and commotion could be heard from somewhere beyond the outside hallway. Aiden buried his face in his hands and could only hope it would soon be over.

The minutes seemed to drag on, but in record time, Aiden saw his mother's face come through the office door. She was somewhat tall with a calming presence, despite her troubled expression. She rushed to Aiden's side, sweeping her auburn hair away from her pale complexion. Despite how much her features greatly contrasted with Aiden's olive-toned skin and dark hair, there was no doubting their connection to each other.

"Are you alright?" his mother asked, her face more wrinkled with worry than usual.

"Yeah, I guess," Aiden said, maintaining his indifference.

"But the firetrucks and the police..."

Aiden stood as his mother forced her arms around him. "Yeah, I know," he said with a sigh. "I, uh, caught a tapestry on fire. This time, I swear it wasn't on purpose."

His mother broke their embrace and glared at him.

"You've only got a month left of school," she said, disappointment dripping from her words. "We'll figure it out. But what am I going to do with you?"

Aiden shook his head and sat back down. He didn't care to recall how many times he'd heard her utter that phrase.

His mother sat next to him and grabbed his face, her brown eyes searching his. "I just don't know what to do," she said, her eyes turning glassy. "You and I have to figure out how to control this thing."

Aiden averted his gaze and remained silent, pulling free from her grasp.

"I don't know if this changes anything," Aiden's mother muttered, her forehead wrinkling in anger. "But no more TV, music, or video games for a month."

"Seriously?" Aiden snapped, as if broken out of a trance. "That's all I have left."

His mother threw him a piercing look. "Aiden Gailhart," she said through clenched teeth, glancing back to make sure the receptionist was not paying them too much attention. "What am I supposed to do? I've tried everything, haven't I? Until we get this thing figured out... This—thing that you do—until you can learn some self-control... I mean, who else can start fires—"

By now, she was so upset that Aiden leaned back, unsure if she would scream or cry. Her thoughts no longer seemed coherent.

"Fine," Aiden finally responded, moved by his mother's emotion. "I'll do what I have to do I guess... But you would punish me on my birthday?"

His mother straightened up and almost laughed, dabbing at her eyes. "It's not your birthday," she said, maintaining a serious tone. "Not yet anyway."

"Dammit."

"Watch your language," his mother chided him. "Anyway, how could I forget your fifteenth birthday? I'm your mother. Of course, you will be spending it grounded with none of your toys..."

Aiden groaned and rolled his eyes.

"He threatened to kill me," Aiden said, watching his mother's eyes dart to the principal's door. "John threatened to kill me this time."

"Kids say all kinds of things they don't mean," his mother replied somewhat casually despite Aiden's somber tone.

"I don't need this place anyway," Aiden sighed. "It's bad enough that they're always calling me a gook."

His mother's head snapped back in Aiden's direction. "You listen," she began with a ferocious gleam in her eyes. "If all you do is care about what others say—I don't care how terrible it is—you'll never get past who they think you are. You'll never be who you're supposed to be."

Aiden sat silently, surprised by his mother's reaction.

"Understand?"

Aiden nodded, feeling as though he were a child again.

His mother stood, straightened up her skirt, and asked the receptionist if the principal was ready to see her now. The receptionist nodded. Aiden slumped back in his chair, wishing he had a hat or something to pull down over his face.

"Wish me luck," his mother said in a sardonic tone.

"It's your favorite part," Aiden muttered, staring straight ahead with an empty gaze.

Chapter 1
Of Agnees and Amblers

In all of Aiden's fifteen summers, he couldn't remember
a hotter couple of months in Philadelphia. His bedroom was
sweltering, despite the fan oscillating at full blast. He had already
resorted to wearing his white undershirt, which was more of a
long tank top, and still he could hardly take the heat. He decided
the best thing to do was not move.

So far, this idea had seemed to work a little, and he stretched
out on his bed, his back soaked in sweat. Beats were emanating
from the stereo on Aiden's dresser as he listened to the latest rap
CD. He tried only thinking of the music, but there were far too
many other things to think of.

Most of them were things he really didn't want to think of.

Despite how school was no longer in session, the events of last
year still taunted him. Once word got out that he was different, it
was a sure sign that he would end up at some other school. Some
other school in some other neighborhood, and his mother would
have to drive out of her way to get him there. Sometimes he
hated that the most.

Some of the guys from school, including John, had caught
him at the store just this morning. They would not let him forget
about the fire.

Aiden wasn't sure how to explain it, but something strange sometimes happened when he felt intense emotion. His hands would swell and burn, and his heart would pound until the compulsion to rid himself of this energy was far more important than anything else. Flames would leap from his hands in bright balls, slamming into anything in their path.

He was very thankful he had never actually hit anybody with one of these energy balls, as he called them, but he had done a fair bit of property damage. Although, when he saw the leering faces of his accusers in his mind, he could almost feel that burning sensation all over again.

"Screw them anyway..." Aiden said, staring at the popcorn-patterned asbestos ceiling.

A knock on the door interrupted his thoughts, and his mother popped her head inside the room. She smiled, but her eyes were tired and her hair was pulled back in a rather rushed fashion.

"Honey?" she said, glaring at the stereo. "Can you turn this down?"

Aiden sighed and rolled his eyes. It took all of his energy just to pry himself off of his bed and reach over to turn down the volume. When he was done, his mother smiled again.

"Someone's here to see you," his mother said.

Aiden's face wrinkled in confusion. "Who?"

"Come on out and see."

"Who is it?" Aiden asked, refusing to move.

"Someone's here from the school I was telling you about."

Aiden grimaced and his shoulders tensed. "That reform school?"

"It's not a reform school," his mother hissed. "Now get out here."

Aiden stood up, clicked off the stereo, and begrudgingly followed his mother out of the room and into the short hallway. Being not very tall himself, he couldn't see past his mother in the narrow space, though he tried. There, in the small living room, Aiden stopped, taken aback.

Before them stood a tall, bearded man with strikingly blue eyes. His long trench coat made Aiden think of those old mob movies he used to watch on late night television.

"Mister Pestler," Aiden's mother addressed the man. "This is Aiden." She gestured to her son. "Why don't you two sit down?"

"Thank you, Lisa," the man said, his voice strong. "Please, call me Vodin. In the Agnec world, everyone tends to be on a first-name basis."

Aiden's mother nodded in agreement, ignoring Aiden's lost expression. Vodin smiled at the woman, then turned his attention to the boy.

Aiden shrugged. He sat down on their old couch while the older man sat across from him on a floral-patterned armchair. Vodin seemed far too comfortable, making Aiden squirm in his seat.

Vodin looked away for a moment, watching Aiden's mother step into the kitchen, but then returned his full attention to the boy.

"Aiden," the man said, his kind eyes taking in the boy's discomfort. "I am Headmaster of the Mount Katahdin Guild School for D'Tari. Your mother's told me a lot about what you're going through."

Aiden was silent, feigning a look of disinterest. He tried to ignore the school's very strange sounding name. He tried to ignore the almost hypnotic effect of the man's youthful blue eyes.

"I hear you've had some trouble at school," Vodin continued, his mouth almost curling in a whimsical smile. "As did I, in the olden days."

Aiden almost smiled, but caught himself. Despite the beard, the man did not look old enough to talk of "olden days".

Aiden's mother returned and handed Aiden and Vodin each a tall glass of lemonade Vodin nodded in appreciation, looking weary in his trench coat.

"Aren't you uncomfortable in that coat?" Aiden's mother asked the man.

Vodin nodded. "Yes, I suppose I am. I hadn't thought about it."

Aiden placed his glass of lemonade on the old coffee table, unsure how cool it was to be drinking lemonade. It seemed like such a little kid's drink to him. Then again, he could feel the sweat gluing his back to the couch... He picked up his glass again and drank deeply.

When he was done, Aiden looked over and realized Vodin had

taken off his long trench-coat. Aiden's brown eyes widened at the sight.

Once Vodin had gently laid his trench coat over the puffy arm of his chair, it was revealed that he wore a kind of suit. It was a casual suit, and looked liked something men wore a long time ago, perhaps in the early nineteen-hundreds, or even before. Aiden couldn't even be sure. He just knew that he'd only seen this sort of thing in movies.

Vodin wore a green sleeveless vest with a high-collared white shirt beneath it, the sleeves of the shirt neatly rolled up just above his elbows. Aiden raised an eyebrow at the Headmaster's pants, which were somewhat tight, tan trousers that tucked into tall leather boots. He averted his gaze, trying to hide his amusement.

Maybe he's one of those historical reenactment weirdos, Aiden wondered.

"Where were we?" Vodin said, looking back to the boy after Aiden's mother had left the room once more. "You've noticed my clothes, I see."

Aiden's eyes snapped back to Vodin's face, his cheeks turning pink.

Vodin smiled. "No matter. It is all part of the culture clash I suppose," he said. "As I was saying, your mother tells me you've been in some trouble."

"I guess..."

"It's alright. Most of us do, when we realize we have something that others don't."

Aiden's face had gone blank.

"I hear you can make fire," Vodin said, his tone matter-of-fact. "Energy, more explicitly. Raw energy that bursts into flame whenever it impacts upon something."

Aiden knew that he looked guilty, but he said nothing. Why would his mother have actually told someone about that?

"No. I can't do that," Aiden mumbled, shaking his head.

"You set something on fire in your school auditorium, I believe..."

Aiden could only stare at the floor.

"It's alright," Vodin said, smiling at Aiden. "So can I. It was one of the first things I realized I could do."

There was a moment of silence as Aiden tried to imagine what Vodin had meant.

"It won't be easy to hear this, but bear with me," Vodin continued. "I belong to an ancient order called the D'Tari. We all have the abilities you have, and in fact, many more. We train children like you at the Mount Katahdin Guild, and help them discover their abilities."

Aiden was listening, his mind exploding with questions.

"Wait," Aiden said, looking around the room as if wondering where the camera crew was. "There's others who can do... what I can do?"

Vodin smiled. "Of course. And more."

"This can't be real."

"I know this can be shocking at first," Vodin said, his tone calm. "So I suppose it's good you're sitting down. I feel I should explain to you some of the basics right now, because, well..." Vodin stopped and made eye contact with Aiden. "You've never had the chance to know."

Aiden wasn't sure how he should feel about that, but he said nothing and simply shrugged.

"The world is full of two kinds of people —for lack of a better way to put this: The Agnecs and the Amblers."

Aiden raised an eyebrow.

"It's a long story, a very long one," Vodin continued. "But I have reason to believe you come from a long line of people whose ancestry belongs in the Old World, a place called Aignesia. Don't bother trying to look it up on any maps of course; It's not there anymore. The Old Worlders are people like you and me, and others, whom you'll also meet. Nowadays, we tend to call ourselves Agnecs. And as for all the New Worlders, we call them Amblers."

"Why?" Aiden cut in, his curiosity getting the best of him. "Why Amblers?"

"It's a very old word," Vodin said, almost laughing to himself. "I think lore has it that Agnecs saw New Worlders as sort of purposeless. Just... Ambling about. It may not be the nicest perception in the world, but it's a name that has stuck, nevertheless."

"So... I'm an Agnec?" Aiden said, trying to keep it all straight in his mind. "You think my family comes from the Old World?"

"Well, yes. At least on one side, it would seem," Vodin replied. "But in this new world, there are Amblers, Agnecs, and D'Tari. Now some Agnecs can be D'Tari, but no D'Tari can ever be Amblers. And you, sir, are D'Tari."

Aiden was speechless, his thoughts overwhelming him. He found himself smiling, to his own surprise.

"The point is," Vodin continued, searching Aiden's face. "That I am thinking I would like you to attend the Guild this year, although I have a little more investigating to do first."

"And this school stuff," Aiden began, his throat getting dry. "I mean, you'll teach me about my powers?" It sounded strange, talking about his powers to someone other than his mother.

Vodin nodded.

"And exactly who are the D'Tari?"

"I suppose we're many things," Vodin replied, looking thoughtful. "Many of us are guardians. Guardians of what's left of Agnec culture and way of life... And I don't want you to get your hopes up, but many times, the burden falls on us to help out the Amblers as well—though such things must be done covertly."

"Like police, or FBI, or something?"

"Deeper than that I'm afraid," Vodin said, his eyes alive as if reliving bitter-sweet adventures. "We are an elite order, Aiden. There are D'Tari all over the world. Though the ranks seem to thin every year, it is our duty to help protect Agnecs and their communities. Because the average Agnec won't have the powers you and I possess. In the past, D'Tari have protected kings and helped tear down tyrants."

"Protect?" Aiden blurted out. "Can I learn to fight?"

"Only if it becomes necessary." Vodin gave the boy a stern look. "We teach defense and technique, but that is least of what we offer. I came here tonight because your mother has told me about your powers, and the problems they have caused.'

"Aiden," Vodin continued, leaning forward and looking into the boy's eyes. "Do you understand what I'm telling you?"

"I think so..." Aiden said, his mind racing. "Agnec is the bloodline thing from the Old World, right? And you think I'm one of them."

Vodin nodded.

"But my powers make me a D'Tari. Just like part of a special group."

"If you decide to come to the Guild, yes," Vodin said, looking pleased. "You will be D'Tari."

"So I do have a choice whether or not to come," Aiden said. "I thought I was being shipped off somewhere..."

"I don't believe your mother would do that to you," Vodin said, looking around the quiet living room. Aiden's mother was still in the other room. "Your mother came to me with a difficult proposition. She doesn't know what else to do, and frankly, I don't think you do either."

Aiden sighed and looked to the floor.

"There's very little the Ambler world has to offer someone like you, Aiden," Vodin said, his tone calming. "At least at the Guild, we can help you find your place in a society that you can contribute to. We can help you put your abilities to good use. We don't just teach powercasting... You'll learn the history and lore of your ancient roots; the properties of the Elves and Dwarves; scrying, healing, prophecy... We even teach the arts, and many other things."

Aiden looked up. "Powercasting?"

"It's what you've been doing with your hands," Vodin explained.

"And did you just say Elves and Dwarves?" Aiden said, before he'd even had time to digest Vodin's answer.

"Yes." Vodin laughed. "Did I not mention them before?"

Aiden shook his head. He looked down again, his heart pounding from a strange mix of excitement and bewilderment.

"Look, I know it's a lot to think about," said Vodin, struggling to get out of the armchair. "Before I leave here today, I have to evaluate your abilities. So let's focus on that."

Aiden nodded, for lack of a coherent thought. He also stood up and now faced the man directly. Vodin placed a hand on Aiden's shoulder. It was much gentler than the firm hand of Principal Sevalis, and Aiden felt a strange comfort in that.

Vodin smiled again. "We can help you discover what it is you need to be," he said. "Because you and I, we're made of the same stuff."

***

Aiden led his mother and Vodin into the brick alleyway between apartment buildings. The heat amplified the smell rising from nearby dumpsters, and Aiden's mother wrinkled her nose in reaction. Vodin gave the woman a sympathetic look.

"My apologies, Lisa," he said, stepping up beside her. "We shouldn't be out here too long."

Aiden stopped in the center of the alley and turned to Vodin with an unsure expression. "So... Yeah. You told me to bring you to a safe place. This is probably the closest I can think of," Aiden said, shrugging.

"Aiden," his mother said, her eyes revealing her worry. "I didn't know you ever came out here-"

"Just sometimes, Mom," Aiden interjected. "There's not much else to do in this hood."

Vodin stepped forward, rubbing his hands. "Well, I suppose we should get started. First, let's make sure there are no witnesses."

Aiden wasn't sure he liked the sound of that, but he stood still and watched as the bearded man held a hand in the air and acted as though he were grabbing an invisible pen. With this unseen implement, Vodin seemed to be writing something. In moments, Aiden could see glowing, floating letters—unfamiliar markings—appearing where Vodin wrote. Aiden's mother gasped and took a step back.

Vodin finished his word with an elaborate stroke, then with a wave of his hand, the word duplicated itself until there were four identical words floating before him. As if scooping water with his hands, he wafted each word in a different direction.

One word swam along and collided with the brick wall to the east. It affixed itself to the bricks and turned black as if it had been written there in ink. One word wafted into the western wall, one to the southern wall, and the last word to the northern wall. In moments, each word was firmly written on the walls surrounding the three individuals.

"These are runes," Vodin explained, taking in both Aiden and his mother's surprise. "I've placed a very simple protection around this nearly-perfect square-shaped space. We wouldn't want someone stumbling by and seeing something they shouldn't, would we?"

Aiden walked to the nearest runic word and examined the details of the markings and the heaviness of the ink. He shook his head, not wanting to believe what he'd seen.

"What do they do?" Aiden asked, standing up and observing the words on the opposing walls from a distance.

"It will create the illusion that there is no one here," Vodin said, seeming pleased by Aiden's curiosity.

"But what about sound?"

Vodin chuckled. "Very observant," he said with a smile. "That was the one downfall of this particular runic formula, but some time ago, I fiddled with it until I found just the right combination. It creates a sound buffer, or muffler, if you will. One might hear something very faintly if they approach, but they won't hear what we hear. Not usually enough to suspect."

Aiden's mother swallowed loudly, seemingly glued to the spot. Vodin looked to her and smiled, despite the mixture of fear andawe on her tired face.

"No worries, Lisa," Vodin said. "We're perfectly safe. I realize you're putting a lot of trust in me at the moment, but I assure you, I'm just taking the necessary precautions."

Aiden's mother nodded, but remained unsure.

Aiden had forgotten whatever skepticism he'd had and found himself in awe of the runes that Vodin had placed on the walls. His mind raced with Vodin's comment about finding the right formula.

"Aiden, my boy," Vodin spoke up, forcing Aiden to pay attention. "Time is of the essence. Show us what you've got."

A cold feeling hit the bottom of Aiden's stomach. "Just like that?" he asked. "I can't just turn it on and off..."

"Come stand in the center," Vodin said, motioning for Aiden to move closer. "And face the far wall."

Aiden stood at the center-most point in the alley and looked at the wall furthest from his mother and Vodin.

"Now what was happening, and what were you feeling when you set fire to the tapestry at your school?" Vodin asked, his tone serious.

"I don't know..." Aiden muttered.

"Don't be embarrassed. We all make mistakes. We all have

emotions."

"Anger," said Aiden. "John..." Aiden stopped and sighed. He clenched his fists. "It was just after gym class and everyone had left, 'cept John. He tripped me and when I got mad, he laughed and called me Half-and-Half... Like he always does."

Aiden's mother turned to Vodin, only to see the intense concentration in his eyes. She raised her hand, but then pulled it back, unsure what to do. Aiden's fist were clenching tightly and his lips curling in anger.

"Go on," Vodin encouraged.

"He called me some more stuff; Said he'd kill me if I ever thought of telling a teacher... I just started seeing red, kind of. He swung at me again, and I felt the energy..."

Aiden stopped and raised his hands outward. As if exploding from the center of his being, the energy raced around his body, through his arms, and blasted from his palms. The energy ball slammed into the far wall with a crack, causing the top layer from a wide circle of bricks to crumble and cascade into a heap of dust and smoke.

Aiden shook his head and found himself blinking for a few moments, but when he pulled himself together, he realized his mother had toppled over backward from the explosion. He rushed to her side and helped her up.

"Are you alright?" he asked, grabbing her hands and pulling her to her feet.

"Your hands," she gasped, still wide-eyed. "They're hot! Did you really do that? I know we've talked about it, but I've never-"

"Yes," Aiden replied, his eyes alive with adventure. "I did do that."

Vodin smiled, standing closer to Aiden. "Such raw power," he said, shaking Aiden's hand. "I want to help you, Aiden. I saw the anger and the pain, but I want to help you gain control of this, so it can be used to help you."

Aiden smiled. "Why would you want to help me?"

"You've got talent, my boy," Vodin said with a laugh. "Do you want to waste that talent on people who aren't worth your time?"

"You mean people like John?"

Vodin simply nodded.

Aiden couldn't seem to stop smiling, despite his mother's worried face.

***

Aiden had spent the better part of a week wondering what things to pack. Vodin had told him to pack light, but Aiden wasn't so sure how light was "light". Aiden could no longer rid himself of the excitement, and he stuffed the last few odds and ends into a duffel bag. He cinched up the bag, now brimming with assorted clothes and personal items, and heaved it onto his bed with a sigh of accomplishment.

"Aiden?" His mother popped her head into the room. "Are you ready? Headmaster Vodin should be here soon. At least, I think soon."

"Yep," said Aiden, still looking around the room one last time.

"Ready. Don't sound so worried, Mom. Geez."

His mother smiled weakly and stepped into the room. "I think I have the right to be a little worried," she said, tousling Aiden's dark hair. "This is something new. Something really different. It'll take some time to get used to."

"I know," Aiden said, pulling away. "But you said I could go, right? I mean, you're letting me go, right? Vodin's paying..."

"Yes. You're going," she said, realizing she was unable to squelch his enthusiasm. "I can't say no now. It's awfully nice of Mister Pestler to pay your way. You need to thank him when he comes."

"Sure," Aiden mumbled, looking around the room once more, still wondering if he'd packed everything.

"It's just..." his mother began, looking around the room with glassy eyes until they landed back on Aiden. "You need to write me. Twice a week."

Aiden laughed. "Yeah, okay," he said, a hint of sarcasm in his voice.

"You better," his mother said, smiling. "I can still keep you from coming back next year, ya know."

"Okay okay. I'll write."

Without warning, Aiden found himself in his mother's embrace. He instinctively tried to pull away, but stopped himself. He returned the hug.

"I guess I'll be gone for a long time, huh?" Aiden said, resting his chin on his mother's shoulder. "I didn't think about that."

24

"I'll be fine," said his mother through sniffles, still holding him tight. "It'll be like that time you spent at summer camp. I'll pick up extra shifts, pay off some bills. Maybe when you come back, we'll be living in a nicer place."

Aiden pulled away, seeing his mother's red eyes. "But this won't be like camp."

"Everything will be fine," she said, stressing each word. "Besides, you almost burnt that camp down, remember? At least this place will be okay with that sort of thing."

Aiden laughed and sniffed, resisting the tears that threatened to overwhelm his vision. "That's the thing, isn't it?" he said, a very serious tone overcoming him.

They looked at each for a short while as if they had both had the same epiphany. Aiden shook his head and blinked for a few moments, then shook it off.

His mother wiped her eyes and looked at him, sighing. "Still doing that..." she said, caressing his face.

"It's just a tic," Aiden said, rolling his eyes. "That's what the doctor said. What am I supposed to do about it?"

"Sorry, honey. I guess I am worried. I wish I could keep you with me always and fix every little thing for you. But... I can't."

After a moment of silence there was a knocking at the front door.

Aiden snapped to attention. "That's Vodin," he said, excitement spreading across his face. "Mom, I have to go. I think you're right; everything'll be fine."

"Of course."

Aiden rushed to the front door and swung it open. Vodin stood there with the same long coat and smile he wore on his last visit.

"Good morning," Vodin said cheerily as Aiden gestured for the man to come inside.

Aiden's mother walked into the living room, wiping her face. "Good morning," she said, putting on a smile.

"I'd love to stay and chat," Vodin began happily enough, skipping past the niceties. "But we really must get going. Aiden, I've got some things I wish to show you before we go to the Guild. I realize it's only been two weeks since we met, but time is of the essence."

"You're sure you can't stay?" Aiden's mother asked. "I can make some tea or coffee."

"Thanks but no. I wish I could," Vodin said, a look of understanding in his eyes. "I really do."

"My bag," Aiden realized and rushed to his room.

He threw on his hooded sweatshirt and pulled the duffel bag onto his back.

"Such impetuosity," Aiden heard Vodin say with a chuckle. "To be young again."

Aiden rushed back into the living room. He could hardly think straight. His mother elbowed him.

"Aiden, show some manners," she half-whispered through clenched teeth.

"Oh sorry. I almost forgot my stuff," Aiden said, realizing he had been rude. "And thank you, Vodin, for paying my way."

Vodin did a slight bow and smiled. "Yours is a special case," he said. "It's not often I meet a student with your circumstances or talent. And from now on, you will address me as Headmaster Vodin."

Aiden nodded.

"But now, we really must go," Vodin added.

Aiden again felt the warm embrace of his mother, and he assured her that everything would be fine.

"I love you," Aiden's mother whispered in his ear. "Remember, don't worry about others. Think before you leap... And write me."

Aiden nodded, her grip so tight that he almost couldn't say much in response. She kissed his cheek and finally let go. The headmaster bid the woman goodbye and stepped outside, followed by Aiden who stumbled on the threshold. Aiden's mother sighed heavily as the door shut behind them.

***

Aiden was suddenly struck with the realization that he knew nothing about this man with whom he was now walking. He felt strangely safe with him, but he didn't really know him. Aiden tightened the straps from his duffel around his shoulders and carried on down the sidewalk.

"My boy, I know this is not easy for you," Vodin began. "Menlir—who you've not had the pleasure of meeting—is the local D'Tari guardian, and he will keep an eye out for your mother."

Aiden nodded, his mind still racing.

"She's safe, and you'll be safe as well."

Aiden followed Vodin down the sweltering sidewalk past the rows of old apartment complexes. The streets seemed alive today, and the traffic almost deafening. The humidity crept into Aiden's clothing and he already regretted putting on his sweatshirt.

"Are you sure you don't have a car?" Aiden asked the older man as they stopped at a crosswalk and waited for the lights to change.

"Agnecs, as a whole, don't really use motor vehicles," Vodin said, looking back at Aiden.

Aiden raised an eyebrow. "How do you guys get around?"

The traffic had stopped and Aiden and Vodin began crossing the street. Aiden saw the heat visibly rising off of the waiting cars and trucks just across from them. He imagined the machines as angry monsters waiting to charge him with hot breath rising from flared nostrils, and the thought reminded him of his younger days. He looked forward again and realized Vodin was several steps ahead of him. He ran to catch up, noticing that Vodin hadn't answered his question.

"We have our ways," Vodin finally responded as they neared the sidewalk. "Walking is of course, always the best for you."

"Sure," Aiden said, nearly yelling over the road noise. "But, what if you need to be somewhere fast?"

The two of them carried on past another row of tall apartment buildings, followed by a gas station and a convenience store. Along these buildings, Aiden could see the occasional tarped window and cracking brick. Everything seemed to be in poor shape. The noise and wind of the traffic hounded them with each step.

"Well, Aiden, this is part of the reason I'm bringing you this way today," Vodin said, glancing at Aiden with a smile. "Sessions at the Guild don't begin for at least two weeks, but I feel that you are in need of some additional tutelage."

Without another word, Vodin led Aiden down the next alley between a warehouse and an office building. Aiden stopped for a moment before he followed the man into the shadows. A sadness spread over him. He thought of his mother. He wondered what good could ever come of going down that alley with someone he'd just met.

"Aiden?" Vodin asked, taking in the boy's sudden change in mood.

"Yeah, I... I think I'm going to stay here," Aiden said, his voice cracking.

"I understand your concern, Aiden, but have I given you any reason to distrust me?"

"No," Aiden said, shrugging.

"Here's my proposition," Vodin began with a glint in his eye. "Just listen to what I have to say, and if it doesn't feel right, you can go right back to your apartment and you have permission to forget everything about this."

"Seems fair I guess."

Vodin relaxed himself up against the old wall of the warehouse and fanned himself with his hand. Aiden stepped into the shadows, keeping his distance, but glad to be out of the heat. It was much quieter in the alley, and Aiden felt as though he could finally think straight.

"I see there's no beating around the bush with you, is there?" Vodin said with a slight chuckle. "As I said, Aiden, I feel the need

to spend some extra time teaching you things you've not had the chance to learn. Things about the Agnec world. I am not some kidnapper here to take you to places unknown..."

It was the honest tone in Vodin's voice that relaxed Aiden. He leaned against the wall of the office building and sighed, unsure of all the feelings racing inside of him.

"It is never easy leaving home," Vodin said. "I left my country at an early age, and then I left home after home after home. But as I said before, at the Guild, I can help you find your way. I know the angst of a wandering mind; a mind and spirit with talent and nowhere to spend it. You're so much like myself at your age."

Aiden looked up, only to see Vodin staring off as if living out a lifetime of memories.

"And," Vodin continued. "Who knows? You might just discover a new home."

Aiden remembered the moment in the alley behind his apartment building, watching Vodin place the runes on the walls... He couldn't help but smile.

"Okay," said Aiden, stepping closer until he was across from the man. "Then I'm ready."

Vodin stood up straight again, his eyes alive with adventure. "Alright then," he said, clapping his hands in excitement. "First thing's first: I'll be taking you into the Agnec Underground. Feel free to ask questions at any time."

Vodin reached out and began writing runes in the air. The runic word floated only for a moment, then he swiped at it, wafting it directly onto the concrete floor of the alleyway. Just as Aiden had seen before, the runes affixed themselves to the surface and turned dark.

"This is called runecasting," Vodin explained. "A fundamental part of the D'Tari way. And there are many, many different kinds of ways to write and cast runes."

Vodin knelt down with a groan and traced the outline of the rune. He got to his feet and backed away in a sudden jolt. The runes glowed, followed by a shaking of the concrete. Aiden also stepped back. A square block of concrete, roughly four feet long and wide, lowered itself down into the ground with a rumble. The result was an open passageway, lit by blue bioluminescent mushrooms.

"So, really," Aiden began, now trying to look down into the passage. "It's magic."

Vodin laughed. "Technically, I suppose," he said, taking the first step down into the passageway. "What Amblers call magic, we might as well call science. But the D'Tari powers we call properties. It's a more specific kind of science that involves the arts as well."

Aiden's heart pounded as he followed Vodin down a concrete slope into the passage. The floor was earthy and the interior dark, despite the glowing mushrooms that were intentionally planted along the wall of the corridor. The brightest point of light was the torch perched on a wooden hook just inside the passage. The air was surprisingly cool, and not musty as Aiden would have expected.

Along the wall next to the passage's opening, there were several markings. They were different than the runes Aiden had already seen, but they still resembled letters of some kind. Vodin studied one of the words briefly, then traced the lettering with his finger. Aiden jumped back, surprised to see the concrete block sliding itself back into place above them, sealing the passage shut.

"As you've probably noticed," Vodin began, seeing Aiden's awed expression. "We did not just now create this passage. I simply unlocked a sealed passage with a special rune. And these special words here," Vodin pointed to the markings on the wall. "Resealed it. It's really not so magical. Quite ordinary if you ask me."

Vodin took the torch down from its place on the wall and began walking along a dim path painted in blue light. Aiden followed closely behind, taking in the sights. The earthy sensation under his shoes had suddenly begun to feel like stones, and a myriad of foreign symbols decorated the walls.

"Stay close to me," Vodin said, his tone serious. "Once we leave this passage, it is important that you do as I say."

"Okay..." Aiden said, unsure how to feel about the warning. "Why? What's beyond the passage?"

Vodin stopped and faced Aiden, the torchlight dancing and flickering across his sincere eyes. "I'd imagine a good number of things; people and creatures that you're probably not used to seeing. Don't be alarmed, and stay close."

"Creatures?" Aiden said, his heart leaping.

Vodin led Aiden further down the corridor. The path began to slope until they reached an empty stone wall. Vodin held the torch close to the left-hand side of the wall, shining the light across some more of the mysterious letters and symbols.

"In we go," Vodin said, tracing the letters with his finger. "Stay alert, and always feel free to ask questions."

Chapter 2
To The Guild

The wall rumbled and slid up into the ceiling, causing Aiden to stand back. His mouth dropped open as he followed Vodin inside. A massive cavern stretched before them, sent aglow by the the blue and white light of over a hundred giant mushrooms. It may as well have been daylight. Though he strained, Aiden couldn't begin to see the far end of the cavern. Its sheer size made him feel so miniscule.

A large roundhouse stood just off to their left, and nearly a hundred different railways crisscrossed from a central point within the building's center. On each corner of the roundhouse stood a large station, each one marked with corresponding 'north', 'south', 'east', and 'west' designations in ornate letters. The railways were busy with wheeled carts hauling passengers at full speed along the tracks.

Aiden shook himself for a moment, wondering if he was imagining things. Just outside each station, there stood a myriad of people and creatures waiting to load a railcar. The creatures caught his eye. Some of them were short and gray-faced with stout bodies, but more human-like than not. Others had the faces and upper bodies of a human, but the tail and legs of a goat.

To further confound Aiden, the humans dressed in a strangely mismatched fashion. Some of them wore old looking suits and clothes like Vodin's, but others wore purely medieval cloaks and tunics. Still others wore a combination of the two, making Aiden want to laugh.

"As in the Ambler world, it's not polite to stare," Vodin said, smiling.

Aiden flushed, then nodded. He realized Vodin was several steps ahead of him, and he rushed to catch up. They followed a cobblestone path toward the roundhouse.

Aiden saw a huddled group of what appeared to be humans standing off to his right. They were all nearly Aiden's height, but looked like adults, though still strangely young. Each with a similar shade of dark skin and variously colored long hair, the people wore elaborately designed cloaks, and remained close to each other.

One of them made eye contact with Aiden and looked away sharply. He felt a sudden pang and stopped walking. The eyes had been beautiful, almost other-worldly. Though he didn't dare look back, Aiden also realized that there was no significant way to tell if those people were male or female. At least not from this vantage.

"Don't stare at the Elves," Vodin said, observing Aiden's reaction. "They only come to the Underground on business, and prefer to keep to themselves."

Aiden risked another look, and realized that Vodin had been

serious. Each of the creatures had long, pointed ears which sloped back, often poking out from beneath their hair. The Elves also had uniquely shaped craniums, which were sort of rounded, yet not so dissimilar to the skulls of humans; At least not so strange that one would notice the difference at first glance.

After moving on, Aiden saw several railcars, loaded with passengers, flying along the nearby railways. The railcars were eerily silent as they glided down the tracks, some were even trollies, but most of them didn't resemble the trains Aiden had seen elsewhere.

Vodin led Aiden past the platforms, across a couple of railway paths, and into the large station designated 'East'. There, he led Aiden through the jostling crowd to the ticket counters. A short human-like creature with a bluish-gray face greeted them at the counter with a gravelly but unmistakably female voice. Vodin handed the bearded creature two gold coins in exchange for two tickets.

Aiden's expression must have given him away, because the creature scoffed at him, "You act like you've never seen a She-Dwarf before."

"Excuse the boy, my good Dwarva," Vodin said with a kind expression.

"Get out of here," the She-Dwarf scowled at them, while gesturing for the patrons behind Vodin to step up. "Next!"

Aiden took a seat next to Vodin in the adjoining vestibule and watched the tracks through a large window. Aiden was up against a brick divider hugging his duffel bag tightly, but on the other side of Vodin, two of the goat-like people were sitting in conversation, while across from them a group of Dwarves sat quietly.

Aiden tried not to stare, but the Dwarves were fascinating. They, like the She-Dwarf at the counter, were all fairly short, having strange ear shapes, and were mostly gray-faced with long hair in complex braids. These Dwarves appeared to be all male with beards so long and thick that it was hard for Aiden to see where their faces ended and the beards began. Nearly all the Dwarves had menacing looking hammers and axes strapped to their backs. It was a wonder they could sit down comfortably, but they seemed to manage just fine.

"Beware the Dwarves too," Vodin said quietly to Aiden. "I won't lie and say they're not a bit temperamental."

Aiden flushed, but tried to smile. "This is all so..." Aiden began, but the words didn't arrive.

"Strange?"

"Yeah," Aiden agreed.

"Which is precisely why I brought you this way, Aiden," said Vodin. "Many of the students attending the Guild live in this world. Well, they live in small Agnec villages and enclaves throughout, to be exact. But nearly everyone utilizes the Underground in some way. These railways stretch far and wide underneath most of the country's largest cities."

"What exactly is the Agnec Underground then?" Aiden asked,

staring out the window.

"You haven't noticed already?"

Aiden rolled his eyes, feeling stupid. "I guess it's a train station sort of thing," he said. "I guess I mean: Why have an Underground?"

"Relax, Aiden," Vodin said, placing a hand on the boy's shoulder. "There are no foolish questions, only those that have not been asked. By now I hope you understand a bit more that when I say 'Agnecs', I include Dwarves, Elves, Fauns and the like, along with the humans from the Old World. Collectively, we are Agnecs, and at the best of times, our goal is to coexist peaceably with each other and with nature. But, well, let's think logically about what modern man would do if they discovered some of these fantastical creatures... These Fauns and Dwarves for example."

Aiden looked across at the Dwarves. He then glanced sideways and caught a glimpse of the goat-men on the other side of Vodin, which now he understood to be Fauns. Aiden frowned.

"If I'm reading you right, you know it would not be a pretty thing," Vodin said, watching Aiden intently.

Before Aiden could react, a railcar pulled into the station with a loud hiss. A well-dressed Dwarf stepped out of the railcar and opened a side door, allowing the passengers to load up and take their seats. The vehicle wasn't much more than a large box on wheels, reminding Aiden of a small schoolbus, and it appeared to have no engine up front.

Aiden followed Vodin inside and realized that the seats were arranged all around the perimeter of the vehicle, creating a strange circle, and were not facing forward in rows, like the cars Aiden had known. They managed to find two seats crammed in between a group of humans to Aiden's right, and the Dwarves from the station to Vodin's left. The railcar was still full of passengers going on to further stops, and when the Fauns came aboard, the small space was packed to capacity. Aiden was thankful for the large windows all around.

The well-dressed Dwarf had already collected tickets, so he closed the side door and took a seat up in the front of the car, facing forward toward a large windshield. The humans on Aiden's right were fully immersed in conversation, and when the Dwarf announced something aloud, his voice was drowned out by the din. The Dwarf shrugged and pulled a tall lever next to him. With a hiss, the railcar crept forward over the tracks.

As they began moving, Aiden turned to Vodin, trying to be discreet. "So it's all secretive? I mean, can Agnecs never reveal themselves to real— er, I mean, Amblers?"

Vodin sighed. "Humans can get along fine in the Ambler world if they want," he said, tilting his head in the direction of the people near Aiden. "Obviously it doesn't work out so well for the others. It was Dwarf ingenuity that has kept the Agnecs safe for so long, and away from the dangers of some Amblers."

Despite there being no engine, the railcar lurched forward at full speed, almost throwing Aiden off of his seat. Vodin steadied him, looking amused.

"Dwarf magic," Vodin said, taking in Aiden's wide-eyed gaze toward the front of the car. "Is a unique brand of its own. Well, it's been nearly three thousand years now... But Dwarves, despite their clan differences, are generally a tight-knit bunch. They built the infrastructures of the Underground, and it stretches across multiple continents."

Aiden raised an eyebrow, his mouth agape.

"So, the simple answer," Vodin continued. "Is no. Agnecs should not ever reveal themselves to Amblers. It would be messy. Too complicated. Nearly three thousand years ago, Agnecs decided to separate themselves from the Ambler world, and we've done a pretty good job of keeping out of sight ever since. Of course, none of that stopped Amblers from retaining their memories of us... Some of the stories you call folk lore and myth, were based on actual incidents. I'm using the word 'based' very loosely, of course."

Vodin chuckled and Aiden smiled. Aiden glanced casually around the railcar. The humans in their strange cloaks were still alive with conversation, talking about everything from the food market to preparing for winter. The Dwarves were still a somber bunch, but the Fauns were lively with chatter. Everyone carried on as though everything was normal.

This is their normal, Aiden realized.

***

Just before Aiden had drifted off to sleep, Vodin had told him to rest a while, musing, "By typical Ambler travel, the Guild would be almost nine hours away, due northeast. But, by Agnec railcar, it should only take us three. This is an express rail after all."

When Aiden opened his eyes again, the feeling returned to his fingers and he realized he was still clutching his duffel bag. The railcar was racing along the tracks at a maddening pace. Outside, the dark tunnels had given way, and now Aiden could see that they were careening around steep mountain sides while mysterious mushroom-lit villages littered a subterranean valley below.

Aiden had grown somewhat accustomed to the speed and balance of the vehicle, but at first it had been jarring. Vodin told him that railcars never hopped or fell off the tracks unless someone with evil intent meant them to.

"Well that's reassuring..." Aiden had said.

Now they were nearly down the other side of the mountain, the valley almost out of sight. Stalactites the size of skyscrapers hung overhead, and in some cases, the tracks raced around them from side to side.

"Oh you're awake," Vodin said, looking over to Aiden.

Aiden sat upright and wiped his bleary eyes, trying to shake off the fog.

"Now let's talk some more about the Agnec world, if you don't mind," Vodin said, a gleam in his eye.

Aiden nodded, still groggy.

"You asked earlier about whether or not Agnecs should reveal themselves," Vodin began while Aiden tried to sit up. "There is something else you should know about that."

Aiden looked up intently.

"The United States government does know about us," Vodin said flatly.

Aiden raised an eyebrow.

"There are laws in place that are supposed to protect us," Vodin continued. "I thought you should know. So, in one sense, we're known, but that is mostly the extent of things. When it comes to helping us maintain secrecy, the government will help cover up incidents, but as I've demonstrated, there's a lot we can do to cover up on our own. And by 'we', I of course mean the D'Tari, since not all Agnecs have D'Tari powers, but I shouldn't forget to credit the Dwarf magic, without which, none of this would be possible."

Aiden stared blankly. "So... What happens to people like me? If I go back into normal, I mean, Ambler society, and something happens by accident-"

"If the government gets wind of it, they will do what they can, and report it to the D'Tari Council, especially if they suspect magical properties," Vodin said, his eyes searching the jostling railcar, then landing back on Aiden. "Which brings me to my next thought: I'm very surprised that no one reported you to the Council earlier."

Vodin went silent, staring out at the blurring rock formations as the railcar sped along the precipice of another mountainside.

"Well, I can't dwell on that," Vodin said after a long moment. "We know about you now, and we're going to help you. That is the important thing."

"So, the D'Tari Council, what do they do?" Aiden asked, his mind racing.

"Glad you asked, Aiden," Vodin said, his spirits lifting. "Excellent question. The Council acts as law enforcement for the Agnec communities—particularly the human communities. Now let me emphasize that there are thousands of Agnecs who do not have D'Tari properties. Many of them have to understand runes and know some runelore in order to go about their daily lives, but most of them cannot do what we do. Or even what you do."

Aiden realized his mouth was open in awe.

Vodin continued, "The D'Tari are a rare breed, and therefore, we train and prepare for everything. Some of us enforce local community laws, but others have a higher calling. Come what may, we have always been there to help Agnecs survive. Even if they don't realize that they need us."

Aiden looked around and lowered his voice, "But what about Dwarves? They have magic, right? Wouldn't they help protect other Agnecs?"

"One might think so," Vodin said. "And though they allow others to utilize the Underground, much of it comes at a price, whether the cost of gold or through extensive political treaties.

Dwarves are cunning and stubborn and often will put the cause of their own kind before the good of others. They built the Underground for themselves originally."

Aiden frowned, shrugging.

"You might think that the Elves would help—they have magic too—but they have isolated themselves from all other parts of Agnec society, except for the rare few who engage," Vodin explained. "Most other creatures, as fantastic as they are, don't carry magic, at least not the way Dwarves and Elves do. Not magic powerful enough to innovate something like this."

Vodin gestured all around.

"So..." Aiden began, looking for the words. "Only humans can be D'Tari then?"

"You might think so, but no," Vodin said, smiling. "The properties are a gift given to those with human DNA, as well as Fauns and Satyrs."

Aiden's face scrunched in confusion. "What do you mean?"

Vodin chuckled as if amused by his own thoughts. "There are more things in heaven and earth..."

Aiden furled his brow. "Horatio..." he half-whispered without thinking. Aiden stopped himself, surprised by what he'd said, then acted as though he hadn't said it at all.

"Thank you for humoring an old man's turn of phrase," Vodin said, energized by Aiden's reaction. "Let me put it simply, even though the Dwarves and the Elves keep to themselves most of the time, doesn't mean they always stay away from humans.

Half-Elves and Half-Dwarves have been known to have the D'Tari properties on occasion—right alongside some of their own innate magic. It is actually quite fascinating."

Aiden sat in silence for several minutes, watching the subterranean world fly past them. It was a lot to take in. He could still see himself showing his powers to Vodin back in the alleyway, and the Headmaster's look of delight resonating joyfully through his being.

"So, you said we're taking this way because you wanted time to show me some things, are there faster ways to travel?" Aiden asked, the realization hitting him.

"Well," Vodin said, grinning. "For D'Tari, yes. For the average Agnec, this is the best way. But more on that later. For now, we start where everyone else does: The basics."

***

The railcar pulled into a station near another large roundhouse. The well-dressed Dwarf at the front of the car pushed the lever forward and the vehicle screeched to a halt, nearly throwing Aiden from his seat. The passengers slowly made their way off the railcar, stumbling onto another cobblestone path surrounded by railways and jumbled lines of commuters.

Aiden stretched his legs and tightened the straps of his duffel bag around his shoulders. Each step seemed like a giant effort to keep from falling. His body ached in strange places.

"I've forgotten how disorienting a ride in a railcar can be, if one is not used to it," said Vodin, patting Aiden on the shoulder.

"You'll adjust, but we do need to keep walking."

Aiden nodded and forced himself to take another step. After a few moments, his body didn't ache as much and he was finally able to walk straight without veering to the left. Though they were still in a massive cavern underground, Aiden thought he glimpsed something overhead. If he squinted just right and looked beyond the bright of the glowing mushrooms, he could almost see something there, just peeking out of the shadow.

Vodin stopped and noticed Aiden looking intently into the darkness above. "Wondering if you can see a roof, are you?"

Aiden did see something. There were roots hanging out of the darkness.

"You're very observant," Vodin said, stepping closer to Aiden. "This is the north-easternmost edge of the Underground, and we're much closer to the surface."

Vodin gestured for Aiden to follow. The two of them continued down the path until Aiden realized there were no more people or creatures around. They were no longer within earshot of the roundhouse or any of the railways. Alongside the cobblestone path, small gardens full of variously colored mushrooms, squash, and other vegetables appeared. The path began to ascend and the gardens on the left gave way to a smoothly hewn stone wall.

As they ascended, Aiden could see a valley forming below to the right. It was full of quaint stone huts, gardens, well-kept fields, and smithies. In a small town square, he could see groups of Dwarves standing casually, talking, and simply going about their business.

Aiden's foot smashed into a stone and he stumbled, feeling the edge of the path giving way. Cobblestones under his feet slid down off the cliff face, and Aiden felt himself slipping. A firm hand grasped his and pulled him back onto the path. Aiden backed himself against the stone wall, panting, and shook his head, unable to register what had happened.

"You are very observant," Vodin said, looking out over the valley below them. "But you've got to discern what to observe first."

Aiden nodded. "Sorry..."

"No need to apologize. Just remember."

With that, Vodin turned and continued walking up the path. Aiden took a deep breath and followed. The path continued to rise until the right-hand view was also blocked by a solid stone wall. At some point, the path had become a torch-lit stairway trailing through a stone corridor, and an iron side-rail appeared on each side of them. Aiden wondered how long they'd been walking, and his legs ached.

"This is the way most of our students would naturally arrive," Vodin said, seeing the fatigue in Aiden's face. "Especially the freshmen."

"So... You like to torture newbies a little bit first?" Aiden said, without thinking, then thought better of it.

Vodin laughed. "We all need some discipline, my boy," Vodin said, chuckling. "Torture..." he mused. "You might work to temper that humor while around the other masters. They're not as easy going as myself."

Aiden laughed, somewhat relieved, although now he wondered what the other masters would be like.

"Nothing is created fully formed," Vodin continued. "We all come from the dust, are molded and cast in the fire... Until we come out a little better, a little more suited to the task each time."

Aiden nodded, though not fully understanding Vodin's words, but trying to focus on the upward journey.

A warm breeze swam through the corridor, and the shift from the cool Underground air made Aiden pause. He could see another light at the top of the steep incline, and he forced himself to keep moving.

"Another reason, of many, that I wanted to bring you out early, Aiden," Vodin said, slowing his pace. "Is because I know you've had no instruction about the philosophy and beliefs of the D'Tari." Vodin took several more steps before he stopped to glance back at Aiden. "We have about two weeks to get you caught up on some of the things that other students already take for granted."

Aiden nodded, unsure how to respond.

Vodin carried on up the stairs. Aiden followed until they arrived at the light source at the top of the incline. They were in a small rounded room with a bright cluster of mushrooms growing from the ceiling. Aiden realized the walls were made of thick wood and the air was pungent with earth and soil. The floor crawled with tree roots, leaving only a small path leading from the downward stairwell to a roughly hewn door.

Vodin walked to the door and traced the outline of some runes on the door frame. The letters glowed and with a click, the door unlocked. Aiden covered his eyes as brilliant daylight invaded the room and Vodin stepped out. Aiden followed, his shoes touching down on dust and pine needles. A vast forest surrounded them, and wide shafts of sunlight filtered down through tall cedars and fir trees. A hot gust of wind engulfed Aiden, making his knees buckle.

Once they were outside, Vodin shut the door behind them. Aiden realized the small room had actually been the hollowed-out trunk of an unnaturally large maple tree. From the outside, the door was hardly visible.

"We're not far now," Vodin said, seeing Aiden's eyes flickering in all directions. "We're nearly as far north as one can be in the United States, save for Alaska I suppose. But follow me, you have nothing to fear."

Aiden gripped the straps around his shoulders, his back aching from the burden of his duffel. He struggled to keep up with the Headmaster. Vodin strolled through the forest, casually moving away spider webs and sidestepping thickets, while Aiden stumbled over fallen branches and imagined the noises of strange beasts at every turn.

They made their way up a fir-lined hill until a dirt path came in view. Vodin smiled and followed the trail, which became increasingly dark from the encroaching trees. Finally, they entered a clearing in the shadow of thickly entwined spruce, cedar, and ash. Aiden was taken aback at the strange structures that met his eyes.

Up against the wildly spun trunk of a giant spruce tree, sat the wooden statues of two giant otters. The statues paralleled each other, sitting like bizarre cats with paws crossed, guarding a space between them, which faced the tree's trunk. Vodin approached the otter on the right and felt along the wooden creature's right foreleg. A runic phrase glowed briefly. Aiden was no longer surprised at this behavior, but he managed to brace himself as a low rumbling began beneath his feet.

The otters began moving, their wooden bodies creaking and moaning as if they were trees readying to collapse. Both Aiden and Vodin moved back as the otters stood on their haunches and faced each other, crossing their forelegs. Their paws crossed overhead, creating an archway tall enough for a person to pass beneath. The statues were now still, as if they had never moved at all.

Underneath the archway, a white mist appeared, writhing and twisting until it formed a solid door. When it was done forming, the travelers went inside. As soon as they had closed the door, Aiden could hear the otters creaking and moaning again.

"They are returning to their original positions," Vodin said, noticing Aiden's look of inquiry.

They were now inside a small octagonal room with no doors

or windows. There was only a candle on a table at the room's center. Next to that candle, sat an open book.

"This is the way everyone must enter the Guild," Vodin said, gesturing to the small room. "Our goal is to keep ourselves inconspicuous, hidden from Ambler eyes of course."

"So being out in the middle of nowhere isn't hidden enough?" Aiden asked with a slight smirk.

Vodin smiled. "We must take every precaution possible," he said. "Sadly, the D'Tari sometimes have enemies. But first things first: In order to enter the Guild, we also must provide a runic pass-phrase."

Aiden observed as Vodin set about scribbling runes in the air, runecasting them onto the open book upon the table. The runes sat glowing on the blank page for a moment, then quickly faded.

They felt another low rumble beneath their feet. The room slowly began to rotate. Gears could be heard whirring from somewhere within the walls. Just across from where Aiden stood, the wall seemed to split, one half pulling away as if being wrenched apart by a giant hand. An old steel door appeared in the opening, and the rumbling of gears ceased.

Vodin strolled forward and pulled open the steel door with a clank, gesturing for Aiden to go ahead of him. Aiden stepped out into the open air, surprised by what he saw. Well-kept grounds stretched out before them. A cobblestone walkway forged a path between tended trees and lawns, until it branched off in many different directions, traveling in symmetrical circles around various stone buildings. "Welcome," said Vodin, smiling. "To the Mount Katahdin Guild."

Aiden glanced at the woods surrounding the grounds. The giant trees were very much like impenetrable walls. He gazed upward, seeing how the tangling canopy of spruce, cedar, and fir trees was perfectly pruned to let sunlight filter in, though it seemed to make a solid roof at the same time.

Vodin walked ahead on the cobblestone path, while Aiden followed, his pupils dilated in an effort to take everything in. They passed an ornate fountain featuring a life-size statue, which Vodin stopped and gazed at.

"Before you know anything else about the Guild, Aiden," said Vodin. "You should know that this is the Guild's founder, Master Porutan the Half-Elf. He was a wise and skilled D'Tari master who risked everything to see this school become an institution. Education and instruction are an important part of the D'Tari way. I'm telling you this because it will be hard work, but it will pay off. Absolutely."

Aiden nodded, still looking at the intense glare of the stone Half-Elf. The stone creature was about Aiden's height, very human-like, wearing medieval cloaks and wielding a sword over its head in a victorious manner. The statue's wild yet joyful expression was so life-like that Aiden stepped back in fear that it would move.

With that, Vodin crossed over to a new path after the walkway branched. Aiden followed, and they found themselves heading toward the largest of the stone buildings.

The main hall was a wide, perfectly circular building in the center of the grounds. All the various cobblestone paths eventually converged right here. A wide halo of sunlight filtered down through the tree canopy and lit the building's circular roof, illuminating the ancient stonework. The building was practically medieval.

"This is the Great Hall," Vodin said, his eyes gleaming. "Some of your classes will take place here, but more importantly, this is where the community meets daily to eat, commune, and start and end each day."

Vodin took a left turn down the path as it wrapped around the great rounded building. After a few minutes of walking past several stone buildings and well-kept gardens, they arrived at a set of identical structures. The buildings stood side by side, each with two spiraling towers to the right and left, each with a thick midsection standing at least five stories high. A cobblestone path connected the two buildings, surrounded by well-tended gardens and some smaller trees.

"These are the student dormitories," Vodin announced. "And the one on the left will be your home for the next three years."

***

When Aiden awoke the next day, he had almost forgotten where he was and how he'd gotten there. It was a sudden knocking that had woken him, and his eyes flashed open, only to see a very different world than the one he had expected. He sat up, rubbing his eyes and yawning.

The room was dim and somewhat long with a fireplace and two other beds, both of which were empty. Daylight was gently filtering in between the openings in the ornate drapery covering the window nearest Aiden's bed. All the beds were organized neatly against the wall, each next to a small table and wash basin. At the far end of the room, one door led to a bathroom, and the other led to a hallway. The design was very functional, and Aiden could tell that everything in the room was very old.

As he stood, the cold stone chilled his feet, waking him up a little bit more. He began to remember the previous night and how Vodin had shown him his dorm room, told him that most Agnecs don't use electricity, and bade him a good night.

Aiden wished he hadn't packed his discman and all those CDs.

The knocking returned, and he looked up at the door.

"Who's there?" Aiden asked, his voice cracking awkwardly.

There was no answer. He pulled on his clothes from the day before and rushed to the door, pulling it open. The hall was empty, save for a stack of clothes on the stone floor near his doorway. He peeked his head into the hall, but the dorms were silent. There wasn't even the sound of footsteps. Aiden shrugged and picked up the clothes.

Closing the door behind him, he threw the clothes on the bed. Something small and papery rolled out of the stack. It was a small scroll, which Aiden picked up and unraveled.

"Dear Aiden," the scroll read, in neat handwriting. "I took the liberty of finding these garments for you! They are traditional D'Tari training garments, plus a cloak for the cold nights. Don't be worried that you will look silly, everyone will be wearing them. We will take time later to go look for other materials you'll need for school, but for now, this will do. Please put on the sleeveless tunic (that's the long rectangular shirt. You tuck it into the belt, but do not tuck it into the trousers!). And also, don't forget to put on the gray trousers. These will serve our purposes for the day, and the heat will make you regret it if you don't. Meet me in the Great Hall at a quarter 'til seven. Headmaster Vodin Pestler. PS. Don't forget the boots!"

Aiden looked over to the grandfather clock sitting in the corner of the room near the fireplace. It was 6:35 a.m. Aiden groaned, throwing the scroll back on to the bed, where it rolled itself partially back up. He picked up the first piece of clothing and held it up in the filtering sunlight near the window.

"Must be the tunic..." Aiden said, examining the long rectangular shirt.

The tunic and the trousers reminded him of the old knights and castle movies he'd seen on TV. Looking back at the clock, he realized he had no time to waste. He pulled everything on, feeling extremely uncomfortable in the trousers, but better that the tunic hung low, then not so great as he fastened the belt over the tunic. After a few moments of struggling with the boots, he sighed and left the room.

It only took a few minutes for him to walk to the Great Hall, but each painful step in the new boots seemed to last forever. The air was still cool and birdsong lifted Aiden's spirits, so he didn't worry about the boots for very long. The large rounded building now loomed in front of him, and though the huge doors seemed ominous, he took a deep breath and pushed them open.

The first room was a foyer, and Aiden's eyes darted cautiously around the empty room. The space was wide, ornate with pictures of past headmasters on the walls, and led directly to another sturdy pair of doors on the other side. Natural light lit the room from a wide window high above the entrance door. Aiden cocked his head, noticing the red carpet which was laid across the stone floor. A large tapestry hung above the double doors at the end of the room. Across the ornate canvas, two runic words sprawled in a very stylish fashion. Of course, Aiden had no clue what they said.

It was very quiet here, but Aiden supposed he should have expected that. Vodin had told him that there were no other students here yet, just some of the masters and groundskeepers. Aiden walked across the room to the double doors, gently placing his hand on the smooth wood. He paused, trying to remember everything he'd seen and heard the day before. Much of it was a whirlwind.

Aiden stepped through the doorway. The main hall stretched before him like an oval, ornate with hanging tapestries rich in color and design. Various symbols decorated each tapestry; one a sword, one a lightning bolt, another a scroll, and still another a musical instrument. The tables were long and rounded, bending to the shape of the room, revolving around a circular table at the very center, where Aiden realized Headmaster Vodin was sitting and enjoying a meal.

"Hello, Aiden," said Vodin as he looked over, wiping crumbs from his beard. "Glad to see you received my note and the clothes." He stood and gestured for Aiden to join him.

Aiden zigzagged though the maze of empty tables until he finally reached the central place where Vodin stood. The tall man gestured for Aiden to sit across from him, so Aiden made his way around until he found a seat on the bench. They both sat down, now facing each other directly.

"Breakfast is the most important meal of the day," Vodin said, smiling and returning attention to his plate full of pancakes and assorted fruits. "Always remember that."

"Sure," Aiden said. He looked around. "Um, so, where do you—I mean, how can I-"

"Oh yes of course." Vodin looked up, shaking his head. "You must be hungry. Where are my manners?"

Vodin reached into his cloak and retrieved a small whistle, which he promptly blew. To Aiden's ears, it had made no sound. At first he thought it must be broken, and he waited for Vodin to give it another try, though he had no idea why Vodin was blowing the whistle at all. The headmaster did not try again, but simply placed the whistle back into his cloak. Vodin smiled, despite Aiden's confused expression.

After a moment, a gentle breeze tickled Aiden's bare arm. He looked over only to see a plate full of pancakes, fruit, and thick bacon floating there. The plate laid itself gently down on the table in front of Aiden.

"Thank you, dear Faerina," Vodin said, nodding to Aiden's right where the plate had once been floating.

Aiden glanced over, this time realizing that a bluish insect-like creature hovered there, carried by two pairs of beetle-like translucent wings. The creature's face looked almost human, despite the large liquid eyes, but the effeminate body likewise was familiar. Aiden slid back on the bench, unable to stop the shock that jolted him.

"Don't be alarmed," Vodin said, smiling to Aiden.

The creature turned to Vodin and bowed, then flew away at such a high speed that it seemed to disappear.

"It's only a Faerie," said Vodin, answering the question on Aiden's face. "Well, she's only a Faerie. I should tell you that we have domesticated Faeries here. Did I not mention that? Through a system of mutual protection, they agree to assist us with various things. They help with the food and some of the chores, and are amazing little delivery-runners."

Aiden caught his breath and looked around. The creature was nowhere in sight. He tried to relax and looked back to Vodin.

"Wow," Aiden said under his breath. "Weird. But kind of cool."

"I had a Faerie deliver your clothes just this morning, along with your wake up knock," Vodin said just before shoveling more pancakes into his mouth.

"I wondered who knocked..." Aiden mused in astonishment.

"We'll have plenty of time to talk about this later," Vodin said, now pointing a fork at Aiden's full plate. "But first, eat."

Chapter 3
Market Street

They entered through a surprisingly small door, one which forced Vodin to hunch, and into a large ovular chamber. All the furniture was rounded, matching the shape of the room, and very large windows covered three of the walls. Vodin closed the door behind them, and Aiden glanced around at the simplicity of the office. Aside from a few chairs, a large desk, a cabinet, and a few other things, there wasn't much furniture. The paintings on the walls were intricate and looked very old, but most of the room seemed hardly lived in.

"The first thing we'll do," Vodin said as he led Aiden into the space. "Is talk a little about your future here."

Vodin's tone had been so serious at that moment, that Aiden froze, a sudden fear overwhelming him. Vodin sat down at the thick wooden desk, straightened up some papers and books, then looked up.

"Well, sit down, my boy. You look terrified of something."

Aiden shook his head, failing to stave off an onslaught of blinking, then sighed when he was done. "You sounded so serious," he said. "...It's nothing. Forget it."

A serious tone of voice usually meant that he was going to be expelled, or worse, but he thought twice before mentioning anything. He had just gotten here after all.

"I realize you've been through some hard times," Vodin began as Aiden took a seat across from him. "I won't lie and say those will end here, but I will reiterate that here, we'll give you the tools do deal with them. I also realize that you've had a difficult time with teachers and fellow students."

Aiden nodded, avoiding eye contact.

"I need you to promise to make an effort to do all you can to cooperate with the masters, and with your fellow students," Vodin continued. "Can you promise me that? Can you commit to the discipline of learning the D'Tari ways and following through?"

Aiden had spent so much time trying to understand what Vodin had been telling him, he hadn't stopped to think that it might be hard work. He took a moment to think about it.

"Yeah," Aiden said, looking up at the headmaster. "I think I can."

"You think?"

"I can. I will."

Vodin smiled. "Alright, well, time is of the essence then," he said, leaning back in his creaky chair. "First, in traditional D'Tari fashion, we teach through two main ways. Each student receives a mentor, and also attends classes taught by other masters. I'll be your mentor, Aiden."

Aiden cocked his head in surprise.

"D'Tari masters can choose whom they mentor, and I've

chosen you," Vodin continued. "You'll meet with me every morning. Well, weekday mornings anyway. When classes start, you'll only be attending those in the afternoons. But the master and student relationship comes before all other priorities. Are we understood?"

Vodin had a surprisingly serious expression, but his eyes appeared to be smiling, even if slightly. Aiden nodded in agreement.

"Very well then," Vodin said, then rifled through the stack of books on his desk. He finally found what he was looking for and plopped a thick leather volume down in front of himself. "Get comfortable, because as I've said, we have some catching up to do."

Vodin gestured to a fold-out desk nearby. It took Aiden a moment to realize the hint, but he promptly got up and pulled the desk next to his chair. Vodin passed Aiden a small stack of parchment paper and a tiny ornate box with a quill sticking out of it. Aiden threw the headmaster a confused look.

"I assume you've taken notes before..." Vodin said, returning Aiden's glance.

Aiden shook his head as if snapping out of a trance, his cheeks flushed. He rolled his eyes, feeling stupid. His fingers brushed the rough parchment, and his eyes were drawn to the intricate quill pen. It was all so strange that at first he just glared at them, afraid to touch them.

Vodin was already turning pages in the massive book before

him, and Aiden looked back up at the headmaster, excited and unsure at the same time. It was familiar like the school he'd known: the sound of pages turning; sitting at a desk; there were even classrooms and something like a cafeteria. But that was where the similarities ended.

"There are some core things we'll be looking at in the first two weeks before classes," Vodin began, his voice ringing out after a long silence, frightening Aiden. Vodin smiled for a moment, waiting for Aiden to compose himself, then continued, "We'll start with the stories you never had a chance to hear as a child—these will be the sort that most of your fellow students will already know. We begin with—you will want to write this down—we begin with the Founding Myth of Aignesia, then we move to the Gifting of the D'Tari Properties, then the Tales of Innish Dorn, then a little bit about Rosh DuKhun, and finally the Tale of A'dhem."

Aiden scribbled feverishly, never quite sure of any of the spellings, but just hurrying to catch up with Vodin's words. At first he'd fallen behind because he hadn't realized that he needed to dip the tip of the pen into the ink, then let it drain for a moment before writing. The first result was an unsightly ink blotch. Vodin was already well along by the time Aiden got the hang of the quill pen.

Vodin had stopped for a moment when he realized that Aiden was taking some time to adjust, but soon continued, "These are the core stories, or narratives, of the Agnec world. They are supposed to have taken place in the Old World, in Aignesia, long before this present world existed. Of course there are plenty of debates about whether or not they happened at all, but for the present, we will focus on the stories themselves."

Aiden looked up and opened his mouth, but decided to first raise his hand. Vodin nodded permissively. "Do you think they really happened?" Aiden asked.

Vodin chuckled. "Well, I don't really know how important it is that I do," Vodin replied. "You see, true myth may or may not tell a literally true story, but myth can certainly contain and impart real truth."

Aiden released a short grunt as he furled his brow.

"I can tell that you're not satisfied with my answer," Vodin said, smiling. "But just the same, if you want to believe these things really happened, then they did. If you decide that they didn't, there is no harm done—as long as you walk away with the truth. All the truth."

Aiden shrugged and scribbled, "Myth - true? Yes? No? Maybe so? Just get ALL the truth."

"Which brings me to my next thought," Vodin continued. "A key principle of living the D'Tari way, is seeking truth above all other things."

Aiden underlined the word 'truth' twice.

"These stories are taught in every human Agnec household," said Vodin, observing Aiden's note-taking. "Even in those who are not D'Tari—so take good notes, write your questions in the margins, and when I'm done, we'll discuss the finer details."

***

Aiden had listened intently to the tale that Vodin told. By the end of that first session, Aiden found himself surprisingly enthralled. So much so, that half way through, he had stopped taking notes.

"Any questions?" Vodin asked, when he was done reading the story.

Aiden looked at his empty parchment and felt a coldness in his stomach. His mind raced back over the things he had just heard.

"Uh.... Oh yeah," Aiden finally responded, grinning sheepishly. "So, in the beginning of the story, Shai existed before everything else, right?"

Vodin nodded.

"And his powers kind of made everything else... I can see that Shai was some sort of god or something, but what is he exactly?"

"Excellent question," Vodin said, his eyes first skimming the page of the book before him, then returning to Aiden. "In the stories, Shai is personified and usually portrayed as a male, though no one can truly say..."

Vodin leaned back in his chair and sighed. "In the short time I've known you, I've seen that you're very perceptive," he said. "Your mother told me that despite your troubles in school, you've never had bad grades, and often have been at the top of your classes. So I hope I'm assuming correctly that you know something about critical thinking and looking for the deeper meanings in what you read. Am I wrong to assume this?"

Aiden flushed and shook his head. "No," he finally admitted. "I guess I did enjoy English Lit and stuff like that."

"Your mother told me you were reading Shakespeare when others were reading comic books..."

"Shakespeare comics," Aiden muttered. "They were comic books based on Shakespeare..."

Vodin laughed. "Nevertheless, Aiden, there's nothing to be ashamed of. You recognized my quote from Macbeth back at the railway station the other day. Most people your age might not have been so quick to make the connection."

Aiden was silenced.

"My point is that if we're going to look at these stories in order to see what they mean for us—for us today—then we need to think critically about the text."

"Alright," Aiden said. "I get it. You want me to look for what's being said underneath all the mythological-sounding stuff, right?"

"I might not have worded it that way," said Vodin. "But yes, exactly. Myth that reveals truth, despite whether or not the stories could be literally true."

"So how does this answer my question about Shai?"

"Well, because there are several theories about Shai," Vodin replied with a knowing look. "You'll want to write this down. In the stories, Shai is more like a venerable old god who mostly does good things; he creates, he gives gifts, but his gifts also get abused and ruined, and he also tends to back away from his creations. In practical understanding and application, Shai is much more than that."

Vodin sighed, as if trying to find the right words. "Shai is a complicated thing to explain, which is admittedly why a lot of people simply do not talk about it. Some say Shai is in everything, and everyone. They say it holds the universe together. Others say Shai is everything and everyone. Such as: I am Shai and you are Shai, but we just don't fully embrace it.'

"Some do stick to the old ideas and call Shai a 'he', or maybe a 'she', but I don't even know if that does it justice—or if it matters. They will say he or she is all powerful, all-knowing, and the like... And that everything Shai does is good. Still there are others who say that Shai was sort of a god who created everything in Aignesia and left it to work on its own without any further contact."

When Aiden was done scribbling notes, he looked up, somewhat confused. "Okay, but what do you really think?"

"After a year, I'll ask you the same question," Vodin said, smiling. "We'll be looking at these stories in different ways and you can look at them critically before you come to your own conclusions."

Aiden sighed and asked again, "But what do you really think?"

"At the risk of having my own opinions sway you too much... If pressed," Vodin began, seeing the look of determination in Aiden's eyes. "I would say that I approach it as an agnostic. If I

am honest, I do not claim to know exactly who or what Shai is.
It is a kind of force, I suppose. Something most of the Amblers
will never quite understand, though some of their belief systems
leave room for such an idea. It is something most Agnecs
don't understand well either. I simply know that Shai works in
application, and as we progress, I'll show you exactly how."

***

That Friday, instead of Aiden hearing the usual Faerie's knock
to wake him up in the morning, he heard an unfamiliar knock.
It had sort of a rhythm to it. When Aiden did nothing, the knock
came again. Aiden crawled out of bed, pulled open the drapes,
and got dressed. He stumbled every other step. When he finally
managed to pull open the door, he stepped back, surprised at
what he saw.

It was Vodin, eyes gleaming as usual, but dressed almost as he
had the day when Aiden had first met him.

"Good morning, Aiden," Vodin said cheerily. "Today we're
going to market."

Aiden nodded, still somewhat groggy and having no clue what
Vodin was talking about. Aiden finished getting ready in a matter
of moments, but Vodin told Aiden to put on his old Ambler
clothes, and without thinking, Aiden changed again. Soon the
two were on their way out of the dormitory, heading down the
old cobblestone path.

The crisp morning air forced Aiden to wake up quickly. The
two of them were half way to the small building that led to the

Otter Gate, when Aiden's brow furled and he stopped. "So, we're not doing our lesson today?"

"We're going to market!" Vodin said just as cheerily as before, but with more volume. "Which, yes, means we're foregoing the usual lesson today. It also means we're going out of the Guild and into the largest Agnec market this side of the country."

"Oh," Aiden said, still pondering the change in routine. He slowly started catching up with Vodin down the walk. "Why are we going to market?"

"I mentioned earlier that we would need to," Vodin said, matter-of-factly. "Don't you remember? Anyway, you'll need some more supplies and school things for the year, and I also thought I'd take this opportunity to expose you to a bit more of the Agnec world. One can sometimes feel a bit isolated all cloistered in the Guild."

Aiden hadn't thought of it like that. He had begun to enjoy the peace and quiet, noticing how different it was from his noisy neighborhood in Philadelphia. Vodin led him into the small rounded room and out through the Otter Gate, leaving the Guild the same way they had entered at the beginning of the week.

"While we walk, let's recount what you've learned this week," said Vodin as he stepped onto the narrow dusty trail between trees.

"Um..." Aiden began, searching his mind while trying to keep up with Vodin's pace. "We went through the Founding Myth— Shai created everything with the help of the phoenix and the lamb."

"Everything?" Vodin probed.

"Well, no," Aiden admitted, almost stumbling on some fallen branches. "He created most of the land and also the first person."

"And?"

"From the first man's hair—which was planted in the ground—the first woman sprouted," said Aiden, realizing how strange it sounded when he spoke it aloud.

"Correct," Vodin said, still walking on ahead. "But who created the Elves, Dwarves, and Faerie-kinds?"

"The Hideyo," Aiden responded confidently.

"And who were they?"

"Um... Oroni?"

"Well, yes, they were part of the race of Oroni, but what else?"

"Uh..."

"They were the Elders, or Elder gods—depending on your view—who counseled with Shai," Vodin chimed in.

"Oh, that's right..." Aiden conceded.

They turned up a steep hill just as a cool breeze came over the rise, carrying the scent of pine and sap through the air. Vodin stopped when he saw a shady grove just before them.

"While we're speaking of Oroni; Now that we've also discussed Sion, who was he and what did he do?" Vodin said, looking to Aiden.

"Sion was usually called the Firstborn of the Oroni," Aiden remembered, stopping beside Vodin to enjoy the view. "He gave the D'Tari properties to mankind and... Centaur-kind.'"

"And what else is significant about that event?"

"He, uh, helped them defeat Resheph..."

"And who was Resheph?" Vodin probed further.

"He was an Oroni who rebelled against Shai... Right?" Aiden said, looking to Vodin for clarification. Vodin nodded. "And... Oh, and then he built the city of Pan... Um, Pand'Ros. Plus he was trying to destroy Shai's creations with an army of Trolls and Orcs."

"Excellent," Vodin said, his eyes smiling. "So we see how Sion becomes the archetypal savior. Part of a race of gods, or god-like beings, who steps down to help the mortals."

"Wait, weren't the Centaurs immortal?" Aiden said, his eyebrow raising.

"Ah, you caught me," Vodin said. "Yes, the Centaurs are immortal, as Shai crafted them from the first man's foot. I believe the quote goes something like: 'Shai looked down and said, I must make a guide for the man. A creature to express my power for him.' Clearly he intended to give humans helpers that would even outlive them."

Vodin looked back out over the grove from the top of the hill. "But some say man was meant to live immortally as well, but we lost that ability when the first man and woman disobeyed Shai and accidentally created the first Orc."

Vodin began walking down the hill, and Aiden followed. "So... Do Orcs really exist?"

"Certainly," Vodin said casually. "Trolls too."

"Are they really as bad in real life as the stories make them out to be?" Aiden asked, making his way carefully down the hill and into the shadow of the grove. "I mean, I read about creatures like that in real-world—I mean—Ambler storybooks. They were nasty then too."

"It's always the extremes that people remember most," Vodin said with a sigh. "The most beautiful or the most frightening. Nevertheless, Orcs certainly have a bad reputation, but don't let this paint your opinion of them before you even meet one."

Aiden felt his stomach go cold. The thought of meeting a creature like that made his mind whirl, and he wasn't sure he liked the idea.

"Relax," Vodin said, turning and patting the boy on the shoulder. "I am just saying, wait until you have all the information before you make a decision. Ah, here's the place." Vodin stopped and stared directly at a tree. "Before we go, I will ask you one more thing about the stories: Do you think Resheph was real and why do the stories need him?"

Aiden thought hard for a moment. "I don't know," he conceded. "But maybe he was real. I guess every story needs a bad guy. Someone to blame. Someone to fight."

Vodin was grinning broadly. "So true, my boy," he said excitedly. "Whether or not he was real, the question becomes deeper than that. Resheph may very well have been real for all we know. Was he an all-knowing, all-evil sort of entity? Not likely. But the story tells us that many things in life can be our Resheph. Defeating our Resheph is the key to being the very best version of ourselves."

Aiden stood back, his mouth open, and his mind in a sort of stupor over Vodin's words. The headmaster began runecasting some words into the air. They attached themselves to the face of the tree and began to glow. In moments, a door frame stood there up against the tree, as though it had been attached to the wood. Aiden shook his head, realizing that there was in fact a functional door standing before them.

Vodin reached forward and turned the knob. "We have to travel by door to the Ambler world in order to reach our destination," he said, looking to a somewhat confused Aiden. "I suppose we could have taken the Agnec Undergound, but this is extremely quick and convenient. Besides, this is how many D'Tari travel. I believe you're ready to see the difference."

Vodin pulled open the door. Aiden gasped when he looked in through the open frame. A brick wall stood several feet away, and the sounds of traffic filled the air.

Vodin looked to Aiden, noticing his obvious shock. "Did I mention, the markct is in Washington D.C.?" he said, reaching out to tug on the sleeve of Aiden's t-shirt.

Aiden shook his head in disbelief, unable to form words.

"But we must get going," Vodin added. "These doors won't last forever."

Vodin stepped over the threshold and onto a paved walk, but

Aiden felt rooted to the spot. He glanced around, smelling the pine and fur trees all around him, hearing the bird song, and then looked back through the open door at Vodin. Despite how much he'd already witnessed of the Agnec world, this still did not seem real. Vodin gestured animatedly for Aiden to come through.

Finally Aiden shrugged and stepped through. The humidity was palpable, and he had almost begun to sweat the moment he arrived. He shut the door behind him and realized it was beginning to fade from existence. Aiden and Vodin had stepped into a narrow alleyway between two buildings. The din of city life echoed throughout the alley from both sides.

"As I was saying," Vodin began, taking in Aiden's pondering eyes. "More often than not, D'Tari will travel by door or some other means of instantaneous travel. At your age, you would need to be accompanied by an adult to even attempt it. Some horrible things can happen to the D'Tari who makes even one little mistake with this sort of thing."

Aiden looked to Vodin with trepidation.

"But anyway," Vodin mumbled, walking away down the alley. "We need to be on our way."

Aiden followed Vodin out onto the sidewalk. The streets here reminded Aiden of some of the old parts of historic Philadelphia, and he knew they weren't all that far from his city. Quaint old shops lined the narrow street, and tourists seemed to be everywhere Aiden and Vodin were. The headmaster did not seem to mind, and he navigated effortlessly through the crowds.

Vodin stopped by a shop front not far from the corner of M Street and Potomac and turned down a very narrow alleyway between two ancient-looking buildings. Aiden followed. In no time, the sunlight began to disappear as the roofs of the buildings seemed to converge overhead.

The further they travelled, the longer the alleyway grew and the darker the path became. After just a few moments, however, Aiden realized they were standing before a door without a doorknob, illuminated by a small candle on the wall. The light had not been visible from the other end of the alley, and in fact, the path had been so dark and strange, that Aiden thought there must be some sort of enchantment going on.

Vodin leaned forward to feel the door, tracing his fingers along a runic word which lit up at his touch, sending a gentle white glow into the air. The lock clicked. He muttered something in a strange tongue, and the lock clicked again. An elegant door handle materialized, and before he touched it, Vodin whispered something in yet another tongue.

The lock clicked one more time.

"This is why I said most Agnecs know something of runelore," Vodin said. "And for those who must approach this place from the Ambler world, they also must know some Elvish and Dwarvish."

Aiden nodded, assuming Vodin referenced the strange languages that had just been spoken.

The headmaster turned the handle and pushed open the thick

door, which seemed more like an iron gate, as the two of them forced their way inside. The door locked itself behind them. Aiden felt as though he was back in the Agnec Undergound, except for the fact that he could see clear sky overhead, and a late summer sun shining down into the alleys, illuminating the cobblestone walkways.

Almost as if he'd stepped backward in time, Aiden saw what appeared to be sixteenth-century storefronts, butcher shops, grocers, black smiths, and a myriad of vendor carts scattered throughout the open square, all hidden from the rest of the world by high walls and buildings. Here Aiden saw mostly Fauns, Satyrs, and Dwarves roaming freely, dressed in any fashion they desired. Even many of the humans wore strange robes, cloaks, waistcoats, trousers, and other clothing that no one would ever call modern.

"Welcome to Market Street," said Vodin. "You'll want to be careful here. It's alright to explore, but just use discernment of course."

Vodin led Aiden through the square and into a small bookstore nestled between a blacksmith and a butcher shop. Thick stacks of books lined a narrow walkway through the store, and bookcases lined every wall from floor to ceiling. Aiden's mouth fell open as he followed Vodin through the maze. There were papyrus scrolls, stacks of parchment, thick leather-bound volumes, and even paper that appeared to be made of sheep-skin, as it still had wool on the backside of it. Books and manuscripts of all shapes and sizes flooded every inch of the store. The place seemed twice as large on the inside as it had seemed from the outside.

Vodin nodded to the kindly-looking Faun who sat behind an old desk, and led Aiden down an aisle designated "Guild Study". The headmaster began perusing the shelves, and Aiden followed, all the while unable to ignore the strange titles he saw, such as Do They Exist? A History of Star Nymphs, The N'Iatari: The Dark Side of Shai?, and The D'Tari Way; An Extremely Comprehensive Guide to Everything.

Finally Vodin found what he was looking for and began pulling a title here and a title there, until he carried a small stack of books. Without a word, he plopped them into Aiden's arms and turned down the aisle. Aiden stumbled, nearly sending the books cascading from his hands. In moments, Vodin had paid for the books, including a leather bag to carry them in, and they were back out in the cobblestone street.

Aiden tugged at the book bag on his shoulder uncomfortably and looked around the marketplace. "Um, thanks... Headmaster."

Vodin looked back at Aiden and smiled, nodding.

Next they went to the ink shop where Aiden was given a special set of quill-pens and several inkwells. They came neatly arranged in a brass case, ornate with runic lettering. Aiden thought it was likely the nicest thing he would ever own. Soon after that, they found themselves wandering toward the blacksmith's.

Aiden had never seen anything quite like this before. The

smithy was nothing more than an open-air forge, the workspace shielded only by a leather tarp. A heavily bearded man wearing a sleeveless tunic was working over the glowing coals, surrounded by swords, knives, axes, shields, and other medieval-looking weapons Aiden did not recognize. The sight was almost alarming, seeing so many weapons alongside the menacingly strong blacksmith at work. Aiden couldn't seem to tear his eyes away from the man's massive biceps and forearms.

Vodin glared at Aiden in warning and led him into the adjoining shop. Blades of all kinds, shapes, and sizes lined the walls, while a myriad of shields, bucklers, helmets, and pieces of body armor were arranged along the stone floors. In contrast to the huge man working the smithy outside, the man behind the desk was small and inviting. He directed them to a small corner of the shop where several barrels stood full of wooden implements and weapons.

"Pick a wooden sword, Aiden," Vodin said, placing a hand on one of the barrels. "Make sure it feels good in your hands. Both hands, because we'll start with the simplest incarnation: The double-handed cross-bar hilt."

Aiden looked to Vodin, raising an eyebrow.

"We've only been talking about people using swords all week," Vodin said calmly. "Why are you surprised?"

"I don't know..." Aiden admitted, unsure how to feel, though he felt a spark of excitement starting to spread.

"Nevertheless, swordlore is a huge part of the D'Tari tradition, whether in peace or war," Vodin added. "This is just your practice sword, you will not be receiving a proper one until next year."

Somewhat hesitantly, Aiden rifled through a selection of wooden swords inside the nearest barrel. At Vodin's encouragement, he tried several of them out, gripping the handle with both hands, and feeling the weight of each one. Vodin explained that a decent sword, even a wooden one, should have a well-balanced blade, yet still be relatively easy to wield by the handle. Aiden finally found one that seemed to fit nicely, and Vodin was impressed by his choice. Alongside the sword, Vodin also purchased a scabbard, a very simple wooden breastplate, and small buckler-type shield for Aiden.

As they crossed the threshold back into the street, they almost collided with a tall woman and three boys all about Aiden's age. Aiden avoided eye contact and intended to keep walking, but Vodin's hand gripped his shoulder.

"Good day, Councilwoman Monadias," Vodin said to the woman.

The woman turned, and as if she hadn't realized, she gave a sudden smile and a slight bow. "Oh, hello, Headmaster Vodin," she said, patting one of the boys' shoulders. "What brings you here?"

"Just helping young Aiden find his school things," Vodin said with a smile and pulling Aiden closer to the conversation. "This is Aiden, my newest protege and Guild student."

The woman flashed a brief and forced smile but said nothing, then pulled a blonde-haired boy close. "This is my son Grant. As you know he'll also be starting this year, along with his friends Charles and Chadwick," she announced importantly.

Aiden glanced at all three boys. The two darker-haired ones must have been twins, though each of them seemed to have a very different demeanor. One beamed with pride, standing tall next to Grant, and the other seemed less interested in the conversation. They glanced over at Aiden, and in typical teenage fashion, they gave him half-hearted nods, then looked away. He wondered what it would be like when they moved into the dorms.

"Very well then," Vodin said, seeing that the boys had all acknowledged each other. "I look forward to seeing you boys in a week or so. It's going to be a wonderful year."

"I'll see you, Headmaster, at the next Council meeting," Monadias said to Vodin, her tone almost cold.

"Yes, of course," Vodin said, nodding. "Farewell."

The two groups parted ways, and Vodin led Aiden further out into the square. Aiden furled his brow.

"I don't know if she likes you much," Aiden said, thinking aloud.

"Again, you are perceptive..." Vodin said with a small grin. "But frankly, I am not here to be liked."

Aiden pondered that statement as they wandered past several carts full of food and hanging clothing.

"She's on the D'Tari Council," Vodin said a few moments

later. "Monadias Griftwalker. She's shrewd and powerful, and not easy to please. So I must always be on my guard," he added, almost absent-mindedly.

Vodin stopped, his face scrunched as if in sudden regret. "As must you, I suppose," he said, looking to a confused Aiden. "We must choose our friends, and our foes, wisely. Remember that, Aiden."

Aiden nodded, still wondering at Vodin's words. Silently, Aiden followed Vodin through the market, amidst the shouting of vendors and smells of livestock. He tugged at his leather bag, feeling the weight of the books, but smiled when he felt the scabbard at his side.

.

Chapter 4
The Shadow

Aiden found it difficult to adjust to the way in which the Guild worked. Vodin had stopped telling the old stories and was now spending much of the mornings meditating with Aiden, as well as exercising.

At first, meditation had seemed strange, but Vodin explained, "All one must do is calm the mind and sit in the silence. Silent contemplation quiets the heart, and when the mind and heart are both quiet, they can listen to each other. When these things synchronize, one's whole being becomes a sounding board for the inner voice, or the light, or the Shai, as some believe it to be. Most importantly, meditating at least once a day can help you gain control of yourself."

Though Aiden was still having little luck seeing the value of sitting in silence—and sometimes finding it mostly boring—Vodin couldn't have picked a better time to begin teaching it, because Aiden no longer lived a peaceful existence in the dorms. Not only were there almost fifty other boys in the dorm, but there were three roommates living with him—though he couldn't remember their names yet. The adjacent girls' dormitory was equally full, and even after a week, Aiden began to see couples springing up as if from nowhere.

Aiden had begun his Introduction to Swordskill classes the first day. After his morning session with the Headmaster, and directly after enjoying his lunch, he was excited to bring his wooden sword, breastplate and buckler to the large field out behind the Great Hall, where nearly all the freshmen students had assembled awkwardly. Aiden was pleasantly surprised to see that Vodin had joined them. In moments, he realized that the Headmaster was the instructor of the class.

Vodin began by showing the students the different parts of the sword. "This, of course, is the blade," he said, gently running his fingers along the flat of his own drawn rapier. "The hilt," he continued, gesturing to the intricate structure protecting his sword hand. "The handle and pommel." He indicated the sword's grip and the rounded bottom tip of the handle. "For our current intents and purposes, this is all you need know.'

"All of you have been instructed to purchase double-edged, two-handed swords," Vodin said, looking around at each student's practice weapon. "Which I see you've all done. Excellent. Every sword demands its own unique way of being handled and fought with, and so we begin with these... Because they are the simplest to use."

At first, Aiden felt awkward holding his wooden sword, but as he stood alongside the other students, noticing their own looks of apprehension, he didn't feel nearly so bad.

"We'll start with simple techniques, mostly defensive," Vodin continued, still holding his own blade out before him. "We'll discuss the importance of swordlore in the pacifistic D'Tari tradition, as well as how D'Tari swords are used for far more than simple combat. We'll use them in runecasting and writing, among other things..."

A student raised his hand. "Yes?" Vodin acknowledged a red-haired boy somewhere off to Aiden's right.

"Did you say pacifistic?" the boy asked, scratching his head. "What does that mean?"

Without missing a beat, Vodin replied, "That means that while, yes, you are learning to defend yourselves with swords and shields and armor, you are not learning for the purposes of killing people... Whether for sport or money or even the whims of some maniacal tyrant..." Vodin paused, his mind seemed to be in a different place, then he returned. "These are tools, made for protecting others, made for discipline. Made for peace. And everyone here must be fully dedicated to using them with utmost responsibility, swearing never to do intentional harm to another creature without justifiable cause."

A silence fell across the group. Students exchanged excited and anxious glances.

"If you're all willing to listen, I'll continue to instruct," Vodin said, demanding their attention. "Yes?"

"Yes," the class said, in near unison.

From there, Vodin sheathed his own blade, which then disappeared, and picked up a spare wooden sword. He began to demonstrate the proper double-handed stance, and how to look at each side and angle of the body as a line to defend. He showed them some simple techniques such as a proper thrust or hack, how to parry, and a basic slash.

"Keep it simple," he said, seeing the students' enthusiasm growing. "Once we've mastered these, in the future, we'll move on to something a little more sophisticated."

He split them up into groups of four where students would practice the techniques on each other. Aiden had more bruises than anything else by the end of that first session, and he had dropped his sword several times. The rest of the week hadn't gone much better, but it was a start.

On Friday, Aiden was thankful to be almost done for the week. He sat quietly, studying the runes scrawled on the chalkboard at the front of the room. Their teacher for Runelore I was Master Flit, a red-bearded Faun, who was at the moment sitting off to the side at a desk and humming quietly. Aiden glanced down at his parchment, trying to compare the letter he'd written to a perfectly formed one on the chalkboard. He sighed, disgusted at his own work.

"Chadwick! Grant!" a voice boomed from the front of the room.

Aiden looked up, realizing that Master Flit had leapt to his feet and was glaring at the boys behind Aiden. Chad and Grant exchanged embarrassed glances and returned to their work. Aiden turned his head slowly, glancing over at them, but making sure they didn't notice.

He had seen them around the dorms, including Charles, but he hadn't talked with them yet. In fact, despite the close quarters, he hadn't talked much to anyone. It seemed as though all of these students were born into Agnec homes, and Aiden could still see the confused glances of his new roommates when they saw his Ambler clothing. He had simply decided to always wear his new Agnec clothes from now on, at least while at the Guild.

"Yes, London?" Master Flit's voice interrupted Aiden's thoughts.

A dark-haired girl near the front of the class began lowering her hand. "Erm, I was just wondering about row six," she began.

Aiden's eyes raced across his own page. He hadn't even begun copying row two.

"The third letter in; Is there two lines there, or is that a small dot?" the girl continued, her face turning slightly red.

"I shall clarify," Flit said in a flat tone. He walked over to the board and followed the lines to row six. "This first letter, the fehu, only needs two upward lines—almost like two upward branching tree limbs."

He drew the character again elsewhere on the board, and several of the students looked to their own parchment as they followed him. Master Flit drew the same character again, next to the first.

"This letter looks the same, but when we add this," he said, placing a small dot above the character. "It becomes veh. Any questions?"

London shook her head, and the class was silent. Aiden sighed quietly. He wondered if the others were as in the dark as he was. He was thankful that he would still be able to ask Headmaster Vodin about these things the next morning.

Something glinted just out of sight, and Aiden realized that London, the dark-haired girl, had been eyeing him. The moment he noticed, she turned her head away. There came a snickering from behind Aiden, and he looked back to see Grant chuckling with Chadwick. They noticed him and Grant nodded as if to say a silent hello.

Aiden returned the nod, then looked back to his own parchment. This class seemed to be taking forever, but Aiden knew it was important if he wanted to learn runecasting. He could feel the warmth of excitement at the mere thought, and he focused in on the strange letters and symbols.

* * *

Somehow, Aiden and Grant's relationship transformed rather quickly, having gone from a nod, to eating together during lunches, to finding things to do on weekends. Charles—who preferred to be called Charlie—and Chadwick were always along as well.

Aiden followed Charles, Chadwick, and Grant along the cobblestone path around the Guild grounds. The air was much cooler these days, and the sun hadn't completely risen yet. The boys were talking quietly, despite the excitement in their voices, and Aiden pulled his cloak around him, chilled from the early morning air.

"Don't spook the Windigo..." Chadwick said, snickering.

"What's that?" Aiden asked, following closely.

"Just a stupid legend. They're not real," Charlie said, glaring at his brother.

"They're real," Chadwick said, besting his brother with a glare of his own. "They look like people—sort of. But they suck blood... Or souls, or something."

Grant scoffed, "Never mind. Let's keep walking." He adjusted the pack on his back and focused them on the path ahead.

Grant led the way, as it seemed he always did. The twins followed beside Aiden, all the while assuring him that they were about to show him something amazing. Grant led them effortlessly through the octagonal room and out through the Otter Gate, as if he'd done this countless times before.

Having not even been at the Guild for two months now, Aiden was surprised at how quickly he'd come to call these boys his friends.

In the morning darkness, they wandered into the wood, and Aiden was struck by both the sense of fear and adventure. Grant led them over a small rise, forcing them to crawl over the massive trunks of several fallen trees until they came down the other side into a grassy ravine.

The twins excitedly led Aiden to the edge of the ravine, and he could see that there was a much steeper drop-off on this side. In fact, the bottom seemed to be covered in shadow. It was almost other-worldly in the blueish-gray twilight.

"Wow..." Aiden found himself saying. "It's cool, I guess. A little anti-climactic though..."

Aiden turned around to face the boys, but was surprised to see the look on each of their faces. They glared at him now, and Grant held a double-edged sword in his hand. This was not one of the wooden practice swords they had recently begun using, but an actual steel blade.

Aiden had almost taken a step back, but caught himself, remembering the deep ravine behind him. He threw them all an incredulous look.

"So... What's going on?" Aiden asked. "And... Where did you get that? You're not supposed to have that."

Grant laughed dismissively and tried to swing the sword around himself, though it seemed almost too heavy for him. "The other night, we broke into the Guild's smithy."

Aiden's brow furled. He hadn't even known the Guild had a blacksmith.

"So... What're you doing with it?" Aiden asked, unsure he wanted the answer, judging by the strange look on Grant's face.

"We thought we'd put you to a little test," Chadwick chimed in as Charlie stood off to the side, looking unsure.

"Let me say it, stupid!" Grant said, throwing Chadwick an annoyed look. He looked back to Aiden. "It's not very often that Headmaster Vodin takes on a student to mentor. My mother hasn't ever seen it happen, and she's been on the Council for years..."

Aiden's eyes raced around, taking in all three boys. At Grant's last words, they all seemed particularly upset. "Well, I didn't make him choose me or anything," Aiden finally responded. "I didn't even know about any of this until, like, last year..."

"Exactly," Grant snapped, holding the sword out. "You don't deserve any of this. You're not even a real Agnec, and you'll never be a real D'Tari."

Aiden's face began to redden as the sting of their betrayal finally hit him. "So, what?" he said, hearing the defensive tone in his own voice, sensing some of his old self returning. "You're going to kill me?"

"Not kill you," Grant said, a determined smirk now crossing his lips. "Leave you to die, maybe."

Chadwick laughed aloud. "You didn't really think you were friends with us, did you?" he said.

"You can't just make the problem go away," Aiden said. "Vodin will still never mentor any of you."

"There are better D'Tari out there than him, you idiot," Grant retorted. "You don't know anything. My mother's on the Council and she could replace him like that." Grant snapped. "Especially after they find that the first kid he's mentored in years goes missing..."

Aiden was silenced, forced to listen to the sound of his heart race.

"That's crazy..." Aiden said, the anger rising in his chest.

Aiden's palms grew hot until each hand had produced a ball of energy that burned like red fire into the chill air. Charlie and Chadwick stood back, but Grant scoffed and held out his blade with both hands. The twins stepped back until just Aiden and Grant glared at each other.

"I don't even know why I trusted you," Aiden said, trying to flush the hurt from his voice. "I don't need you."

"We don't need you here either. The Guild was doing fine without you," Grant growled. "Why don't you go back to your stupid Ambler mommy. Maybe she can whine and complain and get you into another school, somewhere else..."

Aiden ground his teeth. Grant laughed.

"Oh Headmaster, can you help my son? I don't know what to do with him..." Grant did a poor imitation of a woman's voice. "He keeps getting kicked out of schools, wah wah wah..." Grant's face twisted with laughter.

Aiden's rage boiled over and he let Grant have it with both balls of energy. They exploded on the flat of Grant's blade, the blast knocking Grant to the ground, and the blade crashing to the forest floor. Aiden lost his balance, his left foot slipping backward, knocking grass and pebbles loose off the sharp edge of the ravine.

Grant scrambled to his feet, surprised to see that Aiden's energy had melted the sword, leaving it black and smoking. He stepped back to join the twins, while Aiden flailed wildly and struggled to keep balance.

Aiden fell. He closed his eyes, expecting the long fall and then a skull-breaking crack at the bottom. It never came. Instead the fall lasted two seconds and ended in a giant splash. His leg cracked loudly, crushed by his own weight, and he was drenched in freezing water.

When he opened his eyes, Aiden saw all three boys laughing and pointing. The deep dark ravine was gone, and instead, he was sitting in a shallow trench full of cold, stagnant water. Aiden realized it immediately: The ravine had been an illusion, a prank. The pain in his leg was made so unbearable by the stinging cold, that Aiden was fairly sure that tears were running down his cheeks. This of course only made the boys on the bank laugh and taunt him even harder.

"You thought we were gonn'a kill you..." Grant scoffed. "But if I were you, I wouldn't bother coming back."

Aiden ignored him, trying to stand, but his broken leg crumpled beneath him and he screamed. The boys all stopped laughing and stared for a moment, but Grant still snickered. Aiden raised his hand, gesturing for help, but the boys looked at each other with raised eyebrows.

"Let's get out of here," Charlie said to the others, looking nervously from them to Aiden and back.

The others laughed, and Grant threw Aiden a menacing glare before turning away. They took off running over the hill and disappeared out of sight. Aiden looked around, the cold and the pain eating away at him.

As the boys ran away, Aiden could still hear their footfalls through the wood. "I just thought we were gonn'a scare him, not hurt him..." Aiden could hear Charlie say, the boy's voice somewhat shaky.

"Don't worry about it," Chadwick laughed, joined by Grant.

"Did you know who could do that?" one of the boys said, though Aiden wasn't sure whose voice it had been.

Aiden was dumbstruck as the voices faded from earshot. It seemed hopeless, sitting there in the water, drenched to the bone. Each time he tried to stand, the pain in his leg grew worse. He cursed each time he tried. He was just glad that his mom wasn't able to hear him now.

Aiden gave a weak yell for help, but then felt stupid. He thrust himself forward, stretching out his hand for the tufts of grass on the ravine's bank. He moaned, aching from a new wave of pain in his leg, but he knew he had to keep going. He was only sitting in two and a half feet of water, but the pain made everything worse. With one last burst of energy, he thrust himself forward with a splash and finally got hold of the bank.

Aiden had gotten himself halfway out, when something raced by. It would have been silent, if not for the rustling of the undergrowth. He had only seen it for a split second, and at first thought it was a deer or some other animal. He couldn't think about it. He continued pulling himself out of the freezing water, pulling up clumps of damp earth as he did so.

Another rustling came again, this time it seemed closer. This time he'd seen a shadow, a figure. A very human-like figure, concealed in the darkness of the wood. It had sped by, going the opposite direction. Aiden froze, his heart racing.

When no more shadows emerged, Aiden pulled even harder, finally getting both legs up onto the bank. The pain in his leg was excruciating now, but he kept himself from screaming.by thrusting his fist in his mouth. He didn't care that his hand was wet. He tried standing again, pulling himself onto his good leg by grabbing the branches of a nearby spruce.

"You guys suck!" Aiden yelled into the darkness once he could stand, his chest heaving with anger. "You guys-"

But he never finished the inevitable string of violent names he'd wanted to utter. A tall figure emerged from behind a cluster of trees not even ten feet from Aiden. It was taller than any man he had yet seen, but it still looked like a man. It was gaunt and skeletal, with empty eye sockets and bony, clawed hands. It looked like a cloaked corpse, but maybe it was only somewhere between living and dead. The very presence of the thing sent Aiden's heart into his throat, and he felt colder now than he'd been when sitting in the icy water.

Windigo... was all Aiden could think, remembering Chadwick's words from earlier.

The creature hovered slowly, in an unearthly sort of way, toward Aiden. The boy panicked and fell onto his backside, his leg giving way painfully.

The Windigo grew nearer, its slit of a mouth now open to

reveal ugly fangs. Aiden held a hand out to form an energy ball, but he was too weak. Nothing was happening.

He scooted back, risking falling into the water behind him, wincing as his leg throbbed with each movement. The Windigo hunched now, bending toward Aiden as if stalking him like an animal. Its face was menacing. Aiden could feel his pulse rushing, and he looked around frantically for something. Anything.

A dark shadow rushed behind the Windigo. Aiden braced himself for the appearance of more creatures, but only the one remained. The shadow raced by again, this time breaking the Windigo's concentration. Yet again, the phantom sped by, but this time it roared.

From what Aiden could see, the shadow creature looked almost human and almost animal, all at once. The roar was strange. Unearthly. The Windigo shuddered at the prolonged reverberation. In the midst of the wild raging sound, Aiden heard what seemed like words forming.

"He. Is. Mine."

The sound was the most horrible thing Aiden had ever heard, and he bent low to the grass, just hoping the end would come. The Windigo's skeletal frame almost bent in half, shaking as if terrified. The creature turned back into the darkness and faded from sight just as quickly as it had appeared.

The wood was silent.

***

After several moments of staring into the shadows, Aiden braced himself and tried to stand once more. His leg was beginning to stiffen, but that only seemed to increase the pain. It felt as though hot knives were being shoved up inside his leg, directly between the muscle and the bone. He tried to stifle a scream and fell into the grass again.

The sound of footfalls approached, but Aiden resigned not to care so much. There was a pain forming in his head, and he almost wondered if he'd be better off as prey to the bizarre creatures of the wood.

"Aiden?" a familiar voice called.

Aiden moaned and looked up. Vodin stood there with Charlie by his side. Aiden couldn't even manage a word, but he smiled at the sight.

Vodin leaned forward and helped pull Aiden into a sitting position. He looked to Aiden's leg as if he had read the boy's mind. Charlie stayed away, his eyes wide as if in horror. Vodin rubbed his hands together and quickly tore the pant leg open by the seam, exposing Aiden's broken leg.

Aiden no longer felt pain because shock had set in, but the sight of his leg twisted into a normally impossible position had made him grimace. Vodin stood and reached to his side, then drew out a sleek one-handed sword as if from an invisible scabbard. It was a rapier with a complex, swirling hilt design, and the long, thin blade was covered with runes. Aiden shook his head, and for a moment thought that Vodin planned to cut off the leg.

Vodin hadn't noticed Aiden's reaction, instead, he quickly pricked his own finger with the blade, then acted as though he was sheathing the sword. The rapier vanished and Vodin leaned back down. Without losing any time, he began drawing runic words in blood all over Aiden's broken limb. When he was done, he stopped and leaned back on his haunches, looking quite agile for a man who so often spoke of himself as old.

A sharp pain swept through Aiden's leg, followed by a loud crack. Then a wonderful bliss overcame him. The pain was gone, though the bones felt sore, but it no longer hurt when he attempted to move his foot or bend his knee. Vodin helped Aiden to his feet, and Charlie stared at them in awe.

"Um," Aiden finally had the strength to speak. "Thanks..." he said, still amazed at what had happened.

"Let's walk," Vodin said sternly, looking at both boys and making his way back up the ravine.

Aiden and Charlie followed somewhat hesitantly. When Vodin looked away, Aiden glared at Charlie, but the other boy frowned, eyes red with apologetic tears.

"I swear I didn't know how far Grant would take it," Charlie half-whispered. "I didn't know. I didn't know..."

Aiden's face scrunched and he said nothing, but simply followed Vodin up the hill. Vodin led them back into the Guild and brought them both to his office. His expression was unusually solemn.

"Alright then," Vodin said after they had all been seated. "What happened?"

Charlie was silent, but he looked to Aiden as if begging not to be blamed. Aiden sighed.

"I... We were just hanging out," Aiden finally said. "I thought it might be fun to check out the woods, and I slipped and fell in the creek."

Vodin stared intently into Aiden's eyes for a moment, but Aiden had to look away.

Vodin sighed. "Are you sure that's the entire story?" he asked. Aiden nodded.

"Very well then," Vodin finally said, glancing at both boys with suspicion. "Well, I'm just glad you're both fine. Charles, you are dismissed, but find Grant and tell him I want to see him in my office as soon as he can be here."

Charlie stood up, almost shaking from nerves, and nodded. He looked back at Aiden with a thankful yet worried expression just before he closed the door behind him.

"Now Aiden," Vodin began the moment they had been left alone. "Remember what I said about choosing your friends, and foes, wisely?"

Aiden nodded.

"This is your reminder. As your mentor, it concerns me which crowd you fall into."

"Yes... Sir," Aiden said, just feeling thankful that nothing worse had happened, though he realized he was also shaking—

whether it was from nerves, the cold, or from shock, he could not be sure.

"But what happened after you fell?" Vodin asked. "I sense there's more to the story."

"Oh..." Aiden said, but after a pause, he proceeded to tell the Headmaster about the Windigo and the strange shadow creature that had chased it away. When he was done, Vodin looked intrigued.

"You are correct. That was in fact a Windigo," Vodin said flatly. "Nasty creatures. One of this world's primordial oddities. Hmm..." He paused, looking pensive.

"...But what was the shadow thing?" Aiden asked tentatively.

"It seems that you may have had a visit from the unKing," Vodin said, smiling for the first time since Aiden had entered the office.

"Who? What?"''

"Well, legend has it that he's, more or less, Sion's recent incarnation," said Vodin thoughtfully.

Aiden raised an eyebrow.

"If he's visiting you, then just count yourself lucky," Vodin continued, smiling again. "Of course we'll talk more about it soon, but for now, stay out of trouble, get some rest, and stay inside the Guild grounds. Also, go thank Charlie for his help in finding me. If he hadn't led me to you in time, you'd be a lot worse for wear, my boy."

Aiden paused, then nodded, finally smiling a little. Another thought struck him, "Headmaster?"

"Yes?"

"Maybe it's none of my business, but why do you need to see Grant?"

"Well," Vodin began, leaning in as if what he was about to reveal was a secret. "This much I know: He owes the blacksmith a new sword."

***

Aiden changed out of his nicer tunic and into a sleeveless one, threw on a cloak, half-nodded to his roommates—which was nearly all they ever communicated to each other—and headed out into the hallway, determined to be on time for his first day after the winter break. He almost bumped into Charlie and Chadwick as he descended the spiraling stair.

Charlie threw him a sideways smile, but Chadwick glared. Aiden shrugged as the two rushed past him, Chadwick intentionally bumping Aiden with his elbow. This had become the norm. Aiden had slowly come to see Charlie as a friend again, but Chadwick and Grant showed nothing but contempt.

"They're just jealous," Charlie had told Aiden. "Grant's bluffing about trying to replace the Headmaster. He wouldn't do that..."

For all Aiden knew, Charlie's explanation made sense. Aiden's mother had been told of his broken leg, so Aiden had finally told her about Grant and Chadwick too, and she, just like Vodin, had urged him to stay away from them. Aiden had been glad to be home for the short break, but now, back at the Guild, he couldn't wait to get started again.

Aiden stepped outside and shivered, hit by a wave of biting cold air. He pulled his cloak tight around him and took down the snowy cobblestones at a brisk pace. Soon he was surrounded by small groups of students along the walkway. There was an excitement in the air, and although winter had certainly set in, the sun gently glinted through the white sky.

As Aiden neared the Great Hall, he nodded at a couple of the boys in greeting, who nodded back. Just as he made to push open the large doors and make his way inside, another set of hands pushed next to his. In surprise, he realized it was London, the girl from his runelore class.

"Oh, hi," she said, taking her hands off the door, gesturing for him to go ahead.

Aiden nodded, not knowing what to say. He pushed his way through and held the door open for her, along with a myriad of other students who quickly filed in. As Aiden walked through the foyer, London caught up with him.

"How was your break?"

Aiden looked over, surprised to see London talking to him. "Oh," he said, his cheeks flushing despite already being pink from the outside cold. "Oh it was pretty good, I guess."

"Cool," London said, her eyes searching the room suddenly, as if for more words. "Yeah, not much happened on mine either. My parents don't really get the whole Agnec thing."

Aiden looked at her with a raised eyebrow.

London laughed, obviously seeing his surprise. "A lot of
people aren't Agnec-born," she said, smiling. "Some people just
think they're better than others just because they are."

"Yeah, I guess so..." Aiden said thoughtfully, then remembered
the time. "Oh man, I gott'a go."

"What class?" London asked as Aiden pushed open the next
set of double doors before them.

"Powercasting—something or other," Aiden said, feeling
somewhat prideful as he turned into the bustling hall and a flood
of sound hit them.

London looked impressed. "Seriously? Most people don't start
that til the second year," she said.

"I know, but it's what Headmaster Vodin wants... So what else
can I do?" Aiden smiled. "Well... I'll see ya," he finally said with
a half-wave, feeling surprisingly more upbeat than he'd been
when the day began.

They parted ways and Aiden headed to the far side of the
hall, pushing through the jostling crowd of students, staff,
and masters. He reflected momentarily on his encounter with
London, but those thoughts were pushed aside as Aiden entered
another hallway, ascended a busy stair, and finally found his
way into a large room where the chalkboard said, in large letters,
"Introduction to Powercasting".

A beautiful, tall woman with long braids of auburn and an
ornate dress stood near the chalkboard. She had a very serene

expression, despite the chaos in the room. There were no chairs
or desks, so the students seemed unsure where to stand, most
of them haphazardly placing themselves wherever they wanted,
without regard for the others entering the room.

Aiden wandered in, perturbed that people kept standing in his
way or accidentally bumping him, because they were as clueless
as he was. He noticed that the room was wide and very long,
alight by three chandeliers, and at the far end, there were several
paper targets as well as some other materials.

"Students!" a clear, commanding voice bellowed into the
chaos.

The room grew very quiet and everyone looked forward at the
lady near the chalkboard.

"Welcome to Introduction to Powercasting," the tall woman
announced, then smiled gently. "I am Mistress Dorsa as some
of you know, and I'm very anxious to get started. You'll need
to take seats all along this wall here," she said, pointing to the
side of the room with the chalkboard. "We'll face that way." She
pointed to the far end of the room with the targets. "And we'll
jump right in. Please remove any extravagant items of clothing,
jewelry, and the rest, that you'd prefer not to have burned,
destroyed, or otherwise maimed."

Aiden, along with the rest of the class, sat down against the
wall. The students began removing cloaks and outer tunics, along
with other items, and placing them up against the wall behind
themselves. When they had settled down, Mistress Dorsa closed

the classroom door and walked to the center of the room, facing them.

"Some of you were born with this ability, and some of you began developing an aptitude for it later. While some of you may simply want to learn it right now," she began, looking out over the anxious expressions of the students. "Regardless of the circumstances, here you are, and while you're in my stead, there will be absolutely no fooling around." Her tone grew stern. "You will listen intently and do as you're instructed. You will learn to claim these abilities as your own—many of you. Some of you will discover that you cannot possibly obtain them."

Several of the students exchanged worried glances.

"As you all know, the second year is about tapping in to, and understanding, the Innate Properties," she continued. "You will have to feel this inside your very being. Not everyone will, but at least you'll be that much more educated, won't you?"

There was an odd silence in the room as her words sunk in.

"Correction: Not all of you are in your second year, are you?" Mistress Dorsa said, walking nearer to the students. Before anyone could answer, she had walked up to Aiden and looked down on him. "You're the exception, I suppose. Still in your first year. Aiden, is it?"

Aiden nodded, looking horrified and realizing that the entire room was casting a suspicious eye on him.

"Well then, we'll start with you," Dorsa said, offering a helping hand to Aiden. "Since the Headmaster has so much faith in you."

Aiden felt a sudden coldness in his stomach as he stood—with the woman's help—and she led him to the center of the room. She touched his shoulder gently and they stood before the class. His cheeks flushed and several of the students smirked and snickered.

"Headmaster Vodin tells me you're a natural, so there's no need to be worried," Dorsa told Aiden.

Aiden felt as though she must have been sincere, but her tone was hard to read and the weight of all those eyes bearing down on him threatened to overwhelm.

"When I say 'positions', it will mean taking a stance with both arms out, readying to fire," Dorsa said to the class. "By fire, of course, I mean forcing the energy into the palm of your hands and concentrating it on a target. For that is, on the face of it, what powercasting is."

One of the students, a brown-haired girl, began scribbling something down on a piece of parchment, but Dorsa suddenly stood there, blocking the overhead light. The girl saw Dorsa's shadow and looked up, confused.

"Take notes later," Dorsa said, sternly. "This course is about practical application, not theory." Dorsa walked away as the girl hurried frantically to put away the parchment and quill.

"This room has had several runic enhancements, or enchantments—what have you—to protect it, and us, from being completely destroyed. But I warn you," Dorsa said as she stopped and glared at the class, including Aiden. "This does not guarantee every safety and protection. Learning discernment, concentration, and control, is the key to success here. This is a defensive art, not necessarily an offensive one. Many of you will likely use this skill to help protect others, and that, is my recommendation. The combative arts are not for the starting of wars and battles, but for the ending of them."

This reminded Aiden of Vodin's words at the beginning of his swordskill class. He wasn't surprised by this sentiment, but Mistress Dorsa spoke with such conviction that the class was silent with awe. Aiden felt rooted to his spot.

"Now then," Dorsa said, turning back to Aiden. "Assume the position."

Aiden swallowed and took a stance with his arms out and palms up. Dorsa walked around him, adjusting his stance so that his legs were equally apart, knees bent slightly, shoulders up, and palms closer together. As she did this, she explained to the class the importance of the stance.

"You must be prepared to embrace the power flowing through you, as well as brace yourself for the shock of it leaving you," she told them.

When satisfied, she looked to Aiden again. "Alright then, focus on the first target on the far right. Focus. Feel your emotions. Re-imagine the feeling that triggers your energy, and concentrate on funneling that into your hands. If those emotions threaten to overwhelm you, you must control them. You must make them obey."

Aiden's mind went blank for a moment, and he began to sweat, feeling the eyes of the class on him. He took a deep breath, maintaining his stance, and suddenly remembered Vodin's words about sitting in the silence. When Aiden stood still long enough, he didn't think about the others in the room. He only thought about what mattered, and the images of boys from his old school began to surface. Next, he saw Grant and Chadwick laughing and taunting him.

"What are you feeling?" Aiden heard Dorsa's voice.

"Anger," Aiden said, without even thinking.

"Don't let it best you," she said calmly. "Make it obey."

Aiden could almost visualize something like a white heat rising through him, threatening to get into his head. Though it began to swirl chaotically through him, he forced it into his arms and finally into his palms. The target on the far right at the end of the room exploded, taking part of the target next to it down as well.

Aiden shook his head, feeling that familiar sensation when he would normally begin to blink uncontrollably. Surprisingly, the blinking never happened. He smiled and turned to the class, and they no longer gawked and snickered. Several of the students looked on with wide eyes, while others simply smiled.

"The Headmaster was right about you," Mistress Dorsa said, now smiling. "But let's do that again, this time with more control. You'll practice it until it becomes a second nature."

Chapter 5
N'Iatari

Another summer was over, and Aiden had been going stir crazy, waiting to get back to the Guild. He sat in his living room watching television, knowing that any time now Headmaster Vodin would arrive and take him back to a world where most modern technology did not exist.

"Are you all ready, Aiden?" his mother asked, entering the room carrying a laundry basket.

"Yep," Aiden said without looking over, his eyes still glued to the screen as he flipped channels.

"I'm sorry I've had to work so much since you've been home," his mother said, putting the basket down on the couch not far from him. "I wish we could've done more things together."

Aiden shut off the TV and throw the remote aside. "Don't worry about it, Mom," he said. "I'm just glad I could relax. Nothin' crazy happened. That's good, right?"

His mother laughed and began to fold the laundry. "True. So what are you learning this year?'

"Not sure," Aiden said, finally standing. "I'm going to continue powercasting—" He paused, noting the flash of caution in his mother's eyes. She was still not fond of his ability to throw energy from his hands. "But I've been learning runes," he said quickly. "And history, and culture... And other stuff."

Aiden had told her long ago about the Underground, the D'Tari properties, and other Agnec creatures that existed alongside humans, and although she had claimed to believe him, there were still a few talking points they avoided.

"I don't understand it all, Aiden," she had told him. "But I know what you have is special, and I won't stand in the way of you becoming what you're meant to be."

"It should be a pretty cool year, I guess," said Aiden, back in the present, his eyes gleaming.

His mother smiled. "I just wish we had a little more time," she said.

"Oh Mom," Aiden sighed. "It'll be fine. It'll work out."

"I know. Of course it will."

In moments, Vodin was at the door, dressed the same as last year. Aiden said goodbye to his mother and followed Vodin outside into the heat of the day.

As they walked along the old sidewalks, Vodin almost had to yell over the roar of traffic. "Do you remember what you learned last year?"

"Um... Sure. Most of it," Aiden replied, keeping up with Vodin's pace.

"Good," Vodin said, smiling. "I suggest you spend this time re-familiarizing yourself with the key things you learned, because this year, I have some special plans for you."

Aiden felt his stomach tighten. "Special plans?"

"No worries, my boy," Vodin said, stopping to pat Aiden's shoulder. "It's all progress. Any questions before we find a place to draw a door?"

"We're not taking the Underground?"

"No," Vodin replied. "But we are traveling to Market Street to get you some things. Is that your question?"

"Well, no," Aiden said quickly. "Um... I'm sixteen now, and I was wondering: Do Agnec kids get drivers' licenses?"

Vodin laughed, but stopped when Aiden furled his brow. "Sorry, Aiden," he apologized. "But what would we drive? And why bother driving when we can travel faster than any automotive?"

Aiden looked down, his face flushed. "Yeah... I guess that makes sense."

"In some of the Agnec villages, children will drive carriages and ride horses when old enough," Vodin said, beginning down the sidewalk again. "But D'Tari have little need for such things most of the time. Remember, you're a D'Tari first, an Agnec second."

Aiden followed the Headmaster.

"No worries," Vodin continued. "I know you're still trying to understand the Agnec world, but haven't some of your friends at the Guild helped you with that?"

Aiden raised an eyebrow. Other than that business with the Windigo last year, Vodin had not asked much about Aiden's social life. "Um, I guess a little," he replied. "I'm not really close with anyone."

"It's not always easy for people," Vodin said knowingly. "I myself was not the socialite everyone expected me to be. Even now, I would rather have one close friend than a thousand distant ones."

Aiden looked up at the Headmaster, pondering his words.

"Trust me, Aiden," Vodin continued. "Once you've thrown off the burden of others' approval, it's amazing what you can accomplish."

Once they had gone several blocks, Vodin stopped and glared at a simply decrepit house. It was in a complete shambles; the windows and doors were barred and boarded up, the roof was missing shingles—while some areas looked caved in—and the front lawn was overrun with a violent forest of weeds and unruly flowers.

"I must make a short detour," Vodin said, stepping onto the cracked driveway.

Aiden looked around, but simply shrugged. He had passed this place many times in his life while walking to the store, and had never thought much of it. "Why?" he finally asked.

Vodin didn't respond, but simply headed for the side yard until he came to a rough path in the tall grass. He led Aiden to an old wooden gate and easily pushed his way into the backyard. Aiden hadn't thought it possible, but the backyard was even more unkempt than the front. A set of rusting lawn furniture sat out on a rotting wooden porch. What once must have been a small fountain now stood a moss-infested, rust-colored mess surrounded by a swath of tall weeds and cobwebs.

Vodin stopped just before the porch, noting the thick layers of spider webs before him. "You've really outdone yourself, Menlir," Vodin said quietly, looking directly into the shadow of the house, which slumped as if falling off its foundation.

The end of the porch nearest the house—the spider webs, the wooden step, the rot, everything—quickly folded into itself as if space were being bent in half. Aiden jumped back, his heart in his throat suddenly. Despite the rest of the environment remaining broken down and trashy, left within the space that had disappeared, there now stood a clean and well-lit entry way. A Faun stood there, his one-handed basket-hilted broadsword in hand.

"Headmaster Vodin," the Faun said, now smiling. "What a surprise. Come in." He sheathed his sword into an invisible scabbard, and the weapon disappeared, just as Aiden had seen Vodin do with his own blade.

"Menlir," Vodin began, stepping up into the entry way. "This is my protege Aiden. Well, Aiden, what are you waiting for?" Vodin looked back at a confused Aiden.

Aiden shook his head, then looked around. "Uh, sorry," he said, then took a cautious step inside.

"This is Master Menlir," Vodin introduced the Faun. "He is the local guardian for the few Agnecs scattered about this neighborhood. He's also been keeping an eye on your mother for you."

Aiden was taken aback. "Oh, you're Menlir," he said with a look of realization.

"Master Menlir," the Faun corrected.

"Yes, Master. Sorry," Aiden said.

"Nice to meet you finally," Menlir said, taking a very brief moment to appraise the boy.

Aiden nodded.

"What brings you this way?" Menlir asked Vodin as he led them into a surprisingly bright and cheery living room.

Aiden glanced in all directions. He was confused. The house was warm, well-lit, ornate with paintings on the walls, a decorative fireplace, and complete with well-kept furniture. There were no signs of damage or decay as there appeared to be from the outside.

"The outside is an illusion," Vodin said, noting Aiden's obvious question. "Along with many other reasons, it is there for protection."

Aiden nodded, but still astounded at how real he had thought everything was. Menlir seemed amused at Aiden's confusion, but returned his attention to Vodin.

"Let's go in the other room, shall we?' Vodin said, gesturing toward Menlir's kitchen. "We'll just be a minute, Aiden," he called back to the boy. "Stay in here, won't you?."

Aiden nodded in agreement, but watched the tall man and the Faun head into the other room. As the voices trailed off, Aiden wandered around the living room, examining the paintings. Many of them were of ancient looking Fauns with horns of various sizes and thick beards. Aiden looked out the large bay windows, watching the traffic racing by. It was so strange to think that he was inside the old abandoned house. If he were outside, he wouldn't even be able to see these windows. But, here he was looking out through them.

"Illusions..." Aiden thought aloud. He had read about the art of illusioncasting last year. He could see how that might come in handy.

Just like powercasting, making illusions was also considered one of the innate properties, something felt and not necessarily created with runes.

Aiden sighed and got to his feet, the Headmaster and Menlir had been gone for a while now. Aiden wondered what they could possibly be talking about. He slowly wandered over to the edge of the living room, taking care not to trip over Menlir's intricately carved coffee table, and pressed himself closer to the wall until he could hear soft-spoken voices.

"Are you absolutely sure?" came Menlir's voice.

"As I've said," came Vodin's voice in a tentative tone. "I spent the better part of the summer looking into it. Not that I need to explain my family history to you or anything, but we have spoken on the subject. I'd say most of the evidence points in the right direction."

"Alright then," Menlir said, sounding put off. "But is it really wise to trust him with it?"

"I don't see how I have another option," said Vodin. "It will only be a matter of time until my past comes knocking. Shai knows some of our closest friends have been suspicious for some time now that I might be carrying it..."

"But they won't suspect him?"

"Of course not," said Vodin. "Why would they? They don't even know he exists."

"Once you gift it to him, there's no turning back," said Menlir, his tone very serious. "Even if they do find out."

"I'm well aware," Vodin said. "But I'm going to give him the tools to handle this responsibility. I will not last forever, but this great secret must be carried on, no matter the cost. The N'Iatari must not find it. If I keep it with me, it will only be a matter of time."

Aiden relaxed for a moment. The N'Iatari? Why does that sound so familiar? he thought.

Without warning, the Headmaster and the Faun both stepped back into the living room and Aiden panicked, half-running, half-falling away from the wall. The panic seemed to swarm around inside of him and he threw his arms up while landing with a harsh thud on the hardwood floor.

Another figure stood in the center of the room. It was almost like a shadow, but transparent. Vodin and Menlir stared at it, then looked back and forth between it and Aiden with wide eyes.

Vodin leaned over and helped Aiden to his feet with a

surprising amount of strength.

"What are you doing?" Menlir asked, looking almost more angry than confused.

Aiden glanced over to the strange figure, unsure why it was just standing there. Then he realized it moved when he moved. He coughed and the figure faded in gentle wisps of white smoke.

"I don't know..." Aiden finally responded to Menlir's question. "I don't know what happened."

A look of realization spread over Vodin's features, and he smiled. "I think you may have just cast your first illusion."

***

Although Menlir had been eying Aiden suspiciously, Vodin seemed to believe Aiden's story. The boy had explained—though it was a partial lie—that he had simply meant to come talk to the two of them when he tripped and fell. Perhaps Vodin didn't really believe the story, but he didn't seem all that concerned. Instead, the man had explained that the strange figure in the room was an illusion that Aiden had cast.

After they bid Menlir a goodbye and walked away from the house—which still looked condemned and run-down from the outside—Vodin was still beaming proudly. As Aiden followed Vodin along the old sidewalk, his mind raced back to the incident with the illusion, but the Headmaster had said he would learn more as those classes began this year. Even more than that, Aiden thought of what he had overheard.

None of it seemed to make sense, but he wondered if they were talking about him.

In minutes, Vodin had led him to an abandoned alley, well away from the sight of traffic or passersby. With runes, he drew a door along the wall, and when it had appeared, they both stepped through. This was no longer nearly so strange for Aiden. Just as they had the year before, they ended up in an alley not far from the corner of M Street and Potomac in Washington D.C. In just a few short minutes, they found their way into the hidden Market Street entrance.

Despite how Aiden had witnessed all of this before, he still marveled at the vendors' carts and the ancient shops lining the old square. He received a few strange looks from people because he wore his Ambler clothing, but he didn't think too much of it. After they had visited the ink shop, and the book store, Vodin took Aiden back to the blacksmith's shop where they had purchased his wooden practice sword the year before.

"This year you start using a real sword," Vodin said, patting Aiden on the shoulder when they crossed the threshold.

Aiden's heart leaped as they approached a wall of steel blades. The swords were hanging downward from metal hooks in the wall so customers were able to see each sword in full detail. Many of them were double-handed broadswords with crossbar hilts, but each one unique and ornate. Something caught Vodin's eye at the far end of the wall and he led Aiden there.

"Aiden, this is your next step up," he began, gesturing to a section of the wall where several similar swords were hanging.

"But, to be clear, if you plan on advancing in swordskill, this will not be the last step."

"What do you mean?" Aiden asked, still gawking at the glimmering blades before him.

"These are called arming swords," Vodin explained, taking one of the swords off its hook and examining it. "They have a one-handed grip, but maintain a double-edge along with a simple crossbar hilt. This year, now that you've learned how to handle a double-handed longsword, you'll be using an arming sword to learn one-handed technique. Next year, I'll be teaching you how to make your own sword, and that one will be yours... Forever."

Aiden said nothing and couldn't help but wonder what that would be like. He watched Vodin handle the arming sword in a masterful way, and felt humbled. Vodin put the sword back on its hook.

"Time to pick a weapon, my boy," Vodin said with a smile.

Just as he had done with the wooden practice sword, Aiden took his time looking at several different blades. He took more care this time, as Vodin had warned him that steel blades were less forgiving than wooden ones. Finally, Aiden came upon a sword that fit just right. Vodin purchased the sword and a simple wooden scabbard—despite Aiden's suggestion that a wooden one might be too weak for a steel blade—and they were on their way out of the shop.

Once back in the square, Vodin did not lead Aiden out into the streets of Washington D.C. as Aiden had expected, but instead they traveled down an alley and past a place that must have been a restaurant or bar of some kind. The sounds of people talking and laughing followed Vodin and Aiden for a few moments until they turned down another corridor.

The space was narrow and lit by lanterns along the walls every so many feet, but Aiden still could not begin to see the end of the corridor. Vodin carried on ahead, and before long Aiden realized the corridor was exceptionally long. They must have been walking for over a half an hour when finally they came to a door much like the one that entered Market Street from the outside.

Vodin knew the Elvish and Dwarvish passwords to open the special lock, and they entered the Agnec Undergound. Once over the threshold, Aiden noticed how the corridor was well-lit and supported by ornate stone pillars. The path widened and they found themselves walking along a broad avenue surrounded by ancient shops and medieval smithies. Aiden saw the familiar sight of giant luminescent mushrooms along the far walls, alighting the entire cavern as though it were bathed in sunlight.

In minutes, the avenue led them to a railway station and they got tickets for the railcar going northeast. They took seats in a small vestibule and waited for the railcar to arrive. The station was relatively quiet and no one else sat nearby.

Aiden felt a little lackluster. "Why are we going this way when we could just travel by door or something?" he asked, tugging at his duffel bag on one shoulder while adjusting the strap of his scabbard on the other.

"Have you been keeping up with your meditation, Aiden?" Vodin asked, ignoring Aiden's question.

Aiden ground his teeth, avoiding eye contact. "Uh, a little."

"How often?"

"Okay, not often enough," Aiden conceded sheepishly.

"I can't say I'm not a little disappointed, but I know good habits can be hard to form," Vodin said flatly. "We'll get back into that soon enough. But you must stick to it."

Aiden nodded, somewhat dejectedly.

"Patience, Aiden," Vodin said suddenly. "We are taking the railway because you need to continue working on your patience and discipline."

"Oh..."

"Good things come to those who wait," Vodin continued. "And simply because we can do some of the things we do, doesn't mean we always should."

When the railcar pulled up, Vodin led Aiden aboard, and to their surprise, there were no other passengers. The Dwarf at the front of the vehicle announced their departure and cranked the lever back, forcing the railcar to inch forward.

"I suppose this is lucky," Vodin said once the railcar had really gotten moving and they were racing at unthinkable speeds down the tracks. "Another reason for going this way is that it gives us some time to talk before the hustle and bustle of schooling begins."

Aiden nodded, bracing himself for the unknown. Vodin seemed

so serious.

Vodin took a deep breath and finally spoke, "Aiden, some things have come to my attention over the break—most of which I'm still looking into—but in light of current circumstances, I'd like to teach you about some things that are..." He paused pensively. "Well, they're quite advanced."

Aiden's spirits lifted, but he tried to contain himself, wondering where Vodin was leading with this.

"This is also a bit of skill that isn't always smiled upon by some of the D'Tari masters," Vodin added, his face scrunched as if he was struggling to find the words. "But first things first: Do you remember last year, how I healed your broken leg?"

"Of course," Aiden said immediately. He would never forget the incident.

"That is a form of healing based on bloodcasting," Vodin said, shifting uncomfortably in his seat as the railcar jostled. "One must sacrifice blood to help another save blood. Hence, I used my own blood to write the healing runes on your leg. Once the healer's blood has been used to heal another, the healer's own wound will also heal."

Aiden's mouth fell open slightly.

"It is a very ancient and complex part of the properties," Vodin continued, looking out a wide window across from him as they raced out of a tunnel and the outside light brightened up the railcar. "And very useful, as you've seen. But there are other uses for bloodcasting, and many of them have been banned by the

D'Tari Council."

Aiden's eyebrow perked up.

"Many of them are banned, not because they are necessarily evil or dark," Vodin said, reading Aiden's silent inquiry. "They were banned because they are too powerful and can be easily misused and abused. Well anyhow, I bring this all up because we'll be discussing these things this year. Not because I want you to try them, but because I feel it's in your own best interest to understand."

"Is this normal?" Aiden asked, hanging on to his seat as the railcar tipped wildly on the tracks but then corrected itself. "To show this stuff to a sophomore?"

Vodin shook his head. "As I always say: Time is of the essence. I am not exactly sure when, or how, but in my times of meditation lately, I've sensed an urgency to equip you for what I fear may be a difficult journey."

"What journey?" Aiden asked.

"I wish I could tell you," said Vodin. "Sometimes, one just senses these things. Whether it comes from the Shai, or from somewhere else, that is for me to work out. But, to prepare for the worst and hope for the best, I feel I'm making the right decision."

"So..." Aiden began slowly. "Bloodcasting... Have you ever done any of the banned stuff?"

Vodin was silent for a moment, then sighed. "Yes," he said. "I feel that you are old enough to understand. Despite the D'Tari

Council's best intentions, not every single thing is black and white in this world."

With that, Vodin looked around and began to remove his long coat. He quickly took off his vest to reveal a simple tunic, which he then pulled half-way up in the back. Aiden pulled away, surprised at what the Headmaster was doing, but in a moment, it all made sense as Vodin turned his back to him.

Scars, in the form of several different runes, stretched in an ornate pattern across the skin on Vodin's back.

"But it came with a cost," said Vodin, letting his tunic unfurl. "This formula was said to extend my life, and so far it has. I was foolish to think that long life would be the answer to the problems I once had." Vodin stood and began to put his vest and coat back on. "As with everything, we must proceed with caution and progress with knowledge."

Aiden sat still, just taking it all in. He grimaced, thinking of the scars he'd just seen.

"What do you mean, extend your life?" Aiden asked when the Headmaster finally sat down.

"Just that," Vodin said. "I was young... -er, and I sought a superficial means of finding immortality. I'm not exactly proud of it."

The thought struck Aiden that perhaps this was why Vodin had always talked as though he were an old man, despite how he never looked it.

"Moving on, if we may," Vodin's voice broke Aiden's

thoughts. "Let me emphasize that I'll begin this year by translating this new sword," He lightly tapped Aiden's sheathed blade. "And imparting it to you, along with your buckler and some decent armor."

Aiden shook his head. "What?" he said, completely lost. "Sorry, I... I don't know what you're talking about."

"I had to say something to get your thoughts back to the present," Vodin said, laughing to himself. "Sophomore students, granted they have completed a year of learning swordskill already, will not only begin learning defense with real swords, but they get those swords added to their arsenal."

"My arsenal?"

"You've already seen my sword once or twice now," Vodin said, glancing cautiously to the Dwarf driver.

Aiden nodded.

"Well, the reason my sword disappears when I sheath it, is because it is actually returning to my arsenal," Vodin continued. "When we translate an object, we write special runes on the object, and it allows the object to attach itself to us... In our arsenal, for lack of a better word."

"So, it's like storage?" Aiden wondered.

"Something like that," Vodin said, grinning. "Some call their arsenal the Shai, or others believe Shai is what makes the arsenal possible. Now if I have something in my arsenal and I want to give it to you, that's called imparting, or impartation."

"Okay," Aiden said, thinking. "So, you're going to impart my sword to me? And other things?"

"Yes," Vodin said, excitement in his voice. "Your sword, buckler shield, and some armor I found that should work for you."

"Armor too?" Aiden mused. "I didn't know I needed all that."

"Relax. You'll have everything you need."

"Are you going to teach me to translate and im-imp... Uh, impart?" Aiden asked, his mind racing.

"It's not usually something we teach sophomores, but we'll see how you're doing with runelore when get to the second half of the year," Vodin said, his eyes gleaming.

After they had been silently flying along the tracks for a few minutes, swirling around subterranean mountainsides and past quaint villages, Vodin shifted in his seat, looking worried.

"I would like to review some of the things you learned last year, Aiden," he began.

"Of course," Aiden said, although he felt that he had had so much to ponder already that he wasn't sure how much more he could handle.

"But before we begin," Vodin said calmly. "I feel I should probably tell you about the N'Iatari."

Aiden felt himself go cold at the sudden mention of that name. "The who?" Aiden finally said, trying to act as though he'd never heard the name.

"The N'Iatari," Vodin said quietly. "Most Agnecs will generally recognize them as just another branch of the D'Tari, or something similar to us. The N'iatari have mostly the same properties we do, and carry out many of the same practices. And, well..." He paused.

Aiden looked to him imploringly. Vodin sighed.

"I feel it's important to bring them up because you should know that they've been at war with the D'Tari for several centuries," the Headmaster continued, trying to keep his voice quiet. "They seemed to have disappeared for a while, but then reappeared in the last few decades, no longer acting hostile toward us."

"Well, that's good, right?" Aiden said, still trying to read the sudden urgency in Vodin's voice.

"One might think," said Vodin. "Except that I know firsthand that they've not really been gone, but recruiting. They haven't changed their minds about us, they've simply changed their tactic. In recent years, they've begun to slowly resurface in the Agnec world, maintaining that they can live in harmony with the D'Tari—despite their obvious defiance of the D'Tari Council."

A pensive look crossed Aiden's face. "I thought the Council enforced the use of properties," he said. "And if the N'Iatari use properties like the D'Tari, then..." Aiden paused, scratching his head. "How does the Council keep any kind of order?"

"Excellent thought," said Vodin, shifting in his seat. "But there's been no incidents. Well, any recorded incidents. The N'Iatari have supposedly been true to their word as of late. The Council holds nothing against them in a legal sense because nothing against the D'Tari code seems to be occurring. As long as the N'Iatari maintain that they are not D'Tari, and are not committing any of the banned activities, the Council cannot do very much."

Aiden nodded slowly. "So... What's the problem?"

"They are practicing banned activities," Vodin said, his eyes narrowing on Aiden's. "Beyond that, they are secretly building themselves an army of devotees who, I don't mind telling you, are bent on conquering the D'Tari, among other things."

Aiden's eyes widened. "But why?" he asked, hearing his own voice crack.

"Whereas the D'Tari have always considered themselves a mediator between the Agnecs and the Amblers, the N'Iatari disdain Ambler society, and were commonly known to attack any Agnec who dared associate too closely with Amblers. Of course, up until more recently, N'Iatari numbers were relatively low..."

"Why are you telling me this?"

"Here's the rub," Vodin said, again looking into Aiden's brown eyes. "The N'Iatari do not like Amblers or anyone associated with them. But again, they are people just like you and I; It would not be so easy to point them out in a crowd. As long as you're in Agnec society, Aiden, there's a slight chance you could be threatened. I don't want to frighten you, but this is why we train in swordskill and what have you—preparing for the worst, hoping for the best."

Aiden sat back, his head swimming. His heart began to flutter, and he glanced in all directions as if being watched.

"Though the Guild may be one of the safest places to be, and I trust my fellow masters and a handful of others, I am not prone to trust every individual who approaches me claiming to be a friend of the D'Tary way. Be on your guard this year. You can never be sure who may be walking among us."

***

Several weeks had passed since the beginning of the school year, and Aiden felt that he was finally beginning to get the hang of the one-handed sword technique that Vodin had been teaching him. The Headmaster had imparted the arming sword, the buckler, and some pieces of light armor into Aiden's arsenal, and then taught him how to recall each object when he needed it. Having an arsenal had been strange at first, but now it was becoming a second nature.

Aiden locked blades with Grant, as they had been teamed up as sparring partners by Headmaster Vodin. Grant glared at him, trying to force the weight of his blade back. Aiden balanced his stance, his other hand clutching the buckler, and forced away Grant's blade. In that moment, Aiden saw an open path and struck Grant across the head with the buckler, sending Grant's helmet tumbling off into the grass.

Grant fell back, landing on his backside.

"Good use of technique," Vodin said, stepping closer to the two of them. He helped Grant to his feet, despite how the boy withdrew his hand testily. "Aiden, excellent use of the buckler.

Grant, remember to coordinate for each line, and try to see what is not there yet, but always could be. It is about speed and hand-eye reflexes. And keep your mind sharp."

"I know. I know," Grant sneered, brushing himself off, and rolling his eyes as Vodin stepped away.

"Real smooth," Aiden said, smirking at Grant.

The two of them took their positions again with blades out.

"You shut your mouth," Grant growled quietly.

"Begin!" Vodin announced, and the boys began again.

They were supposed to bow to each other and touch blades, but instead, Grant took off at a run, fury consuming his features.

Everything seemed so clear in Aiden's mind. As if time were slowing down, he could see several clear lines of attack and the different possibilities that each line presented. Grant, on the other hand, was grinding his teeth angrily. Wielding his sword with two hands, he raced forward, intending to go for a thrust.

Almost as if he were suddenly someone else, Aiden watched himself step just outside of Grant's line of attack, then bring his blade down on top of Grant's. With his buckler hand, Aiden cut across Grant's bare face. In a second, the blonde-haired boy was face down in the grass. It was all over, and Aiden felt like himself again.

At this point, the other groups of sparring students stopped to see what had happened. Vodin helped Grant to his feet, and Aiden stood back trying to fathom the scene.

"Never fight angry," Vodin said sternly, looking into Grant's dirty face. "And you," he turned to Aiden. "We still have a code to live by. Do not taunt your opponent."

Aiden's moment of victory was swallowed up by Vodin's rebuke. Grant wiped his face off, glaring at Aiden with eyes full of hate. Several of the other students began to whisper, but were silenced by Vodin's sudden announcement that their session was over and it was nearing dinner time.

As Aiden sheathed his sword, watching it disappear along with his armor and buckler, Grant sauntered up to him.

"Next time, you won't have the Headmaster to protect you," he grunted.

"But who's gonn'a protect you?" Aiden retorted.

"Lilit damn you! You stupid little-" Grant raged and rushed at Aiden.

"So it's like that, is it?" Aiden yelled as he took the full brunt of Grant's body slamming into his.

In seconds, they were on the grass encircled by a crowd of excited and concerned students. Aiden struggled under Grant's weight, but he realized quickly enough that the boy was trying to crush him. He wriggled out from under Grant and clocked the boy across the ear. When Grant relaxed his grip, Aiden rolled over and got to his feet. He held his palms up, which had already begun forming glowing balls of energy.

Grant was on his feet with his sword drawn again, and the two boys locked eyes.

"Enough!" Vodin screamed, bursting through the cloud of

students.

Aiden's palms instantly extinguished, and Grant sheathed his sword. The Headmaster grabbed them both by the collars of their tunics and dragged them across the field, away from the others.

"It's time for dinner, and I suggest you all go about your business!" Vodin shouted to the other students, then turned to the two boys, a dangerous look in his eyes. "What is the matter with you two?"

Neither of them answered, but instead exchanged sullen stares.

"Alright then. Grant, you return to your mentor right now, do not go to dinner. You will not return to this class for one week."

Grant returned an expression of mingled anger and disappointment. "He started it," he finally said, glancing to Aiden.

"You rushed me!" Aiden snapped back.

"Enough!" Vodin held his hands up, silencing them. "Until you can both learn how to remove the anger from your sparring, you cannot successfully benefit from swordskill," he said, his tone calming. "Anger and hatred have no place in the D'Tari way. I'm giving you both a suspension from this class for one week."

Aiden's shoulders sloped in disappointment.

"Now, Grant, return to your mentor," Vodin said, thrusting a finger in the direction of the Great Hall. "And Aiden, you come with me."

***

Aiden had never seen Vodin like this. The Headmaster led

them into his office and told Aiden to take a seat. When Vodin sat down at his desk, his blue eyes were wild with a mixture of anger and something like excitement. Aiden slowly sat down, trying to avoid those eyes, his adrenaline beginning to wane.

"What do you have to say for yourself?" came the Headmaster's voice.

"Uh," Aiden began, his eyes downcast. "I don't know."

"You must know something," Vodin said sternly. "I know you well enough by now to know that you do know. Granted, he was taunting you, but you played his game. He was looking for an excuse."

Aiden looked up, realizing that Vodin's tone was not angry as he had expected. "It didn't take much," Aiden quipped.

"True, that boy has a short fuse," Vodin agreed. "But you can't rely on the opinions of others, or the actions of others, in order to determine your own actions and opinions. Do you understand?"

After a moment, Aiden nodded.

"I will be talking with Grant about this, but in the meantime, you are to be careful of your interactions with him," Vodin said, causing Aiden to raise an eyebrow in surprise. "I might have to reassign you a sparring partner."

"Really?" Aiden asked, a sudden hope in his voice. "That's surprising. I thought you'd..." Aiden paused with a sudden caution.

"I would what?"

"I thought you would force us to get along," Aiden said,

feeling stupid that he'd said it.

Aiden watched Vodin's reaction, hoping the Headmaster wouldn't change his mind.

"Normally," Vodin began with a sigh. "I would. But today I heard something just out of earshot—just as the scuffle began—that disturbed me. Something that makes me want to distance the two of you until I can know anything for sure."

"What?"

"He cursed you in the name of Lilit," Vodin said, his voice quiet.

"Yeah... I didn't really understand that. And, who?" Aiden asked, sitting forward in his chair.

"Who indeed," said Vodin, glancing around his office. "Lilit is the central figure of the N'Iatari belief system. Many of them believe she is their god, others believe that she commissioned the Shai to do their bidding, and so forth."

"So, does that make Grant a N'Iatari?" Aiden asked, his mind racing.

"I do not know," Vodin said, stroking his beard. "But it does raise a few very serious questions for me—things which I will have to investigate. So in the meantime, Aiden, keep your distance from him if possible."

Aiden nodded. Then another thought struck him, "Do you think she's real? Lilit, I mean."

"Oh I know she's real," Vodin said straightforwardly. "Is she some some all-knowing evil deity or something? Not likely."

Aiden's brow furled.

"Aiden," Vodin began, his face brightening a bit. "In spite of tonight's incident, I saw some excellent improvement out there. When you focus on the task and remember the code of honor, even in the worst moments, there's nothing you can't accomplish. The privilege of using a sword—remember—is not about proving how strong and how great you are, but about helping others and standing up to real threats, should they ever arise."

Aiden nodded, feeling somewhat flattered and rebuked at the same time.

"Given that I'm seeing this improvement right now, and the sense of urgency I have been feeling as of late," Vodin continued. "And I'm sort of surprised that you have gained so many of the properties so quickly—the other masters tell me you're doing very well in many of your studies—I feel that I need to share something with you."

Vodin slowly reached into his cloak and began pulling a chain necklace up and around his head. When he set it on the desk, Aiden realized that an ovular glass locket sat at the end of the chain. At least the locket appeared to be glass, and was set in some sort of ornate metallic fixture covered in unfamiliar runes. It looked extraordinarily ancient.

"This is a forca locus," Vodin said. "For all we know, this may be the last one in existence, as they come from the Old World. A forca locus, to put it simply, is a container within which to hold a location."

Aiden took his eyes off the locket and threw Vodin an incredulous look.

Vodin laughed. "I know that look. I had the same expression when I first learned of these as well. And perhaps it is a matter of faith, but we do know that there is immensely powerful properties trapped inside this one."

"What do you mean?" Aiden asked, when finally he resolved to follow Vodin's line of thought.

"If there is indeed a sort of place trapped inside this locket, it may be a weapon," Vodin explained. "In the ancient world, there were places, or essences of places, captured and concealed in forca loci, then brought to some future time where they were released for good or ill. These not only capture a location, but whoever, or whatever, was there at the time."

"So what's inside this one?"

"To be honest, I am not exactly sure, but there are certain legends out there. None of which are too precise, so I can not really say," Vodin admitted. "But I do know that there are people who want this, and they must not ever get it."

Aiden shrugged. "Why are you showing this to me?"

"I'm giving this to you," Vodin said, gently pushing the locket closer to Aiden's side of the desk.

"What?" Aiden almost stood up. "Why?"

Vodin's forehead wrinkled. "For many reasons, but one I will share: Over the course of the summer and this year thus far, you and this locket continually reappear in my mind during my times of meditation. The Shai is reminding me, always. It is speaking to me in a way that I haven't felt, well, in far too long. I believe you are supposed to be the next bearer of this forca locus."

"But what am I supposed to do with it?" Aiden asked, feeling as though a new and unwelcome weight was already on his shoulders.

"Never lose sight of it, even for an instant," Vodin said, very solemnly. "Wear it secretly. Never, ever—and I cannot stress this enough—ever let another soul know about it. If you stay in tune with your meditation, there will come a day when you will know exactly what to do with it. But as for me, my time with this has come to an end."

"You said there were people looking for this," began Aiden, noticing the dryness in his mouth. "Who?"

"The N'Iatari," Vodin said calmly.

Aiden's heart fluttered. "Why? What'll they do if they find out I have it? What do I do?"

"Calm down," Vodin said. "If you are wise, they will never know. And should worse come to worst, I have already given you the tools to defend yourself. As long as you are here, you are protected. When you go out into the greater Agnec world with whatever you choose to do after graduation, you will be a master—ready to take on the challenge. I'm quite sure of it."

Aiden felt some hope in Vodin's words, but the task seemed so strange. He pulled the necklace forward to examine it for a moment, then pushed it away.

"What if I choose not to do this?" he asked.

Vodin sighed. "I understand your precaution, I certainly do. I could take the locket back, I suppose, but it would have nowhere to go. You are the one to take it. When I die, the locket gets buried with me, and there is even greater risk that someone could find it and use it."

The thought of Vodin dying seemed strange, but also made Aiden's stomach twist a bit.

"What if someone uses it?" Aiden asked, not sure he really wanted the answer.

Vodin's expression grew unusually grave. "There are a few possibilities, but none of them have a promising outcome."

Aiden was silenced. He looked to the floor, his mind racing.

"Aiden," Vodin began again. "All you have to do is keep it for now. Make sure that no one ever uses it for ill-will, not even yourself. I know it is a big responsibility, but I have faith in you. Now I am asking you to have faith in me."

Chapter 6
The Snowy Day

After several weeks, the locket had come to feel normal around Aiden's neck. He had grown used to keeping it a secret from his roommates as well as classmates, and life seemed to go back to normal at the Guild. Although Grant and Chadwick would still occasionally try to lure Aiden into fights, but he would remember Vodin's warning and walk away.

As they neared winter break and the days grew short and cold, Aiden found himself in closer quarters with the other boys more often than he would prefer, simply because there was not much else to do.

On a snowy Saturday afternoon, Aiden had grown so tired of the atmosphere in the dorms that he went to the Great Hall to do some reading. The massive room was still alight by a central chandelier at the ceiling's center, but what drew Aiden's attention was the fire in the hearth at the end of the hall. He couldn't resist its warmth, and he sat on a bench nearby. Within minutes, he was poring over his runelore lexicon.

"Enjoying your alone time?" a voice came from behind Aiden, making him jolt.

Aiden stood to see Grant, Chadwick, and Charlie just feet from him. Grant was looking smug, along with Chadwick, but

Charlie's face was scrunched nervously.

Aiden tried to hide his apprehension. "Just doing some reading. So if you don't mind-"

"Don't mind at all," Grant said, knocking the book from Aiden's hand.

"C'mon, man," Aiden said, not daring to pick the book off the stone floor. "Just let me be alone."

"Exactly," Chadwick chimed in.

"Okay, what are you talking about?" Aiden finally said.

"Don't you ever wonder why you have no friends?" Grant said, smiling proudly. "Why everyone seems to avoid you. Even your roommates?"

"Not really. I don't care," Aiden said, despite the fact that it had bothered him.

He had always found solace in being alone, but after some time, he finally realized that many of the students did seem very aloof. Not cruel or mean, just always at a distance. Aiden had spent many nights trying not to think about it, reminding himself that he was here to learn.

"They think you're a freak," Grant continued. "They don't want you here."

Aiden's nostrils flared. "They don't, or you don't?" he finally said. "I get it, you don't like me. You don't want me here. Suit yourself, but I have things to do. Just leave me the hell alone."

With that, Aiden swiped up his fallen book and stuffed it in his bag with one fluid motion, pulled his hood over his head and began walking toward the grand double doors that led out of the Great Hall. The hall rang with echoes as the three boys clambered after him.

"It's not that simple," Grant's voice called out as Aiden pushed through the doors into the foyer. "Since you can't really prove how you're connected to any Agnec family, my mother could probably have you thrown out of the Guild."

Aiden stopped and turned, now seeing all three boys standing in the center of the foyer. "Bull," he said, irritated.

"You've been here for almost two years, and you still don't have a clue," Chadwick sneered.

"Vodin won't be able to help you either," Grant added haughtily.

Aiden could feel a heat rising through him, but he shook his head. "I guess we'll see," was all he could muster before he turned and pushed his way out into the freezing air.

As soon as the snowflakes began to cascade before him, Aiden felt a pair of hands shove him from behind. He caught himself, making tracks in the deep snow, and turned around. Grant's sword was drawn.

"Let's do this. Now," Grant said while Chadwick and Charlie backed away against the building.

"Right here, in front of everyone?" Aiden said, almost laughing despite the anger he felt rising.

"Everyone?" Grant said derisively. "Everyone's inside."

"Windows, idiot," Aiden sneered, then turned away down the

white path.

Simultaneously at his back, Aiden heard Grant's unmistakable growl and Charlie suddenly yelling, "Look out!"

Aiden reached for his sword and whirled around, just in time to block Grant's oncoming blade. The metal clacked loudly in the crisp air, and Grant seemed surprised by the force of the blow.

"Not cool," Aiden said, his body now pumping with adrenaline, his buckler now in his other hand. "Attacking me while my back is turned? Very classy."

Grant came again, but Aiden parried, pushing the blade aside and catching Grant in the ribs with the buckler. Grant stumbled but found his balance, gripping his sword menacingly. His face twisted in a rage. As they circled each other, Aiden realized that Charlie was on the ground, looking as if he'd been thrown there. But Chadwick seemed to have disappeared.

Just then, Aiden stumbled backward, a mass of intense cold suddenly consuming him. Chadwick and Grant laughed hysterically, and Aiden realized that Chadwick had tripped him. Aiden struggled to get out of the snow, but seemed to be sinking in deeper with each movement.

"Okay, I think he gets the point," Charlie said quietly, stepping between Aiden and the others.

"Shutup, Ambler-lover," Grant chastised. "He's had enough when he actually leaves the Guild."

Charlie looked as though he were suppressing something very difficult, but he ignored Grant's comment and bent over to help

Aiden up. In one terrifying moment, Aiden realized that his necklace and locket had somehow slipped out from underneath his tunic and cloak. He watched as Charlie caught sight of the necklace. They locked eyes and each looked away. Aiden pushed Charlie with the full force of his might, hoping that the boy hadn't actually seen anything.

Noticeably upset, Charlie brushed himself off and didn't bother trying to help anymore. When Aiden had finally stood up and safely tucked the locket away; Grant and Chadwick were still laughing, but no longer had any weapons drawn. Aiden no longer felt angry, as much as he was concerned over what Charlie had or hadn't seen, but there was no way of really knowing.

"That's your last warning," Grant finally said, his expression very serious.

Aiden stood there, almost numbly. His mind racing over whether or not he had blown Vodin's mission for him. Grant grunted, seeing that Aiden wasn't phased.

Grant scoffed. "Let's go," he finally said, walking away with Chadwick in tow.

Charlie turned an apologetic face toward Aiden, but Aiden could only return a warning glare. Charlie mouthed the words, "I'm sorry.", but Aiden simply scowled.

"Come on, loser!" shouted Chadwick, and Charlie followed the others through the snow away from the Great Hall.

***

Aiden stared mindlessly into his cereal. He was thankful to

be home for the break, but he would always miss the incredible meals served up in the Great Hall. Aiden had only been home a few days, and already he was feeling antsy. He had so many things going on in his mind, it had become difficult to sort it all out.

"Aiden," his mother said from across the table. "Are you okay? You've been a bit listless."

Aiden sighed and looked up. "I don't know," he mumbled.

"You can always tell me," she said, her voice calming.

Aiden forced himself to take another bite of his cereal while glancing through their barred windows only to see the snowflakes falling faster. His mother shrugged, still looking concerned.

"I guess," Aiden finally began. "I just feel blah."

"What do you mean?"

"I still don't really have any friends, and I just wish Grant and Chadwick would lighten up," Aiden said, probing his cereal with a spoon. "I mean, I really think I'm gettin' it—the whole D'Tari thing."

"Do you enjoy your classes?" his mother asked, glad to see Aiden's enthusiasm for learning.

"Yeah, I do. I just-" Aiden paused. Grant's threat had been in his mind all week. "Mom," Aiden looked up intently. "Who was my dad?"

His mother sat back, looking blindsided, but then composed herself. "Where is this coming from?" she asked. "We've talked about this before."

"I know you said he was your boyfriend who died in a car accident—but that doesn't help explain me," Aiden said, his tone demanding. "Was he an Agnec?"

His mother paused, looking down at her feet and sighing. "Alright Aiden, here's the truth," she began, taking a deep breath, unable to meet his eyes. "It was a mistake. I was very young and stupid. I had just moved out here with your Aunt Maggie after your grandparents died... Anyway, I met your dad at a club. He said his name was Wren—although I don't really think that's true. At any rate, well, we made a very stupid mistake and nine months later, I had you."

Aiden sat there, his mind whirling in a mixture of shock and confusion.

His mother continued, hesitantly, "I tried many many times to get a hold of him, but I could never find anyone who had even heard of him. I was desperate and alone, and Maggie had completely disowned me." She paused, a tear streaking down her face. "I was beside myself, but I knew that I wouldn't ever give you up."

Aiden reached out to hold his mother's hand. "Now I guess I know why you don't talk about it very much," he said, still gauging his own emotions. "So... My dad never even tried to find you again?"

Aiden's mother shook her head, trying to compose herself.

"What an asshole," Aiden said, his face reddening.

"Aiden!" his mother chided. "Language."

"Sorry, but who does that?" he said, feeling his sadness turn to anger. "And Aunt Maggie! How could she do that to you? Just when you needed her?"

"I should've never said anything," his mother said, sitting up again, her eyes red. "Maggie had her reasons, not that I agree with them all. But it was me who made the mistake. I was not thinking. Our parents taught us better than that. The point is, Aiden," She grabbed Aiden's hand again and looked into his eyes. "I would still never give you up. Sometimes a terrible mistake can be redeemed... You were my redemption."

Aiden could no longer stop himself and a tear rolled down his cheek.

"When we discovered your powers, I had a new challenge," his mother continued, smiling somewhat as if the memories were flooding back. "I thought I was going crazy, and I didn't want anyone to take you away. By some lucky accident, I met Menlir and he told me about the Guild, but I wasn't sure what to believe. He said you wouldn't be able to attend until you were fifteen anyway, so that gave me some time to make a decision..."

Aiden chuckled to himself. "I'm glad you made the right decision," he said, wiping his face and sniffing.

"I hope so," his mother said. "I just hate being away from you for so many months out of the year."

"It's only another term and then I'll be back for the summer," Aiden assured her. "Headmaster Vodin says I'm doing really well in all my studies."

His mother smiled. "So, there's no hard feelings about your dad?" she asked.

"I guess not," Aiden said. "I just wish I could find out who he was."

"But why?" his mother asked, looking concerned. "Why go through the trouble?"

"Grant said he could have me thrown out of the Guild if I couldn't trace my ancestry to actual Agnecs..."

"Aiden," his mother said, giving him a knowing look. "You, of all people, should know how prejudiced that is. Have I not taught you anything?"

"I know, but what if it's a big deal?"

"Then talk to Vodin about it. It doesn't seem like he's out there to steer you wrong."

Aiden smiled. "True," he agreed. "Do you think he knew my dad?"

"I hope not, for his sake," Aiden's mother said, a hint of bitterness in her tone. "But he may know who he is. I'm not sure, but you can always ask. Just promise me, that if you do find out who he is, you won't go after him."

"Why would I do that?" Aiden asked.

"Aiden," she said, giving him another familiar look. "The past is past, and we all need to move on."

***

The sky was white and thick snow covered the pavement,

except in places where roofs and fire escapes obstructed. Aiden wandered the back alley not far from his mother's apartment. A grey hooded sweatshirt clung to him beneath a dark jacket, and he wore old blue jeans, and a beanie.

Aiden bent on one knee in the snow and pressed up against the side of an icy dumpster. He watched and listened, waiting intently. There was nothing for some time, but he had to be patient. He had been antagonizing a boy who called himself Blu J, and expected him to arrive any minute.

Much of the feud had started three years ago when Blu J had seen Aiden at his old high school. Blu J had just been out to make trouble, but before long, what started as name-calling ended in fist-throwing. So here Aiden was.

This alley was the only passage between Blu J's usual haunt and Aiden's neighborhood, unless of course Blu J wanted to go all the way around. Going the long way would have required a car or a bike, and Aiden knew Blu J had neither. Aiden had been taunting the boy with the fact that he had failed his drive test twice already, and likewise, Blu J had countered with the fact that Aiden hadn't even tried getting a license at all.

Blu J had called him out with a death threat, but Aiden wasn't too concerned. Perhaps two years ago, he would have been scared. Perhaps even one year ago, but now things were different.

He heard a voice in the distance, and braced himself. After a few moments, nothing had happened, but he kept on his guard. A police siren sounded from somewhere far away. It quickly trailed off into some unknown part of the city. Despite the sounds of distant traffic, the snow seemed to force an uneasy silence onto the world around him.

A shadow sped past him. It was gone before Aiden even had the hope of recognizing it.

Aiden stayed quietly where he was. Blu J was not a subtle person, and in this packed snow, Aiden would hear every footstep.

The shadow flew by again, this time closer, and somewhere behind Aiden. He threw his head back, looking for the shadow's source. Again, there was nothing. It must have been a bird flying overhead. A crow perhaps.

Finally, Aiden heard footsteps. Clumsy, awkward steps that told him Blu J was falling directly into his trap. From where he poised, he could see into the alley without anyone seeing him. There was a tall dumpster and a fire escape across from him, and in moments he would see Blu J coming out from behind the dumpster, as it narrowly blocked the entrance from the cross alley.

A tall boy stepped out, just as Aiden had predicted. Aiden held his hands out and fired an energy ball across Blu J's path. The blast singed the boy's jacket and he looked around in a sudden bout of anger and panic. Blu J swore loudly and steadied himself.

Aiden stepped out holding his hands up so Blu J could see the steam rising from his palms. Blu J's dark brows furled and he reached into his jacket. In seconds, he had produced a revolver pistol.

"Hey..." Aiden said, his face painted with surprise. "That's cheating."

"Hey man, what do you call that shit you just did? You're like some sort of wizard or somethin' right?" Blu J replied, tilting the gun at an angle, aiming at Aiden from across the alley.

Aiden smirked for a moment, but caught himself. His tone turned serious, "Where'd you get a gun?"

"Shut up. I have my resources," Blu J snapped and shook the pistol. "You into that dark witchraft shit, man?" Blu J yelled, his expression growing more strained. "Well, call me the exorcist."

"I'm not cheating," Aiden said finally. "I wasn't gonn'a kill you. Just gonn'a mess with you."

There was an awkward silence between them. Aiden had no desire to kill anybody, but he hoped that Blu J was bluffing. Blu J shook the gun even more, as if thinking the mere sight of it would scare Aiden away.

Aiden wasn't sure what to do now. This was a little more than he'd bargained for.

The gun went off with a crack that thundered through the alley. The buckler shield materialized in Aiden's hand and was thrust in front of the speeding bullet. It was almost instinctive somehow. The bullet bounced and ricocheted around the alley until all was silent.

Blu J looked shocked that he had pulled the trigger. He looked even more shocked when he saw the buckler in Aiden's hand. For a brief moment, the boy scratched his face and seemed as though he were about to apologize. Instead, he hardened his resolve and swore.

"That's it man, you're dead!" Blu J yelled, pulling back the hammer and watching the gun's barrel click.

Aiden jumped back behind his dumpster while Blu J retreated behind his. Aiden lobbied an energy ball at Blu J's dumpster and the entire side of it cracked with a bang, much of it melting away. Blue J bolted out from behind it, swearing and running down through the open alley.

As he did so, he managed to turn and crack another shot at Aiden. The bullet buzzed by Aiden's right ear like a mosquito, and he felt an intense anger burning in his chest.

Blu J had almost made it to the end of the alley, when he turned, as if to take aim again. Aiden held his hands out, focusing all his energy into a massive ball, nearly ready to be launched.

Aiden released the energy, bursting full speed at the boy.

Blu J fell violently to the snowy pavement, but Aiden was shocked that the energy ball hadn't struck him. The energy had missed and hit the wall, rattling the old bricks with a loud crack. Then he realized that several men shrouded in white cloaks now stood in the alley. They had appeared, ghost-like from the cold air, and one of them had pushed Blu J out of the way.

Aiden was still processing what had happened when he saw Grant standing before him with sword drawn. Grant was also in a white cloak, and the men—whose faces were covered—slowly came up behind him to face Aiden.

"Grant?" Aiden said in disbelief, shaking his head.

Grant glared menacingly. Blu J picked himself up and looked around, suddenly frozen by the sight of the men. Aiden looked back to Grant, still trying to piece it together.

"What's going on? What are you doing here?" Aiden finally said, taking small steps backward.

"I warned you, didn't I?" said Grant, his blade moving slowly closer.

"Seriously?" Aiden scoffed, despite a sudden nagging feeling inside. "You don't forget a grudge, do ya?"

Grant sped forward with a hacking motion, but Aiden sidestepped it and drew his own blade and buckler. The blades clacked loudly in the freezing air. Aiden could glimpse Blu J running to the end of the alley and throwing his pistol in a firing barrel. In seconds, the boy was nowhere to be seen. But Aiden couldn't think about that now.

Grant cut through the arm of Aiden's heavy jacket—nearly missing the arm inside—and Aiden snapped the boy across the face with his buckler. While Grant was losing his balance, Aiden launched an energy ball into the faces of the nearest men in white and ran to the end of the alley.

The men began to give chase, some of them launching balls of dark energy after him as he raced into a narrow alley. Aiden's heart was pounding. Explosions rippled behind him along the old walls and pavement. He rushed behind a large dumpster and blasted it with a massive energy ball. With a bang, it fell over, half-melted, and its contents flew across the narrow space.

While the men tripped and struggled through the wreckage with Grant lagging behind, Aiden wound his way through the various alleyways and passages between apartment buildings until he came upon his own building. In a panic, he raced up the stairs and into his own apartment.

He slammed the door and set every lock, including sliding the door chain into place. Panting, he wandered into the living room.

"Mom!" he called, between breaths. "Mom!"

"What?" Aiden's mother entered the living room, a look of concern on her face. "What's going on? You're getting snow all over the carpet. What's in your hands?"

Aiden realized he was still carrying his sword and shield. They unraveled into white mist and Aiden fell to the couch to catch his breath, not caring that the snow was melting off of his jacket and onto the fabric.

"No time to explain," he finally said, an intense urgency overcoming him. "I don't think they were far behind."

"Who?"

Just then, there came a knock at the door. Aiden wiped the sweat from his forehead, feeling as though his winter clothes were suffocating him. But he found the strength to stand.

"Don't answer it," he said quietly.

"Why not?" his mother said, her nervous smile turning serious. "What is going on?" she lowered her voice.

"Take a look. Just slowly," said Aiden, as he walked toward the coat rack against the wall.

The knock came again, almost making his mother jump. She slowly went to the door and peered through the peep hole. She backed away, returning to Aiden.

"I don't know who he is," she said. "He's got some sort of white hood on."

"Okay, I think we have to go," said Aiden, taking his mother's coat off the nearby rack and throwing it to her.

"Why?"

"I have an idea who they are... But I really don't want to stay and find out."

"Aiden," his mother said with an uneasy tone, putting the coat on. "Where would we go? You're scaring me-"

"Trust me, Mom," Aiden said, his eyes meeting hers. "Trust me."

The knock came again, but this time, it was more of a pounding against the door. The wood sounded as though it would start cracking in a moment.

"Aiden!" Grant's voice yelled from the other side of the door. "Just come on out, and we can talk."

Not fooled at all by Grant's words, Aiden's mind raced and he fought to stave off his nervous tic. He looked around the living room, desperate to find a solution. His mother was looking to him for answers, and he had none. He didn't dare think about what might happen to her if Grant and the men captured her along with him. The pounding at the door continued.

"Fire escape," said Aiden, his eyes gleaming when he saw the metal ladder just outside their back window.

"Aiden," his mother protested. "Are you sure?"

The pounding had grown louder and Aiden could hear the men shouting.

"Yes. Now," Aiden said, forming an energy ball in one hand, while grabbing her arm with the other.

He blasted out the window and they leaped out onto the metal walkway. His mother gasped and clutched the railing, trying to keep her balance. Something inside the house had exploded with a loud flash, causing Aiden to jolt and his mother to scream. Debris and dust fluttered around the living room and the men in white cloaks filled the space.

Despite his mother's warning gesture, Aiden instinctively launched several energy balls into the living room. The first struck the sofa, the second the table, and after that, Aiden could no longer see amongst the smoke, the flames, and the violent flurry of white cloaks.

Aiden grabbed his mother's arm, trying to ignore her panic-stricken tears, and together they began to descend the frozen ladder, battling a sudden gust of snowy wind.

*****

When Aiden finally led his mother out onto the sidewalk a few blocks over, he noticed the walk had been cleared of snow.

"I don't understand," his mother said, panting. "What's going on?"

"I'll explain, but let's go," he shouted and began to race down the walk.

"Be careful not to slip on the ice!" his mother warned, unable to help herself as she chased after him.

Together they sped down the sidewalk, finally neck and neck. The road had been cleared and the traffic passed them, each vehicle bringing an icy wind in its wake.

"I think these guys want something I have," Aiden said, having to shout over the din of traffic. "Grant attacked me in the alley," Aiden paused as he jumped over a large pile of slush and ice. "But mostly, Grant's just a psycho..."

Aiden's mother didn't say anything, but one glance at her expression told Aiden that she feared greatly for him. He looked back and saw that the sidewalk was empty behind them, but he knew they shouldn't stop running.

"Is he trying to..." his mother finally spoke, her nose and cheeks scarlet. "Is he trying to kill you?" Her words almost faltered.

"Maybe," Aiden said, being honest, despite knowing how much it would frighten her. "I don't know. I haven't figured it out yet, but even Vodin told me to stay away from him..."

In a matter of moments, Aiden saw Menlir's illusionary old shack half-covered in snow just up ahead. He pulled on his mother's arm and the two of them rushed toward the old house. They waddled through the pile of ice and snow in the driveway and into the side yard where the once jungle-like flora was now bowed low, frozen, and covered in a blanket of white. Aiden cracked open the gate into the backyard, which popped and rattled as the ice loosened.

"What are we doing?" his mother finally asked as Aiden shut the gate behind them.

"This is Menlir's house. I just hope he's home," Aiden said, lowering his voice. "He should be able to-"

"Aiden!" his mother screamed and clutched her mouth in shock.

Aiden whirled around, a black mist meeting his eyes, and drew his weapons at once.

The men in white were all around, their cloaks almost blending into the yard's unkempt snowy terrain, though a handful of them had singed cloaks and were nursing small wounds. Grant stood in the middle of the yard, next to one of the men, not far from the old fountain which was now frozen over. The boy's eyes were alive, almost lustful.

Another scream rang out and Aiden whirled around again, only to see his mother struggling against the strength of another man. A gloved hand held her mouth shut, but her eyes were dancing in a furious panic.

"Let her go!" Aiden yelled, his sword out and buckler ready.

"Let me handle it," Aiden heard Grant say to the man nearest him. "I warned you, Aiden."

Aiden turned so that he could see both his mother and Grant

at the same time, quickly becoming unsure which direction he should keep a better eye on. He tried his hardest to hide his fear, but he was near exhaustion.

"You can't run," Grant continued.

"Why are you dragging her into this?" Aiden gestured to his mother. "If you hate me, and want to kill me, then... Fine." Aiden paused, letting the meaning of his own words wash over him. "But don't do anything to her."

"If we wanted to kill you, we already would have," the man nearest Grant said in a deep voice, surprising Aiden.

"I said I've got it," Grant snapped at the man, but the man returned a dirty look. "Anyway," He looked back to Aiden. "Even though I hate you and everything you stand for," he said, licking his lips as if he'd been waiting for some time to say that. "And I do just want you gone... First, you have something we want."

"I don't having anything," said Aiden, his eyes darting around the group of men. They were all tall and strong, and mysterious with their mouths and noses covered.

"Oh I think you do," Grant replied, his eyes searching Aiden's neckline. "I'll take it if I have to, whether you're dead or alive."

"Spare us the drama, kid," the man nearest Grant said, looking to the blonde-haired sixteen-year-old. "Let's just take both of them with us. We don't have time-"

"No!" Grant shook his sword and glared at the man. "My mother said you listen to what I say! This is my time."

The man rolled his eyes as Grant focused back on Aiden.

"So, are you going to give it to me, or do I have to take it from you?"

"If I hand it over, will you let her go?" Aiden asked, seeing his mother still struggling against her captor's grip.

"Come on," groaned a man behind Grant. "There's no time for this! Why'd she send the brat with us-"

"Shutup!" Grant snapped, looking back to the man with a scowl. "When we return, my mother will have you beaten! This is treason."

Aiden stood there for a moment, amazed at Grant's attitude, but then he realized that no one was actually paying attention. In a swift motion, he clocked Grant across the face with his buckler and blasted the nearby man in the chest with an energy ball.

At this commotion, the men broke into a frenzy, and Aiden turned to face his mother's captor. Without thinking, he plunged his blade into the man's foot, and with all his might retrieved it. The man yelped and relaxed his grip on Aiden's mother, but she in turn sent him to his knees with an elbow to the ribs.

"Run!" Aiden told her as the men closed in from all around.

A sharp pain cut into Aiden's shield arm, and he grunted, turning to see the tip of Grant's blade trickling with blood. Grant laughed and prepared to strike again. Aiden dropped his buckler, but managed to block the next blow. One of the men rushed up to Aiden, but Grant gestured for him to stop.

"Let me have him!" Grant told the man.

In retreat, Aiden tripped and almost lost his balance in the snow.

"Aiden!" his mother's voice rang out again.

Aiden turned, seeing his mother racing toward him. The man whose foot Aiden had stabbed had grabbed her and thrown her forward, just before collapsing. Aiden, hardly able to keep his own balance, managed to catch her, despite the searing pain in his left arm.

A burst of dark energy exploded in the crisp air, sending them both cascading into a snowbank beneath a pine tree near the old fence.

Aiden shook his head, feeling slightly dizzy. His mother had landed on top of him, and she seemed unbelievably heavy. She had gone completely limp. Aiden squirmed and wriggled until he finally was able to move her aside and sit up. He made sure she wasn't face down in the snow, but that was all he'd had time for.

The white-cloaked men stood in a semi-circle around the scene, glaring down at Aiden. All of them—save for the man who's foot was trailing blood in the snow—held their swords out.

Before Aiden could think straight, a blinding pain split across the side of his face and he fell back into the snow. Grant was on top of him now with his hands around his throat.

"Give me the locket," Grant growled, reaching a freezing glove into Aiden's shirt beneath his layers.

Aiden grabbed Grant's wrists, but the boy was stronger than expected. He felt Grant grip the shape of the locket and begin to tug the chain. Aiden couldn't believe he had failed Vodin already. Desperation flooded him.

"Vodin!"

The scream had exploded from his lungs until he could no longer breath, his voice echoing into the frozen air and throughout the yard. An eerie silence followed, and one of the men placed a warning hand on Grant's shoulder.

Another man began to write a rune of some sort in the snow with the tip of his blade, but Aiden was too focused on Grant to see what was happening.

Aiden let go of Grant's wrists and clutched the locket's chain, holding it so tight that he felt it cutting into his hands. Grant tried wrenching it from his grip, but the nearest man in white violently pulled Grant to his feet by the collar, leaving Aiden behind. Without warning, the men in white cloaks began to disappear in silent bursts of black mist. One of them held onto Grant as he disappeared. In seconds, they were all gone.

Aiden exhaled a painful breath of air, tears running down his red cheeks. He crawled over to his mother.

"Mom... Mom?"

She was so still. He released a shuddering breath, reaching for her hand. He hadn't realized before that her skin had been somewhat singed. Heat was still rising from her body, but when Aiden felt her wrist, there was nothing pulsing there.

"Mom?" he said again, tears beginning to streak down his face.

Just then, the gate opened from the side yard and Menlir

walked in accompanied by another man. Aiden gazed at them through bleary eyes, unable to say anything. His mind had gone blank and his heart felt shattered. In a burst of tears, he fell on top of his mother's body, trying to embrace her.

"Aiden?" came Menlir's confused voice.

"What's happened?" the other man said.

"She's dead..." was all Aiden could manage to say between sobs.

Chapter 7
The Verdict

Everything was a blur. It took several minutes before Menlir could convince Aiden to let go of his mother's body. Aiden fell back into the snow, just now realizing how intensely cold it actually was. The tears were coming so quickly that he could hardly see, and if he had been able to, he might've realized that the other man was an Elf, or someone very much like an Elf, disguised as a human, wearing mismatched Ambler winter clothes. Likewise, Menlir was also disguised, wearing a winter cap to cover his horns, and a kilt and boots to envelope his goat-like legs.

The Elf approached Aiden's mother and removed his gloves. He laid hands on her neck and began to say something in a language Aiden had never heard. Aiden watched with great intrigue, a sudden hope clearing his vision. His mother's neck began to glow, but then the light faded as easily as it had begun.

The Elf pulled away and replaced his gloves. "I'm sorry..." he said, a sincere sadness on his face. "There is not enough left in her..."

Aiden's tears fell fresh, and he buried his face in his hands, still sitting in the snow.

"Who did this? How did it happen?" Menlir asked.

Aiden could not think straight. Everything inside simply hurt. "The N'Iatari..." was all he could say.

***

The curtains had been closed for almost a week. Despite the gnawing ache of hunger, Aiden had not been outside of his dorm room since Menlir, and the Elf—or Half-Elf, rather—Turlin, had brought him back to the Guild. He wasn't sure how they had done it, because they seemed to all disappear on the spot, and reassemble in the woods near the Guild. But Aiden hadn't spent much time worrying about that, he had been thinking solely about his mother.

The images played over and over in his mind, down to the last detail. Her cries were still in his ears, and her face covered in tears of panic returned nightly, as clearly as if he had just watched it happen. He had exhausted himself trying to imagine how things might have gone differently.

If only I had just handed over the locket, he thought. This stupid thing is the reason she's dead.

He couldn't believe he had almost died defending it. He wanted to take it off and throw it away, but then he saw Grant's twisted face. That evil, hateful, bloodthirsty visage. Aiden knew that if Grant got the locket, he wouldn't hesitate to use it. Throwing away the locket would be like letting Grant win, but Aiden wondered if he hadn't already won.

After all, Aiden's mother was now gone...

A knock came at the door, stirring him from his thoughts. He ignored it, but the knock came again.

"Aiden?" a voice came from the other side. It was Vodin's.

Aiden remained silent, still lying on his bed.

After a moment, Vodin knocked again but this time entered the room as he did so.

"Go away," Aiden groaned, turning on his side, with his back to the Headmaster.

"I realize you're in a great deal of pain right now, Aiden," Vodin said, closing the door behind him. "But you must realize that I only want to help you."

Vodin had said this every day, and every day Aiden had told him to leave. There was something about Vodin's tone that seemed more determined today.

"Your mother's funeral is taking place in about an hour," Vodin said, almost hesitantly. "I think you should come out."

Aiden sat up in surprise. "Funeral?"

"We're still trying to locate your aunt," Vodin said grimly. "The Council has decided, given the circumstances, that your mother should be buried here. More importantly, I thought you would want to come and honor her memory."

It had all happened so fast. "I don't want to talk about her in past tense," he said, brushing a tear from his eye.

"I understand," said Vodin, placing a gentle hand on Aiden's shoulder. "Please come out. The others are very concerned about you. They are hoping you haven't gone mad."

Aiden nodded and began to look for some clothes. When

Vodin left, Aiden was flooded with emotion all over again, but he managed to get himself dressed. In a few minutes, he wandered down to the grounds and followed the crowds until they came to a distant spot in a snowy field near the cemetery.

Despite the gloom in Aiden's heart, the sunshine peaked through the white sky, glinting over the tranquil snow-covered hills. He ignored the distant bird song and pulled his dark cloak tight, trudging through the field until he'd caught up with the gathering crowds.

When people realized he had arrived, there was an uneasy silence. The students gave him a wide berth and he found himself under a large canopy complete with rows of chairs facing forward. Vodin guided him up to the front row while masters and students began to take their seats. Aiden didn't dare look back. He could sense the weight of everyone's collective gaze.

Soon, the whispering began. When Aiden finally gathered the courage to look back and survey the room, his gaze was met with several students looking away abruptly, as if they'd just been talking about him. Charlie and Chadwick were there, and there was no surprise that Chadwick seemed bored. He saw London there too, the girl with whom he shared several classes. Her expression was sad and somewhat confused as well. Nearly all the Guild masters and grounds staff were in attendance, looking equally somber.

Aiden was glad that Grant had not come. The mere thought of him was a disturbing one.

"If you'd all take your seats," Vodin's voice bellowed from the front of the canopied area. "We will get started."

Within moments, the groups of students and masters filtered into the rows of seats and quieted down. Aiden faced forward, realizing that behind Vodin there stood a casket. He felt a strange numbing sensation overcome him.

"We are gathered today to pay last respects to Lisa Gailhart, the mother of our very own Aiden," said Vodin as he looked out over the gathering. "I know that many of you did not know her, but they who are dear to our students are also dear to us. We have allowed her to rest here on the grounds, her memory to rest with our community, just as good neighbors should."

Aiden heard a very slight murmur from somewhere behind him.

"That said, let us comfort Aiden in his time of need," Vodin continued. "Personally, I did not know Lisa well, but I admired her. I admired her for the way that she raised her son, and for the sacrifices she made every day just so he could live a more fulfilled life."

Aiden looked up, seeing Vodin's solemn expression. He sunk into his chair.

"She was strong and determined, and a good mother. After all, these are desirable traits, regardless of whether one is an Agnec or Ambler. Are they not?" Vodin paused, sighing. "Her life was cut short. But in the wake of tragedy, we know that there can still be hope. Her memory will live on in those who knew her. She will never truly leave us. May she rest in the Shai of peace."

There were a few moments' silence after Vodin had finished. Aiden considered Vodin's words, still unable to understand how he felt.

Vodin offered the floor to anyone who would like to speak, but the gathering remained quiet. "Aiden?" he asked, looking over to where Aiden sat in thought.

Aiden shook his head.

"Are you sure?" Vodin asked with a look of consolation.

"There's... Nothing left for me to say," Aiden finally mumbled in an unsure tone, feeling the crowd glaring at him. "No thank you," he added, trying to sound his most polite.

Looking put out, Vodin tried to seem understanding and nodded his head. "Very well," he said. "Let us proceed to the burial."

***

Aiden had never felt more alone. Although nearly everyone at the funeral had given their condolences and paid their respects, he didn't stay long after they completed the burial. He had lost all sense of time, and the most consoling thing seemed to be the darkness of his room. Even his roommates had not returned for a few days, but he had hardly noticed. He hadn't even thought about classes or whether or not they had begun again. No one had sent him any notice.

It may have only been a day later, but Aiden wasn't too sure, when Vodin knocked on the door. When Aiden finally let the

Headmaster in, he realized the man was particularly dressed up. Vodin's expression was so grave that Aiden's mind went blank with apprehension.

"The Council has summoned you to trial," Vodin said plainly, closing the door behind him.

"Trial?" Aiden said, confused. "For what?"

"For the accidental killing of your mother," Vodin replied. "And for the inappropriate use of the D'Tari properties..."

"What?" Aiden's voice cracked. "But I-"

"I know, Aiden, I don't believe you killed her, but Turlin and Menlir both report only seeing you at the scene..."

"Why didn't you tell me?" Aiden nearly yelled, the fear and anger mingling into his tone as he fell back onto his bed.

"Alas, I tried, but you were so grief-stricken," said Vodin, trying to calm the boy down. "I also tried to get the Council to push the trial back a month or so, to give you time to deal with some things." Vodin sighed and sat next to Aiden. "They're afraid."

"Why?" Aiden asked, rubbing his tired eyes and sitting up.

"They've been listening to fear and ill-logic, planted there by a few influential people. Those who are parents are afraid that you will bring harm or bad influence on their children, and others..." Vodin paused. "Well, there are a few others who still cling to their prejudices and fear of the Ambler world."

Aiden felt his heart sink.

"What happened to your mother was heartbreaking," Vodin

said, placing a calming hand on Aiden's shoulder. "I don't believe that it was your fault, and I do believe there were N'Iatari there. The bigger obstacle here is that we have no time, and that very few people believe the N'Iatari are a threat anymore."

"So... What do we do?" Aiden asked, searching for some hint of hope in Vodin's pensive expression.

"You must answer their questions as honestly as you can. Are you sure you've told me everything?"

Aiden nodded.

"Men in white cloaks with their faces covered," Vodin said. "And no one else?"

Aiden nodded, but then shook his head. "Well... Grant was there, too."

"Why didn't you say that before?"

"I don't know," Aiden sighed. "I just... It almost sounded like his mom had more to do with it—I think. The others didn't seem very happy to do what he was asking. I think he was after the locket. I guess I was afraid of what he might do."

Aiden cast his gaze to the floor.

"This puts us in a very difficult position," Vodin said, stroking his beard. "Monadias is currently head of the Council... You might consider not mentioning Grant's involvement. Nor can we ever mention the forca locus."

Aiden looked up, raising an eyebrow.

"Until we can know to what level his mother is involved," Vodin continued, noting Aiden's silent question. "Our safest course of action is to keep it simple. Also, the forca locus, as I have said, is to be kept secret at all costs. How would he even have known about it?"

"I don't know..." Aiden sighed, shaking his head.

"Let us keep the story simple: You were at home, you and your mother were attacked, you tried to get to safety, she was killed, and finally, the attackers disappeared just before Menlir and Turlin arrived," Vodin said, looking intensely thoughtful. "You are still a youth, so their hands are tied when it comes to certain... things." Vodin cleared his throat. "Just remember, you are not guilty. Now are you ready?"

"Not really..." said Aiden, still wiping his eyes.

***

After Aiden had pulled on his best tunic and cloak, Vodin led him out of the Guild grounds and into the Agnec Underground where they spent the next two and a half hours careening down railways and alongside subterranean mountainsides. Aiden wasn't enjoying the scenery or engaging in conversation, his mind was too blurry with thoughts of his mother. It seemed as though no time at all had passed when they arrived at a railstation just beneath Washington D.C.—as Vodin told it—and began making their way down a path into a large valley.

At first the village looked small, but as they walked the old cobblestones, large ornate buildings appeared on all sides, some of them fading distantly into the darkness far above. The streets bustled with markets, carts, noise, and creatures of all kinds.

Aiden found himself admiring some of the ancient store fronts—which reminded him of Market Street, above ground—but he didn't have time to waste and Vodin pulled him along the path.

A massive, rounded building soon loomed before them. It was much like the Main Hall at the Guild, but twice as large and covered in ornate runes and stone carvings of unfamiliar figures and creatures. On the wide double doors at the entrance, the sign read "Council Hall", and Aiden managed to read it just as he and Vodin pushed through.

Aiden had little time to think as Vodin rushed along the marble floors that met them. They sped through a corridor which branched off to several different rooms, but at the end, there stood a heavily armed Satyr wearing a green cloak, stationed at a wide entrance.

"State your business," the ape-faced Satyr said, his voice croaky.

"I am Headmaster Vodin of the Mount Katahdin Guild, and this is my student Aiden," said Vodin, looking somewhat harassed. "We're here for the trial. He is the defendant."

"Alright," the Satyr said, satisfied after looking both of them up and down. "Go on through."

The room was wide and circular, lit by a massive chandelier at the ceiling's center, and the walls were covered in wide, elaborate paintings of everything from ancient battlefields to important looking persons who must have been former Council members. Chairs and rounded pews were arranged in a circular pattern around the room, all facing the room's very center, where a raised dais stood, carved elaborately out of marble and stone. On the dais, an equally ornate, long desk with several chairs behind it stood next to a wide, sideways-facing lectern.

Before Aiden knew it, he was ushered to the front row, nearest the dais, and Vodin took a seat next to him. The several rows nearest the dais had already been filled, and the room was alive with chatter. There was a tension here that Aiden had never experienced, but Vodin's silence was the most unsettling.

A sudden hush fell over the small congregation, and Aiden looked behind him only to see a procession of thirteen individuals in dark robes walking down the aisle toward the dais.

"The Council, as I'm sure you've surmised," said Vodin quietly into Aiden's ear.

The Council members all took their seats behind the long table and faced toward the row where Aiden and the Headmaster were seated. They too shared the grave expressions that Aiden had seen so many others wearing. Aiden also took notice of Menlir and Turlin, seated not far from himself. Then, out of the corner of his eye he saw Grant sitting next to Charlie and Chadwick. His heart seemed to flip-flop when he thought of the accusations they would lobby against him.

Monadias stood from the center of the table and faced the crowd. "The Council is gathered. Let the trial commence. Will the defendant approach?"

"That would be you," Vodin said, placing a hand on Aiden's

shoulder and standing.

Aiden finally stood, and Vodin led him to a box-like wooden podium which stood squarely before the Council's long table, just below the raised dais. In all the racing of Aiden's thoughts, he hadn't noticed this podium until now. Vodin let Aiden into the box and latched the small door shut behind him. Aiden felt small, clasping the desk-like front of the podium and observing how he was boxed in on all sides up to his chest.

Vodin stayed by his side, folding his arms and watching Monadias take her seat.

"Aiden Gailhart," Monadias' voice boomed from the table. "You are hereby accused of involuntarily killing Lisa Gailhart, and practicing the D'Tari properties in a most inappropriate way. We also have reason to believe you may have practiced the properties in front of unauthorized Amblers."

At this, the crowd behind Aiden seemed to shuffle uncomfortably. Aiden tried to maintain himself, but hearing the accusations gave him the urge to jump out of the box and accuse Grant of everything. But, at the very same time, he wanted to break down in tears.

Without hesitation, Monadias called the first witness, and Grant approached the dais, taking his place at the side-facing lectern. Aiden shook his head.

"Being that the witness is my son, I will call Master Fentl to cross examine him," said Monadias, gesturing toward a brown-haired man with spectacles to her left.

The man stood, revealing that he was rather tall, thanked Monadias, and sidled up to the lectern where Grant stood. "Grant, as a point of reference to the character of the accused, would you repeat your experiences with him at the Guild?"

Fentl's accent reminded Aiden of the East Coast upper-crust sort that one might hear at the opera, or on TV. The man seemed confident and serious, and his expression intimidating.

Grant seemed somewhat hesitant at first, but then put on a tortured frown. "I really tried to be Aiden's friend," said Grant, looking over at Aiden, then looking away. "And at first, he pretended to be mine."

Aiden scoffed, but Fentl ignored this and looked back to Grant. "Please explain," said Fentl.

"Aiden acted like he was my friend for a few months at the beginning of last year," Grant began, feigning a sincere tone. "He told me that he wanted to show me something and took me outside the Guild—the whole time acting as if he was my closest friend."

Aiden could feel a dark coldness in his stomach. He thought he might be sick.

"I'm just glad that Chadwick saw us leaving and followed us," Grant continued. "Because instead of doing something fun, Aiden tried to throw me down a ravine. I guess he thought it would be funny or something."

There was a slight murmur in the crowd behind Aiden. "Liar!" Aiden shouted.

"Silence!" Monadias snapped, then composed herself. "We'll have no more outbursts. You must wait your turn to speak your peace."

Aiden's face flushed, and he nodded. He glanced sideways and saw Vodin giving him a reproving look.

"Please continue," Master Fentl said, looking back to Grant.

For the briefest instant, Aiden could swear he saw Grant's smile flicker and vanish, returning to a somber expression.

"So... Chadwick followed and caught up to us just in time," Grant continued. "We sort of fought and then Aiden fell and broke his leg."

Aiden was fuming. How could Grant have twisted the truth so cruelly? And with such a straight face?

After Grant left the stand, Chadwick came up, repeating the same story and only adding his own twist. Naturally he mentioned the small scuffles and fights between Aiden and Grant as though Grant had never provoked any of them. Aiden felt his heart sinking.

When Chadwick left the dais, Aiden watched the boy return to his seat next to Charlie. Aiden half-expected the next witness to be Charlie, but the boy remained in his seat, his gaze downcast. Aiden scowled. In moments, they called Turlin to the lectern instead.

"I was in the area, meeting with Master Menlir about some D'Tari business when it happened," Turlin said when asked why he had been at the scene.

"What business?" Fentl asked.

"As you well know, I am a liaison between the D'Tari and the Elvish tribes for that area. Once a month, Menlir and I meet to discuss the happenings and review whether or not there is any need for added security, and so on. That was our day." Turlin paused pensively, sighing. "I was just walking into the yard behind his house, minutes after we met... And there Aiden was, leaning over his mother."

"And she was..." Fentl probed.

"Already dead," Turlin replied, a look of genuine sadness on his youthful face.

"Did he seem upset?"

Turlin threw the man a surprised look. "Of course," he said. "He was in tears. It took us several minutes to pry him away and find out what had happened."

Aiden could still feel the sting of the snow and taste the salt of his own tears, just listening to Turlin's recollection. He clutched his podium so tightly that his fingers had begun to ache.

"And who did he say killed his mother?"

Turlin hesitated. "The N'Iatari."

The gathering began to rustle and murmur. The tension swelled thickly from behind Aiden.

"Was there any sign of a struggle?" said Fentl, gauging the crowd's reaction.

"There may have been," Turlin said, choosing his words slowly.

"May have been?"

"At the onset, it... It didn't appear as though anyone else had been there. No."

Aiden's mind raced. How could he be lying so blatantly?

"I saw no footprints in the snow, other than Aiden's and another set that was likely his mother's," Turlin continued, looking conflicted. "I did what I could for her, but she was already gone."

Fentl thanked Turlin and called Menlir to the stand. Menlir repeated much of the same story, as well as the notion that there were no other footprints besides Aiden's and his mother's. Aiden's mind whirled and his heart pounded. It didn't seem possible.

"Was it possible that Aiden had done this to his mother?" Fentl asked the Faun at the lectern.

"Nothing's impossible I suppose," Menlir replied. "I don't really know the boy, but I promised Vodin that I would look after the boy's mother, considering how she lived in my jurisdiction. I sent a few Faeries to report on her now and then, nothing unusual ever seemed to happen."

"So, she was an Ambler, is that correct?"

"Yes, and Aiden wasn't raised Agnec," Menlir said, looking around the room. "But what does that have to do with anything? He's one of us now, isn't he?"

"Is it possible his new-found powers simply got out of hand? Perhaps he didn't realize what he was doing?"

"I don't know," Menlir said, scratching his head. "Headmaster Vodin is a good teacher, I can't imagine-"

"Is it possible that in his anger, young Aiden simply forgot the rules—let his emotions get the best of him?" Fentl probed, his voice raising. "Perhaps they were in a heated argument. This boy has a history of letting his temper get the best of him—with both Amblers and Agnecs! And, according to our early investigation, the Headmaster has said that the boy's mother was always wary of his decision to become a D'Tari-"

"Objection!" Vodin's voice bellowed from beside Aiden, causing the room to grow deathly still.

"Yes?" said Monadias from where she sat, looking composed.

"Master Fentl is twisting my words," said Vodin, glaring at Fentl. "I said, initially Lisa was wary, but she seemed to accept it over time. Furthermore, I feel that Fentl is leading the witness towards a conclusion that we can certainly not prove as of yet."

"Objection granted," Monadias conceded with a terse nod.

Fentl, looking irritated, also nodded and dismissed Menlir from the stand. After a moment's settling, Vodin was called to the lectern.

"Is it true the boy has a history of anger?" Fentl began.

"I would call it misplaced frustration," Vodin said, looking fairly calm. "I imagine you would be frustrated as well if you did not understood what you were, or why you did certain things-"

"A simple yes or no would suffice," Fentl interjected. "Is is true that he has been dismissed from a handful of Ambler schools prior to being admitted to to the Guild? Because of accidents involving using D'Tari powers?"

"Again," Vodin began, looking determined. "Those incidents were the result of misplaced frustration. I truly believe he didn't understand-"

"Answer the question!" Fentl barked. "Yes or no? Was he, or was he not, dismissed from several Ambler schools because he abused his powers?"

Vodin bristled, looking at Monadias and the rest of the Council. "Yes."

Fentl smiled slightly and paced near the lectern where Vodin stood. "Is it true that there were fights between the boy and Monadias' son?"

"Yes, but-" Vodin began.

"Isn't it true that Aiden fell into the ravine and broke his leg, just as Grant and Chadwick have testified?"

"Well, yes, I healed the leg myself, but-"

"Isn't it true that you were so afraid of Aiden's powers that you started him in powercasting instruction early? A year earlier than the average student?"

"No," Vodin said, glaring at Fentl. "Not afraid-"

"Did he begin the classes early?"

"Well, yes, but-"

"Thank you, Headmaster, for your time," said Fentl abruptly. "You may stand down."

"Wait just a damn minute!" Vodin bellowed, looking angrier

than Aiden had ever seen him. "If you would stop interrupting, perhaps you would hear the entire story."

Aiden felt the hairs on the back of his neck stand up.

"I wholeheartedly trust Aiden," Vodin continued, ignoring Fentl's look of feigned shock. "Certainly he had some rough edges, but who among us hasn't? I believe when he told me that it was in fact Grant and Chadwick that tricked him at the ravine, I believed him. When he told me that he did not kill his mother, I believe him. When he tells me that the N'Iatari were there, I believe him."

The crowd was silent, and for a moment, Fentl looked unsure of what to say.

"I understand that to many people, trust is only something you can accept with several witnesses or with the exchange of currency," Vodin continued, looking out among the room. "I know, absolutely, that Aiden would never kill his own mother, not even by accident. By the time he was entering his second year, he had already mastered the kind of control one needs for powercasting."

"But is it true that Aiden had few friends?" Fentl asked.

"How many friends do you have?" Vodin asked.

"That's besides the point," Fentl said, caught off guard.

"What does it matter if he was popular or not?"

"By all accounts, even yours, he was mostly a loner," Fentl said forcibly. "Other students stayed away, and no one has stepped forward, besides you, his mentor, as a positive character witness. How can we know that your testimony isn't blinded by your own—possibly fatherly—affection for him?"

After a few moments, Vodin's gaze fell. "I suppose you can't."

Aiden felt himself screaming inside. The heat was rising in his chest.

"Furthermore, Headmaster," Fentl continued, seeing his victory near. "This story about the N'Iatari... It sounds much more like the stuff of legends that you have no doubt put into his head. The N'Iatari of today are most certainly not the N'Iatari of your youth. There's been no activity of this sort for over twenty years."

"No activity that you are aware of," Vodin said, his tone almost seething.

"The Council would know," said Fentl haughtily. "Mistress Monadias," Fentl addressed the table full of Council members. "Members of the Council, I think this will serve to conclude this case."

Fentl returned to his seat at the table, looking smug. Monadias stood and looked to Vodin, her expression was hard to read.

"Headmaster, given your history, I can hardly call you a reliable witness, but you are Aiden's mentor." said Monadias. "I am sure you have put in an excellent effort, but we find that the evidence is hardly in favor of your defense. You may stand down."

Vodin, looking more troubled and angry than Aiden had before seen, left the dais and returned to Aiden's side. Aiden's heart demiGod

pounded in anticipation.

Monadias fixed her gaze on the boy. "Aiden Gailhart," she said, her voice echoing across the room. "Although we do not believe it was intentional, the Council and I believe you are guilty of the crimes with which you are charged."

Aiden felt his knees begin to buckle.

"Given that there is no conclusive evidence to the contrary, and that you are still a minor according to both Agnec and Ambler laws, and given the circumstances, you cannot be charged as an adult," Monadias continued. "You are hereby expelled from the Guild and are forbidden to practice the D'Tari properties. As soon as a proper guardian can be found, you will be returned to the Ambler world..."

Monadias glared into Aiden's glistening eyes. "And I would highly encourage you to not return to the Agnec world, as it is clear that you cannot responsibly contribute to our society."

The room stirred with a tense chatter that continued to grow louder by the moment. Vodin rushed up to the dais.

"This is outrageous," Vodin protested, looking up to Monadias. "Give the boy a chance to defend himself."

Monadias glared down at the Headmaster. "The Council has made it's decision," she said. "This is a very serious crime, and he is very fortunate. We are following the D'Tari moral code, or have you forgotten?"

"Have you forgotten that mercy and a fair hearing are also part of the code?" Vodin snapped back.

"We have been very fair," Monadias said quietly through clenched teeth. "There is a reason you are not part of this Council, Headmaster, and you would do well not to interfere. We'll soon be dealing with you as well..."

Vodin stepped back, an angry and determined look upon his face. Aiden felt himself beginning to blink uncontrollably. He clutched the sides of his box, his knuckles turning white, until the sensation subsided. The situation hadn't changed, and now he realized there were tears in his eyes.

"Master Fentl, administer the trace rune," Monadias ordered the tall man by her side.

Fentl stepped off the dais and sauntered toward Aiden. The Satyr, whom Aiden had met at the door, now stood by Aiden's side. He grasped Aiden's arm roughly and exposed the boy's shoulder.

"What are you doing?" Aiden gasped, surprised by the Satyr's strength.

"This will tell us if you do any complicated traveling," said Fentl, now within feet of Aiden. "Such as jumping or leaving the country."

Fentl held up a hand and began to draw runes in the air. A word appeared and floated to Aiden's shoulder, then turned dark, followed by a brief glow. The sensation was strange, like a tingling on Aiden's skin. The ink remained dark on Aiden's shoulder, and appeared as a tattoo. Aiden's heart fluttered. He tried to wrench himself away from the Satyr.

demiGod

Fentl laughed. "You can't run now. At least not too far."

Aiden glanced over to Vodin. The man looked so helpless. Aiden had never seen him in such a state. He tried again to pull away from the Satyr.

"Hold still, you stupid boy," the Satyr chided, his grip immovable.

Fentl put his hands on Aiden's shoulders, and Aiden felt powerless to stop whatever was happening. The man wrote another rune on Aiden's skin, but this one did not stay as a tattoo. Aiden's sword and buckler appeared in Fentl's hands.

"Hey!" Aiden yelled, struggling again as Fentl placed the weapons on the ground.

"Be quiet!" Fentl snapped. "You didn't think you would be allowed to take these with you, did you?"

"But they belong to me!"

"Not anymore," said Fentl, writing another rune. "You abused those rights."

Aiden's armor and helmet appeared in Fentl's hands now. The man placed them on the ground, then proceeded to cast a rune upon each object. In moments, the silvery sheen that tended to encase translated objects had begun to fade. Aiden stopped struggling, and the Satyr let go.

"Please escort the accused to a suitable location until we can take him to his relative's home," Monadias announced, her voice echoing as if trying to establish some order again.

"My relative?" Aiden croaked as the Satyr opened the box and let Aiden out.

"I'll take him there," said Vodin. "After all-"

"No!" Monadias shouted, standing in alarm. "You are to have no further contact with the accused. He is no longer your student, nor is he your protege, or your concern."

"Vodin?" Aiden asked, desperately looking to the man for some semblance of hope.

"It seems my hands are tied..." Vodin said, looking away.

Chapter 8
Running Back

They had found Aiden's aunt. He wasn't sure how exactly they had located her, but they had. Aiden found himself following Turlin—now disguised as a human—up a cleared path through a complex of nice town homes. It was no longer snowing, but a chill still hung in the air and the surrounding lawns were still white.

They had been traveling since early that morning. Only a day had passed since Aiden's expulsion from the Guild, and he had spent the night in a dank hotel room located in the Agnec village beneath Washington DC. It had been miserable, but Aiden was quickly being overcome by a numbing sensation that was hard to ignore.

After a bit of wandering through the Underground, Turlin had led Aiden here, to a small suburb just outside of Philadelphia. Aiden didn't quite feel himself, and it was almost as though he was outside of himself, watching events unfold that he had no control over.

"Ah, this should be it," Turlin said after a long silence.

They both turned to see the two-story town home at the end of the walk. It was white and pristine, even amongst the snow on the roof and in the yard. Aiden shrugged and Turlin led the way.

After Turlin knocked, a tall, dark-haired woman answered the door and stared at them through a metal screen. "Yes?" she asked, her lips pursing in a less than inviting way.

"Are you Maggie Gailhart?" Turlin asked.

"Yes. Well, Gailhart's my maiden name," she said, looking suspiciously at them, her eyes flitting back and forth between Turlin and Aiden.

"I come from the Mount Katahdin Guild School for D'Tari," began Turlin. "And-"

"Listen, I already give to other charities for troubled youth," Maggie said, shaking her head. "So if you don't mind-"

"Please, hear me out," Turlin cut in. "I'm not here for charity. I'm here because of your sister Lisa..."

"Lisa?" Maggie said, her eyes wide. "What about her?"

There was a moment of silence as Turlin gathered his thoughts. "Well, she's dead," he said slowly. "I'm so very sorry."

Maggie stood there speechless. Aiden couldn't figure out if she was upset or skeptical. Her pale eyes continued flitting between Aiden and Turlin. The Half-Elf glanced to Aiden as if looking for queues, but the boy lowered his gaze. This was never an ideal way to meet up with long lost relatives.

"And you're her boy," Maggie finally said, pointing a skinny finger in Aiden's direction.

Aiden nodded, unsure by her tone if she was accusing him or simply recognizing him.

"Yes," Turlin said. "With Lisa's unfortunate passing, Aiden

here was left to the nearest of kin... And that would be you."

There was another silence.

"Aiden is it?" Maggie said with something near a scoff. "It figures. If she had only listened to me in the first place..." Maggie grumbled, shaking her head. "Come on in. You're letting the in cold."

Unsure how to feel, Aiden followed Turlin inside. Despite the fire in the living room fireplace, it wasn't particularly bright as most of the house lights were off. In the corner of the large room, a small television set glowed and flickered before an old armchair, the sound apparently turned down. The house smelled of moth balls and the bookshelves and credenzas were full of dozens of presumably antique porcelain dolls, clowns, and piglets.

"Take your muddy boots off!" Maggie snapped, pointing to both Turlin and Aiden's feet. "No manners at all, these kids..."

Aiden sighed, plopping his bag down next to a wooden credenza and took his boots off next to Turlin who did the same. They came into the carpeted living room and took seats on the old sofa beside the armchair, being bombarded by the commingled flicker of the television and the fireplace. At the end of the room, a sliding glass door let in a white light, which painted Maggie's face eerily when she sat down beside them in the armchair and clicked off the TV set.

"Do you live here alone?" Turlin asked, looking uncomfortable.

195

"Yes, and thanks for reminding me," Maggie croaked. "Widowed these ten years."

"I'm sorry," said Turlin kindly. "I realize this is asking a lot, but this would be only temporary—if Aiden lived here, that is."

"How did the mother die?"

"Excuse me?" Turlin asked, looking at Maggie's unflinching face.

"How did the mother die?" she repeated, looking perturbed.

"How did your sister, Aiden's mother, die?" Turlin re-worded the question. "Well, it was an unfortunate accident. We believe there may have been some foul play—not on her part—but some... thieves killed her."

Aiden looked to Turlin in surprise, but the Half-Elf ignored him.

"She always was at the wrong place at the wrong time..." Maggie mused. "We wouldn't be in this mess if it weren't for her... Acting like a common whore..."

"Shutup!" Aiden shouted and stood up, making Turlin jump. "She was not a whore! If you hadn't disowned her, maybe we wouldn't be in this mess."

Aiden glared at her, his chest hot. The emotion that had been suppressed by the numbing sensation seemed to be forcing its way through the barrier.

Maggie stood up, noticeably taller than Aiden, with a menacing scowl on her face. "You are your mother's child. Now I see her in you." she said, thoughtfully. "She did have you out of wedlock. You are her bastard, you know that, don't you?"

Aiden glared into his aunt's eyes, seeing nothing but contempt. "My mom's dead... I don't see how she talked so nicely about you, especially since you hated her so much." He looked to Turlin. "I don't need this shit. I'm gone."

With that, Aiden shoved his feet into his boots, leaving them unstrung, and pulled his bag over his shoulder. He threw open the door and headed back into the snowy yard. He was already back to the sidewalk when Turlin rushed out behind him.

"Aiden!" the Half-Elf called. "Wait! Aiden..."

Aiden stopped at the curb, his gaze downcast.

"She's family..." Turlin said, placing a hand on Aiden's shoulder. "Your only family. And we cannot simply leave you out in the cold."

"I'd be better off..." Aiden said, his tears now stinging from the frozen air.

"This will be only temporary, and you'll be of legal age in just a couple of years as it is..."

The thought was simultaneously exciting and horrifying to Aiden. "Don't know if I can last two years with... Her," he said, glancing back at the tall woman now glaring at them through her screen door.

"Aiden," Turlin said, now face to face with the boy. "I haven't known you long, but Vodin trusts you, and I trust Vodin. I believe he taught you a great deal more than you realize. Being a D'Tari often comes with great obstacles, and it is the hard times that either break us or destroy us..."

Aiden stood back, stunned. "You sounded like Vodin just now," he mused. "What about your testimony? Don't you think I killed my mom?"

"No," said Turlin, looking solemn. "I really don't. I was not lying when I said there were no footprints—I really did not see any—but that doesn't mean that someone couldn't have erased them. I..." Turlin sighed, looking sad. "I'm sorry I couldn't do more to help you. Speaking very honestly, the Council has not been right for a while now, and your trial was not fair or balanced by any means. But there's nothing more I could do. Fentl twisted all of our words... And now Vodin is no longer allowed to associate with you..."

Aiden took a deep shuttering breath, his tears falling freely. "What am I supposed to do now?" he said, his voice strained.

"Live here, stay safe, and keep yourself out of the Agnec world for a while," Turlin said, his tone serious. "If Vodin is correct and someone is after you, then this is the best place for you. I'll be keeping an eye on you from time to time, although you might not see me."

Something about Turlin's words gave Aiden some comfort, although not as much as he'd hoped. He shook his head half-heartedly.

"Give it some time. After this all calms down, I don't see any reason for you not to return to the Agnec world," Turlin said, a flicker of a smile on his lips.

"Seriously?" Aiden said, his heart leaping suddenly.

"It's possible," Turlin replied. "But not too soon if you can help it. I don't know what will happen, but keep safe and keep your mind sharp."

Feeling his spirits lifted somewhat, Aiden wiped his tears and headed back to the house.

***

The guest room smelled like moth balls and ancient perfume. Aiden had been in his new confines for nearly an entire day without food, only sneaking out to use the bathroom. Although at first his aunt had hounded him to come out and do some chores, she soon gave up. She had mentioned how this was only temporary and she'd not only be finding him another place to live, but another school to go to.

"And a nice place, not full of weirdos like that Turlin person..." she had mumbled, ignoring Aiden's glare.

His stomach growled so loudly now that it shook uncontrollably. The house was still dark, with only a few lights on in the hall and a fire in the fireplace. Aunt Maggie claimed to be keeping electricity costs down, but Aiden wondered if she was just extremely stingy. Even when Aiden and his mother couldn't afford to pay the electric bill, they had never kept the house this dark during the winter.

He crept downstairs, hearing the TV blaring from the living room. It seemed to be his aunt's constant comfort. With each step, he felt the old stairs threaten to creak. He kept low, straining to hear anything besides the TV, and all seemed quiet. When he finally dared to look over the railing and down into the living room, he saw his aunt fast asleep on her armchair, the television's flickering light illuminating her face eerily.

Slowly he touched down on the floor and began to creep through the room. With the next step, the floorboards moaned. He stopped, looking frantically to where his aunt sat. She was still asleep. He sighed quietly and carried on. Soon he was nearing the television set. The volume was so high that his ears hurt from being so near it.

His stomach growled violently.

"Aiden?"

Aiden froze, his heart pounding. His aunt stood up suddenly.

"I wondered when you were going to come down," she said.

Aiden was surprised by the calm in her voice, and wondered if she was just groggy. Maggie walked toward him and half-smiled. He still hadn't moved, though he wanted to run back upstairs.

"You should sit down and have something to eat," Maggie said. "Unclench boy, I'm not going to hit you."

Aiden smiled sheepishly and resigned to a shrug. He took a seat on the couch, still dreading whatever might come next.

"Let me get you some dinner," said his aunt. "Lord knows you've practically starved yourself. But just this once, then you'll be making the meals around here..."

Aiden threw her a furtive look, and her lips curled into a smile that Aiden couldn't quite read.

Just as Maggie left for the kitchen, the news blared into the room, the exuberant theme song almost deafening. Footage of an apartment complex full of police met Aiden's eyes.

"Welcome back to News on the Hour," announced the blonde anchor woman who now appeared on screen in the studio. "A local woman is missing tonight from the West Heights neighborhood."

Aiden sat back, his heart fluttering as he saw an image of his mother on the screen.

"Investigators find that Lisa Gailhart has been missing for at least three days. It seems that there may have been a struggle, and there has been evidence of a break-in. Police were called when neighbors heard shouts and saw smoke coming from the apartment."

Aiden shook his head, new tears threatening to fall as he watched the footage of his ransacked home being rifled through by policemen and detectives.

The anchor woman reappeared on screen with the image of Aiden's mother beside her. "Due to the violent circumstances of the incident, the neighbors are demanding that officials continue to search. None of them knew Gailhart very well, they admit, but community organizers agree that the investigation could ward off future events like this. Police are asking anyone who knows or has seen Gailhart to please come forward with any information."

Aiden sighed, wondering if his aunt had heard any of the broadcast from the kitchen.

"For those in the area," the anchor woman continued, "Lisa Gailhart is about five-eleven, white, thin, with brown eyes and reddish-brown hair. It is unknown what sort of clothes she may be wearing. At this point, she has no known relatives, and no one else seems to have been missing from the apartment, as officials tells us that she lived there alone."

"What?" Aiden coughed, almost choking on his own saliva.

As the anchor woman droned on with the information, Aiden could no longer hear it over his own racing thoughts.

How come they hadn't mentioned him?

***

Aiden had managed to sneak away to his room after a disappointing microwave dinner, despite his aunt's groaning protests. She had told him that he would begin an entire regimen of chores the next day.

"And it will not be a walk in the park, young man! If you live here, you need to prove yourself," she had said.

Aiden hoisted his duffel up onto his shoulders and pulled the hood of his jacket over his head. There hadn't been much to pack, and now he stood, staring in thought at the closed bedroom door.

"It's worth a shot," he whispered to himself, shrugging.

He raised his hand and began motioning as though he were writing something in mid-air. He concentrated, trying to remember the exact formula, and in moments, the runes appeared before him. They floated to the door and glowed upon the old wood. The door frame glowed briefly, and Aiden stepped back.

He wondered if it had worked, as Vodin had only shown him this once or twice. It had been some time since Aiden had tried to use any of the properties, and he smirked, thankful that he had not lost the ability to runecast. He slowly turned the doorknob and peered through the opening as he pulled.

The smell of pine entered the room, followed by an icy wind. Aiden smiled and pulled the door completely open, his eyes met by a dark forest. A carpet of snow met Aiden's boots as he left the room and stepped into the wood. He shivered, pulling his jacket around himself tightly. He had thought the guest room was cold, but this new shift in temperature showed him just how wrong he had been.

He closed the door behind him, and in moments it had faded. Aiden turned. The wind had died down, and snow was no longer falling. A deep silence came over everything, and Aiden felt a strange emptiness in his stomach. It was no longer the hunger he had felt, but the realization that he had no idea where he was, or how to find the Guild from here.

He could only assume that he was close, but was that true? How could he know? Panic began to swell in his chest.

He took a few steps forward, trying to catch his breath, stumbling through the deep snow until he could see a pale light shining through the trees. He followed it until the pines grew thinner, and finally he pushed his way through into a clearing. Moonlight enveloped him, illuminating everything in that open space. He sighed and looked around.

He could see nothing but trees in every direction. Though he tried, he could not even glimpse a distant mountain top. The forest was thick and dark, and if he stared into the tangles of needled branches, he could imagine them marching on him, like an army of giants.

Aiden thought hard. "How to get to the Guild..." he whispered, his voice sounding strange against the intense silence.

The fluttering of wings made Aiden jump. A dark bird flew past him and alighted upon a nearby branch. Aiden shook his head, regaining his composure. The creature looked like a crow of some sort, and he ignored it, trying to calm his pounding heart.

He was desperately trying to imagine the lay of the land in his head, but the cold was growing so intense that he was beginning to lose concentration.

A clicking noise from off to Aiden's right broke his thoughts. It was the bird. The creature was clicking loudly, turning its head sideways as if to get a better look at Aiden. He looked back, wondering what the creature could be doing. Aiden ignored it again, looking around in hopes that there wasn't something big lurking in the nearby thickets.

The bird cawed, and Aiden jumped.

"Dammit," Aiden said angrily, trying not to be too loud. "What's your deal, bird?"

The creature seemed intent on glaring at Aiden, and after a few moments, he no longer thought he imagined it. The bird was staring, as if trying to communicate something. It cawed and clicked, shaking its head now, motioning again and again to its right.

Aiden approached the bird cautiously. The bird continued the motion, and Aiden could now see what he may have been pointing at. Between the trees, there seemed to be a narrow space, a snow-covered path.

"I need to find the Guild," Aiden said slowly, feeling foolish.

The bird continued its motion, but suddenly fluttered in the direction of the path and alighted on another branch.

"Three years ago, I would've thought I was going crazy," said Aiden quietly to the bird. "But... Out of Fauns, Dwarves, and Elves... A bird giving directions seems pretty normal I guess."

Aiden took several more steps in the direction of the path, and the bird continued to fly on ahead, each time landing on a branch and waiting for Aiden to catch up. Once they made it through the trees, Aiden came to a hill, and on the other side he could see smaller clusters of snowy trees and thickets. The bird, which Aiden had begun to think of as a raven, soared across the clearing and landed on something just out of sight.

Aiden trudged up the hill and slowly came down the other side, only to see the Otter Gate just yards from him. The raven was sitting atop one of the great carved statues, gently cooing. Aiden's heart leaped and he smiled at the bird.

"Thanks..." he said, still feeling a little odd that he was talking to a bird.

Everything was as he had left it. They hadn't even changed the password to get inside, and Aiden managed to get into the grounds without any problems. All was still and silent, and Aiden looked at his watch, realizing that it was midnight already. He made his way toward the dormitory buildings, his eyes darting in every direction, hoping no one would be awake.

Once Aiden was sure no one was watching or following him, he focused on the adrenaline he felt. He had imagined he would be lucky trying to travel by door to the Guild, but he couldn't believe his luck being led to the grounds by some random raven. It seemed almost too lucky.

Aiden steeled himself and entered the boy's dormitory. Aside from a lone lantern in the common room, the place was darker than it had been outside. He glanced around the room, not daring to breath. All was silent. Even the fire had long been gone from the hearth.

Aiden sighed and took a few more steps toward the stone staircase just feet from him.

"Aiden?"

Aiden reached down, as if to call his sword to him, but nothing appeared and he remembered he no longer had it. His eyes searched the room frantically, and he wondered if his mind wasn't playing tricks. The silhouette of a boy appeared, just on the other side of one of the couches. The shape walked slowly forward.

"Aiden?" the voice came again.

"Charlie?" Aiden said as the realization struck him.

"What're you doing here?" Charlie asked, now stepping into the light, revealing his tired eyes, a look of worry suddenly on his face.

It was a good question, and one Aiden did not have a good answer to. He had been so focused on getting back here, with the goal of finding Grant that he hadn't spent much time thinking about what he would actually do. In the end, all he could think of was the hate he now felt. He had had the fleeting thought of killing Grant, but when it came to it, he wasn't sure he could ever do that.

"Where's Grant?" Aiden asked, his eyes determined.

"He's not here," Charlie said slowly, obviously gauging the malicious tone in Aiden's voice. "His mother pulled him out of the Guild,"

"What?" Aiden asked, his anger hurrying to the surface.

"Said things weren't safe here anymore..." Charlie said, his eyes downcast. "I guess a lot of parents are upset at Headmaster Vodin... And you."

"And you..." Aiden said, thinking. "Why the hell didn't you stand up in my trial? You saw what your stupid brother and Grant did to me, and you just let them both lie about everything."

Charlie took a step back. "I-I'm sorry... I wanted to say something," he breathed, unable to look at Aiden. "I... was scared."

"Scared of who?" Aiden said, stepping forward threateningly.

"My brother, Grant... everything," Charlie mumbled, stepping back further. "You don't know what it's like living with Chad—I mean, I love him, but-"

"Well, I don't give a damn!" Aiden said loudly, then caught himself. "Do you know what it's like being accused of something you didn't do? And you told Grant about the locket too, didn't you?"

Aiden tried to rein himself in, but he continued to step toward Charlie.

Charlie was shaking now. "Around your neck? I-I guess I mentioned it... But what's the big deal about that? I didn't think that meant anything..."

Aiden could feel the energy pulsating in his body now, and he brought his hand up, feeling the heat burning in his palm. Charlie had backed himself into a chair and accidentally fell into the seat. Aiden glared at him.

"It meant everything," said Aiden, breathing heavily. He stopped, the energy suddenly dissipating within him. "Now what am I supposed to do?"

Aiden stepped back, leaning against the nearby couch and fighting the tears that threatened to fill his vision. Charlie was horrified and sad all at once. He sat, frozen to the chair, watching Aiden.

Another figure emerged without warning. Charlie jumped to his feet in surprise, but Aiden no longer cared. A tall, cloaked man stepped into the dim light and clutched Aiden's shoulder.

"Charles," the man said, looking to Charlie. "Go up to sleep, and speak of this to no one, do you understand me? Aiden's life depends upon it."

Charlie nodded slowly, a look of shock still on his face. Without another word, he disappeared up the stone steps.

Aiden finally wiped his eyes and dared to look into the man's face. As he'd suspected, it was Vodin.

"Let's go to my office, shall we?"

***

Aiden held his face with his hands, unable to see Vodin across from him through the tears. He tried to pull himself together, and he took a deep breath. Vodin waited calmly while Aiden composed himself.

"Aiden," Vodin finally spoke. "Why did you come back?"

Aiden sighed, sniffing, and finally able to see clearly. "I... I want to know why..." He paused, but suddenly found himself gushing, "Why didn't you stop them from expelling me? Why do they hate me? And what the hell is in this stupid locket? Why do they want to take it?"

"Calm down," said Vodin, raising a hand. "Take a deep breath."

Aiden exhaled harshly and sat back in his chair. "I want to know what's going on, and what I'm supposed to do now."

"I understand," said Vodin, his eyes sad. "I'm so sorry, Aiden. I never meant for any of this to happen. I did what I could, but the Council does not like me much. I have a... Not such a great reputation among them. They seem to be fixated on my past instead of my present."

Aiden raised an eyebrow, but Vodin ignored it. "There are some deep prejudices among the Council these days..." Vodin continued, a bitter tone in his voice. "Something's just a bit off. Regardless, it's something you should have never had to deal with. After all, you're just a student. Why should you deal with all their backwards thinking? For that, I am sorry I wasn't able to help more."

Aiden straightened, unable to ignore the sincerity in Vodin's voice. "You still believe me, right? That Grant was there, leading those men?"

"Yes," said Vodin. "I do. I'm still unsure as to why Grant was there, but I'm looking into it. Currently, the Council is making things hard for me. In fact, well..." He paused, looking pensive.

"What?" Aiden asked, trying to gauge the Headmaster's expression.

"They're pressuring me to resign," Vodin continued. "Monadias has already taken Grant out of the Guild, and she is beginning to push the idea that our Guild has been producing D'Tari obsessed with the darker properties. The sort that are disregarding D'Tari Precepts and Agnec laws, and whatnot..."

"What?" Aiden scoffed. "That's crap!"

"Calm yourself," Vodin warned. "My biggest regret is that I'm unable to complete your training at this time. I just wish I could have introduced you to the D'Tari when there wasn't so much politics poisoning the air. But," Vodin stopped and sighed, looking into Aiden's eyes. "You'll have to learn it sooner than later: Nothing is perfect. Even the loftiest ideals will let you down when you hit the ground running with them."

Aiden scrunched his face in thought.

"There are plenty of Agnecs who just don't understand the Ambler world," Vodin continued. "That misunderstanding leads to fear, and fear, left unfettered, leads to hatred. I can only hope that one day we'll all put the misunderstandings behind us, but until then, there are those who want to bring back the dark glory days of the N'Iatari."

"You told me about this..."

"Yes, I know," Vodin admitted, seeing Aiden's impatient look. "I want to to reiterate it, because I have a good deal of suspicion that there are N'Iatari among us even now. I'm frustrated," Vodin said with a bitter sigh. "Because the threat never felt so ever-present until now."

Aiden had never seen the Headmaster so exasperated yet thoughtful.

"And Aiden, I know it's difficult, but I think you know why someone would want the forca locus. I've already told you."

Aiden felt the locket around his neck beneath his clothing. "I know..." he said quietly. "But I don't want it anymore. My mom's dead because of this..."

"Your mother is dead," Vodin began softly. "Because—from what I've seen of your life—she sacrificed everything to give you a good life, even letting you come here. You tried your hardest to save her because you knew she deserved everything you could offer..."

"It just wasn't good enough," Aiden said, a pain twinging in his throat as tears fell afresh.

"You never had to be," Vodin said. "She would have done anything for you, even step before the flames if meant you would be spared. You know I am right."

Aiden nodded.

"And I know this is hard to hear, Aiden, but the forca locus has chosen you to be its bearer, and you must continue to conceal it at all costs," Vodin continued much to Aiden's disappointment. "The N'Iatari obviously know you have it now... They believe it is connected to Lilit somehow, which means it is a threat if it falls into their hands."

Aiden's chest filled with panic.

Reading his expression, Vodin added, "But don't worry, just stay completely away from the Agnec world. Maybe some day in the future, you will be able to return, and I will try my damndest to find you and continue your training, but for now, you must lay low..."

After a few moments, Aiden wiped his face again and sighed, feeling somewhat uplifted by the thought of eventually returning. Another thought struck him.

"Another thing," Aiden began. "On the news they said my mother was missing, but they didn't mention me at all... It was like I didn't exist..."

Vodin sighed. "Sometimes when a child is raised as an Ambler and then enters the Agnec world," he began slowly, observing Aiden. "In order to keep the Guild and the Agnec world a secret, that child's records and identification are erased from Ambler society..."

Aiden sat back. "What? Why?"

"It's an option we offer the parent," Vodin explained. "Well, to be fair, it is an option granted all of us by the United States government... We are legally protected under secret statutes—but anyhow-"

Aiden sat forward, his mind whirling. "So they just erase everything?" he asked incredulously. "Like we never existed?" He paused and swallowed. "Like I never existed?"

Vodin's eyes were downcast and he folded his hands at his desk. "Your mother felt it would be the best option—to keep you safe, and to keep the local authorities from asking questions," Vodin explained. "After all, when the neighbors wondered where you were all the sudden, and the local school districts did not have you on record, and you were nowhere to be found for long periods of time... It could seem a little suspicious. What would stop police from finding you on file and investigating your mother for your disappearance?"

Aiden was silent. He'd never thought of that before, but he'd wondered why his mother had often asked him not to disturb the neighbors when he'd been home for the holidays or the summers.

"She loved you," Vodin continued. "But I'm afraid she worried as well, and she felt this would be best. Of course, this does put us in a difficult position... Something none of us could have foreseen. You'll have to start over, and we know people who can help you with that, but it might be some time before we can put all the pieces together..."

Aiden had stopped listening sometime around Vodin mentioning how Aiden's mother had worried. He knew she had worried, and he tried to see it from her perspective, though that was too difficult. He thought of that moment at the table when he had asked his mother about his father.

"What about my dad?" Aiden asked abruptly.

Vodin stopped, looking stunned by the sudden change of topic.

"I, I mean..." Aiden stammered, trying to sift through his thoughts. "Maybe I could prove to the Council I had an Agnec father, and they might let me stay in Agnec society?"

Vodin looked thoughtful but equally troubled. "I don't know..."

"I never met him, but my mom said his name was Wren," Aiden said, his mind traveling back to that night not so long ago. "If he was an Agnec, there's gott'a be a way to find him."

"I have done some research," Vodin admitted. "And," he sighed, shaking his head. "I feel that delving too deeply would only complicate things at the present."

Aiden furled his brow and shook his head, almost as if he'd stepped into a brick wall. "Why?"

"You have a wonderful idea there, but if my suspicions are

correct, it would work to heap even more judgement on your head," said Vodin, stroking his beard. "The Council might do something worse. All I can say is that you'll know soon enough who your father is, but try your utmost to not be fooled by appearances."

Aiden sat back, dissatisfied and confused. He had no words to express the anger and disappointment he felt, but all his arguments failed before they left his mind.

Vodin looked over to the grandfather clock and sighed. "Aiden, we have little time, and I need to tell you about one more thing."

Still pondering what Vodin had said about his father, Aiden barely acknowledged the Headmaster's words. He finally managed a terse nod.

"Do you know about demigods?" Vodin asked suddenly.

Aiden looked up, surprised. "I think so."

"In Ambler myth, they are people born to both humans and the gods—part human, part god," Vodin explained as Aiden shook his head in agreement. "In Agnec myth, demiGods—as we emphasize the last part of the word—they are people who possess and hold the capacity to gain nearly all the D'Tari properties."

Aiden looked confused. "Aren't all D'Tari trying to do that?" he asked.

"No," said Vodin, now smiling. "Most D'Tari learn the basics, retain the knowledge, and only develop a few abilities, majoring in at least one of them. But you, my boy, are already fluent in swordskill, powercasting, and illusioncasting... And so far I've seen you excel in runecasting as well as lightcasting and inkcasting. I'm so proud and impressed."

Aiden flushed suddenly.

"You have a greatness in you that I sense rivals the mythical demiGods, but I want you to stay humble," Vodin continued. "Skill is not enough, and a true demiGod will discover that knowledge without wisdom is purposeless."

Aiden sat in silence, letting it sink in.

"That said," Vodin broke the silence. "I have some gifts for you."

While Aiden looked on in curiosity, Vodin stood and walked to a large cabinet near the wall. Aiden had never noticed it there before, and it was currently concealed in shadow. Vodin runecasted some words onto the cabinet and Aiden heard an internal mechanism click. Vodin pulled open the large door and reached inside.

"Here we are," Vodin said, now holding a sword, a buckler, and some pieces of armor.

Aiden jumped to his feet, his face aglow. "What? My sword!"

"Keep your voice down," Vodin said calmly as he smiled and walked toward Aiden. "Yes, I managed to salvage your effects before they were destroyed. I trust you'll need them."

Aiden stood excitedly as Vodin placed runes upon the different weapons and armor. The tools faded into a white mist, returning to Aiden's arsenal. Vodin smiled, but it was a troubled smile, as if there was so much more he wished to say but couldn't. Aiden's spirits lifted when he thought of being able to practice with his sword again.

"Now, you must go," Vodin finally said, looking into Aiden's eyes.

Aiden's excitement dissipated as quickly as it had appeared. "So what do I do now?" he sighed.

"Return to your aunt's house," Vodin said, placing a hand on the boy's shoulder. "But should anything happen, you cannot be afraid to run. Stay alive. Use your best judgment. I trust you'll do the right thing."

Aiden's chest filled with a strange coldness and he frowned.

"This is your chance to start over. For now," Vodin said, his tone so serious that Aiden could no longer look into his eyes. "It's obvious to me that, although I trust Turlin, he's far too busy to keep a proper eye on you... So I have arranged for someone else to guide and protect you."

Chapter 9
Starting Over

Aiden could actually glimpse the stars between the tree tops. Vodin led him out into a small clearing between the snow-covered pines and fur trees after they had left the Guild grounds. Aiden had begun to feel tired, despite his commingled anxiety and excitement. He pulled his jacket tight around him as he followed the Headmaster through the snow.

"He should be here any moment now," said Vodin, stopping to look around at the trees.

A flutter of wings came from behind Aiden. A raven swooped down and landed on Vodin's outstretched arm. Aiden stood back in surprise. Vodin simply smiled.

"Um," Aiden began, unsure how to react. "Is this the guy's pet or something?" he asked, thinking the bird may have been familiar.

"This is," Vodin began. "As you say, the *guy*."

Aiden raised an eyebrow in disbelief. "He's going to guide me?" Aiden asked, trying his best to withhold a scoffing tone. "But he's just a bird."

"What if I am?" the raven croaked, his voice raspy and strange.

Aiden fell back in shock, sinking waist-deep into the snow behind him. The raven fluttered, almost as if enjoying the reaction. Vodin bent down and helped Aiden back to his feet.

"You didn't seem to mind before," the bird continued, resting back onto Vodin's arm. "When I led you to the Guild."

"So you can talk?" Aiden said, his face alive with revelation.

"Of course I can," the raven snapped. "I am a Raven Lord after all, the last of my kind."

Aiden looked to Vodin, seeing a slight look of reproach in the man's eyes. "I... Apologize. And... Thanks for helping me find the Guild tonight." said Aiden to the bird, unable to look into its liquid eye. "I've never met a bird that can talk. Well, except for parrots, but-"

"Yes of course," the raven interjected, sounding irritated. "People are always fascinated by parrots. Have you tried holding an intellectual discourse with those walking tape recorders?"

Aiden shook his head, feeling sheepish. "Sorry," he finally said. He realized now that he shouldn't have been so surprised after all.

"Aiden," Vodin finally began. "This is D'Natis. He is now assigned to you."

Aiden was speechless for a few moments. "For how long?" Aiden finally broke the silence.

"As long as he is needed," said Vodin. "Now, time really is of the essence. Let's draw a door and get you back to your aunt's."

***

When they stepped out onto the well-kept sidewalk, the snow was still there but the air was nowhere near as cold as it had been up in the woods by the Guild. Aiden and Vodin walked side by side, and D'Natis the raven perched comfortably on the Headmaster's shoulder. Aside from the sound of them walking, the neighborhood was silent and still.

As they walked, certain things became more familiar to Aiden and he began to get an idea of how to find his aunt's house from here.

"The place should just be a couple blocks over," he said quietly, pointing west down the row of condos.

"Aiden," Vodin began softly. "This is not the way I want things-"

"I know," Aiden said quickly, although his own tone made him wonder.

"I know the Council has limited me, but I'll do what I can to keep in touch—but it might be some time before I'm able to," Vodin explained. "Are you okay?" he asked suddenly.

"Sure," Aiden said automatically, even though he found himself surprised by Vodin's change of tone. "I guess."

He hadn't had much time to process everything, and now he just wanted to sleep. He would have to think about things as the week went on.

"Then," Vodin sighed. "Here is where I must leave you."

Vodin patted Aiden's back, and almost instinctively, the raven leaped to the boy's shoulder. Aiden almost jumped when he felt the small claws dig into him, but they quickly relaxed and he adjusted to the weight. Aiden wasn't sure how he felt inside, but everything seemed heavy and almost unreal.

"Stay safe," Vodin said, looking into Aiden's eyes solemnly. "Take care." Vodin looked to the raven. "And you, take care of him," he said with a sad smile.

Aiden had no words and could only nod to the Headmaster. With that, Vodin turned back down the sidewalk path, his feet crunching in the snow. The crunching stopped and Aiden turned back, his mind whirling with questions.

"Headmaster Vo-"

The man was gone.

Aiden shook his head in disbelief, but he swore he heard the raven sigh in a human sort of way.

"Let's go on then, shall we?" D'Natis' voice crept closely into Aiden's head, almost tickling his ear.

Aiden sighed and turned back down the sidewalk, trying to keep himself at a steady pace in the patches of both slush and snow. As he progressed, he watched the neighborhood unfold before him, the white walks glittering gently, reflecting the overhead street lamps.

He wondered if the raven would always sit on his shoulder like this, because after a while the novelty of it had worn off. Aiden wasn't sure if he could just ask the bird to move, or if he would somehow offend him.

"Um, this is awkward," Aiden said, laughing nervously for a moment.

"I sensed it too, even though I don't usually pick up on the subtleties of human emotion very easily," said D'Natis.

"I appreciate the help and all," said Aiden, still walking. "But, I mean, do you need to be fed? Or... Do you live in a cage?"

D'Natis scoffed. "I suppose I will let that slide, because you are Ambler-born after all," he said haughtily. "But no. You will not take care of me like some common household pet. I can take perfectly good care of myself, thank you very much."

"Oh. Okay..." Aiden said, sensing some irritation in the bird's tone. "Well, then I guess we're equals?"

"If you want to believe that," D'Natis said in an almost mocking tone. "Then you may believe that."

"Good, then get off my shoulder. It's killing me," said Aiden, trying his hardest not to sound angry. "Stay close okay? Just not on my shoulder."

Silently, D'Natis fluttered into the air and began to soar on ahead. Aiden hoped the raven's presence wouldn't make things even more difficult than they already were. He had no desire to return to his aunt's, but it was the only place he could go.

Aiden soon saw his aunt's doorstep approaching, and as usual, even her porch light was off. D'Natis perched on the light overhead as Aiden slowly touched the doorknob. A glow flittered from somewhere inside. They had seen it through the window near the door.

Aiden stopped and reached down for his sword. This time, he was thankful that it appeared in his hand as he drew it out. Before he could turn the knob, D'Natis made a quiet clicking sound.

"Follow me," the raven said and took off in the opposite direction.

Aiden shook his head, but the bird ignored him and disappeared out of sight around the side of the house. In the dim remnants of distant street light, Aiden cautiously made his way around the house, trying to follow D'Natis' path. He kept his sword out, though he knew it was a risk.

Aiden entered a small gate and stumbled through the snow, despite his efforts to stay quiet. He saw the bird's dark form sitting on the back patio, and Aiden crept slowly up against the house. Birds cawed in the distance, making Aiden stiffen for a moment, but then he kept moving to where D'Natis sat.

D'Natis issued a gurgling croak, which echoed across the backyard, and Aiden stopped in confusion.

"Someone's inside the house," the raven whispered to Aiden.

As Aiden approached the back door, he saw it ajar and found himself staring into the living room where the shades had been torn. His heart sank and he felt the adrenaline abolishing his need for sleep. Slowly, he let his bag fall to the icy patio. Aiden held his sword outward, trying to keep his hand steady, and stepped inside the house. He could hear D'Natis wobbling in behind him.

Aiden stopped, withholding a gasp. A dark form lay haphazardly on the armchair. It was his aunt. In the dim light filtering into the house, all Aiden could see was a pale blood-stained hand and a glimpse of a still, tortured expression on her face. She was not moving and looked as though she hadn't for some time.

The television set was shattered, pieces of its interior were strewn across the floor before it, and it appeared to be smoking slightly. Aiden's eyes followed the trails of broken glass and wires across the muddied carpet until he realized that there were three dark forms standing by the doorway at the end of the room.

As his eyes adjusted, he realized the shadows were men in white cloaks, and they had not yet seen him. They seemed to be waiting for someone to enter through the front door. Aiden's insides ached suddenly and he wanted to run, but something else beckoned him. He wanted to fight. His buckler appeared in his other hand.

"You," one of the men said as he turned.

The others turned and glared at him. Aiden froze, sword still aloft. D'Natis fluttered out of the room and through the open back window. For a moment, Aiden felt abandoned. Had D'Natis arranged this? What was going on?

One of the men launched a dark energy ball straight at Aiden, but the boy managed to block it with his blade. It cascaded back and exploded in the man's face, forcing him back through the window by the door. The shattering glass was surprisingly loud, and Aiden felt as though all of his senses had come alive.

Another man rushed at Aiden, their blades colliding. Aiden held his own and sent the man face first into the couch. The next man raced forward with his blade out and glimmering in the low light. At that moment, a dark form fluttered into the room screeching shrilly into the man's face. Feathers flew in all directions and Aiden fell out of the way.

The men in white found themselves fighting a sudden onslaught of black shapes. A whirlwind of violent sound and black feathers filled the living room, knocking the men to the floor in a frenzy. Aiden held his ears and realized that the biggest black shape was D'Natis, and the raven was beckoning him to follow.

Aiden ducked low, realizing that the massive cyclone actually consisted of thousands of crows. They were everywhere, smashing windows, breaking plates, knocking pictures off the wall, and concentrating all of their collective efforts on attacking the men in white.

After some effort, Aiden crawled out into the open air and found D'Natis sitting on the patio again.

"What the hell is going on?" Aiden said, brushing feathers and debris off of him and standing up.

"I enlist the help of friends from time to time," said D'Natis. "Well, acquaintances anyhow. They are only crows after all."

"Um, thanks," said Aiden, hearing the screams of the men muffled under the violent tumult.

"What are we waiting for?" D'Natis said, an urgency in his tone. "We can't stay here."

With his weapons fading, Aiden turned and picked up his bag, ready to run, hearing D'Natis take to the sky. As he stumbled through the patches of snow, he raced around the house and into the front yard, only hoping that neighbors weren't watching. The raven was already well ahead of him, his silhouette visible by the light of the moon.

Aiden found the sidewalk and continued running. As the sound of frenzying crows began to fade into the distance, one thought began to fill Aiden's mind. Still keeping D'Natis in sight, he raced through the slush, sometimes slipping and sliding, then regaining his footing, only to push himself harder through the darkened neighborhood.

As they reached a main road, the lay of the land changed and Aiden paused, seeing a gas station on the other side of an intersection. Without another thought, Aiden sped across the empty road, keeping his eyes on the small mini-mart by the gas station. As he reached his destination, Aiden almost doubled over, clutching his side and trying to catch his breath. He recovered, looking back across the street.

It appeared that the men in white had not followed them, but Aiden knew he shouldn't stop for too long. He trudged to a phone booth on the side of the mini-mart, while D'Natis perched on its top.

"What are you doing?" the raven asked, glancing back and forth furtively.

"Taking Vodin's advice and starting over..." Aiden said breathlessly and dropped his bag.

He picked up the phone and began to dial, ignoring the bird's rapid movements overhead.

"9-1-1, what is your emergency?" a woman's voice appeared on the line.

Aiden swallowed. "Uh yeah, there's been a break-in, and I think someone might be really hurt..." he said, feeling the adrenaline beginning to wane. He explained the address and in the next breath stammered, "P-please hurry!"

"And what is your name, sir?" the woman asked.

Aiden paused, his heart pounding. "...demiGod."

Part II

Chapter 10
Gryphon Claw

Aiden had been dreaming, although he could never remember exactly what had happened in those dreams.

What he had thought to be a scream quickly melded into the incessant high-pitched tones of his alarm clock, which he struggled desperately to silence. He sighed—it was too early. He smacked the alarm until the buzzer stopped and squinted open his eyes. It would be so much better if he could just stay in bed. He finally made it to his feet and got dressed.

He dreaded thinking about starting his day. It had been a long night, but he had to wake up. At least he tried to tell himself that.

Aiden stumbled into the hallway, shielding his eyes from the natural light that seeped through the blinds in the adjoining living room. He trudged along, trying to adjust, and began smelling something that resembled pancakes. He hoped they didn't taste like rubber this time.

He glared hazily at the wicker table and chairs that sat, ever so unfashionably, in his miniscule dining room. Taking a seat, he grabbed the disheveled Ambler newspaper without much thought. In a moment, he wasn't sure why he had bothered. Naturally, there was nothing but a slew of political mishaps, sports flubs, and fashion missteps. He'd seen it all before.

"Good morning."

Aiden looked up to see his roommate Chuck wielding a spatula, standing guard over the pancake maker. Aiden nodded silently, still groggy.

He'd been up nearly all night long, searching for bail-jumpers in the dark of night. Those backyards filled with dogs and barb-wire fences hadn't made things any simpler. He wished he hadn't taken the job, but it was a job after all. One he did well. He smirked a bit, thinking of the thick wad of bills in his pants pocket.

He returned to his paper.

Another riot had broken out somewhere, Aiden noticed from a short blurb of text on the front page. He was sick of reading the same news. He shrugged and turned the crisp pages, hoping to find something more tantalizing. Aiden sighed, wanting to voice his opinions out loud, but knew that Chuck wouldn't care to listen.

For someone who had essentially been a nobody in both worlds for the last fourteen years, Aiden had always wanted to stay informed of the world at large, but it wasn't always easy. Had it *really* been fourteen years? He looked to the date at the top of the page, only to verify that it was in fact the year 2011. Aiden sighed, willing himself not to think about that fateful time when everything had gone so awry.

Aiden's thoughts were interrupted by a loud crack and the cacophony of shattering glass. Chuck ran out of sight, rushing to see what had happened, just as Aiden stood.

"Hey!" Chuck shouted, a sudden panic in his tone.

Aiden peered into the living room from around an adjoining wall, and saw Chuck on his knees at the mercy of a thin blade. A man in white stood there, holding his sword just inches from Chuck's throat. Aiden reached down to his side, greeted by the familiar feel of his own sword's handle.

Chuck looked worried and unsure if he should say something, or anything.

"I thought you'd be here..." said the man in white—whose face was covered by a deep hood—as he glanced over to Aiden.

"Okay..." said Aiden, his eyes dancing furtively between Chuck and the man in white. "So, here I am. Let him go."

"You were a hard one to track down," the man began. "But we found you. Are you going to come quietly or do I have to convince you a little?"

"And you are...?"

There was no reply.

Aiden could see the man's sword moving ever closer to Chuck's throat, but that wasn't Aiden's biggest concern at the moment. There was something about the sword itself that made Aiden wonder. Chuck began to take a deep breath, as if expecting the blade to take his head off at any moment.

Before Chuck could exhale, Aiden's blade passed through the midsection of the man-in-white's sword. For a moment, it was as though nothing had happened. Then the weapon slid apart in two clean pieces and fell to the carpet. Three of the intruder's gloved finger tips followed.

Aiden stood before the hooded stranger with his blade still drawn.

Chuck was speechless, looking wildly back and forth from Aiden to the man in white.

The intruder clutched his wounded hand, but said nothing. Aiden searched beneath the hood and rune insignia, imploring the stranger's eyes. He saw youthfulness and fear. He flicked his wrist lightly, smiling softly, and his blade began to fade in a white mist.

"So you are N'Iatari... Why you guys always wear white, I'll never know," Aiden said, taking a bold step toward the intruder. "You'd think maybe a royal purple or forest green might be just as... nice?"

No answer.

"Sorry about your finger tips," Aiden said with a smirk.

"I still have the hand, don't I?" the stranger replied without even a grimace.

Aiden smiled as though impressed, but the hooded stranger's eyes grew thinner.

"You won't be so lucky," the man in white spat. He had already set in motion a wild leap toward Aiden, bearing a thick dagger.

The dagger shattered suddenly against the solid, white-alloyed breastplate which manifested on Aiden's chest.

The hooded stranger fell back in surprise but kept his balance. Aiden held out both hands and outstretched his fingers in a basket shape. The energy radiated through him, and he released. Blue energy boomed from his palms and struck the man square in the chest.

The man in white now lay on the other side of the living room, motionless, resting in a crater of drywall and plaster.

Chuck scrambled to his feet, looking panicked. He stammered unintelligibly, eyes still wildly traveling back and forth from Aiden to the fallen stranger. He couldn't seem to gather his bearings, and Aiden kept motioning for him to sit down, but Chuck shook his head.

"I-is he dead?" Chuck finally managed.

Aiden folded his arms. "No. Probably not. He'll have one mother of a headache though."

Chuck looked at him in disbelief.

Aiden sighed, knowing his secrecy was no longer important. "If he was a full-fledged N'Iatari, I might've had to kill him..." he explained, though uneasy about such an idea. "This kid was a trainee. Didn't even have a translated sword yet..."

Aiden inspected the fallen man's body as if admiring his handiwork. Then, as if realizing who he was talking to, he looked back to his roommate.

"Sorry you had to witness this, Chuck."

Chuck was not impressed nor amused.

"As you probably noticed, uh, I can do... It's because I'm..." Aiden stopped and looked at Chuck, whose gaze had almost become transfixed, and not in a good way. "Ah screw it. I'll pack my stuff."

***

This wasn't the first time Aiden had been kicked out of an apartment, and he was sure it wouldn't be the last. If he could only make just a bit more money, maybe next time he wouldn't need a roommate. It took him no time at all to pack his things. In fact, he could fit all his belongings into his duffel bag. He pushed the thoughts of yet another eviction aside, and tried to walk it off.

The Philadelphia streets were surprisingly warm. Heatwaves radiated off of distant cars and pavement, making the scenery dance to an odd rhythm. The sidewalk stretched out before him until it blurred in the horizon of skyscrapers and city parks. Aiden walked along pavement full of cracks where the occasional weed had forced its way through, and the street signs were littered with gang tags and artless graffiti. He stopped for a moment, adjusting the strap on his bag, and took one last mental snapshot.

The streets were surprisingly silent. This decay was no surprise.

Aiden adjusted the locket hanging from his neck. He hated it. He hated how it sometimes burned his skin when his fingers touched it. He hated-

The flutter of dark wings interrupted his thoughts. D'Natis swooped down and landed on his outstretched forearm.

"On the street again, are you?" the raven asked.

Aiden smiled for a moment, looking into the bird's dark eye. "Eh... Chuck freaked out when the N'Iatari showed up... Don't know what to do about it this time."

"The exile's task is never done, is it?" the raven quipped.

Aiden peered out over the endless sidewalk, squinting. "... Never."

Aiden sighed as the bird slowly inched up his arm, finally getting comfortable on his shoulder. "Good thing I have you, D'Natis. I guess we're on the road again."

D'Natis didn't respond, but Aiden assumed the silence was a good thing. It often was. They knew each other too well by now, and for far too long, to let something like language come between them.

Aiden kept walking, his thoughts ablaze. He wondered where they would go, what they would do. Of course, he couldn't let on that he had a few mildly anxious thoughts about seeing a N'Iatari apprentice show up in his living room. This sort of thing had not happened for at least five or six years. He remained calm and steady, trying to balance D'Natis; the raven's ever-shifting talons digging into his right shoulder.

He thought about Chuck. For Aiden, explaining the D'Tari properties to the roommate was always a difficult thing. An avoided thing. Usually it never came up. Sometimes, like with Chuck, it destroyed the living room and caused the roommate to seek therapy. Not only that, but Aiden could only assume that at some point, someone like Turlin would likely have to make a few adjustments to Chuck's memory.

Ever since having left the Guild, Aiden had always struggled with the 'control' aspect of harnessing his D'Tari properties. He couldn't even begin to lie to himself about that. He supposed he could have tried to save Chuck some other way without letting anyone know about his D'Tari abilities...

He looked at D'Natis in the corner of his eye and chuckled to himself.

"What?" the raven asked.

"We're a couple of peas in a pod, aren't we?" Aiden laughed.

"How do you mean?"

"It's no secret that I'm..." Aiden began, trying to think of a funny way to say it.

"Out of control?" D'Natis completed the sentence sarcastically.

Aiden smirked. "Eh, sure. But you're not far off."

The raven cocked his head to get a better view of Aiden's face. "How dare you. I am of noble blood."

Aiden laughed mockingly. "Like that noble time you pooped on that kid's head?"

D'Natis leaped slightly, wings almost fluttering. "He dared to think me a common bird. Me! A Raven Lord! It served him-"

"So who's out of control now?" Aiden said, unable to hold back a smile. "It was a very lordly thing to do..."

"Should I have taken an eye? It's not like the child could sue..." D'Natis calmly retorted. "You and I are about the most protected species on the planet."

Aiden's eye caught the old cemetery they were passing, the tombstones full of very Irish and Jewish surnames.

He knew where this conversation was going, but he still had

to say it. "For starters:" Aiden began. "Protection is only a legal term. It means nothing. Just because guys like Turlin and Menlir occasionally show up and clean up after us, doesn't mean we're protected."

D'Natis' large eye peered directly into Aiden's, as if he were thinking to reply.

"Second: I hate to tell you this, but you and I aren't the same species."

"The bauble around your neck says otherwise," D'Natis said, peering at the locket hanging down into Aiden's shirt.

Aiden glared at the not-so-common bird, unable to make any further debate. He hated that. He stuffed the locket further into his shirt and carried on down the sidewalk. D'Natis was making a victorious clicking sound with his beak. Aiden hated that too.

"C'mon, let's get to the pub." Aiden said, hoping he could spend a few hours forgetting his anxiety.

"Good. I could use a drink," D'Natis replied. "A little bird told me someone wishes to see you there."

"First, ravens and ale don't mix," Aiden huffed, raising an eyebrow at the bird. "Second, who wants to see me?"

"I guess you'll have to find out."

Aiden scoffed and continued walking.

***

Aiden and D'Natis made their way to the Gryphon Claw, a small pub that looked as though it had been built in the 1600s. The journey had taken them winding through the alleys and side streets of the old city, passing through historical neighborhoods and old sites now turned tourist traps. The noon sun was still burning overhead as Aiden finally walked up the rickety steps to the old establishment.

Inside, some of the patrons cast an odd glance or two when they noticed the large black bird on Aiden's shoulder, but no one bothered to say anything. The world inside the pub was dark, and the air thin with the aftermath of cigarettes. A violinist sat in a distant corner, playing Irish reels, while mellow chatter and laughter flooded the room. The walls, the furniture, and all the architecture had retained its old-world charm, and Aiden loved it for that, despite it's propensity for some cliché.

Aiden approached the bar, giving the man behind it—a tall, balding man with a lazy eye—a knowing look. The man leaned forward over the bar, intent on hearing Aiden's words.

"Gryphon's claws make no laws," Aiden half-whispered into the man's hairy ear.

The man nodded, tapped on the bar with satisfaction, looked out over the room, and motioned for Aiden to follow him down the hall just behind the bar. Aiden followed the man into the darkness. He'd been here before, but it had been several months. He never knew what things might occur once beyond this point—especially if certain people recognized him.

The tall man with the lazy eye reached the end of the hall and gave the ornate door several knocks in a specific pattern. After a moment, the door cracked and Aiden was blinded by the light from within. The tall man turned to him and smiled, then left back down the hall.

As Aiden entered, locking the door behind him, and his eyes adjusted, he realized he was looking at Regnir the Half-Dwarf, a short, bearded creature whose skin was the texture of dirt and whose physique was both uniquely human and Dwarf-like. Aiden nodded as Regnir greeted him with merely a grunt.

"Good to see you too," Aiden finally said as the Half-Dwarf returned to his table where he'd been playing cards.

The room in here was much like the room he'd just come from: dimly lit, smoky, and ornate. Of course, in here, met the Agnecs. Aiden glanced around the room, wondering where he'd sit, surprised at how full the small space was. There were plenty of Dwarves in the pub today, a handful of humans, and some other creatures in dark corners Aiden did not bother to spy out.

Aiden suppressed a chuckle.

"What?" D'Natis asked, seeing Aiden's smirk.

"It's funny how obvious Agnec meeting places are sometimes," Aiden said quietly, stepping further into the room. "*The Gryphon Claw*? I mean, c'mon. Even the Ambler part looks like something from some fantasy novel."

"Most Amblers will never guess the Agnecs' secrets. People tend to see only what they desire to see," said D'Natis in his oft sage tone.

Along the bar where a large man tended, sat the two Elves, Ton'r and Nin nac Glennfire. Both of them looked very much alike. Aiden was not surprised to see them, as they were among the very few Elves that would regularly frequent the typical Agnec gathering place. Ton'r was down at the bottom of his glass of ale, and Aiden thought it best to look for a seat elsewhere.

Aiden turned to the right, looking at the far wall where a Faun sat cushioned on a wide divan surrounded by smoke from his hooka. It was Menlir. Aiden made to turn away, hoping he could slink back out the door—as Menlir would not be happy to see Aiden in a public Agnec space—but something else drew his attention.

A beautiful woman sat in a chair across from Menlir. They were in conversation, and Aiden grew suddenly curious.

The woman, dressed in somewhat trendy Ambler clothes, seemed to stand out. Aiden must have been staring, because she caught his eye and approached him.

"Hi," she began somewhat awkwardly. "I'm Megan Rohan," the woman said, smiling as she shook Aiden's hand. "Well, the last name's not too important, as you know," she added, suddenly brushing a strand of red hair from her eyes. She straightened up, as if catching herself, and said, "Menlir and I need to chat with you, if that's alright."

Aiden raised an eyebrow. "How'd you-" he started to ask.

"D'Natis was contacted," Megan replied. "Of course that's how I recognized you." She smiled at the bird just inches from Aiden's head. "Who else has a raven on their shoulder?"

Megan gestured toward a round table against the far wall, away from the other patrons. Aiden tried to smile hospitably, but couldn't hide the strange feeling he had about this.

He stopped and gestured for Megan to wait. "Just a sec," he said, then stepped away.

"You knew about this?" Aiden whispered to D'Natis.

D'Natis cocked his head. "I led you here."

"Like hell you did," Aiden muttered. "Seriously. Do you know what's going on?"

"Perhaps I dropped some subtle cues, or let you take the lead on coming to the pub-"

"Screw that," Aiden said, flustered. "The only thing Menlir's good for is relaying messages to Turlin and cleaning up my mess..." Aiden stopped to glance over at the Faun—whose smile was suspicious. "Last time he wanted a favor, I ended up on a plane to California..."

D'Natis sighed. "I do recall," he said. "But I seek your best interest. Hear him out. If the cause is not worthy, what's so bad about turning him down?"

"Know what it's about?"

"No, but it does sound urgent," D'Natis said, shifting his weight.

"Okay. Fine," Aiden sighed and turned back to face Megan and Menlir.

Megan led Aiden and D'Natis over to a small round table where Menlir had already pulled up a chair. The old Faun looked up at Aiden with something like a forced smile. Aiden sat but did not return the expression.

Once they were all settled, Menlir addressed Aiden despite how Megan was just opening her mouth to speak. "Hello, *demiGod*. I saw your recent article in the *Ol' Rambler*... Still clinging to your theory, eh?" Menlir's words felt like a challenge and his tone was ornery.

Aiden ran a hand through his dark hair, sweeping it out of his eyes. He sighed.

Menlir was stuck in his ways, and at every chance, he had tried to challenge Aiden. Ever since Aiden had begun contributing here and there to the local D'Tari newspaper—under the penname demiGod—his ideas had not been well received, especially by the older crowd. He ground his teeth for a moment, then took a breath. He would not even respond.

Menlir looked a little surprised, but came again. "Nothing to say?" he goaded, smiling.

"Haven't we had this discussion before?" Aiden replied. "I know you were taught that being a D'Tari means you have to follow Sion's Precepts to a tee..."

"He's the source of the properties. How could you not?" Menlir said, his face scrunching in thought.

"Explain how the N'Iatari have the same powers we do then," Aiden said, feeling adrenaline rushing into him. "They don't follow Sion. Or did you forget about that?"

Menlir was silent, looking sullen.

"What if the properties are just *neutral*?"

"Dangerous questions," Menlir snarled, then stopped to look

around the room. "Watch yourself," he said, soberly. "As long as you're in this district, I'll be here for you... But..." he shook his head, frustration painting his features. "I liked you better when you were just a punk kid wandering around—before you fancied yourself some philosopher."

Aiden shook his head, knowing that look. That look of being written off. He hadn't even realized that Megan had chimed in, apparently offended by Aiden and the Faun's sudden back-and-forth.

"Excuse *me*," Megan cut in, her face pink. "I need to talk to you, Aiden." Megan's face now turned the slightest shade of red, oddly complementing her burgundy hair.

Aiden, surprised and slightly embarrassed, sat back. "How did you know my real name?"

Megan composed herself, and gave him a no-nonsense look. "Headmaster Turlin told me," she said, crossing her arms.

If Turlin was involved, perhaps it was important. Aiden nodded and gestured for her to continue.

"Aiden," Megan began. "I've been sent by the Guild. They have a proposition for you," she said, looking somewhat tentative.

Aiden's face scrunched sideways. "I'm going to stop you right there," he said, lifting a finger in protest. "Is this a favor for the Guild, or for the D'Tari Council?"

Megan thew him a confused look. "Well," she said with a pause. "Both, I guess."

"Then count me out."

Megan scoffed. "You haven't even heard what I'm going to say," she said, taken aback.

"At least listen, you thick-skulled Ambler-born," Menlir hissed at Aiden and began to stand.

Megan glared at the Faun. "Master Menlir, that seems unnecessary," she chided, gesturing for him to sit down. "Now, Aiden," she said, shifting her focus.

"*demiGod*," Aiden said.

"Excuse me?" Megan asked, realizing that Aiden was also on his feet.

"I don't think that group of Dwarves in the back heard you yet," Aiden said in an even tone. "If you're going to shout my name, then call me demiGod."

"I'm sorry," Megan said quickly, then took a deep breath. "Aiden," she said quietly. "Please sit down and at least hear what I have to say. *Please.*"

It was her sincerity that calmed Aiden, and he sat down with a sigh.

Megan talked quickly, as if trying not to prolong her point, "As you probably know, the Shadow Congress is re-adjourning soon in Washington. The Guild is sending a liaison, and well—I've been chosen. They would like you to accompany me."

"To represent the Guild?" Aiden sputtered in surprise.

"For protection."

"Protecting you?" Aiden asked, his mind racing. When Megan nodded, Aiden asked, "But can't you protect yourself? I mean, aren't you D'Tari?"

"...Yes," Megan replied, her face turning pink. "I'm D'Tari, but I'm not very skilled in defense or combat..."

"Not every D'Tari's a fighter," said Menlir, only somewhat more civilly than his last outburst.

Aiden thought for a moment. The idea that the Guild had asked for him came as a shock.

Aiden returned to the present, struck by a dark feeling. "So, let me get this straight," he said, massaging the area between his eyes, wondering if he wasn't getting a headache. "The Guild elders want me to babysit you?"

Megan half-nodded, her brow furling suddenly. "Hang on, I don't need you to hold my hand..." she said, defensively.

"I just don't understand why they would ask for me," said Aiden, ignoring Megan's protest. "Has to be some sort of trap," he reasoned, throwing his head back so fast that D'Natis was forced off of his shoulder.

Both D'Natis and Menlir joined Megan as she threw Aiden an incredulous glare.

"How?" Megan asked, confused.

Aiden sat up, sweeping his hair off his face. "I know the Guild wants nothing to do with me," he said, unsuccessfully suppressing a bitter tone. "The Council hates me. Now all the sudden, everybody changes their tune? It doesn't add up. Why? Why would they ask for me?"

Aiden sat in a quandary for a few moments. After all these years, he'd done nothing but relive that horrible week in his mind. That week when everyone seemed to turn against him. Even Vodin had failed him.

"I can only tell you what I know," Megan insisted. "This congressional session is very important—the rights of Agnecs everywhere depend upon it—and I really don't think it's the time to be paranoid..."

"Paranoid?" Aiden laughed. "Who's paranoid? I'm just runnin' the odds here. I can't imagine that they would ask for me, if this were just to protect *you*. And just to watch a bunch of would-be politicians talk and talk while accomplishing nothing? There's plenty of other D'Tari out there. Let *them* play stooge for the Council."

"Aiden," Megan began, obviously holding back some frustration. "Headmaster Turlin told me to seek *you* out. And I don't know what this means, but he said you were highly recommended by Vodin."

Aiden sat back, all of his arguments had suddenly begun to disappear.

"The power of the D'Tari, and the rights of Agnecs, are on the verge of extinction in this country," Megan added, staring into Aiden's dark eyes, emotion hiding in her voice. "Isn't that important enough?"

"I doubt it's all that desperate," Aiden said, though he knew she was right.

Megan's mouth fell open in disgust. "I-I guess I thought Menlir's stories wouldn't be true," she said, as if fighting an inner desire to say something more. "You don't *want* to help defend Agnec rights?"

"What stories?" Aiden asked, glaring at the Faun across the table.

"Of how you're irresponsible," Menlir chided. "You're untamed! You couldn't-"

Megan held out a hand, trying to silence the Faun.

"Says the gambler and the cheat," Aiden snapped at Menlir.

The Faun fell silent.

Aiden felt himself grow hot. He looked to Megan and said, "And what do you mean by rights? What rights?"

"The rights to our lands and our security," Megan replied, her tone growing stern. "The right to be free citizens—some day. I can't understand why you don't think that's worth fighting for."

Aiden's face and ears were now red.

He stood so quickly that D'Natis flinched, almost losing balance. "All this political stuff is shit," he spat.

Megan sat back, silent for a moment, her beautiful green eyes staring angrily into Aiden's. Her cheeks were flushed. Aiden tried to gather his thoughts and make sense of them. He surveyed the woman, realizing, despite her appearance, how young she suddenly seemed.

"How old are you anyway?" he asked her. "Fresh out of the Guild I bet. I don't think you understand how this world works."

Megan made to respond, but Aiden wouldn't let her.

"Go ahead," Aiden continued, feeling the anger in his words starting to burn. "Stand before the Shadow Congress for the D'Tari. It'll be your wake up call. It won't even change a damn thing."

The moment the words had left his mouth, Aiden realized he shouldn't have said them. He didn't really know this girl. She had just pulled at one too many threads.

Surprisingly, Megan sat there in silence. Aiden had expected her to get upset, yell, argue... Do something.

Instead, she took a deep breath and looked up at him. "Enlighten me then," she said calmly. "How does this world work?"

Aiden sat back down in surprise, his anger fading. "Uh, well, alright," he said, gathering his thoughts and realizing that Menlir was smirking at him, as if just waiting to prove him wrong. "From what I know, most times Agnecs keep to their own villages not because they're afraid of Amblers, but because the US government fails to protect them. I mean, how can you expect anything to to be safe when security detail just falls to the common people, or just to some random local vigilante?"

"But-" Megan made to interject.

Aiden cut her off. "What's more, is that the common people have almost no voice. The Council has way too much power, but it does its *own* thing with very little care for the Agnec world as a whole." At this, Aiden bit his lip momentarily, suppressing his frustration. "How the hell can *rights* be enforced when there's no real oversight? The Council says it dispatches D'Tari to be guardians over Agnec villages, but most of the time that's a lie."

"Now hold on," Menlir said, trying to stand but struggling in his seat.

"Sit down," Aiden told the Faun in an annoyed tone.

"Wait a minute! You're off base," Menlir said, giving up on taking a stand.

"But am I wrong?"

"Well..." Menlir began, his ire subsiding. "No. Not exactly," he admitted.

Aiden smirked.

"But the *common people*, as you call them, do have a voice," Menlir added, his face scrunched. "Many villages have adopted a system of voting."

"Good for them," Aiden said, unable to help the sarcasm in his tone. "How many of them have a trained police force? How many of them have any say in the way the Council runs things? How many of them contribute to the Shadow Congress? I mean... What would we *ever* do if the Dwarves disappeared—or worse, all decided to abandon the other Agnecs?"

A moment of palpable silence followed.

Finally, Menlir shifted uncomfortably, clearing his throat. "I hate to say this at all, but we'd probably still have the US government—"

"Yeah, okay," Aiden interrupted, laughing sardonically. "They watch from a distance, making sure Amblers don't suspect. You know that as well as I do. That's pretty much *all* they're doing."

"So, what's your point?" Megan finally said, looking

thoughtful.

"My point is that there's no way to enforce rights," Aiden said. "Agnecs get trampled on. No one seems to care. Going to the Congress won't prove anything, because there's no way to enforce anything. The Council's in bed with the Dwarves—even if it hurts other Agnecs. They're in way too deep—so deep they can't even see what's happening around them. And in the end, it's all bullshit politics to help the rich get richer and feel like they're doing something important."

"That's quite a lovely vocabulary you have there," Megan said, narrowing her eyes. "And a very optimistic view you have of the world."

"Truth," Aiden said, meaning to return her expression, but finding he was unable to look directly into her eyes. "It's the way this world works."

"I think we can change things," Megan said, her tone determined. "We can force the US government to see the problems you're talking about. And with some help," She looked to Menlir. "We can get the D'Tari Council to see the needs of these villages. Hold the Council accountable.'

"Maybe I'm a little naïve," Megan continued, her eyes still locked on Aiden's face. "But I really do have hope that things can change."

Aiden struggled with her positivity, and he began to wonder if they both wanted the same things—just with a different approach. Instinctively, he scoffed. "They'll never change," he said, shaking his head. "I don't want any part in it. The N'Iatari's all mixed up in this too. This is bull-"

"Yes, I've heard your opinion," Megan chimed in before Aiden could finish his sentence, her tone changing.

She stood and leaned over the table, eyes locked on Aiden's with a sudden and fierce intensity. At first, Aiden looked right back, but then realized he couldn't bear to return her gaze. It burned right through him. Menlir and D'Natis were still, waiting for the worst.

"Ambler courts don't care, because we don't exist. It *is* desperate," Megan whispered intensely. "You just admitted that. So are you just being stubborn, or lazy?"

Aiden sat there in shock. He wanted to stand and yell, but something told him not to.

Megan stood back, trying to compose herself. "What worries me..." she began. "Is that *you* are the one they told me to get. *You*... They told me you were the best one for the job." Her words finished in an exasperated laugh. "It's a simple job. I'm just asking for your protection."

Aiden's mind wrestled with her words, and with great effort, he pushed her offence aside only for a moment. "Why am I the best one for it?"

Megan sighed, plopping back down into her seat. "Only Shai knows. Like I said, Vodin recommended it."

"That's right," Aiden said, feigning interest as it all came back to him. "Look," he said, growing serious again. "I don't need this,

I've got jobs lined up left and right," he lied. "Why would I want to go back and be humiliated by the Council and all *their* type?"

Megan sat up straight, gathering her thoughts. "I won't lie and say this is *just* about protecting me," she finally said. "They only tell me what I need to know, but I can tell you that there's been some bad things happening."

Aiden tried to hide his interest, and folded his arms as if to say "*So?*"

"There's been unrest in Agnec Europe," Megan continued, ignoring Aiden's gesture. "I don't know all the details—but I know the Congress is also discussing these issues, and I think they're planning on sending D'Tari overseas, and there's been word of trying to start some sort of army... But as you can tell, we're already short-handed over here. *Our* voice needs to be heard... Turlin said that you might have some input."

Aiden thought for a moment, but forced himself to stand up in defiance, forcing D'Natis to the table. "I don't know you, and you don't know me," he said, momentarily looking around. "You don't know the hell I went through... Sorry, but the Council told me to get lost. Technically, I'm not even supposed to be in *here*." He gestured around the pub. "All the sudden they want me back?" He laughed derisively. "Tell them they can go to hell. Vodin too. Like he's done anything for me..."

Aiden caught himself, his face red. He suppressed a sudden feeling of shame.

"And another thing: You've got to work on your diplomacy,

255

because I don't see how in the unKing's lost universe you'll ever prove anything to the Shadow Congress. Not if *this* is any indication. Nothing personal."

Megan's eyes were somewhat glassy, but she stiffened with resolve.

Aiden turned from the table, with the thought to leave. Megan cleared her throat behind him, and he glanced back.

"I-I'm not leaving until you can give me a legitimate reason for not doing this," Megan said, her voice shaking angrily, her face burning red. "I'm staying right-"

Aiden raised his hand, just inches from her face, and she fell silent.

He could still feel the pounding in his chest. He just needed to get out of this place, and think. He turned and gestured to D'Natis, who instinctively hopped up to his shoulder perch.

When Aiden turned toward the door to leave, purposely avoiding Megan's gaze, Ton'r and Nin, joined by Regnir the Half-Dwarf, were blocking his way. The Elves and the Half-Dwarf looked quite drunk, and the three of them stood there, singing an old bar tune, swinging their glasses of ale.

In Aiden's frustration with Megan's proposal, he hadn't noticed the group's revelry, but he could only see red.

Frustrated, he finally yelled, "What is this? The quest for the One Ring? Get out of my way!"

While the Half-Dwarf and the Elves threw each other sincere looks of confusion, Aiden swept past them—knocking Ton'r to the floor—and left the room, slamming the door behind him.

***

Aiden walked along the old sidewalk, the afternoon heat still stifling. In the half-hour since he'd left the Gryphon Claw, he'd only gone a few blocks, walking slowly while in thought. His mind raced with the strange confrontation. He hardly noticed how hot it was, or the fact that D'Natis was perched on his shoulder nestling in like a hen. He also hadn't noticed that the raven was facing the opposite direction, watching the street behind him.

Aiden hadn't even noticed the smell of humidity in the air—with a possible threat of evening thunder—because his thoughts were with Megan, the impossibility of her request, and on the obvious light in which she had seen him.

D'Natis hadn't said much of anything. He often gave sound advice, but sometimes seemed to know very little about human relationships.

Aiden considered some different scenarios, but then thought of Menlir's words and the apparent stories of Aiden's very un-D'Tari-like behavior.

Perhaps he was a bit selfish, but he looked after himself. And D'Natis—sometimes. What was wrong with that?

But what about the rest of the Agnecs and the D'Tari?

Aiden shook his head. Pain was all that came to mind. He tried pushing it aside. He tried pushing the event aside, but something nagged, deep down.

Sometimes Aiden wished he could just live a normal life, but in truth, "normal" meant very little to him anymore. He suppressed an ironic chuckle, remembering that his wallet was full of both Agnec and US money... His life had been a strange dance between both worlds..

He thought about Megan again. Her face appeared in his mind. He just couldn't seem to block it.

"It's too complicated to fix this way..." he contemplated, not realizing he'd thought out loud.

He could feel D'Natis shifting his weight. "Hmm... Hey," the raven said sleepily.

"What?" Aiden didn't even bother looking, realizing for the first time that he had grown cold from the sweat on his back.

"I know you're brooding and all... But turn around."

Aiden stopped and turned on his heel. There, just beside a street lamp, stood Megan. Her soft features illuminated by a stern expression. She approached slowly, but then her stride grew bold.

"I need you to know something," she said, her tone sincere.

Aiden threw her a look of surprise, but couldn't find it in himself to turn away.

Megan stood closely now. "Unlike your *friends* at the Council," she began. "I do believe the N'Iatari are alive and well—trying to infiltrate various levels of leadership. Shai help me, I won't let that happen. But I can't do it alone, and there's only so much the Guild can do right now."

Aiden made to respond, but Megan continued, "And, the thing is—the Guild elders trust me, but even some of them are a little

258

unsure of whether or not the N'Iatari are doing anything wrong."

"After all this time," Aiden said incredulously, still pondering her words.

"They're close minded, unwilling to change," Megan said. "Most of them fought tooth and nail against you trying to help me. Turlin and I both really stuck our necks out for you."

"I didn't ask you to," Aiden said, feeling the frustration returning.

"I know," Megan said, understanding flooding her voice. "This is very personal for me..." She stopped for a moment, choosing her next words. "My parents were killed by N'Iatari, but the US government did nothing—and of course the Council denied it was N'Iatari. But I saw them..." She sniffed, here eyes glassy. "The white coats..."

Aiden felt his defenses begin to collapse. Glimpses of men in white flashed in his mind, his skin crawling with the remembrance of his mother's scream.

"They destroyed my village..." Megan continued, obviously holding back emotion. "Everything. Master Nutaris rescued my sister and me just before he was killed. Masters Jardun and Turlin were the only ones who believed us—that the N'Iatari had done it. I noticed Lilit's mark on their hoods."

Aiden stood there silently.

"So," she continued, straightening. "I didn't know how much I could say in front of Menlir—he seems a bit nosey—but ever since word got out that I've been chosen to represent the Guild to the Congress, N'Iatari have been stalking me. I'm out to stop them, and—-and they know it." As she finished her sentence, her words almost faltered, as though realizing how frightening the whole prospect truly was.

"He is nosey," Aiden agreed. "And a damn sore loser..."

Megan stiffened, looking almost offended by Aiden's sudden aside. "Maybe I'm just not getting through to you or something, but this is important-"

"I get it," Aiden said, his expression hazy while in thought. "Maybe you do understand some of the hell I've been through. I guess I'm sort of a jerk." He paused and shook his head, torn by various threads of emotion and reason swimming in his brain.

He cleared his throat suddenly. "Alright, who's paying?"

Megan looked up, her surprise evident with the raising of an eyebrow. "What do you mean?"

"Who's paying me to protect you? And how much?" Aiden asked again, this time folding his arms.

Megan took a step back, plagued by a very brief look of disgust, then recovered. "The elders, and I think the Council also-"

"How much?" Aiden cut her off, staring impatiently.

"Five pounds of Agnec gold," Megan said with a sigh, looking shocked at Aiden's sudden heavy-handedness.

"Given the current exchange rate..." Aiden muttered, scratching his chin. "That's almost a hundred thousand in US dollars..." Aiden could feel his insides jumping at the realization, but he maintained a serious expression. "I could buy a lot of sandwiches with that."

"What?" Megan asked, still looking at Aiden with a trace of disgust. "Look... Why didn't you just say this was about the money?"

"You didn't offer me any up front," Aiden quipped. "Since I'm just a soldier-for-hire and all that, why wouldn't I just want the money? Obviously, no one thinks I'm a *real* D'Tari..."

Megan was speechless, staring incredulously at Aiden.

"At least that's what the Council wants to think," he added with a somber tone. "I still need to eat, don't I? And anyway, I still stand by what I said. I don't think going to the Congress will change anything. But I will do what it takes to stop the N'Iatari."

"So you will help?" Megan asked, looking confused.

"Yes," Aiden replied, both excitement and dread welling up inside.

"Good..." Megan finally said, looking as though she was repressing a smile. "And thank you."

"My only stipulation is:" Aiden added. "You do things your way and I'll do them my way, and we'll see who ends up making a difference."

Chapter 11
Home Again

Aiden struggled to wake up for several minutes, sifting in and out of twilight as the sounds of glasses clinking and voices chattering remained yet distant. A knock at the door forced his eyes open, and he sat up.

Regnir's unpleasant voice arose from the other side of the door, demanding that Aiden wake up. The world flooded in suddenly, and he groaned. He had stayed the night in the tiny storage room at the Gryphon Claw, and the previous night's loud revelry had made it difficult to get any rest.

"Is there food out there?" Aiden called to the Half-Dwarf.

"We got ale," Regnir replied coarsely.

Aiden finally got to his feet and pulled his pants on. "Go out and get me a sandwich, will ya?"

After a pause, Aiden finally heard Regnir's irritated tone on the other side of the door, "What do you think this is? A bed and breakfast? Get your own sandwich."

Aiden smirked. "I've got a fiver for you if you get me one. USD... You can buy a lot of smokes with that."

There was another pause. Finally, "What kind of sandwich you want, jerk?"

Aiden suppressed a victorious laugh. After giving Regnir his order, Aiden waited until he was sure the Half-Dwarf was gone. Then he finally left his room and was met by a small crowd scattered across the tables. Some of the regulars were there already, but mostly there were just a few Dwarves and some human-looking types Aiden had never met.

Aiden found a table at the end of the room, and noticed someone had left behind a copy of the Agnec newspaper, the *Ol' Rambler*. He shuffled through the pages. Much of it was the same old same old. Local Agnec meeting houses were dealing with mortgage payments. Others were considering new ways to keep their true natures secret from Amblers. There were politics, philosophy, and safety considerations... Nothing here to surprise.

But something had caught Aiden's eye after all.

"N'Iatari leader to enter talks with D'Tari Council..." Aiden whispered the headline as he read.

Aiden rushed to the article, a dark feeling suddenly striking. He thought about the Guild, since some of the Guild elders were also among the D'Tari Council. As there was only one American Guild left in existence, its leaders had a huge say in what happened to American Agnecs.

But the N'Iatari meeting with Guild elders?

The article wasn't nearly as informational as Aiden had hoped. It was more like a stub, simply mentioning that a currently unnamed N'Iatari negotiator was planning on meeting with the Guild and Council members to talk about the upcoming Shadow Congress.

Aiden wasn't buying it. Negotiator? What did that even mean

in this case?

He folded the paper and set it on the table. Just then, Megan entered the room, let in by the bartender. Megan immediately caught Aiden's eye from across the room and began to approach. Regnir had also trailed inside, wearing a sour expression and holding a small plastic bag. Aiden couldn't decide what made him happier, the girl or the sandwich. His stomach rumbled. The sandwich.

Regnir almost bowled Megan over on his way to the table. They arrived at the same time, but Aiden stood only to greet the Half-Dwarf with the food. He sat the bag on the table and pulled out the sandwich, inspecting it. Megan stopped to watch silently.

"This is ham and cheddar," Aiden chided Regnir. "I specifically asked for summer sausage with provolone."

Regnir's gritty complexion turned a shade of red, but he softened and finally shrugged.

"Got my money, or what?"

Seeing that Regnir was not in the mood for games, Aiden relented, but not without snickering. "Here," Aiden finally threw a five dollar bill on the table. "Get your fix."

As the Half-Dwarf sauntered away, Aiden and Megan sat down. She glared at him.

"Why are you so mean to him?" Megan asked, watching Regnir disappear through the back door. "You know he practically lives here because Half-Dwarves are pariahs in the Underground-"

"I was just helping him out," said Aiden, eye-balling his

sandwich. "Giving him something to do."

"He's not your slave..."

"I gave him some money," said Aiden defensively. "Can I eat now, please? I'm starving."

Megan threw him a disappointed look, but nodded just the same. He nodded in return just before tearing into the sandwich.

"So..." Megan began. "We should probably leave soon."

Aiden stopped to take a breath. "Where we going?" he asked, concentrating on the food.

"The Guild," Megan answered with a knowing tone.

Aiden didn't answer. He couldn't seem to tear himself away from his sandwich.

"When are we leaving for the Guild?" Megan finally asked it outright.

Aiden continued eating. He'd become obsessed with it. He could barely see her anymore, despite how she sat directly across from him.

Megan clenched her fists, frustration building up.

"Are you listening to me?" Megan's voice began to rise.

Aiden could see she was getting upset, so he slowed down a bit. "Um... Yes."

"What did I say?" Megan asked, as if a mother to a child.

"Uh..." Aiden swallowed a hunk of ham. "Something... about the Guild."

Megan glared at him.

"I feel like you're trying my patience right now. Or not listening..."

Megan began through clenched teeth. "Or just stupid."

Aiden stopped chewing. "What did you call me?"

"Good. I'm glad your hearing's not completely gone," Megan said, her ears turning pink "We need to leave for the Guild soon."

Aiden's expression softened. "I'm just messing with you. I know we have to go," he sighed, acting put out.

"Then why-?"

"Relax." Aiden laughed. "Just having some fun."

Megan took a deep breath and gathered her thoughts. "Don't do that again," she said in a very serious tone.

"Okay, you know I'm just not thrilled about going back-"

"But we have to if we're doing this," Megan shot back. "So get over it."

Aiden finished his sandwich in silence, suddenly contemplating how little he understood Megan—or women in general, for that matter. He also resolved that he knew what he had to do and why, but he wasn't going to like it.

***

"We could take the Underground, but that seems risky," Megan told Aiden as she stood in the small back room watching him pack up his very few belongings.

"There are other ways to go, ya know," Aiden smirked, looking back at Megan.

"I suppose," Megan softened, but then arched her back. "Wait, you're not technically supposed to be doing that."

"As if it has ever stopped him," D'Natis said, fluttering from the

267

make-shift cot to a small end table.

Megan looked conflicted. "You're not allowed to travel by door; Since you're in exile, you still have a trace rune, right?"

"Sadly, yes," Aiden sighed. "No jumping for sure—not that I'm any good at it. And I'm not supposed to be in the Underground..."

"Hmm," Megan began, strumming her slender fingers on the nearby door frame. "They did tell me to be discreet in bringing you back."

"The elders didn't even give you permission to bring me back by door?" Aiden asked as he stuffed the last of his clothes into his bag.

"They were..." Megan began, but found herself trailing off.

Aiden raised an eyebrow "Looks like they really believed in you," he scoffed.

Megan was silent. Aiden pulled on his hooded sweatshirt and secured his duffel bag. He double checked the uncomfortably small room, and once satisfied, gestured for D'Natis to come. As the raven settled in on Aiden's shoulder, Aiden strolled past Megan and shut the light off, despite how the woman still stood there in thought.

She scoffed in disbelief. "Hey," Megan shouted. "I think they knew you were too much of a flight-risk, you jerk."

Moments later, Megan had joined Aiden as he sauntered between tables and chatting patrons in the main room. She was obviously a little upset, but said nothing and tried to keep up as Aiden approached the door near the bar.

"What are you going to do?" Megan asked as Aiden finished saying his brief goodbyes to the bartender.

"What are you going to do?" Aiden turned it back on her. "If this is so important, you'd think they'd understand. Or it's not important at all. We need to get there somehow, right? I've traveled by door hundreds of times since exile. No big deal."

Megan shrugged, obviously still conflicted. Aiden simply stepped out into the darkness of the hallway and made his way into the front room where the Ambler pub carried on as if everything were normal.

It was only eleven in the morning, but it was promising to be a hot day. The sidewalks were busy, and cars lurched slowly down the street, threading their way through small crowds of tourists and commuting pedestrians. All the shops along the walk were alive with customers, and the din assaulted Aiden's ears.

After they'd walked a couple blocks, Megan finally spoke. "Alright, well I guess traveling by door is allowed under special circumstances..."

"There ya go." Aiden turned around, feigning excitement.

Megan looked troubled, even still.

"Let's find an alleyway or something out of sight," Aiden said, turning back to lead the way down the old pavement.

Reaching the end of another block, Aiden managed to find a narrow alley between two buildings which kept well hidden beneath low hanging roofs. This end of the block was also relatively quiet, as much of the sector's attraction was elsewhere. He wasn't even sure what sort of businesses these small buildings housed, but neither seemed to be in operation today.

Aiden led Megan into the shadow of the alleyway, pushing himself and D'Natis—who was fluttering to remain perched on Aiden's shoulder—through a forest of stacked boxes and tall barrels. He squeezed into a clearing and saw a rear entrance door on the building to his left. He smirked as Megan finally squeezed in next to him.

"Perfect. We don't even have to make a door." Aiden clapped his hands together.

Megan sighed, looking ill at ease with the whole thing.

"I'll do it," Aiden said quickly. "If they ask, it was my idea."

Megan didn't respond, but simply stepped back. Aiden stood, writing runes, which cast themselves out to the old wooden door. In moments, a glowing runic word sat engraved in the wood, just above the old brass doorknob.

As the white mist faded, Aiden smiled at the look of the runes, then glanced around at both ends of the alleyway. He looked to Megan. Without any further hesitation, Aiden opened the door.

As the three of them peered into the open doorway, they saw a vast wood spread about before them. Their eyes were met with wild waves of fir and spruce trees, the scent of sap and fallen needles beginning to seep into the alley. Rays of mountain sunshine peered down into parts of the forest, creating small havens of light in the midst of an otherwise dark wood.

Aiden looked back out into the alleyway. Even though he'd

done this sort of thing before, the contrast was amazingly stark. He knew they shouldn't waste any more time. He stepped through the doorway and his foot found the forest floor. D'Natis shifted as a fresh breeze slithered through the nearby branches. Megan quickly stepped into the wood behind him, closing the door.

When they turned back, Aiden realized the door, on their side, had been standing up against a large boulder. It was already beginning to disappear, and only its frame could still be seen. That too, would soon be gone.

Aiden braced himself, fighting the memories that flooded him with the onslaught of the familiar sights and smells. He tried to focus on making his way through the haphazard rows of fir and spruce. The forest floor was red and brown with needles, while the way ahead was shrouded by the veil of a thousand coniferous trees, all interlocking randomly. Pockets of sunshine sprinkled through dry branches, illuminating massive spiderwebs across open paths between trees.

Aiden trudged carefully uphill, forcing his way through swaths of needled branches and spiderweb masterpieces. It became so thick that D'Natis finally took flight and began hopping from tree to tree, attempting to see ahead. Megan stuck close behind Aiden.

"Do you know where we are?" she finally asked him.

"Uh..." Aiden shrugged.

"You're supposed to know where you're going when you draw a door," Megan said, repressing an urge to chide him.

"So I got us a little off the beaten path," Aiden admitted

defensively. "It's been a while since I've traveled here."

"Well, let's keep walking I guess," Megan resolved. "Hopefully we're not too far off the path."

Aiden pulled his hood over his head and looked up at the raven who now perched above him on a high branch. "D'Natis! What do you see?"

There was a pause. Aiden pushed through another tangle of branches and let Megan in behind him.

"I see a trail," D'Natis finally called down. "It rounds up the mountain to the northeast."

Aiden stopped and looked up, shading his eyes from a sudden patch of sunlight. "How do you know that's northeast?"

"You dare question my sense of direction?" the raven asked in a self-important tone.

Aiden scoffed. "Forgive me, your majesty..."

"If we keep going the direction we're going, we'll run right into it," D'Natis added, then took flight again.

"I think that's the Appalachian Trail—if I'm not mistaken," Megan concluded, a look of realization lighting up her features.

"You better be right," Aiden said, pushing on ahead. "The Guild shouldn't be far then..."

***

After forcing their way through the wood for what Aiden thought must have been an hour, they caught sight of the trail. Finally the trees cleared and the afternoon sunshine met them full on, forcing Aiden to pull his hood back down. D'Natis hopped back onto

Aiden's shoulder, while Megan stayed close by.

Though the trail was rough, it was also wide enough to be a utility road, winding further up the mountain side. They continued up the trail as the way grew steeper.

"Maybe we should establish some ground rules," Megan finally said in a very diplomatic tone.

"Huh?" Aiden said, focusing on the trail.

"I want to be clear about some things," Megan continued. "If we're going to be working together, you can't be treating me, well, like you have been."

"Like what?" Aiden asked, feeling suddenly defensive. "Excuse me if I'm still not thrilled about all of this..."

"I'd appreciate it if you didn't snap at me like that."

Aiden was silent for a few moments. "Sorry," he finally said.

"In the end, you still chose to do this," Megan added sternly. "I need your help, but I can't force you."

Aiden chuckled momentarily. "I think you would've if you could've."

"Hey!"

"Joking," Aiden said, still smiling. "I'm just joking. You're right, I chose to do this."

Megan relaxed, forcing herself to smile. "Alright, well, then I just wanted to establish that I am the one who does the talking. By that I mean: We're going to be meeting some pretty high profile people, and I'm the one representing the Guild, and I'm the one standing before the Congress. Okay?"

Aiden was silent for a few moments while they walked the trail. "Yeah, okay. I thought you wanted my input?"

"I do," Megan said, her tone sincere. "I'm going to need your help in lots of other ways, aside from just protection."

"How, pray tell?" Aiden asked, smirking.

"Well, research, certainly. I need you to help me figure out how the N'Iatari are mixed up in this, and what they're planning to do."

"Sounds reasonable I guess," Aiden said, then another thought struck. "Did you read the paper?"

"Yes," Megan sighed with a hint of exasperation. "About the N'Iatari *negotiator* meeting with the Guild elders? Yes. The elders are being pretty quiet about it. I don't like it."

"Good to know we're on the same page," Aiden said with a smile.

"On that note," Megan added. "I don't know what's completely in store for us at the Guild once we get there... So please... Just keep your cool, okay?"

"Oh, I'm always cool," Aiden said.

Megan laughed but rolled her eyes at the same time.

Aiden carried on up the hill, thinking about Megan's words. He soon got the feeling that D'Natis was getting the best deal out of this journey.

"Why don't you fly a while?" Aiden asked the raven, stopping to catch his breath.

"Why should I?" D'Natis asked.

"We're doing all the work," Aiden said, pulling a water bottle from his duffel and taking a sip. "This is a steep incline. I should make you walk the rest of the way on those tiny pegs you call feet..."

"These are the perks of being a Raven Lord," D'Natis replied in a mock-regal tone.

"Oh really?" Megan chimed in with a skeptical air.

Aiden allowed himself an amused look in Megan's direction, but focused back on the raven. "At least scout for us a little," he said with a serious tone, pointing out ahead of them.

D'Natis released a sigh from his beak, "Oh alright." The raven pushed off into the air from Aiden's shoulder, steadily rising with each flap. "Humans..." he muttered.

Aiden continued moving forward, trying to pace himself. He kept D'Natis in his sight for a few minutes, but soon the raven had disappeared over a nearby ridge. Aiden took another step, but stopped as something met his ears. He motioned for Megan to halt.

There it was again.

Aiden froze and only hoped that Megan was doing the same. A dark form raced across the trail, out of his line of sight, just a few yards away.

Aiden looked slowly ahead of them, his eyes following the path the form had taken. The trees on either side of the trail seemed intensely dark, especially as a cloud had settled in over the area.

He wondered if he'd been seeing things.

There it was again. A sound, like padded feet gently crushing down on twigs and cones. This time, the sound came from behind them, to the southwest, on the opposite side of the trail.

Aiden looked back to Megan. She remained firmly planted in place, looking to him as if asking what was going on. Aiden remained expressionless. He focused on what lay just a few yards behind her.

A large black bear stood there on all fours, just at the edge of the wood. It stared at the two humans, as if pondering a decision. Aiden opened his mouth, but no sound came out. It only took moments for Megan to realize what he was looking at. Her mouth fell open as well, but no sound could escape.

Aiden heard a twig snap behind him and instinctively he spun around. The dark form he'd seen earlier was in fact a large cub. The bear cub was foraging for food in the foliage just on the other side of the trail. It seemed harmless enough.

Megan finally made a strange squealing whisper and Aiden looked back at the larger bear. Of course, it was the cub's mother. The bear now stood on her hind legs, revealing her teeth as a warning.

Aiden knew that being between a mother bear and her cub was the worst thing they could be doing. He racked his brain for a solution. He wondered if they could simply move out of the path between the two bears. He gestured subtly to Megan and began moving to the side, out of the direct path.

The mother bear stepped forward, landing on her forelegs,

snarling. Aiden stopped, his heart skipping a beat. Megan's eyes widened. The bear roared and lurched forward into a menacing run. She ran straight for Megan.

Aiden threw his hand forward in a desperate gesture. The bear was quickly surrounded by twelve men, each of them making the same gesture and mirroring each other's movements. Each one looked like Aiden.

The bear returned to her hind legs, roaring in confusion at the sight of Aiden's illusioncasting.

Megan almost fell to her knees, but quickly found her feet and ran toward the real Aiden, out of the way of harm. Aiden's illusions taunted the bear until she plopped down again, looking tired and unable to process what was happening. She ran on all fours toward her cub, running directly through one of the mimics—as though it were a ghost. The mother and cub quickly vanished into the shadows of the wood on the other side of the trail.

In an instant, Aiden's illusions disappeared in a white mist. Both Megan and Aiden composed themselves.

"Well..." Aiden began. "That worked out alright. You okay?"

Megan smiled and nodded, but then stopped herself. She and Aiden had locked eyes for the briefest of moments. Megan looked back to the spot where the bears had disappeared, as if wondering when they would return.

"...Thanks," she finally said to Aiden, a small smile forming.

Aiden nodded, but turned to look at the nearby ridge D'Natis had flown past just before. He was feeling something inside, and it had nothing to do with D'Natis, the money, or even the bears. He wasn't sure what it was.

"I guess I was pretty good at illusion-casting... at the Guild," Aiden said, the words forming awkwardly. "Now where is D'Natis?" he quickly added.

It sounded as though Megan had begun to say something when D'Natis—almost as if summoned—came soaring from over the ridge and swooped back onto Aiden's waiting arm.

"The Guild isn't far," the raven said as he held back an obvious temptation to groom his feathers. "If you people pick up the slack, we should be there just before they serve dinner."

***

After the encounter with the bear and her cub, the forest was eerily silent. Megan and Aiden hadn't talked much either, but they stayed close together while trudging up the trail. What had been a slight incline had now become a steep, ever-curving hike up the mountain, and it wasn't long before both Aiden and Megan were finding themselves in need of a short rest. D'Natis on the other hand flew circles around them, chiding them for their lack of energy.

Aiden sat on the edge of the path, staring down at the steep cascade of trees and foliage. He knew they had to keep going, but he felt embarrassed by how far away from the Guild he'd actually taken them. He forced himself back to his feet, adjusting his bag.

D'Natis landed heavily on Aiden's shoulder, weighing him down. "We're nearly there. But we must keep moving," the raven said.

Aiden nodded in a vague acknowledgment, and finally took another step. Megan was close behind him. He still couldn't help notice that she was taking this hike easier than he was.

Aiden wiped the sweat from his forehead. The afternoon sun had begun taking its toll. He wandered up the trail, watching D'Natis glide in wide circles in the general direction ahead of him. Aiden forced himself up the next incline and realized the trail made a brutally steep left turn and traveled further up the mountain.

Aiden stopped and sighed. He wasn't sure if his shoulders could take much more of this.

Just as he heard Megan's footsteps behind him, D'Natis landed on the gravel path before them. The raven quickly fluttered back into the air, soaring into the woods off to the right. For a moment, Aiden was confused, but he quickly realized D'Natis was taking them off the trail for a reason.

A bout of fresh energy hit Aiden and he smirked. He broke off into a run after the raven. Silently, Megan followed, catching on. Aiden burst between the trees, stumbling through thickets and brambles. He did all he could to keep D'Natis in sight. It seemed as though the raven was just playing with him now.

The woods grew thickest here, and daylight began to disappear beyond a roof of tangled branches. Aiden pushed his way through a mess of thick foliage, which had reminded him more of winding his way through a coat closet. Megan stuck close behind him, struggling to slip through the swath of needles and spider webs.

Once they'd stepped through, they found themselves in a small clearing that was nearly consumed in shadow.

When Aiden caught sight of D'Natis again, several more memories came flooding in.

There stood the Otter Gate. As if frozen in time, nothing seemed out of place. D'Natis was perched atop the otter to the left. Aiden stood there for a moment, not really wanting to approach the statues, but he knew he had to.

He could still see himself on that first day when Vodin had led him through this gate.

"Just like you remember it?" Megan asked.

Aiden had almost forgotten that she was there, he'd been so lost in his recollections. He turned to her, but was silent. He turned back to the otters, which almost seemed alive in the relative darkness. Slowly, he approached the statue on the right and ran his fingers along the smooth grain. He placed his fingertips onto the carved lettering and traced each symbol, feeling for every detail.

Just as he'd expected, the wooden creatures shifted and turned, forcing D'Natis to flutter back to Aiden's shoulder. Soon the path was clear and a doorway emerged from the mist. After they crossed the threshold, the sound of the otters shifting and creaking behind them made Aiden stop unexpectedly. He thought of Vodin, no matter how hard he fought against it.

They were inside the octagonal room, and Aiden glared down at the candle and the book. He could still remember the password, and without thinking, he began to runecast the letters onto the ancient pages. As the letters floated to the book, Megan had begun to protest, but it was too late.

An axe materialized from the book and flung itself at Aiden's face. In a split second, it clattered off his raised sword and fell to the ground, reverberating violently through the small room.

Megan released a shriek. D'Natis had lept off of Aiden's shoulder at the first sign of the axe, and was now rolling in feathery circles on the ground. Aiden lowered his blade, now in shock, thankful that he'd drawn it in time.

"Are you okay?" Megan gasped.

Aiden composed himself. "What was that?" he asked, feeling a mix of adrenaline and relief.

"I'm sorry!" Megan gushed. "I thought for sure you would ask for the new password..."

Aiden's face flushed. "I... I didn't even think-"

"You've been gone for how long now? Common sense would dictate that they would *change* the password," D'Natis chimed in, looking up at Aiden.

Aiden was silent, now flustered.

Megan avoided Aiden's frustrated gaze and approached the book. She wrote a rune which floated its way to the empty page, and soon disappeared without a weapon materializing.

Just as Aiden remembered, the room rotated, gears whirred, the wall split, and a door appeared. It was as though nothing had changed, but then again, there was no reason for them to change something that seemed to work so well.

Aiden took a step forward, but Megan put out a cautious hand. Aiden's forehead scrunched, but he stepped aside curtly and let Megan go first. She placed a hand on the door, and firmly stated something in a language Aiden didn't recognize.

The door clicked and cracked open.

"We've reinforced a lot of the security around here with Elvish charms," Megan said, smiling slyly as she grabbed the door's long ornate handle. "It's amazing some of the old Elven languages the linguists re-discovered..."

Aiden hadn't known that. He shrugged as Megan pushed the old door open wide enough to let them all through.

What else has changed since I've been gone? he wondered.

With D'Natis back on his shoulder perch, Aiden and Megan stepped from the small room and out into open air. The Guild grounds were just as Aiden had remembered them. The trio wandered along the old cobblestones, surrounded by well-kept lawns, and Aiden was struck by both a sense of nostalgia and terror. His stomach felt as if all the Earth's gravity had disappeared, but he continued walking.

Megan walked ahead on the path, and Aiden followed her hesitantly, now beginning to wonder if this had been the right decision. D'Natis seemed upbeat, although silent. They passed the old statue of Master Porutan the Half-Elf, and Aiden nodded to it, as if it understood his internal struggle somehow.

The grounds were silent, aside from the sounds of classes being held out on the training field quite some distance from them. The trees, the shrubbery, and all the buildings looked as untouched as they had the day he'd first arrived as a curious fifteen-year-old.

As if viewing things through a strange haze, Aiden found himself striding up to the Great Hall. It too was the same as he'd left it. He dreaded going through those doors.

"Ah... Home," Aiden sighed begrudgingly.

Chapter 12
Turlin's Request

No sooner had they wandered in through the large wooden doors of the great building, that sounds of conversation and clinking dishes filled their ears from just beyond the foyer. The foyer was empty, and Aiden hesitantly following Megan into the wide room. Aiden sighed, noting that the old red carpet and the hanging tapestry hadn't changed at all, although they were worse for wear.

Just as they were half way to the double doors at the end of the room, through which they could hear a multitude of people, one of the doors swung open.

"Master Fentl," Megan addressed the tall man who'd just entered the foyer, her voice suddenly cautious. "We just got here—"

"I can see that," the man said indifferently, then looked to Aiden. "Well, she finally found you, did she?"

Aiden paused, surprised to see the man, and balling his fists suddenly. "Yeah," was all he could say.

"Fascinating," Fentl said with a knowing smirk while appraising Aiden.

"What?" said Aiden, fighting the urge to relive his trial. He could still see a younger version of Fentl standing at the lectern, leading on the witnesses with loaded questions.

"Oh," Fentl paused, amused. "It's just that you look nearly the same as you did all those years ago."

Aiden feigned disinterest. "Oh?"

"Yes, but what's more is that you have the same lost expression on your face," Fentl continued.

"You two know each other?" Megan asked, confused by Fentl's words.

"Yes," said Fentl, almost smugly. "Was an unfortunate event." He sighed. "Well, Aiden, good luck on your endeavor. I do hope you can find your way-" Fentl paused and leaned over to whisper into Aiden's ear, ignoring the raven on the other shoulder. "-back to that Ambler hell-hole where you belong."

Aiden stood back, appalled by both Fentl's words and by his breath, which smelled of hookah smoke and fish. Megan looked at the two of them confused, but Aiden did not want to alarm her, so he composed himself.

Fentl shifted his gaze back to Megan. "How did you get back so soon? I didn't expect you this quickly," he said, as if trying to repress a sudden worry.

Megan swallowed for a moment. "Well... Yes. But I knew it was urgent."

There was an awkward pause as Fentl glared back at her, as if he fought the urge to say something. The master soon composed himself. "Well, the Headmaster will be pleased. He's just inside— I assume you're looking for him."

Aiden's face scrunched. Master Fentl's smile seemed forced as he made a half-bow to Megan. Silently, the man left the foyer, leaving Aiden and Megan in the center of the empty room once again.

Aiden cleared his throat, still feeling a burning in his chest but trying to shrug it off. "Why is he here?" he asked, not hiding his disdain.

"He teaches here."

Aiden's brow furled. "Wonderful," he said sardonically.

"I know he's sort of strict and kind of a pain as a teacher, but what's the problem? If you don't mind me asking," Megan said, observing his tortured gaze. "What did he ever do to you?"

Aiden laughed, as if to stop himself from swearing. "He led my trial proceedings," he said slowly. "Let's just say I never got a chance to defend myself."

"Surely there was some-" Megan made to interject, looking both concerned and surprised.

"Nope," said Aiden with a very stoic tone. "Not a single word. He didn't leave the witnesses a lot of wiggle room either."

"Hmmm," Megan hummed almost skeptically. "I'm sorry," she finally said somewhat awkwardly. "But we probably should-"

"Probably should go get this over with," Aiden finished her sentence, gesturing in the direction of the main hall.

Just then, the double doors at the end of the room opened again, and a cacophony of sounds began to filter into the foyer. A Faun's horned head emerged from behind the doors. Megan beamed and walked toward the end of the room.

"Aiden, this is my mentor, Master Jardun." Megan was eager to introduce the two of them as the doors shut and they remained in the foyer.

Jardun was a Faun's typical height—a couple of feet shorter than Aiden—with curly dark hair and beard, and a tunic that accentuated his muscular build. Aiden greeted him with a casual nod, but the Faun was glaring at D'Natis and sighing. Even D'Natis released a small sigh that sounded all too human.

"Yes," D'Natis hissed. "We've met."

"You have?" Megan asked, surprise painting her features.

"Yes..." Jardun agreed, clearing his throat. "Unfortunately."

Aiden sensed the tension in the room, feeling the bird bristle and dig into his shoulder where he perched.

"D'Natis," Jardun caught the raven's eye. "Good to see you again," he said with a clearly false civility.

D'Natis stirred and tilted his head for a better view of the Faun, thinking nothing of the pain his talons were causing Aiden's shoulder. "Very gracious of you to say so," he responded with equally feigned manners. "Don't worry about your dark secret, I won't speak of it. I'm but a dumb beast, and you, after all, are my superior."

Aiden couldn't help but smile. He felt so proud that some of his sarcasm had finally rubbed off on the old Raven Lord.

Megan looked dumbfounded.

Aiden's curiosity got the best of him. "So what happened between you two?" he asked, looking to the raven. "How come you've never mentioned this before?"

"Should you tell it, or should I?" D'Natis said, glaring sideways at Jardun. "Which would you rather hear," he added, addressing Aiden and Megan. "His story, or the truth?"

Jardun scoffed. "Now's not the time."

"Of course not," D'Natis said, his feathers ruffling. "My lineage is no concern of yours."

Jardun's cheeks flushed. "This is not the time. And it wasn't my fault," he said through clenched teeth.

"Excuse me," Megan chimed in, looking anxious. "I don't know what happened between you two, but now we really do have to meet with the Headmaster."

Jardun cleared his throat and dropped D'Natis' gaze. "Thank you," he said quietly, looking to Megan, and for a moment, there was a sudden vulnerability in his expression.

D'Natis made an angry clicking sound, but said nothing more. He felt like dead weight on Aiden's shoulder.

"Now that you're here," the Faun said to both Megan and Aiden, a new confidence overcoming him. "We have a lot to discuss. Thankfully everyone's still here, having their meal."

"Hopefully just the important ones anyway..." Aiden muttered through grit teeth, still thinking of the confrontation with Fentl.

Megan nodded and followed as Jardun forced open the doors to the main hall. Aiden and D'Natis followed. The four of them were met with a whirl of voices followed by cutlery and cups clinking in no particular rhythm. Several of the masters sat eating their meal at the room's long central table. Jardun led Megan and the others around tables full of feasting students and servile Faeries, to that central table, and each of the masters stood once they noticed the presence of the visitors.

The smells and sounds threatened to recall Aiden's memories at every turn. He even saw that the hanging symbol-clad tapestries had not changed at all. He readied himself for whatever would happen next, especially as Turlin's face came into view.

"Ah yes," said Turlin, who wore the traditional long blue robes. "Welcome back Megan. And I see you've accomplished your task." He smiled as he put a gentle hand on Megan's shoulder.

Megan blushed happily and bowed to the Half-Elf.

Aiden half-smiled as Turlin's eyes met his. "Been a while, hasn't it?" he said, nodding to the Headmaster.

"Yes," agreed Turlin. "Too long I suppose."

Headmaster Turlin gestured for Jardun and the guests to all take a seat. As they did so, he looked to the other masters at the table, saying, "Aiden, you remember Mistress Dorsa and Master Flit, don't you?"

Aiden nodded. The two masters looked very nearly the same as they had when he had attended. Mistress Dorsa was still tall and beautiful, and Master Flit had more grey in his beard now, but like most Fauns, he looked relatively young even in old age.

The masters sat down and politely resumed their meals. Aiden's stomach rumbled just looking at their plates. All three masters had fairly large helpings of fileted fried trout with sides of baked potatoes and asparagus.

"Long journey, was it?" Turlin asked Megan.

"Sort of," she said, giving Aiden a sideways glance. "But it all worked out."

Turlin noticed Aiden staring at the food and smiled. "Oh, forgive me. It is dinner time after all. Let's get you all something to eat," he said, standing and turning, his bright eyes searching for something across the room.

Turlin gestured to someone outside of Aiden's sight, and then sat back down. Aiden watched Turlin, waiting for his next words, and felt the familiar sensation of D'Natis nestling into his shoulder. He wondered how long the Headmaster would keep him waiting before he decided to explain the situation.

"Aiden, are you alright?' Turlin looked up from his plate. "You seem tense."

Aiden's mouth opened in surprise. "Uh... Well, I guess I was wondering about everything..." Aiden got to the point. "What am I doing here? I mean, Megan's told me some things-"

"Yes," Turlin said, politely interjecting. "A man of action. I remember that about you. First, let's not let business sully a good meal."

A gentle Faerie appeared at the table and laid large plates of fried fish, potatoes, and asparagus in front of both Aiden and Megan. Aiden nodded to the creature, but the Faerie returned with a blank expression before leaving the table. He recalled how strange it had been the first time he'd been served by a Faerie. It still seemed odd.

Aiden dug into his food, thankful for the first home-cooked meal he'd had in months.

***

"Now that we're all settled," Turlin began after they had eaten in silence for some time. "Let's all get up to speed, shall we?" The Headmaster's eyes landed squarely on Aiden.

"The Shadow Congress will be convening in a little over two weeks," Turlin continued. "Aiden, I'm unsure how much you know, but the Shadow Congress consists of both Agnecs *and* Amblers. There are representatives from over 100 nations, federations, and tribal confederacies worldwide, from both Agnec communities, and from various Ambler political bodies... In other words, you'll be seeing a few *actual* congressmen... And women," Turlin said, adding the last bit when he saw Megan's expression.

Aiden nodded.

"The United States is poorly under-represented by any D'Tari who might be involved," Turlin added. "Dorimar nac Heartwood is a high ranking representative from the Elvin Council of the Eastern Seaboard, and the current liaison between the various east coast Elf tribes and the D'Tari... If anything, he could prove to be a useful ally. Remember that name, Megan."

Megan nodded.

Turlin swallowed another bite of food, then continued, "I can't promise any excitement." Turlin smirked in Aiden's direction. "You two must attend both the General Assembly and the Peacekeeping and Security Council sessions."

"How does that work?" Aiden asked suddenly.

"I think it's fairly straightforward," Turlin replied. "The General Assembly can last anywhere from two weeks to a month; this is when all the delegates and representatives come together to discuss the issues: Security, Agnec secrecy regulation, Ambler relations, conflicts between tribes, education, and the rest. Then there's usually the house-cleaning bit where they vote on adding or removing members from various councils, budget issues, and what have you."

"Sounds exciting," Aiden said lazily.

Turlin smiled, despite Master Flit's look of irritation at Aiden's remark. "I told you I could not promise any excitement. But there are some serious issues on the docket this time 'round, and we are blessed enough to be holding the Congress in the US this year."

"They don't always hold it here?" Aiden asked.

"Oh no. It rotates every four years to various locations around the world," Turlin replied. "Some of the more serious issues this year seem to be related to the United States and Europe though, so we're making sure to be as involved as we can. But the D'Tari sort of have an interesting standing," Turlin sighed. "We're not considered a unique tribe or nation, so we don't have the same status as others in the assemblies.'

"The D'Tari Council has a permanent membership on the Peacekeeping and Security Council, but they only have so much input... And are often controlled by the overarching resolutions, with only so much authority of their own," Turlin said, his hand slowly forming a fist as he began to glare angrily at his near-empty plate.

"The Council..." Master Flit scoffed from the corner of his mouth.

Turlin gave the Faun a sideways glance, but then continued, his tone evening out, "So, Megan, your job is to ally yourself with the liaisons as much as you can, because although the D'Tari Council has its own place of input, individual Guilds are not nearly so lucky."

"What do you mean?" Aiden asked, really trying to absorb the Half-Elf's words. Despite himself, he was growing fascinated.

"As individual Guilds, we have to take our case to the Council, then, *if* the Council decides to take up our cause, they take up the issue during the Congress," Turlin explained. "We've already pleaded our cause with the Council, and with a majority vote, they agreed to take up the cause—but they demanded that we send a representative of our own."

"Huh," Aiden wondered. "Is that normal?"

"No," Turlin sighed. "The two dissenters in the Council were— as you could well guess—Master Fentl and Mistress Monadias."

Aiden bristled just hearing the name of Grant Griftwalker's mother.

"Monadias, still being the Council head, claimed they had no one to send for the task—despite how I know they'll be sending a few of their own to be present at the assemblies. So... here we are," said Turlin, folding his arms.

"Nice to hear the Council hasn't changed much," said Aiden sarcastically, sitting back in his seat.

"Megan," Turlin said, looking to the woman intently. "Our first focus is Dorimar. We need the Elf vote, and I think, according to my sources, we already have a decent majority of support from the International Confederation of Blue Dwarves, since they're usually the Council's first priority."

Aiden rolled his eyes. "Can't do much without being buddies with those guys..."

Turlin ignored Aiden's remark and looked into Megan's eyes. "Megan, I've taught you what I can in the ways of diplomacy, and you have a thorough knowledge of how the politics work. Are you willing to commit to this task?"

Megan swallowed so hard, Aiden could almost see the lump in her throat. There was a pause. Turlin's question had reminded Aiden of Vodin's request of commitment all those years ago.

Megan nodded. "Yes," she said. "I am willing."

"So," Aiden chimed in. "What exactly is our cause?"

"That brings me to the next point I meant to make," Turlin said, his expression a little brighter now. "As you probably guessed by what the name implies, the Peacekeeping and Security Council sessions deal with the protections for Agnecs, solving conflicts, and all those sorts of things. This is where members who have a big enough vote can actually create legislation; even task forces— hence why the D'Tari are involved. We once were a pivotal part of these sessions, as many D'Tari were utilized for solving militant conflicts. Of course, that was a long time ago...'

"As it is, the sessions normally last about as long as the General Assembly. Now, the big issue we have, well," Turlin paused, looking pensive. "Is that we have to convince the various members of Congress—first in the Assembly, then in the Security Council— that the N'Iatari are on the move—and not for the better. We need to convince them that the N'Iatari are actively working to infiltrate levels of leadership. They're finding Agnec villages to infiltrate and destroy. They're showing up in various parts of Ambler society and killing innocents..."

"We hear tell that a series of Ambler murders on the west coast is actually linked to N'Iatari activity," Mistress Dorsa chimed in, looking somber. "And this isn't an isolated thing. I wish it were."

Turlin nodded in whole-hearted agreement. "Furthermore, sources tell us that various N'Iatari guilds are appearing across the country," he added.

"N'Iatari have guilds too?" Aiden asked, surprised.

"Why not?" Megan said. "Makes sense to me."

"We need to keep on eye on a congressman named Philip Regis," Turlin said, his eyes thinning at the mere mention of the name. "He's a US senator, but he's also an Ambler liaison to the Shadow Congress. He's... Well, he openly supports the N'Iatari, and has campaigned for them throughout the years."

Aiden almost choked while trying to swallow a piece of potato. "Wait... I, I think I've heard of him," he said, between chews.

"I'm sure you have," Turlin sighed, almost with a reluctance to say what came next. "If you've followed any of the Agnec papers, I'm sure you've seen his name once or twice."

"But he's an Ambler?" Aiden's face scrunched in confusion. "Why would he try to campaign for the N'Iatari? I mean, why does he even care? How does he even know about them? How does he even know about Agnecs at all?"

"There are a few Amblers, a slight few, mind you, that are aware and accepting of our kind. This doesn't shock me, although it is a little unusual for an Ambler to step into the Agnec world politically. Any other Amblers attending the Congress will simply be observing, more than anything else," said Turlin thoughtfully. "As for the N'Iatari... You must remember that they have not been in the Agnec eye for some time. Most Agnecs believe that the N'Iatari are either no longer an organization, or that they are relatively comparable to the D'Tari now—trying to be a force for good.'

"As for Regis, he calls himself an informed Ambler; one who still identifies as Ambler, but claims to sympathize with the Agnec cause. Ever since the 1970s, Regis, and others who've worked with him, have campaigned for a *peaceful* N'Iatari. The N'Iatari promote freedom and just causes... so they say."

Aiden shook his head.

"We do what we can to educate other Agnecs about the N'Iatari's dark secrets," Turlin said, seeing Aiden's reaction. "And certainly the students here know the truth, but the Agnec world must know as well. Apparently now, Philip Regis has a new plan: He's going to propose new legislation to create an international militia to protect Agnecs..."

"To be fair, that doesn't sound so bad," Megan chimed in.

"True," Turlin agreed. "On the outset, it has all the appearance of keeping Agnec communities safe. Our sources tell us, though, that he's going to propose training recruits with a combination of both D'Tari *and* N'Iatari practices. He's going to make them one army, and they'll spread across the globe."

At this, Master Flit jumped into the conversation, his face turning pink with indignation. "I don't need to tell you what this really means," he said, his voice shaking. "He's building an army to conquer the Ambler world. He wants to take us with him, and he wants government money to do it."

There was something about extreme zeal that always rubbed Aiden the wrong way. He finished another bite of his asparagus and sighed. "If I could play devil's advocate here," Aiden said, wiping his face with an ornate napkin. "Let's try to look at this objectively... On one hand, maybe he is trying to build an army to fight Amblers with dark properties, but what if he really *does* just want a bigger fighting force, to protect the Agnecs? Ya know, from actual threats?"

Master Flit looked momentarily befuddled, as if someone had just spoken a heresy. Mistress Dorsa, on the other side of the headmaster, seemed more thoughtful, but remained silent.

"While I appreciate your perspective, Aiden, I wish I could

believe this was a positive thing," Turlin said, sitting back from his own empty plate. "But given Regis' past, I don't think it is. You know as well as I do, that the philosophy of both N'Iatari and D'Tari are far too different for this to end well."

"I'll give you that," Aiden had to admit. "If N'Iatari weren't trying to kill me so often, I could probably be convinced otherwise." After a moment, Aiden thought aloud, "What's the deal with Regis? Is he really just an Ambler with a passion for Agnec rights, or just a suit with a price tag?"

Turlin stopped and gave a fleeting, but knowing, glance to Mistress Dorsa.

"He's an agent of Lilit, I'm sure of it," Master Flit jumped in once more.

Turlin smiled and placed a peaceful hand out in front of the red-bearded Faun's chest. "Flit, this hasn't been confirmed or denied."

"I don't think we need to worry about that old myth," said Aiden, almost under his breath.

Master Flit seemed suddenly incensed.

"Even the greatest myth can drive men toward darkest zeal," said Turlin, his bright eyes burning through Aiden's. "Anyway, Aiden," Turlin continued, ignoring Master Flit's offended expression . "We don't know for sure about Regis. Megan will need your help in researching him. We believe the senator is going to promote legislation to start this army at the nearest opportunity. At this point, the D'Tari Council says it has heard no such news—or at

least, that's what I was told by Monadias—and they have no plans
to object."

Aiden looked dumbfounded.

"It is essentially up to us. Well, technically Megan, to stand
and oppose the legislation on behalf of this Guild," Turlin said,
glancing over to the woman. "And Aiden, it is your highest duty
to protect and help her with her task. Megan," He looked back to
the woman again. "Ally yourself with Dorimar, raise awareness of
the issue—because knowing the way things work, there's a chance
they'll try to sneak this in as quickly as they can—get Agnecs on
the street involved if you must. You need to be able to provide
some sort of evidence or testimony to the fact that the N'Iatari
are not who Regis says they are. Convince the Security Council.
Simple? Simple. Now if you'll excuse me-"

"Hold on," Aiden cut in before the Headmaster could stand. "I
was told there'd be compensation?"

Turlin looked somewhat put out, but he still managed a smile. "I
was wondering if you might ask," he said. "Yes, you'll get what is
promised, but only after the task is done. In the meantime, all your
living expenses will be arranged and paid for."

Master Flit seemed even more irritated than usual at Turlin's
words, but Aiden smiled, though his mind whirled trying to process
all he'd just heard.

"What a horrible thing to have to help the Guild out of respect
for the D'Tari and the Agnecs," Master Flit snarled, standing to his
feet and glaring at Aiden.

"Calm yourself, Flit," Turlin said to the Faun. "It is not our place to judge his heart. Even this can be used for good."

Aiden had been about to stand and confront Master Flit, but Turlin's words had stopped him. He wasn't quite sure how to respond now.

"Now if you'll-"

"Wait!" Aiden stood and interjected again. "Sorry, but so does this mean you remove the trace rune and I'm officially back from exile?" There was somewhat of an excitement in his voice that he couldn't help.

There was a pause. Turlin turned, looking a bit weary, but then smiled. "I told you that someday, you might be able to come back," he said. "Congratulations. I suppose today is that day."

Aiden smiled and pulled up his sleeve, exposing the complicated rune on his shoulder and making D'Natis flutter.

Turlin began drawing runes in the air. "I'm sure you've dreamed of this day," he said, chuckling. "And there you are."

The runes attached themselves to Aiden's shoulder, forcing the trace rune to fade. In moments, the new runes faded as well. Aiden took a freeing breath and thanked the Headmaster.

"Now, if you'll really excuse me," Turlin added once again. "I have several things to get done this evening. I must be off."

With that, the Headmaster stood and left the table. With the sudden absence of a trace rune, Aiden felt happy. Looking across at Masters Flit and Dorsa, he noticed they glanced at him warily. Even Jardun was looking at Aiden still, as if trying to make sense of something. Megan seemed to be lost in thoughts of her own, and D'Natis hopped to the space on the seat next to Aiden.

Aiden was struck with a sudden thought, "I read that the N'Iatari are meeting with the elders—here."

"Yes..." Master Flit nodded with a look of disgust, as if he'd found something even more appalling than Aiden's pay to scoff at. "Regis and some of his...*friends*... are meeting with the Headmaster and the others. I'm sure they'll be asking if the Guild will support his legislation, but we are all prepared to reject it."

Aiden nodded to the old Faun.

***

After several long minutes of contemplation, Aiden found himself staring at the little food left on his plate. He wondered what came next, but before he could say anything, a girl stood directly behind Megan. Her presence almost startled him. Megan turned around and smiled widely, despite a still looming look of concern in her eyes.

"Hi Red," the girl said, smiling back at Megan. "What're you doing here? Did you realize that you actually failed and have to come back for more classes?" the girl asked, snickering.

"You wish," Megan said, standing. She was not much taller than the girl.

"Hi Master Flit, Mistress Dorsa..." the girl greeted the masters, turning to each one respectively, taking a more reverent tone, as if she had just realized they were present across the table. "Master Jardun," she likewise looked to the Faun on the other side of

Megan.

"Who's your friend?" Aiden heard the girl whisper into Megan's ear.

"Oh, Aiden, this is Dora... my sister," Megan introduced them, almost hesitantly for a moment.

Aiden nodded coolly. The girl blushed and grabbed a lock of her long brown hair, twisting the split-ends around her finger in tight curls. Aiden couldn't help but notice that Dora was beautiful, slightly more full-figured than Megan, and somewhat tall.

At that moment, Megan stiffened and said, "Uh, I'll be right back. I need to talk to the Headmaster."

It was so sudden that Aiden could only watch as Megan caught up with Turlin who was passing by, leading him to an empty table just a few feet away.

In the meantime, Dora sat down in Megan's empty seat next to Aiden. He noticed how she looked him up and down, but then dropped his gaze when he looked at her.

"So... How do you know Megan?" Dora asked, taking on an air of someone much older than she looked.

Aiden smirked. He watched the others at the table lose interest very quickly. One quick glance in the direction of Masters Flit and Dorsa told him that they had already left. Jardun remained in his seat, his eyes rolling into the back of his head. Dora seemed eager to hear Aiden's response, so much so that she seemed oblivious to the world around her. She even somehow seemed to miss the large raven sitting next to him.

"We work together... now," Aiden finally responded.

Dora's pupils dilated. "Interesting," she said.

"Not really," Aiden thought aloud.

At that moment, Aiden heard Turlin's voice carrying over from where the Headmaster sat with Megan. "I chose you, because you have experienced the N'Iatari firsthand," Turlin said, his tone confident.

"But I'm not brave... I'm sort of an emotional wreck sometimes..." Aiden heard Megan start to say, but was interrupted by Dora who was not done gawking at Aiden.

"Are you two... together?" Dora asked, noticing that Aiden was gazing over at Megan and Turlin's table.

Aiden was taken aback, then laughed. "Oh no!" he coughed. "I mean, no," he added, more seriously. "No. I uh, no. Just friends."

Dora's face lit up.

"Yeah," Aiden sputtered, but then realized how close Dora seemed to be sitting. "I uh. No, not together. In fact, neither of us are really with anyone at all, that I know of." He fiddled with his thumbs awkwardly. "I'm definitely not planning on it. Being with anyone right now. That's for sure. I'm sort of too busy with my current assignment," he finally added, which was the truth of course, but he'd only said it in hopes that she would take the hint.

Dora was silent, but still gazing. She kept tilting her head as if trying to force some words, but nothing came. Aiden pretended not to notice while he finished up his meal.

In those moments of silence, Aiden heard Turlin's last words of encouragement to Megan, from the other table: "You can do this, Megan. I know you can. By the power of the unKing, I know you can. And you will. You must find that inner strength."

"Well..." Dora's voice interrupted Aiden's eavesdropping. "I guess it was nice to meet you..."

Without another word, Dora walked away. Aiden sighed in relief.

Megan returned to the table red-faced and wiping her eyes, but Aiden pretended not to notice. Jardun and Aiden both stood to meet her, and Jardun offered to take them to their quarters.

***

Jardun led Aiden, D'Natis, and Megan back out onto the grounds just as the sky was beginning to dim. Aiden watched as students left the great hall in small groups, returning to their respective dormitories for the evening. It was strange watching the students wander. They all seemed so young, despite how many of them were taller than him.

There was a refreshing breeze in the air, and now that he'd stuffed himself, Aiden felt comfortable for the first time in hours. It was a surprising feeling, given how much he had dreaded returning to the Guild. He felt somewhat soothed by the fact that neither Turlin nor Flit seemed to hold the D'Tari Council in very high regard.

Jardun stopped ahead of them on the path and momentarily glared at D'Natis, then looked to Aiden. "We've prepared rooms for you both in the teachers' quarters," the Faun said with little expression in his tone, but then glared back at D'Natis. "And you, D'Natis... I don't assume you'll be sleeping indoors...?"

"I see what you're playing at," the raven scoffed, raising himself up on Aiden's shoulder, feathers ruffled. "Don't want the filthy bird staying inside, do you? Think he might just upset someone?"

Jardun stroked his short beard and sighed. "No, why would I think that?" he said, now rolling his eyes. "I just wondered if you needed—"

"Don't bother explaining," D'Natis snapped. "I'll find a nice quiet tree, away from you." D'Natis shook out his wings, stretching them, and making Aiden shiver from the sudden rush of wind. "I'll see you in the morning, Aiden," the raven said, a streak of irritation clearly lingering in his tone.

Aiden nodded, though confused at D'Natis' reaction, and the bird pushed off into the air, soaring into the canopy of evergreens above them. Aiden sighed and shook his head. Megan just stared up into the trees with a perplexed expression. Jardun seemed to have already moved on, though he grunted and mumbled, and was heading further down the old cobblestones.

"Hey," Aiden addressed Jardun as he caught up with him along the path. "Whatever happened between you two... Must've been serious."

"Let's not speak of it," the Faun grumbled.

"Just saying... It's been a long time since I've seen D'Natis that angry," Aiden said.

"If he doesn't want to talk about it, then drop it," Megan growled, stepping up beside Aiden and elbowing him in the ribs.

Aiden held his tongue, but released a grunt.

Jardun led them through a maze of different stone buildings until they came to an orderly row of quaint circular shanties with thatched roofs. Each building was about the size of a small room with a fireplace, and built with stone bricks. There were twelve shanties in all.

Jardun led them down the path until they reached the two buildings at the very end. He directed Megan to her shanty, which was on the left, and Aiden to his, on the right. Aiden opened the door of his shanty and peeked inside, just as he saw Megan doing the same with hers.

It was small, and practically medieval as far as comforts went. The tiny round room was illuminated by a solitary candle sitting on a rough end table. There was a stone fireplace, a wooden floor, and a bed that appeared to have a straw mattress. He had stayed in worse places. It would have to do. After all, he would only be here for a day or two at the most.

Aiden dropped his things onto the bed and came back outside, seeing that Jardun was still there. Megan was coming back out as well.

"Not bad," Megan said, seemingly genuine.

"It's not much, but it is functional after all," Jardun said, and smiled for the first time since Aiden had met him. "You'll be safe here for the next couple of weeks, most importantly."

Aiden shook his head, thinking he'd heard that wrong. "Couple of weeks?" he coughed.

"Headmaster Turlin was a bit scatter-brained tonight," Jardun said, turning to Aiden. "But he meant to tell you that he wanted me to catch you up on some training."

"Catch me up?" Aiden scoffed.

"Yes. You never completed your third year." Jardun gazed at Aiden, his dark eyes piercing. "Now we can't fit an entire year's worth of lessons and mentoring into the time we have, so Turlin asked that *I* give you the... er, abbreviated, version."

"No one told me this," Megan added in surprise. "But it couldn't hurt."

Aiden made to protest, but couldn't find the words. He'd spent so many years trying to forget this place and move on.

"I don't need any more training," Aiden said stubbornly, surprising himself by the calm in his own voice.

"Only a fool can make absolute statements," Jardun said, shifting the weight on his goat-like hooves. "This is part of your mission, the one you agreed to by coming here with Megan. She needs protection. She's already been attacked by assassins three different times in the last month. Once it was quite serious—"

Megan lifted her hand to stop Jardun, turning pink suddenly.

"You didn't tell me that," Aiden said, turning to Megan in surprise.

"I told you they were stalking me," Megan said, avoiding Aiden's direct gaze.

Aiden could feel his blood boiling. At first he'd been mostly upset at the thought of staying at the Guild for longer than necessary, but now he could only think of the men in white cloaks and Grant's smug face.

"Alright," Aiden answered Jardun at last. "Let's get this over with."

"My other students are usually more enthusiastic about it," Jardun quipped.

"That was almost a joke," Aiden said with a mixture of slowly fading anger and sarcasm. "But I wouldn't quit your day job."

With that, Aiden mumbled something unintelligible and stepped into his shanty, slamming the old wooden door behind him.

Chapter 13
Stepping Up

The tangled underside of a thatched roof blurred into existence nearly six feet above him. The old wooden frame croaked as Aiden finally sat upright, rubbing his face with his hands. He had not slept well on the old straw mattress, and his vertebrae popped with every movement.

A fierce knocking suddenly rattled his brain.

"Wake up!" came a voice from the other side of the door.

It was Jardun.

"Oh Lord..." Aiden groaned, looking across the small room.

"Be in the Great Hall in five minutes," Jardun barked.

Aiden agreed in a lackluster tone. The waking world had already begun to filter in as he could hear Jardun's hooves crunching along the old cobblestones and dry needles. Bird song filled the trees and the smell of pine and sap was strong. The morning air was still freshly chilled and crept draftily into the old shanty—something Aiden noticed the moment he tried to get dressed.

He stopped, and as if jolted by a sudden premonition, Aiden slowly opened his front door and looked down. As he'd suspected, Jardun had found him some traditional clothes to wear during training, or just for being around the Guild. Not only did the clothes bring back some memories, but Aiden felt strange slipping them on once again.

Finally, he stepped out of the shanty and closed the door behind him. He squinted in the sudden onslaught of sunlight filtering down through the foliage canopy. He adjusted his tunic and fiddled with the leather belt at his waist. Taking a deep breath, he looked around and began his journey.

Aiden walked along the path, trying desperately not to wake anyone in the shanties. He really didn't feel like talking to any of the masters, at least not more than he needed to. He followed the path around until the central building was in sight. He briefly wondered where D'Natis was, but then imagined the raven was out finding food of his own for the morning.

Aiden stopped on the path as the circular building dwarfed him, casting morning shadows behind it. He took a deep breath, not wanting to admit that what he felt wasn't frustration anymore, but fear. Aside from the N'Iatari trainee, he hadn't really fought with someone skilled in the D'Tari properties for some time. He hadn't kept up on practicing some of the skills required of him. He had not continued his meditation...

Inside the Great Hall, Aiden's ears were assaulted by the same din of mealtime traffic. He was glad to see that Jardun was the only one sitting at the masters' table, and Aiden took a seat across from him, acting as casual as he could. Jardun didn't say much, but advised Aiden to eat a good meal, warning him that he'd need his strength.

Normally Aiden would have made some sort of crack or joke,

but Jardun's expression was grave, so Aiden kept to himself and finished his oatmeal and assorted fruit.

When they were done, Jardun silently led Aiden out of the Great Hall and down the cobblestone path until they reached the training field some ways away. The field was empty, aside from some of the equipment sheds. Jardun silently walked to a central spot in the well-kept grass and drew his sword. The double-handed longsword had, like all D'Tari blades, materialized as if from nowhere. It almost seemed too long for the Faun, but he wielded it expertly. The morning sun glinted off the blade, causing Aiden to blink.

Jardun looked to Aiden. "Today," he said, his eyes appraising Aiden. "We evaluate your abilities, and see which things need to be... brushed up on."

Aiden didn't like the sound of this, but he too began to take a ready stance as Jardun moved slowly toward him. The Faun's blade was now in position, aimed toward Aiden as if ready to strike.

"What're you waiting for?" Jardun said, a strange adventuresome look in his eye. "Defend yourself."

"I don't want to hurt you," Aiden said, stepping back. "Not yet anyway..."

"Steel sharpens steel," Jardun cried as he lunged toward Aiden.

Aiden stumbled back, managing to draw his sword. The two blades clattered loudly in the morning air, and Aiden caught his balance again.

"We're doin' it like that huh?" Aiden said, recovering from his surprise.

"Show me what you're made of," said Jardun enthusiastically, returning to the forward position. "No holding back."

"Okay, but that's your call..." said Aiden as his buckler materialized in his left hand.

Jardun attacked again, but Aiden blocked with both buckler and blade, forcing the broadsword sideways with some difficulty. As Aiden saw his way clear and made to strike, Jardun forced the broadsword back. Aiden saw it just in time and stumbled backward.

Jardun laughed, but Aiden returned, this time punching away Jardun's blade with the buckler. In that split second, Aiden thrust and managed to catch Jardun in the shoulder. The Faun growled and hoisted the broadsword back, narrowly missing Aiden's shield arm. Jardun stopped.

"Not bad," he said, his face a mixture of chagrin and excitement, looking to his shoulder. "Just grazed me." He shook the arm. "It's obvious our weapons are unevenly matched, but I see you remember Vodin's training well. I also see you've got some runes on your blade," Jardun smiled almost mischievously. "Let's see what assets you've added to your swordskill."

"Uh... You asked me to not hold back..." Aiden said, feeling a little bad to see Jardun's shoulder bleeding.

"It's nothing," said Jardun. "Had it been a double-handed sword, I might be worried..."

"Vodin always did say that double-handed swords were less superior than one-handed..." Aiden said, smirking as he took position.

Jardun smiled too, but seemed a bit irritated at the remark nonetheless.

The Faun lunged again, but this time Aiden threw an energy ball at his legs. Losing momentary control of his sword, Jardun launched a ball back with one hand. To Aiden's surprise, Jardun's ball flattened into a shield-like shape, collided with Aiden's, then reflected it back toward him. The grass exploded just as Aiden jumped out of the way.

Still in shock at the actions of Jardun's energy ball, Aiden managed to keep his balance with his buckler and sword out. He'd never seen anything like that, and the look on his face must have betrayed him.

"That was quick thinking," said Jardun, now moving closer with blade in both hands again. "But also sort of cheating when it comes to our current purposes."

Aiden smiled. "Just tryin' something."

Instead of coming forward to strike, as Aiden had expected, Jardun suddenly reached down and stroked a runic phrase etched into his long blade. The broadsword glowed and released a steady stream of bright fire. Aiden jumped aside, stumbling and rolling in the grass. A trail of flames followed him, turning the shards of grass brown.

"Dammit, man!" Aiden yelled. He'd not been ready for that.

He jumped to his feet and found a runic phrase etched onto the blade of his own sword. Stroking it, he watched water gush forth in a thick stream. Aiden ran forward, dousing Jardun's blade, then turned toward the flaming patches of grass. In moments, the flames were gone and the smell of smoke remained.

"Very nice watercasting," said Jardun, looking impressed. "Seems a bit advanced, considering how you couldn't have possibly taken third-year classes."

Aiden stood back, making sure there were no more cinders hanging about the grass, and took a deep breath. "Well, I've done a lot of reading since then. I just sort of figured it out."

Without warning, the broadsword swept Aiden's legs. He fell onto his back with a thud, realizing he wasn't cut at all, just aching from the sudden fall. He looked up, seeing Jardun ready to strike again.

"You must always be ready," said the Faun, raising the long sword. "You don't get second chances in a real fight."

The blade came down, but Aiden rolled aside. With a surprising amount of strength and speed, Jardun hacked at him again, but Aiden rolled in the other direction. Each time the blade came down, bits of grass and dust flew into the air, covering him.

Aiden, still on his back, thrust his buckler out in front of him just as the broadsword bore down. With a loud crack, he felt the small shield split, and as Jardun withdrew the blade, the buckler unraveled into a white mist. Aiden thrust his blade forward, feeling desperate now, as well as angry.

"I thought this was practice!" Aiden yelled, not bothering to hide his anger.

"Practice staying alive," Jardun replied, forcing Aiden's sword out of his hands.

Aiden rolled sideways, again evading a blow from the broadsword. His own sword had gone flying somewhere just out of reach, and he felt trapped here on the ground. He rolled onto his back again, just in time to see Jardun's sword coming down. With little recourse left, Aiden kicked his feet out, as if to catch the blade, but at the same time, he launched an energy ball directly into Jardun's hands.

Jardun screamed and the blade fell haphazardly. Aiden caught the flat of it with his boots, but balanced it with his still smoking palms. He kicked out and launched the broadsword as far beyond him as he could muster, hearing it clunk somewhere behind him in the field.

Jardun reeled, now looking a bit angry himself, blowing the smoke from his blackened hands and grumbling. Aiden jumped to his feet and began looking for his fallen sword, afraid that it had returned to his arsenal already.

"Are you trying to kill me?" Aiden yelled, incensed.

There was no sign of his blade, so he reached down and drew it from his arsenal, where it had obviously returned. Jardun was silent, but glared calculatingly at Aiden. Without a word, the Faun reached up behind his shoulder. A quiver full of gleaming arrows appeared there, alongside the metallic bow that had materialized in his hand.

"Seriously?" said Aiden with an incredulous tone.

Jardun placed an arrow to the string. He certainly was not joking around. Aiden tried to call his buckler to him, but it would not appear, and Aiden wondered if that was because it had been damaged. Instead, he called his armor to him. A white-alloyed breastplate and helmet quickly materialized and Aiden took a defensive stance.

Aiden had not called his full armor to himself in so long that he had almost forgotten what it felt like to wear it. It was sturdy and unnaturally strong, and at the same time, more flexible and comfortable than it should have been.

As the first arrow flew, Aiden concentrated. Things seemed to slow, if just by a nanosecond. He knew he couldn't run, but he had determined not to. With a swing of his blade, two pieces of arrow clattered harmlessly to the grass behind him.

"Are we done now?" Aiden asked, feeling shaken.

Jardun's expression softened. "I won't lie. I'm impressed. Not many people can stop an arrow like that at point blank range," he said, lowering his bow. "But you may be a bit rusty with some things. All in all, I am pleased."

"I'm so glad your highness is pleased," said Aiden, lowering his sword.

Jardun raised the bow again, setting another arrow to the string.

"Okay okay!" Aiden yelled, raising his sword instinctively. "Can we stop this?"

Jardun smirked. "Of course," he said, letting the bow and arrows vanish from his hands. "And thank you for not blasting my hands off with that fire ball," Jardun added.

Aiden smirked. "I toned it down for ya."

"I trust you know that I wouldn't really hurt you. If I had wanted to, I would've taken your legs off when I had the chance. And if I had hurt you, I am also a healer."

Aiden shrugged, not all that reassured. "I can heal myself," he said defiantly.

Jardun seemed taken aback. "I refuse to believe that," he said. "Most people only excel in one or two areas, but here you claim to be skilled in nearly everything..."

"Well, I was never great at the old *seer* thing..." Aiden smirked. "Other than self-fulfilling prophecy. Thought I'd leave that sort of thing up to *your* type..."

Jardun threw Aiden an annoyed look. "Healing takes extreme patience and concentration. Not to mention it takes blood to heal blood."

"What? I'm just that selfish?" Aiden scoffed. "And anyway, how are you gonn'a test it? Hurt yourself?"

Jardun didn't answer. "We have a week," he said, his tone changed. "Two, tops—to get you up to snuff. I also have some new things to teach you as well."

Aiden, seeing that it was safe, let his armor and sword disappear, sighing. He yawned, hit by a fresh bout of sleepiness from the fitful night.

"How's your illusionry?"

Aiden shrugged.

"Well, let's see it," Jardun prodded. "They told me you were skilled with it."

Aiden stretched his hand out and concentrated. Just as he'd done with the bear and her cub the day before, he produced illusion versions of himself in a circle around Jardun. They mimicked his movements. Jardun smiled, but then stepped forward, trying to touch one of the semi-transparent images. His finger went through it as if it were water.

"Not solid," the Faun said with a frown. "Can you not produce a solid illusion?"

The mimicks disappeared. "Uh... No," said Aiden, confused. "Didn't know that was possible."

"This is third-year stuff," Jardun sighed. "Looks like we'll have to brush up on this as well. Also, you'll need a new sword. I'll teach you how to forge it."

Aiden looked confused, distracted by Jardun's sudden change of topic.

"Do you not remember your training?" Jardun asked, looking irritated. "Didn't Vodin tell you that you'd have to take the next step up and build your own sword?"

Aiden stood pensively. The initial thought had surprised him, but now that he thought about it... Vodin had told him that, at the beginning of his second year. It was strange to think of parting with this sword though. He had made the blade his own. Aiden almost felt embarrassed somehow, that all these years, he'd been using an arming sword. A training sword. No self-respecting D'Tari would use their training sword forever, that much he knew.

"I guess he did," he finally admitted, looking sheepish.

"It's time to move on," Jardun said seriously, moving closer. "From what I gather, you've been keeping yourself sharp fighting Ambler criminals and the like. That's all well and good, but that is absolutely nothing in comparison to what you could face on the road ahead."

**

Aiden walked toward the Great Hall, returning from the training field. Small groups of students passed along the walk before him, and he observed them as he drew near. Sometimes he wondered what it would have been like to live a normal Agnec life. To have been like all the other students.

Master Fentl's hawk-like face came into view as Aiden neared the large building, pulling him violently from his recollections. The two of them locked eyes for the briefest of moments, then passed each other, avoiding eye contact. Aiden shook his head, passing a small cluster of female students as they chatted noisily on their way to lunch.

Aiden stepped into the Great Hall in the midst of a typical lunch period. It looked as though the masters' table had been nearly abandoned by now, but Megan was sitting at its far end. She was all alone. Aiden waded through the circular aisles full of busy tables and finally placed himself across from her.

Megan looked up from her copy of the The Agnec Chronicle,

a more widely-read paper, smiling. "Oh, hi," she said softly, and somewhat cautiously. "So how was your first day?" she finally asked in a playful tone, as if she were a mother asking a child.

Aiden laughed weakly. "Fine I guess... I think Jardun was trying to kill me though," he said, his tone lighthearted.

"Rough training?" Megan asked, putting the paper down.

"He was just pushing me to my limits; at least that's what he said," said Aiden, feeling tired. He sighed. "I don't really know what I signed up for..."

"But I think you do," said Megan, eyeing him. "At the beginning of every student's training, we were asked to make a commitment, come hell or high water. I doubt your mentor skipped over the tradition."

Aiden tilted his head in unwilling acknowledgement. "Yeah... True," he said reluctantly.

"Plus, you're not making me feel any better about my job," Megan added. "If Jardun's worried-"

"Isn't Jardun always a little worried though?" Aiden interjected. "He seems the type."

"Sort of," Megan admitted. "In case you haven't noticed, so am I. Probably more so than him. And anyway, who knows what we're up against in terms of what the N'Iatari are planning..."

"Yeah," Aiden said dully. "Well, we know about the possibility of an army," he added. "And it just doesn't feel right. Like, I get the idea—and it sounds nice and all, but..." Aiden scratched his head and brushed his hair back. "Not if the N'Iatari are involved."

"Exactly," Megan agreed, smiling. "Speaking of the N'Iatari, have you seen this?" she asked, pointing to her paper.

A headline from the *Chronicle* read: "D'Tari Guild Elders Reject Undisclosed N'Iatari Proposal."

"I guess it's official," she said, letting Aiden take the paper so he could read it.

"When did this happen?" Aiden asked, looking back up at her, an eyebrow raised.

"Last night," Megan replied. "I guess it wasn't much of a meeting. You and I both fell asleep so early," she explained, trying to stave off Aiden's look of incredulity. "I mean, it was a long day. I had no idea the meeting would take place last night."

"That must've been the important thing Turlin had to get done," Aiden mumbled. "What actually happened? This article doesn't say much of anything. Doesn't even say what the proposal was."

"Turlin says that Philip Regis arrived—he had some others with him, I don't know their names—and met with the Guild elders and masters... And that was about it I guess. The proposal was rejected almost completely."

"Almost?" Aiden said, looking back up again after skimming the article in the paper.

"Well..." Megan sighed slowly. "Master Fentl was absent..."

"What?" Aiden said incredulously. He stopped, realizing his outburst had caused the inhabitants of nearby tables to stir. "What?" he repeated, lowering his voice.

Megan could only shrug and nod. Aiden's own sour expression

temporarily disappeared when a Faerie arrived and placed a plate of food in front of him. He nodded in thanks.

"I don't know why I'm surprised," Aiden said, examining the contents of his plate. "He and Monadias have already chosen to be ignorant of the whole thing."

"So, without Fentl's vote, Regis has apparently decided to go forward proposing it to the Shadow Congress—which we knew he was going to do anyway—but still," Megan continued. "I've tried to give Master Fentl the benefit of a doubt, but-"

"I can't," Aiden said sharply. "Man's a power-hungry prick."

"That seems uncalled-for," chastised Megan. "I know you're still bitter about your trial, but I'm sure he felt he was just doing his duty-"

"Duty?" Aiden spoke up. "Duty to who? The D'Tari code? To Shai? Or to Lilit?"

"That seems a hefty accusation," Megan retorted, now irritated. "I know I don't know the whole story, but not everyone who wrongs you is going to be N'Iatari. No one is perfect, but that doesn't mean you can just demonize anyone you dislike."

"That's right, you don't know the whole story..." was all Aiden could say, although he knew she was right.

"Okay," Megan said hesitantly, sensing the tension in Aiden's tone. "Well, you just can't know about a person I guess."

"You just can't prove what you think you know about a person... More like it," Aiden muttered, then took a bite of his mashed potatoes.

There was a brief silence while Aiden ate, then Megan cleared her throat. "I realize this may not be easy for you," she said. "But we're in this together, okay? I need your help, and protection. We need to work together."

"So why can't Jardun protect you?" Aiden asked, his tone sincere. "I mean, I guess I'm still trying to understand why they need me."

"I realize maybe we haven't given you perfectly straight answers," said Megan, looking pensive. "I don't really know as much as I wish to either, but I know Jardun's still busy teaching—as are other masters—and all I know is that Vodin demanded that you were the right one for the job."

"But why?" Aiden asked, his tone vulnerable. "And where the hell is Vodin? Why isn't he here?"

"I don't know... And he hasn't been here since, well, since you were exiled."

Aiden shook his head, scrunching his face in thought. For the first time in a long time, he actually wanted to see his old mentor, and to talk with him, but there seemed to be no answers as to how that could be done.

Megan looked at him, appraising his current state of intense thought. "I'm sorry for whatever happened to you here," she said, her tone soft and sincere. "But you're obviously back here for a reason. I don't think you would've come back if there wasn't something important for you here..." She stopped, looking tentative.

Aiden made to protest, but he could see the sincerity in her eyes.

"I know I was being forceful about things when we first met, but still... No one's keeping you here," Megan added.

There was a prolonged silence. Aiden was hoping Megan would change the subject or realize she had something to do, but she seemed just as fixed as he was. He kept stuffing his face, unwilling to think about what actually bothered him. Coming back here felt as though he had given up somehow. As though he'd given up on defying the D'Tari Council, and now he would simply be a stooge for the corruption that he was certain existed in the system. Furthermore, his chest burned with rage whenever he thought of the Griftwalkers, and he knew that if he ever laid eyes on Grant again, it would be near impossible to control his need for revenge.

But here he sat, back at the Guild, fighting every sight and smell, knowing that to give in to the memories would somehow defeat the part of him that had never given up. Maybe he had grown bitter. He had never really had a great plan, but avoiding this place had been a part of it, especially after five years had passed without word from Vodin or even Turlin. After a full fourteen years, he had lost far too much faith in the D'Tari.

Back in the present, Aiden wished for Megan to go silently, but she seemed to be reading his thoughts and then defying them. He concocted a shallow answer simply to irritate her.

"I guess I could just use the money..." Aiden finally muttered.

"You couldn't find another job, something less important?"

Megan said, obviously incensed. "For the money?"

Aiden was silent.

"I, I'm sorry," Aiden finally said, when his plate was near empty.

Megan looked up in surprise. "For what?"

"For being an ass the other day when we first met," he said. "The thought of reliving what happened... It was all too painful. I..."

Megan was silent, looking surprised, still watching Aiden with interest.

"I didn't know how to react," he continued. "The last time Menlir called on me for a favor for the D'Tari, I thought I was doing something helpful and it turned out to be a joke—one that got me into hot water with the Feds and the Council. But the last time I was here, really doing something with my life... I failed. And everyone failed me.'

"But I think I know why I'm going to stick through this," he added in a suddenly positive tone as he fought back the tears that threatened to surface. "No one can convince me that the N'Iatari are something different... Something good."

Aiden scrunched up his face, knowing it must be obvious now that he was emotional. He avoided Megan's gaze, fighting back thoughts that were daring to haunt him. He felt something brush the fingers of his left hand which had been sprawled out on the table.

To Aiden's surprise, Megan's fingers slowly intertwined with his own.

***

After lunch, Jardun found Aiden and led him out of the Great Hall and across the grounds to one of the outlying structures. It was a tall stone building in which the interior was supported by a staircase spiraling upward, while each landing branched to a different room. As Aiden climbed the stairs, he realized these rooms were full of students being taught by instructors.

The Guild was in its first month of classes, and there was a sense of excitement in the air. As he passed closed doors and caught glimpses of class sessions through the small windows, Aiden's senses came alive with memories of his time here. Though this building was not familiar, it reminded him of other classes he had attended on the grounds. He shook his head, trying to focus on the present.

Jardun took him to the top of the stairs. The top room was bright and airy, daylight bursting in through the open window. The contrast to the dark staircase forced Aiden's eyes to adjust. In moments, he realized that the walls were covered in ivy and rows of plants were nestled in a trough along the window. Paintings of pleasant scenes and grand portraits broke out from beneath the ivy in certain places. The floor was relatively clear, to Aiden's surprise, and he followed Jardun inside and took a seat before an ancient wooden desk. Jardun sat behind the desk.

"So..." Aiden began, unable to stop looking at the decor. He could sense that the walls were breathing. "This is your office, huh?"

Jardun nodded. "This is how this is going to work," he got straight to the point, gazing into Aiden's eyes.

Aiden took a seat at the sound of Jardun's matter-of-fact tone.

"Your day will begin with a physical challenge," Jardun continued. "The afternoons will focus on your mind."

Sensing the intensity of Jardun's demeanor, Aiden wanted to protest, thinking about how Vodin had always done things the opposite way, but found himself simply nodding.

"I'm surprised you have nothing to say about this," Jardun said, sitting back in his chair. "No remarks? No jokes?"

Aiden furled his brow. "If I wanted to say anything, I would say it," he said in a clear tone. "Why would I say anything?"

"Well, I hear you've been writing about D'Tari philosophy..." Jardun said, as if probing. "And coming to your own conclusions, regardless of what a lot of others have to say about it."

"And you're going to tell me that I'm wrong?" Aiden said, confused but a little offended.

"Having some articles printed in a local paper doesn't make you right."

Aiden scoffed. "Being narrow-minded doesn't make you right either," he retorted.

"Look," Jardun began, trying to calm his voice. "We may disagree on some things, but I feel you should know as much as you can, especially in the event that you do go up against Lilit."

"You mean the mythical character that N'Iatari blindly

worship?"

"Be a little open-minded, alright?" Jardun said, still calm. He paused, then changed his tactic. "I have no doubt you still remember some of your D'Tari history—I hope," Jardun said, placing a large dusty book on the desk before him.

"All of it."

"All of it?" Jardun said in disbelief.

"In Aignesia's First Age," Aiden began, mock-reciting. "Sion the Oroni gifted the D'Tari properties to the kings of men and Centaurs. Nearly five thousand years later, in the Fourth Age, Innish Dorn went on to become the most famous D'Tari warrior of all... Blah blah blah... And then he became the quintessential incarnation of the hero myth."

He couldn't help but smirk at Jardun's quizzical reaction.

"It's disrespectful," Jardun said, shaking his head. "You may know the stories, but there's so much more than that, and has been since then."

"I was hoping there would be," Aiden said, taking a more serious tone. "It seems like all Agnecs do is cling to the myths of the Old World. Nothing that's true for the now."

"Truth?" Jardun said, then released a half-hearted chuckle. "It can be all true for the now, as you say, if you just know how to dig."

Aiden was bemused, though somewhat reminded of Vodin.

"But for now, we must focus on the *crash course*," the Faun said with a hint of disdain while opening the thick volume on his desk.

"It seems like you know all the Old World stories, so let's go on to what we know of the New."

Aiden shrugged, although deep inside he was eager to see if there was anything interesting yet to learn.

Jardun paused, looking up at Aiden. "First off," he began. "Have you kept up with your meditation?"

Aiden was taken aback by just how much the Faun had sounded like Vodin. There was no reply.

"I'll take that as a no," said Jardun, looking disappointed. "Another thing we'll be working on..."

***

Aiden had been training now for two days, and Jardun had mostly focused him on physical conditioning in the mornings, then meditation and history lessons in the afternoons. Although Aiden's body ached all the time now, he wasn't complaining about the muscle definition he saw developing in his biceps and abs.

Aiden stepped out of the Great Hall, following the dark-haired Faun onto the cobblestone path. They had just finished with breakfast, and without much more than a grunt, Jardun had told Aiden to follow. They arrived shortly at a green lawn strewn with several stalls and wooden buildings. Around the smaller buildings stood wooden balance beams, makeshift racks full of equipment and practice weapons, and various tools.

"We're switching gears today," Jardun said, clearing his throat as he stopped on the path ahead of Aiden.

Aiden stopped in surprise, then looked around wondering if he should expect something to jump out at him.

Jardun walked out into the lawn and looked at some of the balance beams. "Today, we need to begin working on the more advanced practices."

Aiden steadied himself.

"May I see your blade?" Jardun asked, stepping closer to Aiden.

Aiden hesitated. Finally he reached down to his side and drew out his sword from the nothingness. He held it up, watching it gleam in the slivers of early morning sun. He admired it for a moment then handed it to Jardun.

Jardun held the flat of the blade across his hands, also admiring it. "Thank you. I assume Master Vodin gave you this?"

Aiden nodded.

"Do you remember how he did it?" Jardun asked, still inspecting Aiden's blade.

Aiden sighed. "Uh, yeah," he said thoughtfully. "He gave me a special runic formula to etch onto it."

Jardun traced the complex symbols along the blade's center. After his finger had gone the length of the word, the blade began to unravel into white mist. Aiden's eyebrow raised at the sword's actions.

Jardun looked to Aiden with an almost smug smile. He gauged the expression on Aiden's face. "You didn't know you could call your sword back to you that way, did you?"

Aiden shook his head sheepishly.

Jardun walked further out into the grass again. "You obviously excelled in the basic D'Tari defenses: Swordskill, powercasting, and a bit of illusionry... But prior to the third year, most masters won't teach their students how to translate for themselves."

"So how's it work?" Aiden said, shifting on his feet.

Jardun wrinkled his brow at Aiden's impatience.

"And the runes you've already etched onto your sword—those can be helpful, but that's simple stuff compared to what we're going to learn now," Jardun added quickly, stroking his beard. "It's good that you already have a rudimentary grasp of runecasting though. That will help."

"Rudimentary?"

"We'll start small," Jardun said, ignoring Aiden, walking near the wooden stalls, his eyes roaming in all directions. "Here," he finally said, picking up a leather ball from a work table.

Jardun walked back to Aiden and held the ball out with one hand, while lifting his other hand as if writing in mid-air. "First I'll write the rune that symbolizes the *starting*, as you should already know how to initiate a runic formula..."

Aiden nodded. The Faun wrote a small runic phrase which leapt from the air and onto the leather surface of the ball.

"The actual phrase we use differs for each object, but it essentially gives a description of the object and the reason for its use, and how it can be called to use," Jardun said, smiling to himself. "There. But instead of the usual rune that completes a phrase, we use the rune that symbolizes our own names," Jardun added, writing the last rune in the air. "It creates a relationship between the object and yourself. Any questions?"

Aiden shook his head pensively. Although, he grew slowly angry at Vodin for not having explained these things so long ago.

Jardun held the ball up, looking at the runic phrase he had just written, which now stood imprinted on the leather surface. He ran his finger along the length of the phrase and just as Aiden's sword had, the ball began to vanish in a white mist. Jardun took a few steps back and assumed a stance, looking ready to throw something. He pulled his throwing arm back, and the leather ball appeared in his hand. He followed through and let the ball fly until it was on the far side of the field.

"As I'm sure you must have witnessed, but maybe didn't understand why," Jardun continued. "If the translated object stays out of your possession too long, it will disappear and only come back when you call it again."

"I know," Aiden said, feeling a little insulted.

"Or if it gets damaged or broken, it'll disappear, then come back only if you call it... But it might take a while," Jardun carried on.

Aiden made to say something, but realized that this explained why his buckler had been gone for so long after it was damaged.

Jardun looked at Aiden, giving him a sly smile. "Because," he continued, self-importantly. "What we are really doing here is immortalizing these objects. They'll never completely break or damage or anything as long as they are in your Shai."

Aiden stopped. "Let's just call it my arsenal, shall we?"

"Touchy," Jardun said, looking amused. "I see there's another philosophical difference we have."

Aiden ignored the Faun and glanced over to where the leather ball had landed, and sure enough, it was beginning to evaporate into a white mist.

"So... Can I translate anything into my arsenal?" Aiden asked, an almost mischievous smirk forming on his face.

"Well..." Jardun began thoughtfully. "Yes, and no. Whereas all things are possible, not all things are permitted. The D'Tari Council may slap you on the wrist now and then for certain practices," he said, looking to Aiden, "But terrible things have happened to the D'Tari who experiments too broadly with translation..."

"Like what?"

"Just for example, someone once tried translating their cat," Jardun said, grimacing. "It wasn't pretty."

Aiden mirrored the Faun's expression.

"But let's get started," Jardun said. "Time is running short."

Chapter 14
Further Education

Aiden spent the afternoon learning translation. At first it was a matter of learning and memorizing formulas for various objects, but when it came down to it, Aiden discovered that he had to create these formulas on his own.

Aiden didn't want to admit it, but he was actually enjoying himself.

He began translating all sorts of objects, from weapons to farming implements to furniture. Of course, with this process, Jardun taught Aiden how to un-translate things. Otherwise Aiden might have had an entire arsenal full of random, even useless objects.

As Aiden was learning to un-translate objects, he accidentally un-translated his own sword. It looked so odd sitting there on the grass, completely mortal again. Aiden re-translated it in no time at all. He was catching on so quickly, that at one point, he even caught a look of unexpected pride on Jardun's face.

The following day, Jardun began teaching Aiden how to *impart* translated objects into another person's arsenal. It was much simpler than it first seemed, and Jardun demonstrated by transferring his own blade to Aiden by runecasting a special formula directly onto Aiden's body. The process was painless and the runes wore off of Aiden's skin in moments. Now Aiden was able to summon Jardun's blade, as though it were his own.

Of course Aiden had to give it back, which he learned how to do rather quickly, but not without a little struggle. Jardun did not seem to appreciate Aiden's sense of humor, and Aiden finally and begrudgingly returned the blade.

Aiden's mind was alive with thoughts and ideas concerning his newfound D'Tari skills. Over the next day or so, he began practicing translation on almost every object he came across. He discovered that translating something gave the object a superior quality, a power that wasn't quite there before translating. This quality was something that he'd taken for granted before, but now appreciated, as he began to master the translation process.

After yet another day, they met again in the morning out on the training field.

"Today, we're going to learn modification," Jardun began, clearing his throat.

"And that is?" Aiden asked, no longer feeling so resistant to Jardun as a teacher. He was now openly eager to learn.

Jardun found the leather ball and placed it on a table in one of the small sheds and beckoned for Aiden to come near.

"Modification is sort of like translation," Jardun began, looking back and forth from the ball to Aiden. "But of course, as the name states, you modify objects to do certain things. Observe."

Jardun lifted his hand and began runecasting a formula which naturally floated to the surface of the ball and imprinted itself.

Nothing seemed to happen, but slowly the ball began to change shape. Its leathery sinews warped and moved until finally the ball went from being circular to being ovular. Aiden raised an eyebrow.

"So... You can turn a baseball into a football... Nice..." Aiden said, his sarcasm masking his approval.

Jardun scoffed, but now he did so lightheartedly, smiling at Aiden. "This was just an example," he said. "This can get very complex, depending on the kinds of actions you want to take place. Modification can essentially mean *anything* is possible."

Aiden had a mischievous look in his eyes.

"Again, anything is possible, not all things are permitted..." Jardun reminded him.

Jardun began again by showing different sorts of modifications to the ball, starting off with the simple, and ending with the complex. He first turned the ball into a block shape, but in the end, he had turned the ball into a working radio, despite the fact that the exterior retained the leathery appearance of the ball.

Aiden was wide-eyed in disbelief, and at a loss for words.

Aiden's first attempts were fairly clumsy. Despite the straight-forward nature of runecasting, the formulas for modification had to be just right, or the object could be damaged, or worse. Aiden tried working with the ball, but after having gotten one rune wrong, the ball burst its leather seams.

Jardun picked up the ball, saying, "The beauty of modification, is that it's not just a fun way to change things, it serves best as a way to fix things..."

Jardun cast a rune which immediately sewed the leather skin back onto the ball. He picked up the ball and examined it, admiring his work for a moment.

"Let's try again."

***

The masters had all left the table and it was just Aiden and Megan once again. He looked across to her, and realized that they had finally grown somewhat comfortable with each other. He was still making up his mind about her though.

This had become their routine at lunch and dinner: After all the masters left the table, they talked about the day.

"How did things go today?" she asked in a familiar tone.

"Not bad," Aiden said, deciding what to eat off his plate next. "We did modification today. I think I'm getting the hang of it."

Megan looked back with interest. "Oh I love modification," she said excitedly. "Sort of opens up new worlds of possibility, doesn't it?"

Aiden smiled. "So..." he paused. "How come you never learned-"

"To fight?" Megan finished his sentence. "I just never could get the hang of swordskill. But, that's me and about sixty percent of D'Tari trainees actually. Not as many people are as good with the martial arts as you are, ya know..."

Aiden blushed at the compliment, and Megan caught herself, as if realizing what she'd said. "So," Aiden began again, trying to hide his pleasure. "What area did you major in, then?"

"Well, music has always been big for me," said Megan, pushing her empty plate to the side.

"Music?" Aiden said, unable to hide his surprise. "The D'Tari have music?'

"It's a third year option—but I, well, it just really consumed me."

Aiden was pensive. He wondered what sort of things he'd missed by not being at the Guild longer, and felt an anger beginning to return.

"Also, I really have a disdain for unnecessary violence," added Megan.

Aiden looked at her, thinking of Vodin's pacifism. "I guess that's the D'Tari way, right?"

"It should be, not that all types think that way. Why? What's your take on—well, just fighting in general?"

Aiden cocked his head. "I use it to survive," he said flatly. "Sometimes I wish I didn't have to, but the knowledge has come in handy. I've never really had the leisure of not fighting..."

Megan was silent, as if skeptical of Aiden's attitude. There was a silence, as Aiden thought better of what he might say next. He had always felt justified in doing what he'd done to survive, although he also felt torn by the fact that it was unnecessary violence that had killed his mother. But then, he thought of the locket, and the reason why the N'Iatari had used violence to begin with. He had often tried to avoid the question of when violence was necessary, because it sometimes seemed just too complex to deal with.

"I just thought of something," Megan began, pulling Aiden from his thoughts. "Where's D'Natis? Have you seen him?"

"No," said Aiden, his eyes downcast. "Not since that first night. I hope he's okay. I looked for him the other night, but couldn't find him."

"I suppose he's still upset about that thing with Jardun," thought Megan aloud.

"Yeah... I still don't know what that's about."

"D'Natis won't tell you?"

Aiden shook his head. "Jardun won't tell you?"

Megan shook her head.

"Well what about the Shadow Congress?" Aiden said, switching topics rapidly. "When do we leave?"

"Whenever you're done training," said Megan, eyeing him. "Jardun said something about a week, maybe less. I know there's a formal banquet sometime before the sessions start."

"Formal?" Aiden said, pushing his empty plate away. "Are we talkin' black tie?"

"Relatively," said Megan, smiling at Aiden's obvious discomfort with the idea. "The entire event is pretty dressy, so... just be aware."

Aiden moaned. "Oh alright... Least I'll look sexy."

Megan laughed. "Yeah okay," she quipped in mock disbelief. "But seriously, you do need to be on good behavior. I've been an ambassador to all sorts of events like this, and frankly, there are a lot of snobs out there."

Aiden's interest was piqued.

"But now we're dealing with Agnecs from all over the world," Megan continued. "Even look at someone the wrong way, or say something wrong, and they'll decide that you're not worth listening to. To make matters worse, we're sort of a podunk little Guild compared to the training centers of Europe."

"Ever been to Agnec Europe?" Aiden asked, enjoying Megan's passion for her job.

"I've never been anywhere outside the US," she said with some regret. "But anyway," she perked up. "We need to be 'on our game', as the Amblers say. I've been working on the proper protocol and etiquette with Headmaster Turlin every night."

"I wondered what you two were up to," said Aiden, thinking of how he usually trudged off to his shanty after dinner every evening, so tired that he fell asleep moments after getting inside.

"Speaking of which," said Megan, looking at her wristwatch. "I should get to his office."

Aiden felt a sudden and new disappointment at her words, but he tried to hide those feelings. "Oh yeah," he said, standing as Megan got to her feet. "I've got to get some sleep. More modification tomorrow, and Jardun said something about forging a new sword."

***

Jardun and Aiden spent the next morning on modification. Aiden had finally begun to get the hang of it, as much of the work involved memorizing formulas for the most basic modifications, but he also thought of crafting his own. It was going better than he'd expected.

Jardun brought a large leather-bound volume to the work desk. "This book contains all the basic formulas you'll ever need for modification," he said, slamming the thick book down on the wood. "From it, you can also form the foundations of your own formulas."

"Thanks," Aiden said, with some awe.

Before Jardun realized what was happening, Aiden sent some runes onto the book and translated it into own his arsenal. The Faun scowled at him.

"Fine," he huffed. "Borrow it, but I'll want it back at some point."

Aiden smirked.

Soon, with the help of the book and some practice, Aiden was able to change the leather ball into a clock-radio, almost like the kind he'd seen in Ambler stores.

As Jardun worked with him, Aiden tried to modify nearly as many different objects as he had tried to translate. Jardun was bemused, but felt the need to continue changing items back, as if "fixing" them. By the time Aiden had modified almost twenty or so objects, he was struck with a new thought.

"If I can make something into a radio, I can make something into a camera..."

"That seems pointless," scoffed Jardun, though he seemed to be repressing an amused expression. "Why would you do something like that?"

"You never know when something might come in handy," Aiden said, ignoring the Faun's skepticism.

Aiden searched intently for a common object. It was the only time in his life he wished he wore glasses, because he knew they would be a perfect object for this experiment. Although he knew he risked destroying them as well. Finally, he settled on his wristwatch, and using the book he'd been given, he began crafting a set of runes for a new and unique formula.

It was nearing noon, and through lots of trial and error, Aiden felt as though he had made real progress.

"If I may make a suggestion," Jardun interrupted. "Some of the D'Tari masters can use their illusioncasting to project images, almost like photographs or videos—or what have you—onto walls. Perhaps this can be your method of reviewing what you've captured?"

Aiden smacked his forehead in revelation. "Brilliant," he praised the Faun. "I was wondering if it was possible, but you just made it clear."

"Then consider this your final project for modification," said Jardun, smiling.

Feeling like a proud student again, Aiden set to work, trying one rune after another until he had worked out the kinks. Finally, his stomach rumbling with hunger, he pressed the button on the side of the watch—the one which normally would set the time—

and the device hummed gently. Aiden smiled, and was especially happy that the humming was not too loud. He and Jardun looked at each other, both somewhat excited. He pressed the button again, and the humming stopped.

He pressed the second button—one which he had created anew— and from the watch's surface, a shimmering, semi-transparent blue-tinted image emerged. It was much like Aiden had imagined a hologram to look like: A miniaturized three-dimensional moving image of both Aiden and Jardun and their immediate surroundings. Aiden frowned.

"It's not really projecting right," he said, noticing that the image was centralized over the watch's glass surface.

He angled his wrist, turning the watch to one side. His heart leaped when he realized that this movement stretched the image, depending on the angle. He walked toward the far wall of the work shed and angled his wrist until he achieved the right effect. The image amplified itself and stretched across the wall, using it much like a projector screen. Aiden smiled widely.

Jardun congratulated him, "Wonderful effort, I suppose you're more innovative than I gave you credit for."

Aiden thanked him with a nod, then continued fiddling with the watch. He twisted the first button—originally meant as a way to roll the clock hands forward and back—but now, the projected images could be rewound and fast-forwarded, like a video.

He frowned again. "The only thing is, there's still no sound," he said.

"I'm sure we can fix that soon enough," said Jardun. "But we should get some lunch, and then, we're off to make a sword."

***

At the far end of the training field, stood the smithy. Aiden had never seen it up close before. After a satisfying meal in the Great Hall, and a pleasant chat with Megan, he followed Jardun out to the field's edge where the rounded open-air tent stood next to a large, covered forge.

"As per Vodin's request, though I don't know why," Jardun began, looking at the metallic implements hanging from wooden racks inside the tent. "I was instructed to help you forge a swept-hilt rapier. Vodin thought it would best compliment your particular style."

Aiden could not hide his sudden happiness, despite Jardun's obvious dislike of the weapon and technique. Silently, Jardun pulled on a leather apron and threw one to Aiden. Unquestioning, Aiden donned the protective material. In moments, the Faun led Aiden over to the forge, which was already intensely hot and must have been fired up for quite some time. He handed Aiden a pair of thick gloves.

Jardun pulled a large piece of metal up onto the forge, and held it there, shifting it and balancing it with prongs and a long pan until the metal glowed white and red. When the glowing metal almost looked as though it had turned to clay, the Faun placed the pan atop an anvil.

"We need to shape it," he said, looking to Aiden. "Concentrate,

347

and put those gloves on."

After a brief pause, Aiden put on the gloves and slowly began shaping the thick material. It was an awkward sensation, because he couldn't seem to get the shape exactly as he envisioned. He could feel the heat rising and beginning to burn the areas around the flame-proof gloves. When Aiden had only gotten a short way through, Jardun sighed and grabbed Aiden's wrist.

"We need to start over," he said calmly. "It's taking too long and the metal is too cool by now..."

Aiden stepped back and looked at the metal he'd been working. It was a strange, misshapen mess. "Dammit," he muttered.

"Consider this a lesson in patience," said Jardun, smiling, as he pulled another long piece of metal back onto the forge.

Soon, Aiden managed to shape the material into something that actually looked decent. Jardun helped him fashion the edges until the metal was long and thin. The Faun handed Aiden some prongs.

"While the metal is still malleable, we work on the next part."

Aiden was confused, but decided not to question it. He helped hold a new pan and watched Jardun start the process over again. Once that metal was hot and soft, they poured it into the first pan, and Jardun began mixing the alloys together.

"Now, we reshape," said Jardun with a smile.

It was as if something clicked, and Aiden understood. The two of them stood there shaping and molding the metals until they began to smoothly coalesce.

"The first metal we used is steel, the kind we call Sweet Iron," said Jardun as he worked. "It forms the core, but the second metal was another kind of steel—a slight variation, but with much higher carbon content. So," he paused, wiping the sweat from his brow. "We wrap this around the core, like so."

It wasn't long before the two metals had become one, and Jardun had cut away the dross in order to create a long and sleek blade. Aiden, with Jardun's guidance, worked a variety of delicate and decorative details into the face of the blade. This took a great deal of patience, because the blade had become so long and thin. He also managed to etch in his name written in decorative runes.

"Now we temper it," said Jardun, slowly placing the blade over the forge after it had significantly cooled. "Get that bucket of water ready," he said, looking to edge of the tent.

After several minutes of careful observation, Jardun nodded and Aiden dragged the bucket closer to the forge. Quickly, the Faun dunked the blade into the bucket, sending steam billowing. After a moment, he drew up the sword, admiring the look of the hardened steel.

"Is it done?" Aiden said, unable to hide his eagerness.

"The handle feels nice," said Jardun. "But you try it. See how it works for you."

Slowly, Aiden took the sword and felt the smooth grip. He was fascinated as he appraised the sleek metal, amazed that just a short while before, this had been just an ugly hunk of material. He balanced the blade on his finger by the fulcrum, surprised by how well balanced it was. He gave it a quick slash in the air, and smirked.

"Oh this'll do," he said, excited. "This is so much lighter and faster than my arming sword..."

"You are Vodin's pupil after all," said Jardun, rolling his eyes. "Give me a heavy longsword any day. I like to feel something in my arms."

Aiden ignored the comment, still admiring the blade.

"Now we create the rest of the hilt, and it's all yours," said Jardun.

***

"With any luck," said Jardun as he led Aiden to the training field once more in the quiet of the morning. "This will be your last day of training."

Aiden smiled, a sense of accomplishment running through him.

"You've been here only a week and two days," continued Jardun. "Who knew you could learn anything so quickly?" he said with an unexpected smile. Aiden threw him a mock glare. "But anyway, Turlin says he needs you and Megan to attend that banquet Friday evening. So we need to make this count."

Aiden nodded, still not looking forward to attending the banquet, but having resolved that this was all part of the mission.

"I won't lie. I had my reservations about teaching you, but you've done very well," said Jardun, but then he caught himself and his tone changed. He cleared his throat. "Today we work on scrying and illusioncasting."

"Scrying?" Aiden asked, quietly. The word was familiar, though he had no clue what it meant.

"Though I doubt some masters would have a problem teaching this to their students, I consider scrying a bit of a moral gray area," said Jardun, choosing his words carefully.

Aiden's face scrunched, wondering if the comment was intended as a jab at Vodin. He ignored it though, curious to see what Jardun had to say.

"Scrying is the art of listening—really listening in. Sometimes called Second Sight; It takes a great deal of concentration to focus in on what you want to hear. But when you've mastered it, you should be able to hear things from great distances, and through sound-proof walls, and the like."

Aiden stood silent with interest.

"I wouldn't normally teach it, but I feel that it may be useful to you on your mission," Jardun said, looking a bit harassed.

"How's it work?"

"As with meditation, you need to clear your mind, and close your eyes," Jardun began. "Focus your ears on the thing you want to hear."

Aiden closed his eyes, and after a few moments, he heard the call of a mocking bird some ways away. He tried thinking of nothing but that sound, but he was reminded too much of D'Natis. Where was D'Natis? The sounds of other birds began to cloud his hearing, followed by the gentle breeze rustling the treetops. His concentration was broken.

"Nothing's really happening," Aiden said, feeling a mix of worry and frustration.

"Keep trying," said Jardun calmly.

Aiden tried to clear his mind again, but could not stop thinking of D'Natis, then he thought of Megan, then of the upcoming banquet. He sighed.

"It's a difficult skill to acquire," Jardun admitted when Aiden opened his eyes. "An innate skill that can be learned if practiced. Though some never do find it. It's so simple that it makes itself difficult."

"Hard for me to concentrate," said Aiden.

"Well, how do you expect us to move on to illusioncasting?"

"Because I already know how to do that," said Aiden, reminding himself of his sixteen-year-old self.

"Practice scrying whenever you get the chance," Jardun said sternly. "If it's meant to be, it will come eventually. Use it responsibly of course."

Aiden nodded, and felt his spirits lift when he realized that the Faun was moving on.

"I'm eager to get on to illusioncasting anyway," admitted Jardun as he stepped further out into the field. "Scrying's not my strength, and well, I've already mentioned my reservations about it."

Aiden nodded, tucking the idea of scrying away in his mind for later.

"Take a stance," ordered Jardun.

Aiden stood as if ready to enter combat, assuming this was what the Faun had intended.

"I noticed your illusions were simply replicas of yourself. That's great for fooling wild animals—as Megan has reported—but will do nothing against a skilled N'Iatari. Can you do anything else?"

Aiden flushed somewhat, but concentrated. He threw his hands forward and a semi-transparent bird swooped down at Jardun. It passed through the Faun with ease, then disappeared.

"Can't get the damn raven out of your mind, can you?" Jardun said, turning to Aiden.

Aiden sighed, wishing he wasn't so distracted. "I haven't seen him all week, and I'm... I'm worried."

"And you blame me?"

"A little bit," admitted Aiden. "I kind of actually can tolerate you now, but what the hell?" Aiden said, feeling his frustration mounting.

"It's not my fault he went off the way he did," said Jardun.

"It's your fault he's upset in the first place, though," Aiden shot back. "Whatever happened between you guys."

"According to him," said Jardun, now with some anger in his tone. "I'm not about to go into this with you right now," he added, trying to calm himself. "What's between D'Natis and I, will stay between us. What's between you and I, is a mentor and student relationship. That is all."

Aiden paused, glaring at Jardun. "Let's get this straight," he began. "I may be your student right now, but you are not my mentor."

Jardun stopped, looking somewhat taken aback. "But after all you've said about Vodin. Megan told me-"

"Screw that. Yeah I haven't always liked him," said Aiden. "And I've been pissed at him and Turlin for not keeping in touch; Pissed at the Council for what they did to me... But," he stopped, the anger subsiding. "Vodin's my mentor. I realize now that he had the best intentions. Even if the shit did hit the fan."

Jardun nodded, unable to say anything in return.

"And he assigned D'Natis to me—who I trust, with my life," Aiden added with a determined tone. "So, excuse me if I take his word over yours about what went down—whatever the hell it was."

Jardun sighed. "I respect your loyalty to your friends," he said calmly. "That's the mark of a good D'Tari."

Aiden half-nodded. "Thank you."

"I... hope D'Natis is okay," Jardun added, mustering sincerity. "I would like to continue our lesson now, because well, you've got the skills. But I'd like to see them go further."

Aiden nodded, composing himself, and took the stance again.

"This time, consider focusing on another sort of animal, and then project it right in front of you," said Jardun after a moment.

Aiden obliged, and a large cat appeared before him.

"Hold it," Jardun said. "Concentrate until the cat becomes solid. You've got to really focus on what you want it to do."

Aiden focused, though other thoughts tempted to break his concentration. He watched the cat, making it move about slowly, but it seemed no more solid than before. Jardun stepped closer and stick his finger through the illusion.

"Still not solid," he said. "Focus."

"I'm trying," said Aiden, feeling as though his head had begun to hurt.

"The N'Iatari won't give you this long to make it work," said Jardun, walking around the cat. "You know that."

With one last bit of effort, Aiden made the cat jump at Jardun, and for a brief instant, he could have sworn the creature had become a solid. Jardun fell back, but then the cat passed right though him.

"Dammit!" yelled Aiden, letting the illusion disappear.

"I felt something," said Jardun, getting back to his hooves. "Which means you're on the right track."

***

Aiden awoke early the next day, only to hear someone at his door, knocking vigorously.

"What?" Aiden answered with a yawn, annoyed as he pulled the old door open only to feel the morning air dampen the room.

The sky outside was still dark. Jardun stood there with a somber expression. He held a crumpled mess of black feathers in his arms. It was D'Natis. Aiden's heart sank as revelation washed over him. It felt like the bottom of his stomach had fallen out.

"D'Natis! What happened to him?" Aiden asked, trying to grab the wild bundle out of Jardun's arms. "What did you do to him?"

"I found him in the wood," Jardun said as Aiden took the bird and placed him gently on the bed. "I think his wing is broken..."

355

Aiden quickly lit a candle, scorning Jardun to move out of the light because the Faun's shadow was falling on D'Natis' crumpled form. Aiden inspected the bird. D'Natis looked so helpless and still. He was still breathing, but weakly. He seemed unconscious, perhaps in shock, and it did look as though his left wing was broken.

"Where did you find him?" Aiden snapped at Jardun.

"I told you. In the wood," Jardun replied defensively, closing the door behind him. "I think he fell from a tree. He was right in the shadow of this large-"

"Screw it," Aiden interrupted, trying to move the candle closer to D'Natis without getting it too close. "I'll ask him myself."

"Is he...?"

"Yes, still alive," Aiden said.

There was a horrible silence as Aiden bent over the raven. He sighed and reached over to where his duffel bag lay on the stone floor. In seconds, he produced a pocket knife and flipped it open, still observing the bird's slow breathing. Aiden's stare was so intense that Jardun stepped back, looking unsure.

Aiden flinched as he pricked the tip of his thumb with the small blade. He dug in until blood was running thickly, then retracted the blade and closed the knife, throwing it to back into his bag. Quickly Aiden took his thumb and began to write a runic word in blood upon D'Natis' broken wing.

"Don't just stand there," Aiden snapped, finally looking back as if remembering Jardun was in the room. "Go get some water!"

Aiden watched D'Natis' limp form for several intense minutes. He'd hardly noticed that Jardun had gone. He wasn't sure what to think, but he felt as though he could scarcely breath.

When Jardun returned, Aiden wiped his face with his sleeve and held his head down to the bird's tiny chest. The raven's breathing was no longer so shallow. In another minute, D'Natis began to move restlessly, his left wing twitching as if life were flowing back into it.

D'Natis' large eyes opened and he gazed up at Aiden. For the briefest of moments, the raven actually brushed his head affectionately up against the man's outstretched hand.

Aiden had almost forgotten that his thumb had bled profusely all over the bed sheets. He no longer felt the pain, and simply looked down, smiling at the bird. Aiden exhaled a sigh of relief, stopping himself from wanting to caress and hug the bird. D'Natis was still a Raven Lord, and that sort of thing was simply not done.

"You gave us a scare..." Aiden said, not wanting to sound like a father, or worse, a pet-owner. "What happened?"

"I take it you healed me," D'Natis said, his voice still a bit weak.

Aiden nodded, then looked to his own thumb with the realization that the wound had closed up, now that D'Natis had been healed.

D'Natis finally managed to get to his feet, but then maintained a roosting position on the bed. He croaked quietly, looking over to where Jardun stood.

"I'll admit I was upset... And just wanted to stay out of sight until you were done," D'Natis said, glaring for a moment at the Faun, whose expression was a mix of awe and sadness.

"I had found a nice place out in the wood," D'Natis continued. "It reminded me a lot of my old nest not too far from here, long before I'd met you. Everything was fine for most of the week." D'Natis coughed. "Water, please."

Aiden turned to Jardun. "Did you bring the water?" he asked in a demanding tone.

Jardun silently handed him a bowl of water which Aiden placed in front of the raven.

"Thank you," D'Natis said after a few moments. "But some time a few days ago, I saw a large shadow speeding through the wood. I was looking for food and I was attacked."

"By what?" Aiden asked.

"A Windigo," D'Natis replied, still shivering. "I didn't have time to get up to my tree. I didn't even hear the beast approaching... I'm supposed to be smarter than this. I am a Raven Lord after all."

Aiden shook his head. "Don't worry about it," he said softly. "It's not your fault, right?"

D'Natis shuddered. "The fall broke my wing," D'Natis continued. "I saw that shadow again, and it must have spooked my aggressor. The Windigo fled, and I was left to die there in the shadow of my tree."

Aiden tried to wrap D'Natis in a blanket. "Wait, so the shadow wasn't the Windigo?"

"No, I don't think so," said D'Natis weakly. "If anything, it was helping me, I suppose."

Aiden could clearly see the Windigo that had attacked him when he was only fifteen, and how it too had been spooked by a strange shadow creature.

"I'm... glad that everything's alright," Jardun finally spoke up, looking uncomfortable.

"Oh, you are?" Aiden said, standing. "If it weren't for you, he wouldn't have been out in the woods like that."

"I thought we discussed this. You can't possibly blame me for this," Jardun said, his expression stern. "If it weren't for me, he'd still be out there."

"What the hell happened between the two of you anyway?" Aiden finally said, his tone rising. "All those years ago-"

"No," D'Natis cried, trying to shift positions uncomfortably.

Aiden rushed to the raven's side and wrapped the blanket around him again. "Save your strength," Aiden said softly. "Just relax."

"We cannot speak of this now," D'Natis said. "But perhaps I was being a bit foolish,"

"And petty," added Jardun with a tone of indignation.

D'Natis released an angry squawk that echoed throughout the small space. "There's nothing petty about being alone is there? Nothing petty about being the last of my kind! And it's all your fault."

Aiden had never seen the bird this angry before, and he was almost positive D'Natis would fly across the room and peck out the Faun's eyes, if he had had the strength.

Jardun was silent, but his face grew red.

The silence was broken by someone knocking at the door. Aiden, frustrated at both Jardun and D'Natis, walked toward the door and swung it open. Megan stood there, wrapped in a warm bathrobe. Aiden was suddenly very aware of the fact that he was only wearing his boxers and a t-shirt, but he did not have much time to think about it.

"What is all the shouting about?" Megan asked, her eyes dark from sleep and her short hair disheveled.

"Drama," Aiden said, closing the door after Megan entered.

Aiden quickly pulled on his pants and sat back down on the bed next to D'Natis. Megan took a closer look and gasped at the sight of the raven and the blood-stained bed sheets.

"What happened?"

"He's okay," Aiden said, still feeling waves of frustration toward the feud between the raven and the Faun.

"I believe you now," Jardun said sheepishly to Aiden, after a moment.

"About what?" Aiden said, his tone indifferent.

"About being a healer..."

Aiden calmed somewhat. Jardun's comment might have bounced off of him, but Aiden only slightly acknowledged it with a nod. D'Natis' condition, as well as the strange shadow creature, were still heavily on the forefront of his mind.

Aiden looked to Megan as she gazed helplessly at D'Natis. "He'll be alright. Just needs some rest," Aiden said, then looked into the raven's large eyes. "Just sleep now, D'Natis. And stay close, because we're leaving as soon as we can."

***

While D'Natis rested back in the shanty, Jardun took Aiden for a walk while the sun was still low in the sky. Aiden had hardly noticed how the weather had been growing rapidly cooler, until today. He couldn't think of much else beside what had happened earlier that morning, and how torn he was between almost wanting to like Jardun, and the loyalty he had to D'Natis.

"I apologize for what happened this morning," Jardun finally broke Aiden's thoughts. "I was only trying to help."

"I know," Aiden admitted. "Sorry... I panicked."

"I feel the need to tell you that you should work on that temper, and start showing some respect," said Jardun.

Aiden made to protest, but Jardun's words were sincere, despite how old-fashioned and strict they might normally seem.

"But I'll also say that I'm proud to have been your teacher, at least for a time," the Faun continued. "You obviously know what you're doing, even if you missed some steps along the way."

Aiden's cheeks flushed, and he couldn't find the words to respond.

For a few silent moments, Aiden realized the two of them were walking the long way around the grounds. A way which would eventually take them back toward the Great Hall, and finally to the Headmaster's office. It was only a matter of time before Aiden and Megan were meant to leave, but he knew that Turlin had insisted on one last briefing.

"I know we haven't had time to go over all of New World Agnec history," began Jardun after some minutes. "But I hope now you have a more balanced view."

Aiden's mind switched gears. "Well, before now, I've only heard the story of how A'dhem opened the forca locus and ended the War of All Worlds, but I didn't know that Sion translated himself in order to become the unKing."

Jardun nodded.

"Can someone really do that, though?" Aiden asked, thoughtfully. "Could someone really translate themselves into their own arsenal, and survive?"

"Well, Sion was an immortal," said Jardun. "It's not implausible. Legend says that he became part of the fabric of the universe itself, somewhere between man and animal... Somewhere between earth and star dust, I suppose."

Aiden marveled at Jardun's words, but couldn't ignore his own natural skepticism. "And that stuff about Lilit, I still don't know."

"What stuff?" said Jardun, smiling as if knowing what was coming.

"How could she have survived Resheph's death? How in the world could she have been his daughter?"

Jardun chuckled. "That's why we call it legend, but sometimes we also call it faith. It's not so important to understand every detail, as much as it is to know the finer points. I personally believe Lilit is real because, well, because I believe Shai is real, and that the story of how Agnecs came to be in the New World is also real."

"So, that's your faith without proof, huh?" said Aiden.

"I see proof in the fact that I hear from Shai in my meditation, but also in that I exist. I see proof in that the N'Iatari are so dead-set against everything that follows Shai. They're afraid that he's real as well."

Aiden was a little off-put by the absolutism in Jardun's tone. "I don't know," said Aiden, breathing in the cool air. "I need more proof. And don't tell me the proof is in these powers. There's a science to these abilities that could simply be part of the way the universe works—and Amblers just haven't figured it out yet."

"Interesting thought," said Jardun calmly. "And I agree, but as I also see the universe as something that emanated from Shai, then your point is moot."

Aiden shook his head in confusion.

"Shai is the foundation—much like the basic runes you've learned and mastered—and from Shai everything expands outward into existence."

Aiden's mind seemed ablaze. Vodin, in all of his lessons, had never talked this deeply about his beliefs.

"Furthermore, because we come from him, he is also a part of us, and we are a part of him," said Jardun.

"But if following Shai, or communing with it—or whatever—is about helping people and doing the right thing, then what about, you know, all the shit in this world? All the evil?" said Aiden, his insides fighting each other.

"Much of what we perceive as evil, is only evil because we don't like it," said Jardun as they began to turn a corner and the Great Hall came into view. "Death is not evil, but murder is. Natural death brings rebirth. Everything dies so other things can live. It's the cycle of existence. People who intentionally do evil things are not really evil by nature. It takes some time for them to become blind to the Shai within."

"What about love?" Aiden said, surprising even himself. "I mean, even some D'Tari teach that some kinds of love are wrong. And what about all the evil in this world done in the name of love?"

Jardun smiled. "Love is the reason," he said softly. "That we exist. I know a lot of us forget this simple thing. I for one, experience a deep presence of Shai whenever I feel love, and I feel that somehow the two are eternally bonded. So how can any true love be wrong? Where there is resentment, jealousy, fear, and rage that leads to hate... There can be no real love. What many people call love is not true love at all."

Aiden thought of his mother. She had always been what love meant, and he would have done anything to save her. He wondered if the feelings he had for her were at all truly connected to a sense of Shai—whatever that could even mean. He held back a tear, walking in silence. Jardun's words echoed gently in his mind for a few minutes.

Soon, they were walking into the Great Hall and finding their way into Turlin's office. As Aiden entered the ovular room, he half-expected to see Vodin behind that desk, but was met by the dark-skinned Half-Elf instead, followed by Megan who sat across from him.

"Ah now we can begin," said Turlin as Aiden sat down beside Megan. "Master Jardun, thank you, but this only concerns these two now," he said, looking to the Faun.

Jardun nodded, although looking somewhat put out. He addressed Aiden, "I'm sure I'll see you again some time. Try to remember all that you've learned."

Aiden, still deep in thought, nodded. "I will," he replied, unthinking. "Thanks."

With that, the Faun disappeared and the door closed. Turlin looked to both Megan and Aiden, his expression hard to read.

"Before you leave," Turlin began quickly. "There are some things you should know."

Megan looked worried, and Aiden tried to push Jardun's conversation from his mind for the moment.

"As you know, some of the D'Tari Council are not too thrilled that we're sending you along to the Congress," continued Turlin. "Even some of the masters here are a bit touchy about it. They're not convinced of anything, and want to avoid causing a scene. Nevertheless, I know you both are firm believers in our cause. You both have good reason to be convinced that the N'Iatari are doubtless a threat.'

"Our sources tell us that the N'Iatari are currently under the helm of Lord G'nehon. Apparently, he and Senator Regis have some sort of connection, and of course Regis denies any negative press concerning the doings of G'nehon."

"Why is that name so familiar?" Megan said pensively.

"Sadly, you may know that name because G'nehon was the man who led the attack on your village," Turlin said to Megan. He sighed.

Megan's face changed, as if reliving scenes of horror. "Yes," she said slowly. "I heard them shouting his name... Proudly."

"Apparently though, even the D'Tari Council is not convinced of G'nehon's involvement," Turlin said with a frustrated tone. "Now, more than ever, do I understand Vodin's frustrations with the Council."

Aiden sat up, thinking about the Headmaster's words.

"As I've said, the only reason you two are even getting passes into the Congressional sessions is because the majority of the Council voted on it. Had some other people gotten their way... Well, I might've sent you anyway, but it would have come at a cost. At any rate, we met with Senator Regis, and I cannot deny that his way with words and mannerisms will be hard to counter. He seems to know the workings of the Agnec world only too well, and now that we understand more fully his plans..."

Megan sank in her seat. Aiden could tell that she was slowly spiraling into a panic.

"Well, to sum up, he proposes that a united militia be formed from all the D'Tari and N'Iatari Guilds. Not only that, but it would also create a budget for this process—one that would slowly edge out this Guild, as most of the money for upkeep and facilities would go to a common purse. But, being the last known D'Tari Guild in this country, most of the actual money would end up going to N'Iatari Guilds.'

"I've looked at the rough outline, and I noticed that he wants to designate tuition fees—regardless of which Guild they're actually paid to—into a fund that would dispense it out evenly to all the Guilds."

"Doesn't sound like such a horrible idea, in theory," said Aiden, although he still distrusted the N'Iatari.

"In theory, it could work, if it were truly even. But the proposal seemed much more like a business plan than a guide for governance. If only we were as equally profitable as those other Guilds," said Turlin. "But we're simply not growing. And who decides which money goes to what Guild? Eventually, the bigger Guilds receive more attention, and the smaller ones disappear. I wish it didn't come down to this—the money, that is."

Aiden was suddenly reminded of his own payment, which he had eagerly thought about at first. It no longer seemed all that important.

"But it's so much more than that," Megan chimed in. "Maybe they're making it about money, but we know it's about what they stand for... And what we stand for. I mean, how could we just let them overtake us like that?"

"I appreciate your zeal," Turlin said, smiling. "But to make things worse, I wasn't very partial to their plan for the governance of the militia itself. There was also a clause that caught my eye; Something about being able to co-opt the militia as a police force. Again," Turlin nodded, seeing Aiden look as though about to comment. "It does sound like a good idea on paper... But Regis proposes that he and Tilli Rosen create a new organization to govern the military force. Of course, it would be sponsored by the Shadow Congress, naturally..."

"Tilli Rosen?" Aiden asked.

"Yes, like Regis, she's also a self-proclaimed 'informed Ambler'," said Turlin flatly. "She's been his campaign partner and aide for a while now, and we have little to no information on her background—but she seems to have some considerable appeal to other Agnecs in the Congress."

"Hmm..." Megan hummed. "So, they wouldn't let the Peacekeeping and Security Council govern this new militia?"

"No, they propose forming a new council that would oversee everything independently. I fear they would essentially treat the Guilds as a breeding ground for new recruits, channeling graduates directly into their own services, especially when one takes into account the ambition of this concept." Turlin sighed, looking suddenly worried. "As we suspected, they want this to be an international project, one that would supposedly unite all those who use the properties, but so far, I've heard no consensus on the general philosophy or ethics being employed."

Aiden could hear the anxiety in Turlin's tone.

"With the press ignoring any negative N'Iatari activity, I fear there could be many who wouldn't so much as bat an eye at this idea. After all, who wouldn't want to create a system that could help protect Agnecs a little more efficiently? As I recall, Aiden, that's part of your complaint, is it not? That we don't have a unified system; we're just independent villages protecting ourselves?"

Aiden perked up, then saw the sincerity in Turlin's eyes. "Yeah, partly," he agreed. "But at what cost do we sacrifice our independence just to feel safe? I mean, I cannot trust the N'Iatari. I just can't. If I knew nothing about them, I would probably jump at a chance to vote for something like this."

"Exactly," said Turlin. "Regis feeds on people just like you."

Aiden threw him an offended look.

"That is to say, people who want change for the better. People who are a bit fed up with the old way we've always done things," added Turlin. "Those are not bad things to want, but we must know exactly why we want them, and how to make them happen. I'm never too prone to trust a politician myself..."

Aiden nodded in full agreement.

Chapter 15
Banquet of Shadows

Megan, Aiden, and a recovering D'Natis left the Guild grounds at just before noon. In nearly fifteen minutes' time, the trio found themselves stepping out of a door onto a cracked sidewalk. It was an alleyway right behind what sounded like a wildly popular club. The throbbing music was so loud that Aiden swore some of the bricks in the walls were shaking.

Aiden straightened the bag on his shoulders, making sure that D'Natis was still sitting comfortably. He was glad to be back in *normal* clothes again. Megan followed closely, also in her Ambler clothes, looking behind her only to see the door they'd just traveled through as it began to evaporate.

Aiden stared from one end of the alley to the other. The area was surprisingly clean, and very deserted. The music continued throbbing from inside the building behind them, and he of course expected to see people congregating around such a place, but there was no sign of life.

Megan examined the pavement several feet from them. In moments, she discovered that she'd been standing on a downward slope that led beneath street-level.

"Here we go," she said, smiling.

Aiden watched as Megan traced a rune alongside the concrete

slope. Slowly, the ground began to open. Small, blue lights lit the path before them as they descended into the space, the sunlight fading fast from sight. Once on level ground, Megan traced another rune beside her on the wall, and the pavement ceiling above them slid closed seamlessly. They wandered through the dimly lit stone hallway. Aiden could feel D'Natis shifting restlessly as they walked further downward.

"So..." Aiden began, his eyes glancing in all directions, despite the fact that there was little to see. "Do you know where we're going?"

"Mostly," said Megan in a fairly confident tone. "There's really only a few good ways to get there, and I thought we'd take the Underground. Shouldn't take long."

"Aren't we already in D.C.?" Aiden asked as they slipped through another stone door and beheld a huge railway roundhouse.

"Yeah, but we have to go in from the Underground side," Megan persisted. "Or else they might get a little suspicious. Besides, it's just a few minutes by railcar."

Aiden shrugged.

As they walked toward the roundhouse, crossing tracks and passing a thin line of waiting patrons, Aiden saw some unfamiliar creatures. They were short with gray skin tinted green. They looked almost reptilian but were most certainly mammals, with stringy hair and grimy black claw-like fingernails.

"Don't stare at the Orcs," Megan whispered to Aiden as they took their place in line.

"First time I've seen them... Ever," Aiden admitted. "Didn't know they were allowed out in public."

"The Confederation of Orc Tribes finally pushed through a resolution in the last Shadow Congress," said Megan, as the line began to progress. "They made a treaty with the Blue Dwarves. The move back into the public eye has been slow but steady."

"No conflicts? Or anything?"

"Nothing serious to speak of, no," said Megan. "I think they've just been seriously misunderstood over the years."

"I'd still be cautious," said Aiden instinctively, ignoring his mother's words of warning against assuming prejudices—which echoed in his mind suddenly.

"You just can't know about people," said Megan with a knowing glance.

After Megan bought their tickets, they, along with several others, crowded into the glass-chambered vestibule to wait for the railcar. Aiden was reminded of that first day he and Vodin had done this very thing, and how surprised he had been at the speed and relative silence of the railcars. Before Aiden had much time at all to delve into the memory, the railcar pulled up and the passengers piled inside.

Soon they were flying over the tracks, the vehicle tipping and swaying, but never derailing. In mere minutes, Aiden began seeing signs, posted along the rails, saying things such as *'To Congressional Meeting Hall'* or *'Delegate Lodging'*. The railcar came to a halt, almost throwing Aiden from his seat, and several passengers stood. Megan led the way.

As they stepped back onto the old stone pavement, Aiden wondered, "Why couldn't we just have traveled by door into the Underground—or jumped, or something—to where we need to be?"

"Impossible," said Megan, leading them onward at a brisk pace down the old stones. "As a security measure, the Dwarves put a block on that sort of thing—well, also at the coercion of the Peacekeeping and Security Council. I mean, if that was possible, then just about anybody—by anybody of course, I mean, rogue D'Tari, Elves, Dwarves, Dark Faeries, whatever—could just jump right into some random village whenever they wanted and do whatever they wanted..."

"I see what you mean," said Aiden as they began heading steadily up a rise.

From the rise, they could see quaint stone villas below emerging from the stone itself. Despite the fact that they were underground, the homes seemed to have a rustic charm about them, surrounded by well-tended gardens full of giant illuminating mushrooms. Aiden realized he was looking down into a small valley which held a village, complete with shops, pubs, and other establishments.

Before Aiden had realized it, they approached an ornate doorway covered in various runic symbols. Megan traced one of the runes, and the door slid open for them. Once past another stone hallway, they found themselves in a dark room that smelled much like a basement. A small light told Aiden that their path was ahead of them up some steps. Megan led them up the rickety stair and knocked on the door.

A loud series of clanking sounds—like the undoing of locks—sounded from the other side of the old door. A large, bald man with a huge matted beard peered out through the cracked door. "Gowry Tavern and Inn," the man croaked. "Have a reservation?"

"Yes," Megan said, at first put off by the man's demeanor. "For the Mount Katahdin Guild, I'm Megan—Headmaster Turlin sent a lettercast."

"Lettercast?" said the man, then slammed the door for a moment.

"Quite a way with people," mumbled Megan as she threw a cautious glance to Aiden.

"You're one of those D'Tari types," said the man as his face appeared again. "Yeah, we got it. Come in."

Megan and Aiden stepped over the threshold, D'Natis still on Aiden's shoulder. As they entered the room, Aiden wasn't at all surprised to find that the place looked much like the Gryphon Claw back in Philly. Pipe smoke filled the room, Agnec patrons laughed and drank at the bar, and ornate paintings of Old World types covered the walls. No one seemed to notice the newcomers.

"Here," said the large man, his huge fingers placing a skeleton key into Megan's hand. "Room's at the top of the stairs, just through that door. End of the hall." He pointed them toward the old door at the end of the busy room.

"Just one room?" said Megan, confused. "I was under the

impression that there would be two-"

"You want the room or not?" the man barked. Apparently, he was not used to people questioning him.

"We'll take it," said Aiden, appraising the man. "It's good. Thanks."

"They call me Barty the Keep," said the big man, as if feeling forced to introduce himself. "If you need anything, ask for me..."

Megan nodded and led the way through the room of patrons, as if wanting to distance herself from Barty as soon as possible.

"Yeah, I doubt he would come running too quick, even if we did ask for him," Aiden muttered.

After they passed through, Aiden closed the door behind himself, but not without first seeing the large man staring after them, Barty's dark eyes particularly following Megan. Now inside an old foyer, they ascended another rickety stair, only to find an upper level full of rooms.

"Room 12," said Megan, looking at the number on the key. "Right here."

Megan found the door at the end of the hall. After a few moments' struggle, she managed to get the door open with a loud click and a creaking whine.

The room was very small with only a wrought-iron bedstead, a night stand, and an old wardrobe. There was also a small window with rays of sunlight filtering in through the cloudy glass. It was the first daylight Aiden had seen in an hour or so, and he was at least thankful to have a window. Otherwise, the room reeked of mildew and the bedspread seemed questionable, but he'd been in worse places.

"Well," he mused, still standing in the hall. "At least this part's above street level."

Megan appraised the room, frowning. "I guess it'll have to do..."

"So..." Aiden said, sighing. "Tomorrow's the banquet, right?"

"Yep," said Megan, still staring at the tiny room in thought. "Look," she began, her tone changed. "This is awkward... I guess I thought there would be two rooms-"

"No big deal," said Aiden as D'Natis hopped off of Aiden's shoulder, landing atop the wardrobe. "We're both adults."

"Yeah," Megan said, sheepishly. "Let's set some ground rules..."

"I'll take the floor," Aiden instantly conceded.

***

Aiden had been extremely tired from a long day when he first hit the pillow, and thought he'd drifted into sleep for a moment there, despite the hardness of the floor beneath him. He was soon reminded of why D'Natis usually slept outside or somewhere else. The bird had been nestling for a while in a small pile of top sheets Aiden had pulled off the bed, but at some point had grown restless and began wandering around the room. Aiden kept hearing the sound of tiny claws scratching around on the old wooden floorboards. He could feel the reverberations beneath him.

"Can you stop that?" Aiden asked in an irritated whisper, trying

377

not to wake Megan.

"I realize you're tired," D'Natis said quietly. "But after all, you know my routine. Also you were the one who wanted me to stay inside tonight... So I say this without apology: Get over it."

After Aiden had finally gotten back to a semblance of restful sleep, he was disturbed again by the drunken stumbling of someone in the hall outside the door. In moments, the person had found their key and eventually the correct room, and tumbled inside, slamming the door behind them.

Aiden was angry again, but finally managed to calm himself. The rest of the night was marked with the occasional and very random sounds of revelers from downstairs, odd noises from the outside streets down below, and the general creaking sounds which the ancient house naturally made. In the midst of this rough night, Aiden began to wonder if he hadn't been a bit spoiled by sleeping in the peace and quiet of the Guild for the last week or so.

"Hey," came Megan's gentle voice after Aiden felt as though only two minutes had passed. "Time to get up."

Feeling as though he must have been dreaming but not remembering, Aiden sat up, his back aching from the hard floor. Megan was already dressed and tidying up the room.

"We have a couple things to get done today, before the banquet," said Megan with a focused tone.

"Like what?" Aiden said, yawning as he finally stood, the vertebrae in his back popping loudly.

"You don't have a nice suit, do you?"

"Crap," Aiden said with a sigh. "No, because I hate wearing ties."

"Well, then you'll love what we're doing today..." Megan said with a knowing smirk.

Aiden scowled, knowing what that meant. Having slept in his clothes, he just needed to freshen up. In moments, they were closing the door behind them and locking it with the ancient skeleton key. Megan led them down the hall, D'Natis once again on Aiden's shoulder.

Soon they were out on the Ambler street, where Megan led them on to a busy lane full of sidewalk shops and boutiques.

"Where am I supposed to find a suit?" Aiden asked hesitantly.

"Well...." Megan smiled. "I read about a nice little place up here..."

"An Ambler shop?"

"Yeah," Megan conceded. "But that's fine. Some of the money the Headmaster gave me was converted into Ambler bills. Should be enough."

Aiden nodded, accepting that this was happening after all. He said nothing, though he wanted to.

After fifteen minutes or so of walking along the old shops, Megan's face finally lit up. Silently she tugged at Aiden's arm and they wandered inside a small storefront shop to their left. It was the sort of place Aiden would have never even approached unless extremely provoked.

Of course, now it was different. He reminded himself of his

mission.

He felt less awkward about the whole experience because Megan was by his side. Mannequins in nicely tailored suits stood all around the store, casting sophisticated poses in all directions. Unsure where to start, Aiden stopped to look at one of the well-dressed mannequins, unknowingly being approached by an employee.

The man—who was dressed almost as nicely as the mannequin, aside from being less formal—was suddenly by Aiden's side. "Uh, sir," the employee began in a cautious voice. "We don't allow animals or pets of any kind in this establishment."

Aiden had almost forgotten about the large raven on his shoulder. D'Natis glanced sideways at Aiden.

"Oh, sorry..." was all Aiden could muster as he turned back toward the front door. "Be right back," he told Megan as he passed her on his way out.

"Sorry, D'Natis," Aiden told the raven once outside. "Just give me an hour or so, okay? I have to give these snobs my business. Alright?"

"I am not your pet," growled D'Natis, his feathers bristling. "Make sure he knows that."

"Alright," said Aiden, smiling at the bird. "See ya in a bit."

With a terse glance, the Raven Lord set off into the sky, surprising a small crowd of passing onlookers. Aiden wandered back into the shop and found Megan, who was already talking to the employee.

"He's so touchy sometimes," Aiden mumbled to Megan.

In moments, the employee, though still looking at Aiden as if he somehow would produce another large bird into the store, began to help him look for a suit. It was a new and weird experience for Aiden. He had never had someone go find all the pieces to a suit and then make sure that it fit him in all the right places.

After some trial and error, with input from Megan, it all seemed to come together. Aiden stood there appraising himself in the mirror.

"Not as bad as I thought..." said Aiden to himself, no longer caring that Megan stood there off to the side.

The single-breasted lapel jacket was comfortable and lightweight, and the white collared shirt was equally so. The pleated pants seemed like they would be useful for any sort of swift movement, and even the dress shoes seemed sturdy despite their elegance. Better yet, everything was dark gray while the tie was black. Aiden had asked them to find him a longer, black coat to go with it, just to complete the look.

After all, if he was going to be the bodyguard, he might as well have some sort of style.

"It's sort of amazing..." said Aiden, still looking at himself in the mirror.

Megan's cheeks were turning slowly pink.

"What do you think?" Aiden asked her.

She released a slight cough. "Looks good," she said after an awkward moment.

***

Aiden and Megan took their time wandering back through the shops and the streets. Aiden could not stop thinking of Megan's expression when she had first seen him in the suit. He began wondering about her. Who was she really?

"So, what do you do... I mean, for fun?" Megan's voice broke through Aiden's thoughts.

He stopped, surprised. She had beaten him to the very question he'd meant to ask her. "Uh, not much I guess," he said. "I read... and write, sometimes. You?"

"The same," she said, looking unsure what to say. "Of course music, like I told you before. What kind of things do you write?"

"Sometimes just things on my philosophy about the D'Tari and the Shai... Things like that."

"Cool," said Megan, smiling. "I'd like to read them sometime."

"Yeah..." said Aiden, feeling suddenly strange. "Sure. I mean, I don't think you'd find it all that interesting."

"Oh," said Megan, looking suddenly put out. "Well, I might. You never know."

"Yeah..." Aiden wanted to change the subject. He knew that if Jardun's beliefs were any indicator of the things he'd taught Megan, then there was a chance some of his, Aiden's, views might not be well-received by Megan. Thankfully, he saw the street-side front of the Gowry Tavern and Inn—which to all Amblers, just looked like a run-down hotel and pub.

D'Natis met them out front, perched on a lamp post. "Having

fun are you?"

"Where were you? Why the hell didn't you come back?" Aiden asked the raven, holding out his arm as a perch.

"Just thought I'd stretch my wings a bit," D'Natis quipped. "Especially after that night with you." He landed on Aiden's arm, then hopped to his shoulder.

Aiden rolled his eyes as the three of them approached the tavern's old double-door entrance.

"Tonight I'm gonna pry open that window and let you roam," Aiden resolved.

"Good... Don't know why you didn't think of it before," D'Natis sighed. "Sometimes the greatest solution is the one right in front of you..."

Aiden rolled his eyes.

The old tavern was as rowdy as ever, and just like the Gryphon Claw, the front room was for Ambler types. It looked just like a rustic old pub for people who enjoyed the look and the ambiance, but as the trio gave a password and entered a secret side door, the sights and sounds gave way to the Agnecs who were even louder and wilder.

Megan turned suddenly to Aiden, "Well, we've got a few hours, and not to embody the stereotype," she began with a slight laugh. "But I need some time to get ready."

"For the banquet?"

"No, for combat," she chided jokingly. "Yes for the banquet. I'll be upstairs."

Aiden grinned sheepishly. He watched her ascend the old staircase, suddenly lost in her movements.

D'Natis pecked at his shoulder.

"Ow! What was that for?" Aiden asked the bird, glaring at him.

"Getting chummy, I see..."

"Just friends," said Aiden without thinking, though his gaze wondered back to the stairs in search of Megan. "Just friends..." She had disappeared. "Oh well. I guess we can hang down here for a while..."

They entered the pub and took a small table in the corner, watching people laugh and drink and go about their business. In a far corner opposite them, Aiden saw three Orcs sitting with some Dwarves. He tried to see what they were doing without seeming obvious.

"Foul creatures," said D'Natis quietly, forcing Aiden to look away. "I'm surprised to see them here. The Underground is certainly one thing, but here..."

Aiden raised an eyebrow. "Not a fan then, huh?"

"Not really," said D'Natis. "It's especially a bit disheartening, considering they were at bloody war with the Blue Dwarves not even ten years ago. Banned from all public meeting places and whatnot..."

"I didn't know you followed any of that," said Aiden pensively. "You never seem all that interested in politics."

"Or perhaps I just pay more attention than you realize," said D'Natis with a serious tone. "Nevertheless, I cannot trust them.

The Raven Lords have spent more time keeping Orcs in line than most other Agnecs... And they were not fond of us."

"Speaking of Raven Lords," said Aiden, looking into the bird's large eye. "What were you actually doing today? Were you upset?"

"Perhaps," admitted D'Natis. "But I let that go after a bit. Typical Ambler policy anyway. No, I encircled the streets and made some connections, as you might say, with the local creatures. Mostly crows and squirrels."

"Oh, okay," said Aiden, his face still scrunched in wonder. "Any thing I should know?"

"Not much. Some crows on Third Street indicated that the night life around here is nothing to be desired when it comes to human activity... Lots of crime I suppose. Perhaps I'll know more tonight, as I intend on going out a while."

Aiden hummed and they sat in silence for a while, simply taking in the atmosphere. The Dwarves and Orcs carried on, but not much else seemed to happen at that table. Aiden had begun to notice that Barty the Keep, the large man they'd met the night before, was watching them intensely. The man simply gazed, almost as though not realizing it. Aiden decided not to pay it too much attention, though it unnerved him a little.

After some time, he checked his watch, realizing that the afternoon had been slipping away. He would have to begin getting ready for the banquet soon.

Finally, with D'Natis on his shoulder, he rushed back upstairs with his garment bags and began readying for the banquet. He struggled to pull on the pants and the shirt, and in no time had pulled on the suit jacket as well.

"Damn monkey suit..." he muttered while struggling with the tie.

"What was that?" asked Megan from the other side of a foldable dressing screen.

"Oh nothing..." said Aiden, not realizing he'd said it aloud.

Finally, he stood there, dressed and looking at the mirror. Though he actually liked the suit, Aiden felt far too out of place wearing it. He straightened out his pant legs and brushed out the wrinkles of his dark coat.

"Ready?" Aiden asked Megan.

"Almost," she said. "I can help you with your tie again."

"No, it's good."

"Uh huh," she said, suppressing a laugh. "Be out in a minute."

D'Natis hopped up to Aiden's shoulder.

"What're you doing?" Aiden asked, brushing the bird back to the bed.

"What I usually do...?"

"But c'mon, this is the nicest coat I've ever owned," protested Aiden.

"What's more important?" said the bird coolly. "Fourteen years of friendship, or some stupid coat?"

"The coat," said Aiden, smiling mischievously. The raven threw him a disarming glare. "Fine," Aiden conceded. "Hop on."

"It's only until we arrive, anyway," D'Natis assured him, fluttering to his shoulder. "Then, I'm going to do a little snooping around the perimeter..."

"So, how do I look?" Megan asked as she appeared from behind the screen.

Aiden turned, his mouth falling open slightly. His mind went blank at the sight of Megan in a form-fitting sequined black dress. It wasn't particularly low cut, but just enough. Her red hair seemed to pop from the contrast, and it was obvious that she'd spent some real time on that as well.

His pulse quickened and he stammered for a moment. "Great," he finally managed to say with an uncontrolled smile.

Megan's face turned slightly pink, but she composed herself. "I hope I look ok," she added thoughtfully, coming out into the center of the room and straightening his tie. "It's good to make a first impression... But I'm sure you'll impress some people with this suit," she continued, as if just thinking out loud.

"With you by my side, they won't be lookin' at my suit," Aiden responded enthusiastically, his cheeks flushing as the words left his mouth.

***

Aiden and Megan stepped back into the Underground after passing through the basement of the Gowry Tavern and Inn. Aiden had been under the impression that the Shadow Congress was being held somewhere above ground, but Megan assured him he was wrong and led them out through the old ornate door. Instead of heading back toward the railstation from whence they had arrived only a day ago, they walked east along a cobblestone path.

The village came into view once more, and they took the path down into a wide valley bordered by rising hills and rocky corridors on all sides. The path began to widen into a road, and soon, Aiden realized something.

"Why is this so familiar?" he thought aloud.

"We're going to Council Hall," she said nonchalantly. "That's where the Congress is being held. I thought you knew that."

Aiden felt himself go cold. "No," he said with a scowl threatening to surface. "I didn't..."

Aiden could feel what little enthusiasm he'd had beginning to fade. What little confidence he'd felt because of his new suit, or what excitement he'd had to have Megan on his arm—it was all disappearing, and now images of Monadias and Fentl flashed in his mind. He walked on ahead with such terse movements that D'Natis flapped off his shoulder.

"What's a matter?" Megan asked, seeing that Aiden had begun walking swiftly down the hill before them.

"Let's get this over with," said Aiden, suppressing all the memories.

D'Natis glided gently alongside Megan. "They held his trial here," he said quietly, though Aiden could still hear. "Best not talk about it."

The journey to Council Hall was not far, and after entering the village and passing a myriad of vendors closing their carts for the day, they began to see signs of gathering crowds further along the main road. The light from the giant mushrooms, visible in the distant corners of the valley, had begun to dim—signifying the arrival of evening—and lamps were slowly being lit along the village streets. The large rounded building finally loomed into view, accompanied by an ornate sign reading '*Banquet of Shadows*' near the large double doors at the entrance.

"Here I take my leave," said D'Natis, fluttering from Aiden's shoulder. "As always, I'm your eye in the sky..."

Aiden forced a smile and nodded as the bird rose into the air, soon disappearing amongst the surrounding buildings.

The walk down had relieved some of Aiden's steam, but now he tried to calm his nerves as he pushed through those doors. It was strange seeing so many people—humans, Elves, Fauns, and Dwarves alike—crowding into that building looking relatively upbeat and dressed in their finest attire. The atmosphere was so very different than when last he'd been here.

Megan slipped a small piece of parchment into Aiden's hand as they found themselves in a long line filling the main corridor.

"What's this?" Aiden asked, examining the piece. It was blank with one Dwarvish phrase embedded in it.

"Our tickets," said Megan, smiling as she revealed her own small piece of parchment.

Aiden shrugged and moved along as the line progressed. There were two Dwarves at the door, reading and tracing the special symbols on every delegate's ticket as they approached. The line moved along quickly, and Aiden could hear someone announcing something just inside the room beyond.

After the Dwarves examined Aiden and Megan's tickets, the two humans entered the main circular hall. It looked much as Aiden remembered it, although the room was teaming with delegates and officials in mid-conversation. The raised dais was still at the room's center, but decorated festively, and over a hundred rounded tables were placed around it, each with place cards and an ornate centerpiece.

A well-dressed Faun near the entrance gently took Megan's arm. "You'll need to be announced," he said, facing the room. "May I present D'Tari liaison Megan Rohan of the Mount Katahdin Guild," his voice suddenly boomed out into the room. "And... a guest."

The room gave a gentle applause. As the Faun smiled and turned away, Megan's face flushed. "I should be used to that by now," she said sheepishly. "Let's find our table..."

Another Faun quickly offered to take Aiden's coat, and was obliged. "Wow," thought Aiden aloud. "Fancy..."

The lights were somewhat low and the room was mostly lit by the glow of a thousand elegant candles. The decor had a sort of otherworldly feel about it: the walls, centerpieces, and chandeliers were covered in ivy, multicolored and translucent orchids, chrysanthemums, dahlias, and other varieties of flower. After a few moments, Aiden realized that the glowing mass writhing and swirling near the ceiling was not an enchantment or a light show, but instead was almost an entire colony of fluttering Faeries.

Aiden and Megan slowly made their way through the excited crowds—amidst hearing new arrivals being announced to the room—wending through the decorative tables until they found their seats. They sat at their table, which was still empty, a feeling of excitement in the air.

Megan turned to Aiden, looking anxious. "Okay, now what?" she said.

"Relax," he said, smiling. "I guess we just enjoy it for now."

Aiden sat back for a moment, and realized that he could not take his eyes off of Megan. Despite her anxiety, she was aglow. He felt more relaxed just observing her as she watched the room. This place no longer felt like the same room he'd been tried in so long ago, and he began to wonder if she wasn't on to something with all her talk of hoping to change things for the better through diplomacy.

Over the next ten minutes, the crowds seemed to do an intensely slow dance around Aiden and Megan's table. Many of the delegates came to introduce themselves to Megan. There was Dothrak of the International Confederation of Blue Dwarves, who wished her well; Then came the Fauns Sarmos and Terma, one from the Common Alliance of Satyrs and Fauns, and the other from the Faun-Satyr Coalition; Finally, Jhon, Terri, and Darby from the Agnec Nation human tribal federation approached with some kind words for Megan. Some of them shook Aiden's hand, but most of them paid him no attention. Amidst the crowds, Aiden was sure he could see the Orcs from the tavern seated at some far off table, looking sorely out of place.

Finally, a handsome dark-haired Elf in emerald dress robes sauntered over to the table. "I am Dorimar," he announced in a kind tone. "From the Elvin Council of the Eastern Seaboard."

"Oh yes," said Megan, smiling as she stood to greet the Elf.

"Please, sit down," said Dorimar, gesturing to her. He pulled up a chair next to her as she did so, ignoring Aiden on Megan's other side. "I believe you and I have a common goal during this Congress," he began, observing Megan. "We both desire to see the rights and freedoms of Agnecs preserved."

"Naturally," said Megan, choosing her words wisely.

"I was told your particular goal is to object to Senator Regis' proposed legislation," said the Elf, his voice lowering. "I might be persuaded to join your cause, as I am no fan of the N'Iatari myself."

Megan smiled, both surprised and relieved. "Of course," she said, an eager tone escaping. "The more support, the better. Do I need to talk with your, uh, your superiors?"

"No," said Dorimar flatly. "I will take care of those details. As one might say, I am a rare breed, considering how few Elves want to make alliances with humans, or even D'Tari for that matter. But I feel there is a common good here, one that must be defended, thus why my... superiors—as you say—have sent me as liaison."

"Okay," said Megan, still smiling. "Let's plan to meet after the sessions start, and we'll make a plan."

Dorimar chuckled slightly. "Oh I love how you humans can turn a phrase. It's settled then. I trust you'll enjoy the banquet."

With that, the Elf stood, bowed slightly, and turned back into the crowd. As he walked away, Aiden couldn't help stare after him.

"He seems..." began Megan, as if unsure how to express herself.

"A little too friendly," said Aiden, without thinking.

"Perhaps," she said, looking to Aiden. "But if he's willing to help us, we're off to a better start than I'd hoped."

After a few more moments of chatter, the crowds began to disperse to their tables and the dais at the center of the room lit up. A gray-haired Faun, wearing a double-breasted black and green waistcoat with silver buttons and odd coat tails, stepped up to the podium on the stage. After adjusting a box to stand on, the Faun could finally see over the podium, and he looked with bright eyes out over the quieted audience.

"Thank you for coming to our special event tonight," the Faun's voice shook ever so slightly. "I am Lord Dervin fen Fendiloch, the master of ceremonies. We are pleased to host this event, held at the beginning of every quadrennial Shadow Congress, ever since its founding in 1946." He cleared his throat politely. "Tonight," he continued, his ancient eyes roaming across the sea of faces. "We are reminded of our hope and our struggle in the midst of uncertainty. The desire to see a cooperative world of Agnecs, a place of equal and civil rights, and to create a shining hope for our children, and our children's children."

Aiden looked over to Megan, only to see her face shining with a deeply intent kind of joy. Aiden had to admit, the old Faun had a way with words. Another quick survey of the room revealed to Aiden that four figures in black suits stood ominously, each one stationed at a far corner. He was nearly sure he knew what was coming.

"In light of this present, and future, hope," the old Faun continued, his voice unwavering. "Let us work to that end. Let us strive to create a brighter tomorrow. Right the wrongs. I grant you all the best of luck as you prepare to enter into what is already proving to be a challenging session." There was a slight murmur in the crowd, but it passed quickly. "But tonight, we celebrate our future victories, and revel in the company of good people. So, without further adieu, let me introduce to you the leader of our gracious host country—the United States—President Robert Johnson."

The room applauded loudly as the Faun stepped aside and a tall, balding man walked out onto the stage. As the old Faun re-adjusted the podium for the President, Aiden's own suspicions had been confirmed. He knew the Feds when he saw them.

The President had the appearance of a thin man, except for the odd-shaped beer belly, and despite his awkward stature, his presence seemed to demand attention. His olive-toned complexion was bright with enthusiasm as he waved at the audience and gestured for them to calm down.

"I remember when he ran," said Aiden to Megan as the clapping began to die down. "The media wouldn't stop freaking out about the fact that he's half-Japanese... I'm half-Japanese, or whatever, and what's the big deal?"

"You're also not running for President," said Megan firmly, her voice lowering. "People just don't know how to handle anything that they deem different. I've been in the Ambler world enough to know that their media likes to keep things more entertaining and less informing..."

Aiden smiled, knowing just how right she was. "Are Agnec politics any different?"

"I used to hope so..." said Megan, trailing off as the President took the podium.

"Thank you. Thank you, so much," the President said when the crowd had finally grown silent. "Thank you as well, Lord Fendiloch," he added, turning to where the old gray Faun stood just off the stage. The President returned his attention to the audience, still smiling. "It's an honor to be here tonight. It's truly an honor to be part of such a diverse and important event, an event which has the power to shape the lives of people—all kinds of people—not only in the United States, but throughout the entire world.'

"In the next two months or so, I hope to see the Agnec world come to several resolutions. Resolutions that will remind us all to respect one another. Resolutions that will enforce and maintain the peace among not only the Agnec world, but also among Agnecs' interactions with my world. I know I come here as more of an outsider than anything, but what happens here concerns me greatly. I do not pretend to know all the obstacles that your world must overcome to achieve unity, but I feel that if the Agnec world were to fall into chaos, very quickly my world would follow suit. We all desire stability in our societies, along with peace and justice, and I feel that both worlds have the same common desires and values. We all desire to maintain that stability in each respective realm.'

"But tonight, let us all enjoy the festivities as we gather together in what one could call the most undeniably diverse gathering in the recent history of this great country," continued the President with a smile. "I promised Lord Fendiloch I would keep this short, so to that end, let us all work together to create a stable and united future for the Agnec world, and for all other worlds as well."

The room applauded, and with a slight glint of unease—as if he'd just caught sight of some Orcs in the crowd—the President stepped down from the stage, met by all four of his secret service agents.

With that, the banquet began.

***

As the evening dragged on, Aiden decided that he didn't know how to relate to these people. As the meal arrived and the music played, several people were talking to Megan and seemed to take her seriously. Aiden was glad for that, but he was almost completely ignored.

It seemed as though most people, if not everyone in the room, were reveling in just as much pomp as anyone reportedly did in the *normal* Congress. Lord Dezmer, a surprisingly well-to-do Half-Elf, sat across from Aiden and Megan, and could do nothing but talk about his large mansion.

"Naturally I've festooned the walls in the formal dining room with my collection of Elvish seashells—they've been passed down in my family for so many generations, they're practically prehistoric," Lord Dezmer gushed enthusiastically. "You must come see them sometime," he said to Megan. "They're full of so many ancient enchantments, I'm sure I don't even know what they all are."

Megan could only smile and nod, but before she could say anything, Farrima, the woman opposite Lord Dezmer, chimed in. "Oh if you can appreciate that, then I'm sure you would love my estate. It's above ground, but far out of Ambler sight. We have a sprawling four-hundred acre piece of land. And horses! I love to ride, do you? I remember just last week, Lord Fendiloch visited and was so enthralled with everything, that he said he wondered why we weren't holding the Congress there..."

Aiden felt like sticking his fingers in his ears.

In the midst of things, he spied a dark-haired man in a very modern suit coming across to their table. The man, though older and graying, struck a youthful and oddly familiar impression in Aiden's mind. He, much like the President, also seemed to be of some Asian descent. The man greeted the others at the table, politely interrupting, before turning to greet Megan.

"Philip Regis," the man said with a congenial smile, offering a hand to Megan.

"Oh..." Megan stood, surprised but trying to maintain a light air.

"Senator, I'm Megan. I'm so sorry I missed you on your recent trip to the Mount Katahdin Guild-"

"No worries," Philip said, smiling. "Yes, well, it's a shame that the Guild elders and myself could not come to a better agreement."

"Well..." Megan began, but trailed off, realizing it was best to say nothing.

"Again, no worries," Philip continued. "Once the sessions get started, perhaps I can convince you to see things as I do."

Megan could only smile.

"But let's forget that business for now," the Senator said lightheartedly. "It's time to forget about all this politics business and enjoy the night!" He laughed and helped Megan back into her seat in gentlemanly fashion. "And you are?" Philip looked to Aiden.

Aiden was surprised by the attention. "demi-I mean, Aiden," he replied, still not used to announcing his real name in Agnec circles.

Philip stared for a brief moment, then regained his composure. "Of course, the elders told me about you as well. Aiden *Gailhart*, correct?"

Aiden flinched at the name. "Correct," he said, his face a mixture of confusion and a forced smile.

After another odd moment, the Senator continued, "Well, I'm sure we'll be seeing more of each other. Until then, enjoy your evening."

With an uncomfortable nod of the head, Philip Regis suddenly left the table and wandered into the crowd, being quickly side-armed by a rather attractive blonde woman in a red gown.

"Gailhart?" Megan looked to Aiden, bemused. "I thought you were one of those people who had no last name... Sort of like Cher or Bono," she said with a chuckle.

Aiden bristled for a moment, then calmed himself. "I didn't know you knew about Cher or Bono," he said, trying to sound at ease. "Kind of trendy for an Agnec girl."

"I was raised by Amblers til I was fifteen," said Megan quickly, watching the Senator disappear. "It's not like those celebs are the latest thing to come across the wire. So..." She paused, looking back to Aiden. "What's wrong with your last name?"

"Nothing," said Aiden, lowering his voice, unable to hide his offense. "I just... don't use it anymore. Plus, how did Regis know about it anyway?"

Megan shrugged. "Maybe Monadias mentioned it," she said casually. "I'm sure it's listed in the records of your trial..."

Aiden shook his head, not wanting to delve too far into the memories again.

"Who was that woman I wonder," Megan thought aloud, looking back into the room, finding Senator Regis again. "Was that Regis' wife?"

"Ah no," Lord Dezmer chimed in. "That would be Tilli Rosen. His wife and children do not appear to be here..."

"Hmm..." Megan mused. "I guess that makes sense..."

"Some say she's an Agnec," the Half-Elf added. "Rosen, that

is. Some of us wonder if she was afraid of her Agnec identity and only recently revealed herself."

"They seem friendly," Aiden said, gesturing toward Senator Regis and Tilli without thinking about what he was implying. "Uh, I mean, in a business sort of way."

The Half-Elf smiled, as if having his own opinions on the subject, but said nothing.

Chapter 16
The Opposition

Aiden sat on the floor in their room, leaning up against the old wall, the hard wood making his backside ache. Megan had fallen asleep hours ago, and despite his anxiety, he felt somewhat comforted by the gentle sounds of her breathing.

Although it had been a long day, he once again found it hard to sleep. This time it wasn't so much that the guests at the inn were so noisy—though they were—nor was it that D'Natis was restless, because he was outside roaming the night. It was something else.

Philip Regis had used Aiden's last name.

He couldn't push it from his mind. Though it seemed that the last forty-eight hours had been a blur, Regis' brief appearance was disturbingly crystal clear. And why did the man seem vaguely familiar? He knew he had never met the Senator before. He had never even seen pictures of him.

Megan was likely right, that the elders or the Council had told Philip Regis about Aiden. But that would seem as though the Senator had taken an interest in Aiden... And why would he do that?

The floorboards creaked suddenly. Aiden looked up into the darkness, certain elements of the room aglow with the moonlight that filtered through the window. His thoughts fluttered away.

After a moment, there was another creaking sound, this time much closer than the first. The doorknob was slowly turning.

Aiden stood, drawing his blade. He thought of waking Megan, but the door knob was turning more swiftly now. Hoping to not be heard, he rushed across the small space and hid behind the door.

It slowly opened, and the light from the hallway flooded inside. The shadow of a tall, hooded man stretched across the room, falling on Megan's sleeping form. The man stepped inside, closing the door—without realizing that Aiden stood just inches behind him. Silently, the man reached down to his side to find a blade appearing there.

"Too easy," the man muttered and began to raise his sword.

Megan's eyelids fluttered open and she gasped at the sight of the moonlight reflecting off the man's blade.

A blue ball of energy struck the intruder's back, sending wild shadows and colors dancing about the room. The man grunted, smashing face first into the floor on the opposite side of Megan's bed.

Megan shrieked and threw herself out of bed, rushing toward Aiden.

"What's going on?" she asked, finding time to throw on her robe.

Aiden stumbled to the nightstand and turned up the oil lamp until the room came into focus.

"We have a visitor," said Aiden, his blade still drawn.

The hooded man swore and pulled himself to his feet. His cloak was white with the runic insignia for '*Lilit*' on the forefront of the hood. His blade had disappeared in the chaos. Though his face was enshrouded in shadow, Aiden could sense the man's look of indignation.

Without warning, the man launched a ball of dark energy at Aiden. It seemed to suck all the light from the surrounding air as it flew. Megan ducked and Aiden swung the flat of his blade at the ball, lobbing it back toward the intruder. It missed and blew through the window. Glass and windowsill shattered, scattering about the room and falling to the street below.

In another split second, Aiden raced forward, striking the man's leg. A spurt of blood hit the old wooden floor. The man grunted and clutched his leg, but said nothing.

"Who sent you?" Aiden finally said, his voice full of adrenaline, his sword steady.

"You'll know soon enough," the man said, his thinning eyes visible now.

"I don't want to have to hurt you," Aiden said, thrusting his confident blade beneath the man's chin. "Who sent you?"

"Lord G'nehon sends his compliments," the man said, his voice raspy.

"Well, that answers that," Aiden mused, making sure to push his blade's tip a little closer to the man's throat. "And I'm pretty sure I know *why* you are here..." Aiden continued, side-glancing to Megan who was very ill at ease. "But how did you know-"

"That's all you'll get from me," the man in white snapped,

pushing aside Aiden's blade with a gloved hand. "This is only the beginning."

In the same moment, Aiden felt a fist fly across his ear. His head searing with pain and ears ringing wildly, he struggled to keep his footing. The intruder briskly turned toward the shattered hole in the wall where the window had once been. Aiden regained his balance and thrust again with this sword, catching the man in the calf of the leg. The man yelped and stumbled out into the night air.

Megan grabbed Aiden's arm and they staggered to the window just in time to watch the man fall helplessly toward the pavement with blood glistening in an airborne trail behind him. Instead of the expected crack of the pavement, the man disappeared in a sudden rush of black mist.

"Dammit!" Aiden yelled, just as D'Natis swept toward them from the darkness.

"Rough night?" the bird said, his large eye glistening in the light of the street lamps.

***

The morning after the incident in their room, a short old man with few teeth knocked on Aiden and Megan's door. The man was accompanied by Barty the Keep, and greeted Aiden with a furious tone.

"You need to leave the premises of my establishment," the man said, his lips wrinkling coldly over a nearly vacant mouth. "You've drawn too much attention here! You can't stay."

Aiden was still groggy. "That's a nice wake up call," he said, feeling heat rising in his chest. "This woman was almost murdered last night, and you're throwing us out?"

Megan shook her head, yawning. "Aiden, just tell them we'll go... It's not worth it."

Barty was glaring at the pair of them as if stewing on murderous thoughts.

"Fine..." Aiden said finally.

Soon, Aiden and Megan were walking along the sidewalk out on the Ambler streets. D'Natis was once again perched on Aiden's shoulder.

"What now?" said Megan, yawning again, looking disheveled.

"We think fast..."

After another five minutes or so, Aiden saw a hotel on the next street corner. After taking some time to change their clothes in the bathrooms of a nearby restaurant, the two of them wandered into the hotel lobby wearing their nicest clothes. The concierge at the hotel first began to protest being paid in cash, but then was astonished at Megan's thick bundle of twenties.

"We have the money," Aiden told the man. "Even if we're here for weeks..."

The man stared for several moments, as if considering how many hundreds the bundle must have amounted to. Finally he consented and gave them a room.

"Keep the change," Aiden said, having handed the man an extra fifty-note on top of their fee.

Once they stepped into the elevator, Aiden smiled, feeling smug. "I've always wanted to do that," he said with a laugh. "That was pretty pimp."

Megan glared at him.

"No, that's not what I meant-"

"I know what you mean by it," she said, rolling her eyes. "I still don't like it, so please don't say it."

Aiden stopped, and nodded slowly in apology. Things remained awkward for the remainder of the ride, but soon they walked into the hotel room to observe and drop their things on the beds.

"Nice place, huh?" said Aiden finally.

"Nicer than the Gowry Inn," agreed Megan. "Alright, come on. We have to head back to the Underground. I'd like to hit the library."

"There's a library?" said Aiden, confused. "I don't know about you, but I'm tired. Plus I need to let D'Natis in. He's been waiting."

He walked to the window, slowly slid open the glass, and popped out the screen. Aiden put his fingers in his mouth and whistled out into the morning air.

"Yes, the big library is right next to Council Hall. There's some things I'd like to research before the sessions start... So who is this Tilli Rosen anyway?" Megan added, as if the thought had been nagging her just beneath the surface. "I mean, no one seems to really know..."

"I know," Aiden agreed, turning back to Megan, thankful that the awkwardness of their moment in the elevator had passed. "I think it's weird enough that one Ambler seems to be so involved in the Agnec world—but two?"

"I guess it takes all kinds," said Megan, sitting on the bed behind her.

The fluttering of dark wings announced D'Natis' arrival at the windowsill. "We must find some better system," said the raven. "I must have circled the building twice just trying to find you. Unfortunately, I at first landed on the wrong sill. Some people would be wise to close their windows while they do that sort of thing..." D'Natis shuddered, his feathers rippling all over.

Aiden laughed, but caught himself. "Hey," he said, struck by a thought. "Would you be willing to go on a little research trip for us?"

"Oh I suppose," D'Natis said, sounding put out. "But first, a nap."

"Wish I could say the same," said Aiden, but Megan's expression told him there was no such chance.

"D'Natis," Megan began, approaching the raven calculatingly. "I would really appreciate it if you could... Maybe, head to Tilli Rosen's hometown and do a little snooping for us?"

***

Everything had been quiet since Aiden and Megan had moved into the hotel room. No one had broken in. No one had tried to attack them in any way. The event had left Megan somewhat shaky for a day or so, but she allowed herself to get lost in preparing for the Congress.

On the Monday following the banquet, the Shadow Congress was set to begin. Megan discovered that there was another entrance into the Underground that would allow them to avoid the Gowry Tavern and Inn. It took them somewhat out of their way, but they arrived just in time, now coming from the northwest side toward Council Hall.

Much of the lightheartedness seemed to have gone out of the delegates as they crowded into the corridor on their way into the main hall. The huge room was no longer beautifully decorated, but now seemed rather dull, as long, segmented tables curved around the central dais, cascading back to the end of the room.

Wearing his dark suit without the long coat, Aiden ushered Megan into the room feeling more suspicious than ever about the multitudes of people shuffling around them. He nearly brushed shoulders with one of the President's Secret Service agents in passing. The agent stopped and turned.

"Hey there, *demiGod*," the agent said in a sharp tone, shaking Aiden's hand suddenly. "Staying out of trouble?"

Aiden only nodded, and then continued ushering Megan to her table—which was more like a long desk where other delegates sat, shuffling through their papers and looking at their watches.

"What was that about?" said Megan, glancing back to the agent.

"Just someone who had to clean up one of my messes a while ago..." Aiden sighed. "Don't worry about it now. Just focus on this stuff," he added with a slight smile. "Hope it goes well."

Megan smiled back, and Aiden left to take his place at the far back of the room, making sure to place himself somewhere nearest the aisle with the best access to Megan's table.

Lord Fendiloch took the podium and quieted the room just as he'd done at the banquet, but this time it was to announce the opening of the General Assembly. One by one, he announced the various representatives in attendance—a process which took half an hour.

As the old Faun began to announce the agenda for the day's session, Aiden glanced about the room. At a table on the other side of the dais, he spied Senator Regis and Tilli Rosen seated next to one another. They were both busy looking through binders on the table before them. Another quick survey also revealed that the President had been seated at a specially enclosed box in the far back of the room, accompanied by two agents. Aiden shook as someone else caught his eye. Mistress Monadias and Master Fentl were also in attendance, some ways off. They seemed to be glaring over at Megan.

Aiden clenched his fists. "Seriously?" he muttered to himself. They wouldn't object to Regis' proposal—they even denied they knew about it—but then they just show up anyway?

"Much can happen in four years," said Lord Fendiloch as he neared the end of his opening statements. "So there is much to review before we can move on to new business."

***

Aiden felt as though his legs were dead after that first day of sessions, as there were few breaks and only brief moments for him to run to the bathroom when he'd needed to. As for the sessions themselves, there had been no new business, no proposals, nothing. Although Aiden supposed he shouldn't be surprised, he wondered when Regis would begin talking about his proposal.

As Aiden made to escort Megan from her table, Senator Regis and Tilli Rosen approached them.

"Miss Rohan," Regis said, gently touching her arm. "First, I wanted to say that I'm so sorry about what happened to you on Friday night. I hope you're doing okay."

"Oh," said Megan, taken aback. "Uh, yeah, I'm fine. Sort of shaken, but fine. How did you-"

"Second," Regis continued as if he'd not heard Megan beginning to speak again. "I'd like you to meet my partner and aide, Tilli Rosen."

Megan, forced to change her train of thought, smiled politely and offered a hand. "Oh yes, glad to finally meet you."

"Likewise," said Tilli with a confident air. "Philip says you're here to oppose our proposal," she added with a lighthearted chuckle.

"That was our intention, yes..." said Megan slowly, off-put by Tilli's straightforward approach.

"Don't worry about it," said Tilli, smiling. "I, for one, am confident that you'll have a change of heart. But if not, no worries... I mean, all this politics business; It's nothing personal. You win some, you lose some."

Senator Regis smiled, but looked almost worried about Tilli's words.

"Who's this?" Tilli asked, now appraising Aiden.

"Oh, this is Aiden," said Megan. "My- my friend."

Tilli took Aiden's hand and smiled. "Wow, aren't you a looker," she said, moving in close. "Strong silent type?"

Aiden's face was flushed. "Only sometimes..." was all he could manage to say.

"Well, we need to get going now," Regis chimed in, gently taking Tilli's arm.

"Nice to meet you both," said Tilli. "It'll all work, you'll both see. You'll come around..."

Once the Senator and Rosen had disappeared among the crowds, Megan looked to Aiden, her eyebrow raised in confusion.

"What the hell was that?" Aiden finally said, looking irritated.

"I don't know..." said Megan. "And... how did Regis know about the attack?"

"Megan, there you are," another voice chimed in before Aiden could think.

"Dorimar," said Megan, smiling now. "I wondered if I'd see you today."

"Yes, sorry," the Elf said as he nearly knocked Aiden aside just stepping between him and Megan. "I'm seated with the other Elvin representatives." He gestured to a section of tables further along on the other side of the room. "I was wondering if we could meet tonight... To discuss..."

Dorimar stopped, as if realizing Aiden was there at his shoulder.

"Oh I'm sorry," said Megan, looking suddenly flushed. "Dorimar, this is Aiden, my, uh-"

"Her protection, assigned by the Guild," said Aiden, making eye contact with the Elf—though he found it hard to stare for too long.

"Oh I didn't see you there," said Dorimar in seeming surprise. The Elf looked back to Megan, hardly acknowledging Aiden's presence. "We need to discuss a strategy. As far as I know, in a day or two, the floor will be open for new proposals, then next week, they begin voting..."

"Okay," said Megan, looking somewhat flustered. "Let's meet at my hotel room-"

Aiden shook his head vigorously, just out sight from Dorimar. Megan paused.

"On second thought," said Megan, smiling awkwardly. "Let's meet at the library—the one here just across the way."

"I'll meet you there in twenty minutes," said Dorimar flatly. With a slight bow, he walked away, still failing to acknowledge Aiden.

"What's the big deal?" Megan asked, lowering her voice so only Aiden could hear.

"You're too trusting. We don't even know if this guy's really helping us or not," said Aiden. "I don't want him knowing where we're staying."

***

The Old World Library of History and Legal Records was very quiet as Aiden and Megan wandered through the ornate front doors. Dorimar met them just inside the lobby, ignoring a stone desk where a Dwarf librarian sat reading a dusty volume.

"Should we go to the congressional records?" Dorimar said, once again ignoring Aiden's presence. "I thought it might be a good place to start."

"Okay," said Megan, though sounding unsure. "Although I've looked in there a bit already, and-"

"Follow me," Dorimar announced. "I know this library well."

"I know where it's it," said Megan.

The Elf did not seem to be listening as he stepped onto the first stair. A giant staircase spiraled before them, serving as a backbone for the seemingly bottomless, rounded building. Instead of moving upward, they were moving downward. On each ornate landing, they could see that books lined the walls from floor to ceiling. The place smelled of dust and age, and when Aiden looked down over the creaky railing, it seemed as though the stair went on forever.

When finally they reached the fifteenth-floor landing—now many feet deep into the earth—Dorimar led them into a dimly-lit section of dusty shelves that were labeled "*Shadow Congress Records*".

"So," Megan began, pulling up a chair at an old desk near the shelves. "I wanted to start by looking up records from the

414

International Agnec Court of Justice—I need to find as many N'Iatari-related incidents as I can."

"Interesting approach," remarked Dorimar, also taking a seat. "Alright, if you feel that Senator Regis is connected to the N'Iatari-"

"You don't?"

"I feel we should first approach this by showing how fiscally wasteful and poorly regulated the plan would be," said Dorimar. "Can you agree?"

"Not a bad idea," said Megan. "But first thing's first... I need to ask: Why are you helping me? I mean, what can possibly be in this for you? Especially because I know that Elves in general prefer to be left alone. If Regis starts a militia, it doesn't affect you at all, does it?"

"Fair enough," said Dorimar. "You're correct in believing that my motivations are not nearly so in tune with yours. We have reason to believe that Regis may be planning on coercing the Elves to get involved in his militia experiment. I'm uncertain as to whether or not he's N'Iatari, or whether or not that's even an issue—I'm more concerned at what it could do for the Elves around the country..."

Megan sighed. "I suppose that's fair. But you'll still help me?"

"Yes," Dorimar said, nodding. "I'll search through the treasury records—as this will likely be the first thing to come up—and you may continue trying to prove the N'Iatari connection... If you like."

Megan nodded, but looked somewhat slighted. Aiden shook his

head, reminding himself to not get involved, but fighting the urge to say something to Dorimar. He wasn't sure what he would say, but something about the Elf's demeanor certainly rubbed him the wrong way.

"I'll just be over here..." began Aiden, sitting at another desk a little ways from them. "Just hangin' out."

"Thank you Aiden," Megan said apologetically. "I realize it's late already, but bear with us."

It wasn't long until Aiden began drifting in and out of sleep as he unwittingly bent over the desk in front of him. He could still hear the low voices of both Megan and Dorimar carrying on as if they were a mile away, despite how he knew they were just feet from him. He gasped for breath as if breaking from a sudden slumber, and couldn't be sure if his eyes were open when he saw it.

A shadow had passed near him.

It had been fast but human-like. Wordlessly, he stood and scanned the library, his eyes flitting from shelf to shelf, exit to exit.

"Aiden, what's a matter?" Megan asked, turning.

"Uh... nothing," Aiden said, still desperately scanning the room. "It's fine. You two stay here... I'll be right back."

Aiden had hardly bothered to look back at Megan's confused expression. He had the immediate but inexplicable feeling that Megan would be safe for the time being. Looking around, it became apparent that the room was completely empty, save for the candle-lit corner where Megan and Dorimar sat. Aiden seemed to float through the room as if weightlessly, past large bookshelves and ancient oak cabinets, moving close to the shelved wall and into the shadows of the corner.

He followed along the far wall, realizing in moments that what he thought had been a corner was actually a doorway adjacent to the adjoining wall. It was very dim here, and he pressed his ear closely to the old wooden door. He could hear muffled voices, though the words were still unclear.

He slowly cracked the door, but paused. The voices had stopped, but in moments, they began again. The corridor within seemed dark with only a patch of light flickering somewhere at the end. Aiden crept inside, keeping as quiet as humanly possible.

"What about him?" Aiden heard an earthy voice mutter.

"We can't harm him," a gruff voice responded, irritated. "Lord G'nehon has plans for him."

"Of course..." the first voice added, sounding just as put out.

Aiden stayed close to the wall, clinging to every bit of shadow he possibly could, and avoiding the dancing candle light that whimsically swayed in the corridor. He stopped when he saw the silhouettes of two people; one the short and stocky build of a Dwarf, and the other that of a large, burly man. The man's profile seemed all too familiar.

"So back off, Cardibran," the large man said, sniffing the musty air. "Don't even try to get the girl either... Not yet."

"Why not?" the Dwarf said, scoffing. "She's nothing to him."

"That's what you think," the large man said, bending down to poke the Dwarf in the chest. "G'nehon's got his reasons. All I know is that he needs her to get to him..."

"You know something else, don't you Barty?" the Dwarf sneered.

In the pause that followed, Aiden suppressed a gasp of realization. The large man was Barty, the keeper of the Gowry Tavern and Inn.

Barty sounded less confident, mumbling something unintelligible. "I can feel you in my mind, you bastard," he growled, but his words trailed off. "Alright!" Barty finally said as if in pain, his large silhouette stepping threateningly toward the Dwarf. "Lord G'nehon said something about keeping the girl occupied for now. He said the Senator needs her right where she is. That's all I know," Barty finished, growling.

"Interesting. And so disappointing," Cardibran the Dwarf said in a hissing tone. "I hate waiting, and watching..."

"I also don't understand why you couldn't have met me at the tavern," said Barty.

"Too many witnesses," replied Cardibran. "Too many people flowing in and out of there connected to the Shadow Congress. Honestly, they're your best customers right now."

Barty shrugged. "My only customers right now... But why here?"

"Frankly, I like the dark," chuckled the Dwarf. "Furthermore, you know I run this operation—or did you forget? I'm here at the dark lord's command of course. I control information, and that, my friend, is priceless."

"Are we done?" Barty grunted. "I got business to attend to."

"Yes, sure," conceded Cardibran. "But I still can't believe you let them out of your sight, you idiot."

"It wasn't me, I was just doing my job. I would've kept them there if I could—Boss man said they were giving us away! Who's the asshole that sent in the assassin?"

The Dwarf growled. "That was an unfortunate misunderstanding, but he's been dealt with. Stupid Griftwalker, thinks he knows the plans..."

Aiden felt his heart leap.

"Time to go," Cardibran continued. "Don't let yourself be seen until you're well away from the library... Or I swear..."

The two nodded to each other and shifted, as if looking in opposite directions around the corridor. Barty grunted and began heading in the opposite direction down a bend in the hall that almost seemed too small for the man. To Aiden's dismay, the Dwarf turned, as if in thought, and then walked in Aiden's direction.

Aiden fought the urge to call his sword, and pushed himself up against the wall even further until he felt as though he had become somehow a part of it. The Dwarf walked slowly through the shifting darkness, having left the candles burning at the end of the corridor. Aiden knew that Dwarves had excellent eyesight, no matter how deep the shadows. It would only be a matter of moments until the Dwarf saw him.

Cardibran stopped just a foot away from Aiden, at eye-level with the half-kneeling man. He sniffed the air suddenly.

"Hello?" the Dwarf said, almost hesitantly.

Aiden held his breath.

"I can almost taste you," Cardibran said, turning and looking directly into Aiden's eyes.

Aiden didn't dare move, though his every urge told him to. It was odd. Cardibran stared directly at him for a few moments, then looked away as if not seeing him at all.

Cardibran snarled in irritation, straightened up his clothes, and finally walked to the door sighing. In a moment, he was gone. Aiden waited a bit longer before he finally allowed himself to take a breath. Convinced it was safe, he stretched, his legs cramping from the awkward position, and left the corridor.

He snuck back into the library and quietly returned to his seat at the desk just feet away from Megan and Dorimar. It was almost as though nothing had happened. Megan acknowledged his return, but focused back on her discussion and reading.

Aiden's heart pounded as he contemplated what he'd just overheard. There was hardly any doubt in his mind that he and Megan must have been the subject of discussion, but who was this Cardibran? And how did Griftwalker fit into everything?

Most puzzling of all: How was it possible that Aiden had been eye to eye with Cardibran, and the Dwarf had not seen him?

Aiden would tell Megan all about this later, but he didn't dare mention it now, in front of Dorimar.

***

Aiden stood at the back of the main hall as the congressional sessions proceeded. He couldn't believe that it was only Wednesday. It felt as though time had begun to slow.

After the incident on Monday, Aiden and Megan had discussed several things, but still had no answers. It all ended in conjecture. Obviously, Senator Regis was connected to Lord G'nehon somehow, and he was tracking Megan's movements... But how? And could they prove any of it, besides taking Aiden's word for it?

Aiden watched intently as Lord Fendiloch finally opened the floor for new proposals. After several minor incidents were noted and various issues laid out, Philip Regis finally stood, and was given the floor to speak.

The Senator had a certain charm about him, there was no denying it. He smiled, thanking the old Faun as he took the podium.

"Today, I speak on an issue of grave importance, and I hope that you'll all bear with me," he began, looking into the audience. "The way of the Agnec world is fraught with danger, despite the best attempts at living peaceably. Despite their best efforts, most villages—whether Dwarf, Elf, human, or even Orc—can only defend themselves as best they can. I know that you're probably looking at me, knowing that I am but a concerned Ambler—though I'm proud to be a part of this amazing meeting of minds and cultures—and I'm sure you're wondering how I can know anything about the Agnec world. That's a fair question.'

"Let me assure you: I've been involved with the Agnec world for over twenty years, doing everything I can to promote unity amongst Agnecs, as well as keeping the important individuals informed—such as the President," he smiled, looking back to where President Johnson sat. "Keeping them informed of the things that are important to the sanctity and safety of the Agnec world.'

"That said," he continued. "I've done my research, and I've seen a serious problem with the relative safety of the average Agnec village—especially when it comes to the human residents. In many cases, especially with above-ground locations, or Agnec children attempting to attend Ambler schools, we see discrimination. This is not only a little slight here, maybe a little bullying there—no, this has ended in murder, destruction, and a very real oppression.'

"Now statistically, I have proof of these facts: For Agnecs who live above-ground and have at least some connection to the Ambler world, one in every five children is bullied for being *different*. Ten in every twenty are refused certain rights that normal Amblers are easily granted. Five in every thirty are discriminated against by Ambler police, accused of dark practices, misunderstood, et cetera. Furthermore, the murder, suicide, and sexual assault rate of above-ground Agnecs is higher than the same events in your average local Ambler population. This is outrageous! And I haven't even touched on what many *Underground* Agnecs have to deal with.'

"This isn't at all to say that Amblers are the problem—of course not. I seek unity between Amblers and Agnecs. I wish that the small percentage of Amblers who do know about this world, could be as I am. But frankly, what laws the US has in place to protect

Agnecs... simply are not enforced. But how could they be?"

Aiden found himself nodding in agreement, then stopped himself.

Regis continued, "Ambler-on-Agnec violence is a very real issue, unfortunately. Most of the time, Amblers are unaware that these Agnecs are part of a bigger community of course. We must maintain our secrecy, yet we must maintain our safety as well. Of course... I say this as one who feels so akin to you that I count myself among you," Regis added, as if realizing he misspoke. "To make things worse, most Agnecs will not fight back, only to preserve that secrecy—but at what cost?'

"Furthermore, the Underground villages can be at just as much risk. My research shows that a great deal of violence between Agnecs has been occurring lately, and my friends, I know we can all agree, that this needs to stop!" He hit the podium, his voice rising. "We need to come together, despite our differences... But as it is, the average human Agnec village has a much higher rate of crime, murder, and sadly, the inability to defend itself against the onslaught of say, an attack from outside the village.'

"Despite the best traditional efforts of our D'Tari friends," He glanced, smiling, toward Monadias and Master Fentl. "I am proposing the creation of a more efficient and united defense system that would assign highly skilled and well-trained teams of individuals to serve and protect Agnec villages."

There was a slight murmur in the crowd, but Regis maintained a positive expression, licking his lips before his next words.

"Ultimately, in three phases, my proposal entails a necessary budget, a restructuring of training guilds—where yes, we would certainly incorporate the D'Tari—and the formation of an independent council to oversee the operations. I appeal to the congressional leadership, in hopes that you will allow me to carry this proposal on to the Peacekeeping and Security Council for a final vote.'

"Now I know there have been conflicts and misunderstandings in the past, but I appeal to you," Regis said, looking out over the sea of men, women, Fauns, Elves, Dwarves, and a host of other creatures. "You, those whose bloodlines draw their origin from the Old World, and you, the D'Tari, the N'Iatari, and anyone else who has ever called themselves an Agnec... I ask you to see what good can come from putting the past behind us and moving forward in unity, in order to create a more peaceful world."

Aiden could see Megan shifting uncomfortably in her seat, but the rest of the room broke into loud applause. Senator Regis smiled, again thanking Lord Fendiloch, and left the dais, returning to his seat next to Tilli Rosen.

It wasn't exactly that everything the Senator had said was pure gold, but it certainly was the way he had said it. There was a twinkle in his brown eyes, a knowing and shrewd smile on his face. His enthusiasm was infectious. Aiden almost wondered if he himself could have been persuaded, had he not known better.

Lord Fendiloch stood with a pensive look on his face. "If anyone is against the moving forward of this proposal, let him speak now.

Otherwise, we will plan to vote on this matter next week, without contestation."

After a brief murmur spread across the room, Aiden saw Megan stand tentatively. Several heads turned, as if in surprise.

"And your opposition?" Lord Fendiloch addressed her.

Megan's face grew somewhat pink, but she took a deep breath and spoke, "I oppose this proposal on behalf of the Mount Katahdin Guild. I fully represent the majority opinion of the Guild elders and masters."

Aiden saw Megan make a terse movement with her hands, as though she was fighting to keep them from shaking.

Lord Fendiloch scanned the room. "Is there any other opposition? There must be at least two in order to-"

Dorimar also stood from across the room. His deceptively frail figure had appeared from behind a table just across from Megan's, and when he stood, she beamed at him.

"I also oppose this proposal, on behalf of the Elvin Council of the Eastern Seaboard," Dorimar said, his voice projecting much louder than Megan's had.

Lord Fendiloch almost seemed surprised for a moment, but fixed his expression as blankly as he could. "Very well," he said, glancing around to see if anyone else had stood. "Senator Regis, you will make your full proposal in a week's time, and at that time, the opposition will have prepared their cases against."

***

As the room began to empty at the end of the day, Aiden kept a keen eye on Senator Regis. He kept him in his peripheral vision while walking up the aisle to meet Megan.

"Well, that went as well as anyone could've guessed..." said Megan, looking somewhat relieved. "Ready to call it a night?"

"Yeah," said Aiden, distractedly. "Sure..."

As they slowly trudged through the shifting crowds back toward the exit door, Aiden continued to watch the Senator. Regis seemed on a similar trajectory toward the exit, but was caught up by various people stopping to chat.

Aiden couldn't keep his mind off the Senator's speech.

He was forced to look away as he and Megan left the room, making their way through the crowded corridor. Several Dwarves were giving Megan an odd look in passing, and Aiden wondered if it was because of her opposition to Regis' proposal. Megan seemed to be ignoring the attention much better than Aiden, but soon none of it mattered as they stepped out onto the village street. They were greeted by a cool breeze and the soft glow of lanterns illuminating the ancient structures around them.

Heading toward the northwest, the two of them strolled silently along the old cobblestone streets, ignoring the small groups of passersby who left Council Hall behind them.

Aiden was still stuck on Regis' speech. "It's not the worst idea, you know..." he finally said.

"What?" said Megan, after a moment.

"Creating a designated force to police and defend Agnec villages..."

Megan stopped, her face visibly changed in the shifting shadows. "Aiden," she sputtered. "What are you saying? You agree with Regis now?"

"No," Aiden backpedaled. "No, I don't agree with him—not if he's connected to the N'Iatari... I just feel like," Aiden could see Megan's glare, and he continued walking in order to avoid it. "I just agree that it's a great concept. I mean, you've heard me complain about the same stuff he pointed out. There's no way to enforce the laws that exist..."

Megan sighed—but Aiden couldn't tell if it was from exasperation or simple exhaustion.

It was silent for the next few minutes as they passed old stone villas surrounded by dark gardens. Patches of large cropland were slowly becoming visible in the distance, but the lanterns grew fewer and fewer along the way. They could no longer hear the distant chatter of voices or the occasional squeal of wagon wheels from the center of the village.

"Maybe you could suggest an alternative?" Aiden finally said as the way began to climb upward toward a stone wall.

"An alternative..." Megan began, her face visible again by the light of the lanterns which hung on the wall. "To his plan? You mean, a way to keep the concept, but defeat any abuses of it?"

"Something like that," Aiden said, smiling.

"Hmm..."

As they faced the wall, this time Aiden traced a rune and the stone door slid open seamlessly. He was finally getting used to using this route instead of entering the Underground by way of the Gowry Tavern and Inn, even if they had to backtrack a little each time. Once inside, Aiden could sense the wheels turning in Megan's head, and her mood had lightened some. They ascended a flight of stone steps until they came to another door.

After stepping up into a dark alley behind a cafe, the stone door slid closed. Seeing that it was safe, Aiden and Megan stepped out onto the open sidewalk surrounded by small Ambler shops and restaurants. Though there was some nightlife here, no seemed to notice the random appearance of two people from the alley. Aiden took the lead, taking in the fresh night air and watching his shadow dance as each street lamp passed overhead.

It wasn't long before the hotel building loomed into view, its upper levels cascading into shadow and only slightly illuminated by a handful of sporadically lit windows. Here the streets were quiet, save for a distant siren. Aiden was feeling somewhat more optimistic about things as they approached.

"Maybe you weren't wrong after all," he said, almost jokingly.

Megan scrunched her face in confusion. "About what?"

"Maybe things can change after all-"

He stopped at the sound of footsteps and glanced into the shadows across the street from the hotel. Megan froze, mostly reacting to Aiden.

"Hang on," he whispered, pulling Megan closer to the building and turned his back to the street side. He suddenly realized their faces were very near one another.

Megan blushed, then composed herself. "What's a matter? What're you doing?" she demanded, keeping her voice down.

Aiden glanced over his shoulder carefully. A man came into view, well-dressed and simply strolling along with a confident gait. Aiden felt his insides leap.

"It's Regis," he whispered in revelation.

"Are you sure?" Megan asked, unable to see past Aiden.

"Positive," said Aiden, his mind working fast. "Okay, I'm going to tail him. This could be our chance to see what he's up to. You should be safe once you're inside the room, and-"

"What?" Megan blurted, almost too loudly. "I'm not staying in the room while you get to do this. No way," she insisted incredulously. "We're in this together, come hell or high water. Plus, you're protecting *me*, right? You can't just leave me alone!"

Aiden made to protest, but he was unable to get past her impenetrable gaze. "Fine," he conceded. "But if something really bad happens, get the hell out. Okay?"

Megan nodded, then stopped, suppressing a smile. "Or we'll just see what happens..."

Aiden turned his head just in time to see the Senator's form turning a corner down the next street. Aiden nodded to Megan and the two of them crossed the road, making sure to keep to the shadows once they were on a sidewalk near some old buildings.

Aiden tried to be aware of the occasional passerby, but there didn't seem to be any as of yet. They trailed Regis from as far away as they could before he would begin to vanish from sight.

Although the streets were empty, the air seemed loud from a nearby thoroughfare, and the resounding traffic covered what little there was to be heard of their footfalls.

Soon even the street lamps seemed to dim, and many of them no longer worked. As they crossed beside overpasses, they began to see shabby tents where homeless people had obviously bunked down for the night. The air grew cooler and Megan's arm slowly slid into Aiden's. This action had gone almost entirely unnoticed, as Aiden concentrated on the distant form of the Senator.

Aiden soon began to wonder why the man was walking at all. Regis was a United States Senator. He had a car, didn't he?

After another ten minutes, Regis turned left into an alleyway, and Aiden was relieved that something seemed to be happening. Aiden pulled Megan off to the side and stayed close to walls alongside the sidewalk. Keeping track of the alley where Regis had disappeared, Aiden pulled them closer to that opening, seeing a small beam of light shining out from some distant point inside.

Cautiously, Aiden and Megan peered into the opening between buildings, only to see a wide space full of stacked boxes, crates, and wooden pallets dimly lit by a lantern at the far end. Regis was there, looking in the opposite direction, as if observing something in the far shadows. As the Senator reached the midway point, the lantern light illuminated the way, forcing Aiden and Megan to crouch, just enough to avoid its rays.

In moments, two men in white cloaks appeared before Regis with blades drawn.

"Senator Regis, I presume?" said one of the men in an alert tone.

"Of course," Regis replied calmly. "I have a meeting with Lord G'nehon. I'm sure you're aware of it."

"First, you know what to do," said the first man, keeping his sword forward.

"Of course," said Regis, lifting his hand in a writing motion.

The Senator wrote a a small runic word in the air and wafted it toward the far wall as though it had been blown by the wind. The ornate symbols glowed momentarily, then faded. The bricks in the old wall behind the men in white began to shift and rearrange themselves until a passage appeared.

Megan opened her mouth to gasp, but no sound came out. She cupped her mouth, looking to Aiden with wide eyes. He returned a confused look.

A short, stocky figure came into the alley from within the passage. The two men in white stepped aside to let the newcomer pass.

"Cardibran, my favorite lackey," said Regis, approaching the Dwarf. "What news do you have for me—from the interchange at the library? I hope you've been paying attention..."

"Of course," the Dwarf sneered. "It seems like Lord G'nehon has a bigger following than we thought."

"Than you thought, perhaps," corrected Regis. "I am not surprised."

"I just think that you might be underestimating the vote—I

mean-"

"Oh I'll take care of the opposition. No worries there. And if Lord G'nehon's building an army across the pond—as they say— he can do it here as well. Soon, we'll have all the support we need. With Rosen on our side, no one can stop us, not even Turlin's doormats."

"I'm going to move in closer," whispered Aiden.

"Just scry," said Megan.

"I suck at that. Just stay here, and if the shit hits the fan, you know what to do..."

Before Megan could protest, Aiden had crouched as low as possible, snaking himself into the alley behind a stack of boxes. He tried to move in even closer, still unable to see the faces of the men in white. The shadows were far too penetrating.

Aiden tried to shift his weight, but realized he'd stepped on a piece of broken pallet. It ground against the pavement as he tried to place his foot elsewhere. He stopped, realizing the noise had resounded in the alley. Everyone had frozen for the moment.

"Cardibran," Regis said to the Dwarf suddenly. "Come with me. We have a few things to discuss."

With that, Regis and the Dwarf disappeared further into the shadows and through the passage, their footsteps fading beyond the alleyway. Aiden realized that he'd likely missed his opportunity and made to turn back, but the men in white remained on guard, not far from him. He tried as noiselessly as he could to nestle between a stack of crates, hoping to go unnoticed.

The light from the end of the alley blinded him from an opening between crates. Everything began to topple with an ear-shattering crack. Aiden found himself falling, his face and arms being battered and torn by the wooden containers. The wood was cracking open. Liquids and masses of unseen objects were splattering into Aiden's face. His scream was muffled beneath the chaos and darkness.

A pain burst into the back of his head, illuminating his mind with a thousand colors. In seconds, everything had gone black.

Chapter 17
Toad's Corner

The darkness slowly began to give way, and the light at the end of the alley seeped in. Aiden could feel someone lifting the crates off of him. With each shift, his body ached.

He had almost forgotten what he'd just experienced, but it all came back to him in seconds. He dared not move.

He couldn't be sure that the liquid soaking his clothing wasn't blood. Everything hurt, but he suddenly realized he could feel his right arm, which had been crushed down to his left side. He tried to wriggle his other parts subtly, just to make sure everything was in order.

"I think he's still out," Aiden heard a man say.

"Once we get these things off him, tie him up. Gott'a ask him some questions just to make sure," came another man's voice.

Both voices were hovering right over him. Aiden's face hadn't been fully uncovered yet, but it was only a matter of moments. He kept his right hand steady, waiting for just the right instant. His heart pounding.

He closed his eyes as the crate above his face shifted and moved. He could see the light in the alley through his closed eyelids, and the darkness of a shadow falling over his face in the next moment.

"Yep..." said one of the men, clearly lingering over Aiden's body. "Still out. Stupid son of a bitch. Didn't even see it-"

The man moaned suddenly as a blade struck his left arm. Aiden leapt to his feet, struggling a little as the weight of various liquids sloshed off his body along with debris from the crates. The first man was struggling to back away, gripping a bleeding arm, while the other stood, surprised, but managing to draw his own sword.

Wordlessly, the armed man attacked Aiden, but he was blocked by Aiden's buckler and countered. Their blades clattered in the darkness, sending sparks in all directions. For some time, it was just Aiden and the first man dueling, but he knew he would have to end it soon. When he'd had the chance to look, he noticed the injured man had disappeared.

Aiden reached forward and felt for a rune on his blade. A blast of flame lit up the alleyway, setting the N'Iatari's white cloak ablaze. With a whip of his wrist, Aiden's blade squelched its own flames, and he watched for a moment as the man dropped and rolled in panic, still wrapped in bright fire. Aiden turned to the street side of the alley, hoping he could leave.

Two more men in white cloaks stood there, stopping Aiden cold in his tracks. The injured man must have sounded the alarm...

Aiden looked back to the end of the alley and saw two more cloaked men blocking the passage. One of the men closest to Aiden drew his curved blade, and by way of watercast, doused the burning man, extinguishing the flames entirely. In moments, the burnt and smoking man struggled to his feet and stumbled out of the alley and into the opened passage.

"Well... Shoot," said Aiden, his eyes scanning every detail of the alley, and Megan was nowhere to be seen. "Looks like this is going to be fun..."

The man with the curved blade stepped closer, then laughed for a moment. "Hmm... It's a small world," the man said, watching his blade glint in the thin light. "I thought I recognized your fighting style... Aiden."

"Huh?" Aiden grunted, thoroughly confused, still holding his sword aloft.

The large man lowered his hood to reveal a head of long blonde hair, which reflected the small patch of moonlight seeping down into the alley. Aiden squinted in the darkness, trying to see the man's face. In a moment, his eyes widened with furious revelation.

"Grant..."

"Mmhmm," the large man agreed casually. "Just call me Griftwalker, the N'Iatari aren't so strict on the whole first-name basis thing. I wondered if we'd ever see each other again, and here we are, on opposite sides of this thing. No surprises. Huh, you don't even look a day over twenty, maybe twenty-five..." he mused. "They told me a D'Tari was in the alley, didn't know it was you... And with a fancy new sword," he added, noticing Aiden's newly-forged rapier.

Aiden changed tactic, fighting his urge to lash out violently. "I seem to have heard something about you being mixed up in all this," he said, slowly lowering his left arm as if to check the time on his watch. A thought had struck him. "Well, what the hell have you been up to?"

"I'm not here for the small talk," Griftwalker sneered. "What are you doing here? And on who's orders?"

Aiden took a quick moment to twist the knob on his watch, pressing the button, though he pretended to be fiddling with it as if unthinking. "Funny, I should ask you the same question," he replied. "A bunch of N'Iatari in an Ambler warehouse at night... Nothing suspicious about that."

Even though it was now half-hidden beneath a thin beard, Aiden could still see Grant's boyish face as though it were yesterday. He fought back against the memories and tried to focus on the moment.

"So tell me, *Griftwalker*," Aiden said slowly. "What have you been doing with the N'Iatari all these years? Catching some rays in California? Killing some innocent people?"

"I guess you've done your homework," said Griftwalker. "I don't mind admitting that killing those Amblers was a lot of fun, but mostly it had to be done. The Dark Goddess is back, and G'nehon will stop at nothing to do her will."

"But why would you possibly need to kill Amblers? What does it prove?"

"I'm not going to dialogue with you right now," Griftwalker growled. "We had our reasons, but you'll be dead in a moment, so I wouldn't worry..."

Griftwalker looked to the other men and barked, "Move!"

All four men approached Aiden at once. A flower of brilliant flame bloomed from the center of the men, setting all four of them ablaze. When they had all doused each other, Aiden had vanished from the center of the circle.

One of the men collapsed in a pile of broken and shattered crates. The others turned to see that Aiden stood up against the opposite wall, smirking in the dim light.

Aiden lobbied a double blast of fireballs at two of the men. One of them dodged, while the other took the blast fully in the face and flew into the opposite wall. When the man slid down and collapsed to the bricks, his body had left a small crater.

Griftwalker and the other man now rushed Aiden with blades flying. All three blades rang at once, sending sparks into the air and lighting up the alley.

"Ready to join your mommy?" Griftwalker taunted. "I can still see the look on her face when she died-"

"Shut up!" Aiden screamed, knocking the other man's blade away and glaring at Griftwalker.

Aiden felt a blade rip through his shoulder. Griftwalker laughed in his face.

Ignoring the pain, Aiden threw all his weight behind his buckler and sent Griftwalker to his backside, and the man's blade flying off into the darkness. Aiden could feel a rage beginning to consume him.

"You son of a bitch!" Aiden yelled with rapier ready to strike, no longer able to control himself. "Do you know what kind of hell I went through because of you?"

Aiden made to strike him, but the other man's blade cut in from the side. Aiden swore, forcing the opposing sword away. The cloaked man conjured a fire ball and sent it flying, but Aiden dodged and the wall behind him cracked from the explosion. Aiden swung around and thrust his blade through the man's thigh.

In that split second, Aiden knew that he should stop, but he could only see red. In the next moment, his thin blade had struck through the man's neck. The man gurgled and crumpled into a bloody heap as Aiden retracted his sword.

Griftwalker had already clambered to his feet with sword ready. He and Aiden stood, glaring at each other. For that single moment, Aiden almost glimpsed fear in Griftwalker's eyes.

Their swords clashed, echoing throughout the alley. Aiden saw a burst of red and blue lights alternating wildly across the alleyway. A siren burst from somewhere just outside on the street. Both Aiden and Griftwalker froze, seeing the look of surprise in each other's faces.

"This is the Police. Stop what you're doing and come on out with your hands where we can see them," a megaphone squawked into the alley as the men heard a myriad of car doors slamming, equipment jingling, and guns being readied.

All of Aiden's anger began to fade, and he could only imagine what the cops would think when they saw the bodies in the alley. Both he and Griftwalker were still motionless, frozen, and glaring into each other's faces with blades connected. In that brief moment, Aiden wondered if they could work together.

"Correction," Griftwalker sighed.

The man's fist crashed into Aiden's left eye, sending him to his backside, his blade falling into the shadows.

"Hell has only begun for you," Griftwalker snarled, crossed himself in an unfamiliar hand gesture, and quickly faded into a swath of black mist.

Aiden cursed and picked himself up.

"This is your last warning," the megaphone squawked again. "Come out now, or we will use necessary force."

"Screw this," Aiden said, turning to the wall and beginning to write runes in mid-air.

In a moment, a door appeared before him. He threw it open and stepped over the threshold just as a rush of tear-gas canisters blew into the alleyway.

Aiden stepped out of the door and into dark shadows somewhere just outside of his hotel.

Clutching the wound on his arm, he knew now that he should have been more specific with Megan about what to do, but he hoped that she'd be here.

"If only I knew how to jump or lettercast..." grumbled Aiden, unable to help himself as he stumbled back against a wall and slid to his backside. "Or wouldn't it be amazing if Agnecs used cell phones?"

"Aiden?"

Aiden sighed in relief as he saw Megan race toward him. Her face was lined with worry.

"Are you okay?" she asked, kneeling at his side, looking shocked at his appearance. "As soon as I saw the crates collapse, I got to safety and sent Jardun a lettercast..."

"Did you call the cops too?" Aiden asked, realizing now that the pain in his arm was growing more intense.

"Um, yes," she said, awkwardly trying to help him to his feet. "But I'm probably not the only one. I heard sirens, did they show up?"

Aiden nodded, wincing and finally standing.

"Well, let's get inside."

Without thinking about anything except his desperate need to get upstairs, Aiden sloshed through the lobby and into the elevator with Megan's help. They staggered into the room, slammed the door, and Aiden collapsed onto one of the beds.

***

Aiden could feel himself falling in and out of consciousness. He could hear Megan talking to him, but he wasn't sure what she was saying. Lights danced frivolously in his mind's eye. When his eyes opened again, he could have sworn Jardun was there, but then things fell back into darkness once more.

It seemed as though only moments had passed when Aiden finally sat up looking around the room, the morning sunlight already bleeding in through the window. His head was pounding, his eye black and blue, everything ached, and his shoulder was bandaged.

"Um," said Aiden, seeing Megan enter the room. "Hey, what

happened?"

"Oh I'm glad to see you're awake," she said kindly, coming toward his bed. "Jardun thinks you may have gotten a concussion. You were pretty out of it. He healed your arm too."

Aiden slowly felt along his arm where the wound had been, and he peeled back the bandage. The wound was gone, despite the remainder of dried blood on the inside of the bandage. He sighed, his head still pounding obnoxiously.

"Where's he now?" Aiden asked groggily.

"Had to get back to the Guild, but he wishes you the best of luck."

"Well... I feel like shit," he finally said.

Megan went to the mini-fridge and began rummaging for something. "We've got some soup here. You should try eating something."

Aiden nodded, though the thought of food was a little unsettling. Finally, the events of the night before began to return to his mind. He looked to his watch, a chill of excitement running through him. He turned the dial until satisfied, then pressed the play button.

A three-dimensional image appeared from the watch's face, making Megan jump. "You scared me! What is that?" she blurted.

"Just a little something I'm testing..."

And they watched as Aiden played back the fight between himself and Griftwalker. But there was no sound.

"Dammit," Aiden swore, pressing the button again. The images faded. "I still haven't figured out how to capture sound..."

"So... did he die?" she asked, looking concerned.

"The other guy?" Aiden asked, all the sights and sounds beginning to sting his mind. "Yeah," he said with a sigh. "Can't see how he would've survived. I don't know how I feel about that. First time I've actually killed someone..."

Aiden stared off into the ceiling, feeling something like shame beginning to bite at him.

Megan pulled up a chair next to Aiden's bed, looking both understanding and concerned. "Well, you were defending yourself. I mean, it's sort of what you trained for, isn't it? What else could you do?"

"Guess so..." Aiden said with a nod. Vodin's teachings on pacifism would always be with him, just beneath the surface. He shrugged, hoping to think about something else for a while.

"If you want to work on fixing your watch, you've got time," Megan said, reading Aiden's discomfort. "I didn't really have to be at the sessions today, so you can just relax and focus on this."

Aiden sighed, not wanting to be reminded of all they had to face with the Congress, but he nodded, thankful for how accommodating Megan was being.

"Besides," said Megan, sitting back. "Now we know that there's a connection between Regis and Lord G'nehon, as well as Griftwalker..."

"Griftwalker also told me he was connected to the murders on the West Coast—of course didn't explain why, but why would he?

He mentioned the Dark Goddess. Said she's back," said Aiden pensively. "Three guesses who that is."

A light tapping on the windowsill caught Aiden's attention. He glanced over and almost rolled off the bed. D'Natis stood on the windowsill, balancing skillfully.

Aiden gasped in a mix of surprise and joy as Megan rushed to open the window. The raven hopped from the sill to the table in front of Megan. D'Natis staggered somewhat, looking tired. His large eye finally rested on where Aiden lay, his look full of unspoken words.

"D'Natis, are you alright?" Aiden asked, wondering why the bird was looking a bit off.

D'Natis finally hopped to the table nearest Aiden's bed and lowered himself, folding his legs up inside his feathers. "I'm fine," he said slowly. "Just tired I suppose."

Megan made a face similar to that of a child finding a wounded animal. "Do you need anything?" she asked in a soft voice. "Water?"

D'Natis paused, then agreed to the water. Megan went hastily to the kitchenette.

"What happened to you?" D'Natis asked, eyeing Aiden suddenly, as if just realizing what he saw.

Aiden looked at himself, remembering that he was still covered in multicolored paints and splashes of blood. The bed was an absolute mess, and Aiden knew that his face was badly bruised.

"Uh... Long story. Don't worry 'bout it," Aiden shrugged.

"So..."

"What did I find out?" the raven cut him off. "I'll tell you. You should note that a lot of Agnecs no longer take kindly to talking Animal Lords... I suppose my kind are the thing of legend to some *people*." He ended the sentence angrily, his tongue lagging as if his throat was intensely dry. "This has not been easy."

Megan placed a mug of water in front of D'Natis, and the bird paused to drink.

"I went directly to Senator Rosen's hometown of Camden," D'Natis continued after draining nearly half the mug. "I talked to everyone that could possibly know her in the Agnec world. At least I tried. That was no easy task, mind you. And many of them were not friendly nor understanding. I got the sense that she was relatively unknown." He sighed and shifted his weight on the table. "Thankfully, when I went to the local hall of Agnec records, the librarian was nice enough to let me peruse the documents. According to the Agnec census data, well, Rosen has never lived there... Certainly wasn't born there."

"Hmm..." Megan mused. "What if she was actually from somewhere near Camden, but not actually there?" Megan wondered aloud, looking thoughtful.

"I too had the same thought, and conducted further research, checking every possible Agnec meeting place I could find," D'Natis chimed in. "For someone who is supposedly so prominent on the political scene and loved by Agnecs, she certainly has left no trace—especially with Agnecs."

"I wonder how that's possible..." Aiden mused, stroking his chin. "There has to be a paper trail, and a bunch of local supporters... I mean, who even appointed her to office?"

"I suppose now you'll have to do this the Ambler way..." Megan said, sitting back. "Use the internet."

"I'll have to do it?" Aiden asked, surprised.

"Yeah," said Megan. "I'm still researching the N'Iatari as well as preparing for my presentation next week. I'll do my thing while you do yours, right?" She smiled, seeing Aiden's look of disappointment. "Anyway, there's bound to be a lot written about her in the Ambler papers and online, right?"

***

It was already the weekend and the Congressional sessions were closed until Monday, so Aiden and Megan found themselves at the local public library.

"Well, this is bunk," said Aiden, after a few hours of research. "There's absolutely nothing on Rosen—anywhere. Nothing about her family, nothing about her position, nada."

Megan frowned, gesturing for Aiden to join her at her computer, and he wandered over, shrugging. "Well, put a pin in that for a moment," she said, her eyes still locked on the screen. "This..." Megan said quietly while Aiden stooped beside her to get a better look. "I thought you should know about."

Megan was on a local news site, and across the top of the page, the bold headline read, "Philly Politician Accuses Stalker of Local Police Scuffle".

At first Aiden thought nothing of it, but Megan forced him to read the rest of the article. Of course, he ended up kicking her out of the seat so he could sit up properly to read.

The article followed, "Washington, D.C., — At around 10:20 on the evening of the 5th, local police officers were called to investigate near the Art-Supply warehouse just two miles from the Pentagon. Neighbors had reported hearing fighting and shouting in an alley near the warehouse, including booms and odd bangs which they thought may have been gunfire.'

"The alert level was raised however after two officers arrived on the scene and called for backup. One of the first men to arrive on the scene was Officer James McOwen, who initially admitted that he called for backup the moment he saw a trail of blood coming out of the alley. 'There was several small explosions. The alley was lighting up, even though it didn't sound exactly like gunshots. People were fighting and shouting. It was the use of deadly force for sure,' McOwen said in an initial statement.'

"When backup arrived, police were baffled to discover the alley empty, save for the remains of an as-of-yet unidentified security officer. The full report has not been released by a coroner, but initially it was said that the man's throat had been slit and there were burn marks on his face."

Even though he was confused at why they were calling the man a security officer, Aiden knew it was the man he had killed. He felt a horrible pang of guilt creep inside him, but he continued reading to himself, "Several thousand dollars of property damage have been estimated in the wake of the scuffle. 'The place was a mess,' said McOwen. 'Crates and containers shattered and spilled everywhere, paint and supplies all over the walls and the ground... Blood everywhere. There were these charred black spots like someone had been throwing fire, and if that wasn't crazy enough, water. There was puddles everywhere too.'

"This, as odd as it is, might have gone unnoticed by the press at large if it weren't for the involvement of Philip Regis, a Philadelphia, PA Senator whose hotel is only blocks from where the incident occurred."

Aiden almost felt nauseated, only imagining what would likely come next.

He continued reading, "The Senator was walking back to his hotel that very night, and suspected he was being followed. 'I've been attending a local conference for the last week or so,' said the Senator when he broke this story to us exclusively. 'I've seen the same man almost every day on the street, it was only a matter of time I suppose.'

"'My security detail reported the incident to me,' Regis continued, sounding confident but looking, as any man would, shaken. 'I felt that I should alert the area to watch out for him.' According to the Senator, he tried to shake his stalker by walking to the hotel a different way, which must have led the stalker into the wild confrontation with the warehouse security. The details are still unclear. As of this point in time, Regis' stalker is to be considered armed, dangerous, and highly unstable.'

"According to the Senator, the man has short dark hair, is about mid-height, thin build, light-skinned, and looks as though he could be of some Japanese or Chinese descent."

Aiden couldn't bear to read the rest. He leaned back in the uncomfortable office chair and closed his eyes. It was strange reading about himself. Of course, it was extremely out of context, which threatened his calm, but he knew he should compose himself. There were too many Amblers around. He released a sigh which ended in a growl.

"Are you ok?" Megan's voice finally broke Aiden's thoughts.

"It's like doing something really stupid, and then finding out the entire world was watching..." Aiden said, finally looking back to her.

"So... the body they found-"

"Yep," Aiden nodded. "Well, you saw me kill him in the playback from my watch... But why are they calling him a security guard? He was N'Iatari. And why did nothing else get discovered? I mean, what happened to the bodies of the others? And Regis went through that passage with Cardibran..."

"That's just it, though," Megan chimed in, her mind whirling. "Obviously they didn't want the passage discovered. It must have closed itself before the police went in the alley... And someone must have quickly changed the clothes on the body..."

"It just seems too convenient," said Aiden, thinking aloud. "I know the N'Iatari are good at covering their tracks," he added, thinking of how his mother's murderers had left no footprints in the snow. "But that's a quick change. The cops were right there."

"Seems the most likely explanation," said Megan. "Yes, I saw the man you fought. And who's to say the N'Iatari couldn't have conjured up a quick rune to disguise the body at the last moment? Those other men weren't dead were they? Maybe someone dragged them in the passage before the police actually made it into the alley?"

"That just means that someone might've been watching me escape..." realized Aiden.

"And Regis knows it was you following him..."

There was a silence between them for some time, and Aiden returned to his research, while Megan returned to a large volume she had borrowed from the Agnec library.

"I'm such an idiot," said Aiden, after another ten minutes had passed. "Here's the US Congressional records... If you just know how to search... I guess I sort of missed out on the whole internet thing growing up..."

When Aiden was finally able to locate Rosen's listing, the name was displayed in a very small font, under '*Special Presidential Liaison to Minority and Ethnic Communities*'...

"This would explain why," Megan surmised. "Even though the members of the Shadow Congress know her, they aren't too familiar with where she's from..."

"Even Fendiloch didn't want to say anything..." added Aiden. "If you ask me," he continued. "I would take some stock in that '*and*' placed in Rosen's title... She's the President's watchdog for the minority communities—that's well, you know what that means. *And* she's the watchdog—likely Regis' watchdog—for the *ethnic* communities, and in this case, that probably means *us*."

***

Aiden walked along the sidewalk through the market district, with D'Natis nestling on his shoulder and Megan nearby. The mid-day atmosphere was alive with tourists and locals walking in every direction, entering street-side shops, and investigating the vendor kiosks. Aiden strolled slowly, doing some reflection.

Megan's presentation was only a day away, and they had some lobbying to do. Aiden wasn't very thrilled, but given that it was his job, he agreed to go along. When he heard Dorimar would be joining them, he now wanted to be there... just in case.

Aiden hadn't walked far when his thoughts broke at the sight of a man standing just off to the side near an alleyway observing a store front. He stopped, seeing that the man's back was turned to him. The man's frame was slim yet muscular, his stature short yet somehow not diminished. It was Dorimar. The Elf—who could easily fit into human society if he tried—looked out of place in the street clothes, and he wore a yarn beanie on his head, which brazenly failed to match the rest of his clothing. The beanie had mostly served to cover up the Elf's distinctive ears and cranium shape, but even so, Aiden almost laughed.

"Dorimar?" Megan said quietly, approaching the Elf.

"Yes, Megan," Dorimar said, smiling subtly at her. He turned as if thinking to acknowledge Aiden, made a terse movement with his neck, then looked back to Megan.

Aiden's face scrunched, though he wasn't surprised at being snubbed. He stopped when he realized Dorimar's hand was gently caressing the small of Megan's back.

Aiden stepped closer, and he could see Megan smiling back at Dorimar, her white cheeks blushing. Aiden clenched his fists, and found himself moving in. He came in between the woman and the Elf, forcing his presence so abruptly that D'Natis hopped off his shoulder. Aiden acted as though he was looking at the items in the store front window. Although he had no clue what he was looking at, he could only think of Megan and Dorimar.

"Hey!" Megan said, surprised at Aiden. "What're you doing?" she asked in an awkward half-whisper.

Aiden turned around, seeing an annoyed look on Dorimar's dark face. "Just looking," Aiden answered Megan, though he was eyeing the Elf.

"Let's enter the Market, shall we?" Dorimar said, sidestepping Aiden and gently taking Megan's arm.

Megan threw Aiden a confused glance, but Dorimar led the way, purposely avoiding Aiden's gaze. D'Natis hopped back to Aiden's shoulder, himself a bit ruffled.

As if instinctively, Aiden noticed that the cross street ahead of them was M Street. The alley suddenly grew familiar as he followed after Megan and Dorimar, a cold feeling sitting in the bottom of his stomach. As if reliving some old dream, the way grew long and dark, stretching unnaturally before them. Soon they stood before a door without a handle, shadows dancing slowly in the candle light.

As Dorimar turned into the flickering light, Aiden noticed that the Elf no longer wore the funny looking beanie, or the street clothes. Now he donned a more traditional traveling cloak and his head was uncovered. He had changed so quickly that Aiden knew the Elf must have done it through magic.

Dorimar opened all three locks by tracing the runes and reciting the passwords in both Elvish and Dwarvish. He gave a smug smile as the handle appeared, while Aiden grimaced.

Soon, Aiden found himself following closely behind Dorimar and Megan as they walked along the store fronts, observing the various goods on display behind the old glass windows. They had entered Market Street, with all of its Old World charm and noise separated from the New World by only a few feet of brick wall.

"So, who are we meeting with again?" Aiden asked Megan quietly, hoping that Dorimar would not hear.

"A small group of various representatives who have agreed to hear our cause before tomorrow's vote," said Dorimar importantly, before Megan could even respond.

"What he said," she told Aiden, nodding to the Elf. "You met most of them the night of the banquet," she added in an upbeat tone. "Don't worry about it. That's for me to do."

Soon they turned down an alley, leading away from the main market, and a dark door led them into a pub. The interior was much the same as that of the Gryphon Claw, the Gowry Tavern and Inn, and other Agnec establishments Aiden had seen. A sign post hung just inside the door frame, reading, "Toad's Corner".

At the far end of the busy room, in a dimly lit space, three individuals sat around a table. Megan waved to them and made to lead the way, though she was forced aside as Dorimar barged past her.

"Rude," Aiden commented sideways to D'Natis.

"Aiden," Megan soon said after greeting the female Faun at the table. "You remember Sarmos from the Common Alliance of Satyrs and Fauns."

Aiden nodded to the Faun, while Dorimar looked suddenly perturbed.

"And Dorimar," Megan introduced the Elf quickly, her face flushing at his reaction. "From the Elvin Council of the Eastern Seaboard."

The Elf bowed slightly, though looked less than enthralled.

Megan composed herself, introducing the others, "And this is Dothrak from the International Confederation of Blue Dwarves," The stout creature bowed, maintaining a stony look. "And Jhon from Agnec Nation," she finished while the tall human male smiled casually, shaking Aiden's hand and bowing respectfully to the Elf.

"Ahem," coughed the raven on Aiden's shoulder.

"Oh yes, I'm so sorry," said Megan, looking nervous by her mistake. "This is D'Natis, the Raven Lord."

The raven hopped off of Aiden's shoulder and made a slight

bow, his tail fathers lifting slightly behind him. "Last of the Raven Lords," he added regally.

Jhon jumped slightly in surprise, but then happily acknowledged the raven, while the she-Faun and the Dwarf did not look surprised in the least by the talking bird. Dorimar remained stoic, but eyed D'Natis for a few moments, as if he too had not previously realized the raven's true nature.

Now that the introductions had been made, they all took seats.

"I hope you don't mind if we get straight to the reason we're all here," said Megan, shifting in her wooden chair. "I hope not to be too forward, but also, as you know, there is an important vote tomorrow..."

"Of course, of course," said Sarmos with a genuine look. "Let's get to it."

"First of all," Megan said, after taking a calming breath. "Thank you all so much for taking the time to meet with us... And for showing interest in our cause. We're all concerned, actually, that although we think Senator Regis' proposal sounds like a great concept, we feel that it could turn into a system that would be too easily abused."

The she-Faun and the man nodded slowly, while the Dwarf remained fixed.

"But, I've also set out to prove my concerns over Regis' connections to the N'Iatari—well, let me rephrase that," Megan continued. "I'm concerned with his connections to a particular N'Iatari... Lord G'nehon."

"And I," Dorimar chimed in suddenly. "Have added my support, but my contribution is mostly in that not only do I feel that the proposal has too many loopholes, but financially it doesn't make sense for the long term."

"Yes, there is also that," agreed Megan. "So what I'm saying, on top of all that, is that the system Regis proposes would have an independent council that could easily run the gambit of decisions with no checks and balances needed for distributing the kind of military and police force that he wants..."

"You're concerned that Regis would abuse this system?" asked Jhon. "How so? And why?"

"I'm concerned that anyone could, in theory," said Megan. "It would be completely independent, without any oversight from an outside council or body. Who's to stop someone from funneling D'Tari or N'Iatari graduates into some sort of... army of mercenaries?"

"Naturally that would depend highly on the motives of the governing council," said Sarmos pensively. "Are you sure this is not borne of paranoid thinking? Haven't the N'Iatari proven to the Agnec community that they are just another branch of the D'Tari? Their organization has not shown any ill will towards anyone in decades."

"Hasn't it?" said Aiden, fighting back his own feelings.

"Steady," whispered D'Natis.

"You have proof of the N'Iatari's misdeeds?" the she-Faun asked, surprised.

"Yes, as a matter of fact, I do," said Aiden, resting his watch arm on the table. "Should I show them?" he asked, looking to Megan.

"I'm not sure-" said Megan, looking suddenly flustered.

"This is not part of the presentation we agreed on," said Dorimar to Megan.

"I'm not sure what that will accomplish at the moment," Megan told Aiden finally. Before he could respond, she turned back to the others. "We do have eyewitness accounts," she said firmly. "Both Aiden and I have been victims of N'Iatari attacks—both led by Lord G'nehon actually—and furthermore, we have reason to believe that Regis is connected to him."

Before anyone could respond, Megan continued, "Though the reports are sparse, there's a small amount of data to suggest that something strange is going on—and maybe it's only a faction of the N'Iatari, not the whole organization itself—but as I said, it's especially concerning to me that Regis is heading up this proposal, especially because of his connections. I mean, he's made no statement about the philosophy or values behind the uniting of D'Tari and N'Iatari-"

"Yes, but perhaps he has a statement that's not been made yet," suggested Sarmos.

"I think it should have been mentioned in his introduction then, don't you? At any rate, as a D'Tari myself, I can tell you that the two organizations—well, let's face it, the two cultures—have very different ideas about a lot of things. And Regis has made no accounting for this."

There was a moment of silence as Megan's point sunk in.

"I have one question," Dothrak the Dwarf, after having been silent the entire time, finally spoke. "What business is this of yours, Dorimar, that you should be involved?"

Megan looked surprised at the intensity with which Dothrak had spoken. Dorimar shifted in his seat, but looked back at the Dwarf with a fixed expression.

"My people have reason to believe that Regis may next call upon us to join his militia, or to help police various Agnec communities," said Dorimar. "Furthermore, he, like most D'Tari," He looked over to Megan with something of a stern look. "Tend to rely upon Elvish tongues and enchantments for various protections. If Regis seeks to truly fortify his force, then it's only logical that he would want our assistance—something which we do not all believe we need to give."

Dothrak's greyish brow wrinkled in offense. "Why wouldn't they ask my people for help first? After all, the Agnec world is still using Dwarvish charms for most protections, and you Elves are content to stay away, aren't you?"

Dorimar released a hollow laugh. "We enjoy our privacy, yes, but it's ridiculous to imagine that your magic is better than ours. Isn't it?"

The Dwarf scowled. "No," he said, the hint of an angry tone beginning to rise. "We're the reason the Agnec world is still standing, no thanks to your kind."

"Cling to your gold," said Dorimar, his voice slightly raised.

"Cling to your gold is all you people do. You're not really here to help anyone, save for reaping the benefits!"

"You said it yourself, that your own intentions are solely focused on your own people!" Dothrak retorted, beginning to tug at his beard in irritation.

"At least I am honest about it," said Dorimar. "You worthless little earth worms are nothing more than gold-hoarding con men!—to use an Ambler term—why don't you all go back to counting your money and leave the politics to the rest of us?"

Megan glared at Dorimar, partly angry, partly in shock. The Elf's face was now red, but no more red than Dothrak's cheeks had also become.

The Dwarf stood, shouting a curse in Dwarvish. "Lest I challenge you to the death, this conversation is over," he spat.

Dorimar scoffed as the Dwarf stomped away from the table and disappeared through the door frame at the front of the room. The table sat in shock, staring at Dorimar.

"Well..." said Aiden quietly. "That went well..."

"Okay," Megan began slowly. "Let's just take a moment to cool down, and maybe get back to the issues at hand. Okay?"

Dorimar was silent.

"So, as I was saying," Megan continued, trying to gauge the rest of the people at the table. "I feel we have enough information to make a case for at least some concern, and if there's enough of a case against, perhaps we can stop Regis' plan from going on to the next batch of sessions... Or at least perhaps the Congress elders will demand that he modify it enough before it does."

"My concern is this whole N'Iatari business," said Sarmos, watching Dorimar in the corner of her eye. "As you can see, we're still a realm divided by class and racial differences. Won't the N'Iatari-D'Tari divide be seen as petty? Perhaps as a ploy to stick to old stereotypes?"

"Not if we can prove what we know," said Aiden.

"What say you, Dorimar?" the she-Faun looked to the Elf.

Wordlessly, Dorimar looked away with a terse jerk, stood, and sauntered off to the bar at the front of the room, looking still furious.

Megan scoffed, biting her lip angrily. "I'm so sorry," she said to Sarmos. "I- I-"

"I don't hold you accountable for his actions," said the Faun in an understanding tone. "But I need some more time to consider your request and I need more evidence."

"But the vote is tomorrow," said Megan, a hint of desperation in her voice.

"I'm not easily bought like most politicians," said Sarmos, standing. "I think you have good intentions, and I don't ask for any petty thing in return for my vote—but I do suggest that you reconsider who you call partner."

Megan sighed.

"Nothing is final on a matter like this until the Peacekeeping and Security Council sessions—so we have until then," continued Sarmos. "I wish you the best of luck, and we'll keep in touch."

With that, Sarmos left the table, her hooves clunking on the old hardwood floor.

"Well, Jhon, you've been awfully quiet," said Megan, looking over to the man. "What are your thoughts?"

"I'm more inclined to side with you against Regis," said Jhon with a thoughtful expression. "I realize my vote may not swing things completely in your favor, but it's what I can do."

Megan smiled, obvious relief painting her features.

"I've looked at some of the proposal, and the budget certainly needs to be changed. Furthermore, I think, with some further investigation, we can conclude what Regis' connections really are... Because I'm curious about those myself. I want to see the D'Tari succeed if they can. I have... fond memories of them protecting my village from Orcs. You live by a moral code that I respect, one that seems to be built into the Agnec world... I don't really know, nor have I heard much good about the N'Iatari... So, yes, count me in."

Aiden smirked. He felt warm inside just watching Megan's face light up.

"Thank you so much," gushed Megan. "This means a lot to us."

"My pleasure," said Jhon, standing from the table.

With that, the man made his way out of the room. Once he had left, Megan's eyes fell back onto Dorimar—still sitting at the bar near the door. She sighed, all her joy quickly disappearing.

"Permission to speak freely?" Aiden asked as they left the table,

D'Natis hopping back to his shoulder.

Megan nodded.

"Dorimar is a douche."

Megan gasped. "Aiden! Don't say things like that," she chided. "It's complicated between Elves and Dwarves. You know that."

"Yeah, but he just really screwed this whole thing over."

Megan didn't reply. They arrived at the bar and took seats next to Dorimar, spinning slowly on the old bar stools. The Elf silently sipped ale from a large pint, as if still stewing on the encounter with the Dwarf. Megan looked to Aiden as if she too had no clue what to say next.

"Dorimar," Megan said finally. "I guess we should probably leave now..."

The Elf raised his hand gently as if to shake off her suggestion. "I suppose I should apologize to you," he said. "But it serves us right, trying to do any sort of reasoning with a Dwarf."

"Well, it doesn't matter anymore anyway," said Megan. "I've got a presentation to prepare for, so..."

"Ah, if you'll excuse me for a moment," Dorimar interrupted, ignoring Megan. "I need to talk to someone."

Before Megan could protest, Dorimar had left the bar and walked across the room to join another Elf's table. Aiden hadn't even noticed that table until just now, as some of it was obscured in shadow.

"Well, he's well-connected," Aiden said, sensing Megan's frustration.

Megan simply watched with incredulous disappointment.

"I need a drink," Aiden finally said, turning back around to face the bar, only to realize the bartender was nowhere to be found.

"Excuse me, Miss," a man's voice came from next to Megan, making Aiden spin around to face the room again.

A man with long black hair and a pale complexion stood there in traditional dress, his shoulders covered by a traveling cloak. He looked into Megan's face with a concerned expression.

"Have you seen my son?" the man continued. "He's only about yay high," He gestured with his hand, indicating about four feet tall. "Has black hair, green cloak? His mother's worried sick. Been missing for an hour..."

"No, I'm sorry, I haven't," Megan replied with a voice of real concern.

"Drat," the man said, frustrated, glancing around the pub. "Well, if you see him, please let me know. Here's his picture..."

As Megan made to stand, the man pulled a roll of what looked like parchment from his cloak and unraveled it just inches from her face. A powder fluttered from the parchment, bursting into Megan's eyes and mouth. She coughed and sputtered, clutching her throat. Aiden leapt to his feet, drawing his blade, but found himself cushioning Megan's collapse, gently laying her on the floor.

She was trembling and starting to choke. Her body flailed and flopped, and Aiden felt himself go cold with panic. The gagging noises echoed through the room, alerting the other patrons of the tavern. People at the tables began to rise, wondering what had happened. The room grew noisy.

The black-haired man glared triumphantly, his face twisted suddenly. "Even now, Lilit has already won," he said, his tone adamant, and then burst from the room at full speed.

Megan's face was already bloodless and her breathing labored. She had nearly stopped struggling. Dorimar was quickly at her side, glaring into Aiden's face as if somehow he, Aiden, had been responsible for the attack.

"I'm not sure what that stuff was," Aiden said, trying to keep the panic out of his voice.

"An old assassin's trick," Dorimar said with a scowl. "Her windpipe's blocked, but we can't blow it out... That would only make it worse."

The Elf placed a hand on Megan's throat and began muttering an incantation. In moments, the blood seemed to rush to her face and she sat up coughing and gasping. The feeling returned to Aiden's chest as a rush of emotion hit him, but then he stiffened again.

"The assassin!" Aiden realized, standing now with sword drawn. "D'Natis, watch her, alright?"

D'Natis, who had been standing on the bar, made to respond, but was thwarted as Dorimar stepped forward.

"*You* stay with her," Dorimar barked, placing a hand on Aiden's chest as if to stop him from taking another step. "I'll go after him."

"It's *my* job to go after him!" Aiden protested, swatting Dorimar's hand away.

"No, it was yours to protect her, and what a grand job you made of that," Dorimar quipped, his gaze piercing Aiden's.

"Get him!" Megan suddenly spouted from the floor where she sat, leaning up against the legs of her bar stool, still spluttering. "Just do it!"

Aiden bent down to hear her, checking to see if she was really okay. The bartender had appeared and was bringing her some water. D'Natis glared at Aiden, but he couldn't see why. When he stood back up a moment later, Dorimar had already disappeared.

"Dammit!"

Aiden flew out the door and into the dark corridor. His pulse quickened, a sudden rage racing through his veins.

Chapter 18
Man Against Elf

Aiden could see the tail of Dorimar's cloak as it whipped around a corner, and he raced to catch up. He found himself running down a dark corridor, well away from the market place. He was right on Dorimar's heels, and the Elf flinched, seeing Aiden out of the corner of his eye.

"Go back!" Dorimar said.

Aiden did not answer, but pushed himself to catch up to the Elf. The two of them were almost neck and neck, and Aiden could finally see the assassin out ahead of them. The black-haired man, his cloak tailing wildly behind him, was racing with dangerous momentum over the old stone bricks. The corridor was dimly lit by wall lanterns placed at intervals, sending strange shadows dancing around them.

"Go back!" Dorimar said again to Aiden.

"No," Aiden refused, beginning to pant from his effort.

Save for the sounds of their boots clambering across the bricks and the rough panting of the two humans, the passage seemed as though it should be unusually quiet. The corridor, which now rounded at the top as though it were a tunnel, seemed to go on endlessly.

The would-be-assassin grasped at his side and began to slow

ahead of them. Aiden watched Dorimar speed up, as if gliding on some invisible machine for a moment. The Elf drew his sword from beneath his wind-swept cloak. It was a sturdy, gleaming Elf-wrought metal, which Aiden hadn't before noticed on Dorimar's person. Aiden pushed himself to keep up, his own sides aching now, and likewise drew his own blade.

Aiden rushed forward, his sword not far from the man ahead of them, but Dorimar's blade fell into the way, blocking it with a loud clang that echoed throughout the tunnel. The assassin turned back to see what had happened and stumbled over the bricks, straight on his face.

"Idiot!" Aiden yelled, as the two of them staggered to a violent stop.

"He's mine to deal with! You should be back with Megan," Dorimar said, with one eye on the confused assassin and another on Aiden's livid face.

For a moment their swords locked, but Dorimar looked ahead of them and let his blade drop to the bricks. It clattered loudly, confusing Aiden. The assassin had gotten to his feet and was beginning to run again, and Aiden prepared to follow. In that moment, there was a swift, wild movement off to one side. Aiden stopped. Before he could see what had happened, the assassin yelped and collapsed.

When Aiden turned back to Dorimar, he saw the Elf easing his grip on a bowstring, the arrow nowhere to be seen. When he finally caught up to where the assassin lay, he saw Dorimar's arrow in the man's back. The black-haired man was motionless, blood beginning to pool beneath him.

"Great..." Aiden said, gasping to catch his breath and clutching at his aching side. "Nice going. I thought he might've been good to question..." Aiden coughed, glaring at Dorimar, who approached, looking barely winded. "But whatever..."

"If you had just stayed back there," Dorimar said, his face twisted with anger, despite a restrained calm in his tone. "You would not have distracted me."

Aiden was bowed now, still trying to catch his breath. "Oh come on," he panted. "You're an Elf. You could have put that thing right between his heart and his lungs just to keep him alive long enough to ask him anything... I think most D'Tari could have..."

"I don't miss often, but when I do, I admit it," Dorimar said, his face still contorted. "And if most D'Tari could have, why didn't you then?"

Aiden couldn't think of a time when he had ever seen an Elf show this much rage with such an expression. Aiden's own face had turned red with both anger and embarrassment.

"Oh shit," Aiden said as he looked up, then back down the tunnel they'd just traveled. "Megan..."

Mustering whatever energy he had left, Aiden sped back down the tunnel. The journey seemed just as long on the way back. He followed the tunnel until it became the passage, and then as it drew to less of an incline, it became the corridor again. He turned right and finally saw the door of the old pub. He grabbed the ancient door jamb, propping himself up in the open doorway, and tried to catch his breath.

Everything aching, Aiden staggered into the pub. The sudden silence was jarring, and his own breath was cut short when he saw what stood before him.

A bearded man in a white cloak stood there in the center of the room. He stood behind Megan, with one hand tugging her head back by the hair, and the other clutching a dagger poised to slit her throat.

Megan seemed to be alright, besides the laboring breath she was forced to take with her head in that position.

The patrons in the room had mostly stood and moved toward the back, looking frightened and remaining still. A couple of mothers shielded their children's eyes in fear of what might happen. D'Natis stood on the bar, his feathers ruffled and his beak slightly open as if he'd been ready to attack. Everything was eerily still.

The bearded man gazed at Aiden as if about to say something, but remained silent.

"So what do you want?" Aiden finally asked, unable to stand the quiet.

The man laughed. It was high-pitched and alarming as it broke the silence, only increasing the sense of inevitable horror beginning to slide into Aiden's chest.

"I only want to see the look on your face when she dies..." the man said in a high tone, his eyes sparkling with something between determination and demented joy.

Aiden's brow knit. He would have to think fast, but nothing was coming to mind. "You must want something," he said, trying to keep eye contact with the man.

"Give up," the man said slowly. "Go home. None of this is any of your business..."

Aiden raised an eyebrow. "What, specifically?" he asked in a cautious tone.

"You and the little lady here are in over your heads now, but perhaps you can be spared if you were to simply give up. Politics isn't really your area... Why don't you just go home?"

The N'Iatari man was still glaring at him with those wild eyes and unwieldy beard, daring him to approach. Aiden knew he couldn't, not just yet. Nor was there much he could say.

"Who sent you?" Aiden finally asked the man. "Was it G'nehon?"

The man laughed, his tongue flicking like a lizard's. "Asking questions won't stall the event, demiGod," the man said, tugging harder on Megan's hair, forcing her to yelp.

Aiden stepped back, pushing aside his first inclination to react.

"Why are you calling me that?" Aiden asked.

"Word's out on you. It's only a matter of time until the entire Congress will know of your shame. No one wants to believe a junior ambassador and an outcast who murdered his own-"

"Not so fast!" Aiden spouted, unable to help himself. Megan's face was alive with fear and confusion. "What do you think you're accomplishing with this anyway? Any moment now, my Elf *friend*," Aiden made a sour face. "Will be here, and there'll be two of us. You sure you're ready for that challenge?"

"It'll be too late," said the man with a smile. "She's no good alive. Not really," the man continued. "But I'd rather have *you* dead even sooner."

"Then take me, and let *her* live," Aiden said, holding his hands out slowly.

"That's no good either," the man said, tightening his grip on Megan. "You both need to die. Yes..." the man trailed off, his eyes gazing as if seeing things beyond Aiden. "That seems the only way it'll fix things."

Aiden was silent, watching as the man seemed to be working things out. Aiden hoped he hadn't just helped him figure out a course of action, but it seemed as though he just might have. The man glared at Aiden again and began pressing the blade into Megan's exposed neck. She began to scream.

"That'll work," the man said, beginning to laugh. "As long as you refuse, she dies slowly. Your choice."

Aiden felt cold and helpless, watching the man slowly press the blade into Megan's neck. Dark droplets were beginning to seep from the cut now.

The air behind the man distorted slightly, as if pieces of reality were breaking apart. In that space, Dorimar appeared, as if pulling himself out of another dimension. In one swift movement, he wrenched the N'Iatari man's arm back and away from Megan's neck, and the woman collapsed to her knees. The N'Iatari blade clattered against the wooden floor.

Aiden ran forward to catch Megan, dragging her away, as Dorimar attempted to stifle the attacker. Aiden pulled Megan back toward the bar. Her neck was covered in scarlet now, the cut bleeding unhindered. Aiden paid no attention to the loud struggle going on behind him in the center of the room, but instead scanned the bar for something. Megan was colorless again, and although Aiden had directed her hand to her throat to compress the wound, she was too weak to hold it there on her own.

Aiden burst from the floor and grabbed a whisky bottle from the top of a liquor shelf just behind the bar. Glass flew in all directions, littering the floor with shards and a wave of alcohol, causing D'Natis and the bartender to jump in fright. Aiden had shattered the bottle over the edge of the bar, and without warning, he jammed one of the jagged edges into his own outstretched arm. He returned to Megan's side, his arm spurting red.

Quickly he formed a runic word upon Megan's neck, using his own blood. Although for several moments, it was hard to see, but soon Megan's cut no longer bled. The color returned to her face, and her chest rose and fell in regular patterns. She seemed unconscious, but her pulse was normal again. Aiden exhaled a sigh of relief, watching his own wound begin to seal itself, leaving a sudden scar.

When he turned around, he was both relieved and frustrated at what he saw. The N'Iatari man lay dead on the wooden floor, and Dorimar was cleaning his blade.

***

"You're sure?" asked Dorimar, as he looked to Megan.

Megan nodded, much to Aiden's chagrin.

Dorimar smiled. "Well, as you wish," he said, feigning disappointment. "Why don't you go back to your hotel and get some rest? You should be resting."

Megan shook her head slowly to disagree, her neck still hurting. "I'll be fine," she said quietly.

Dorimar looked somewhat frustrated for a moment, then composed himself. "Very well then," he said, then turned back down the aisle toward his seat.

"Lovely person..." said Aiden, glaring at the Elf as he walked away.

He and Megan stood at the back of the main room in Council Hall, watching the shifting crowds of delegates and representatives file into their seats. Megan tugged gently at the scarf around her neck, sighing.

"Are you sure you want to stay?" Aiden asked, seeing how she was uncomfortable.

"Yes," she said, her throat somewhat raspy. "Just everything's sore from yesterday... But," she added with a smile. "I have you and Dorimar to thank for being alive."

"You've already said that... a few times," said Aiden, trying to keep himself from blushing. "Just my job."

She watched Aiden as he resumed glaring at Dorimar across the room. "I know you don't like him, but he is helping—and he helped saved my life. That's something, right?"

"Yeah," said Aiden slowly. "But he also killed the men who could have given us info..."

Megan frowned. "You're not saying you think he meant to? He was just defending himself—and me—right?"

Aiden threw her a skeptical glance and shook his head tersely.

"Well, I find it hard to believe that it was intentional," said Megan. "And anyway, who else is going to give our defense today? My throat's still killing me."

"Let me do it."

Megan shook her head. "Sorry, but no. Look, things are starting—I need to take my seat now."

Visibly upset but maintaining his composure, Aiden nodded and watched as Megan walked down the aisle to her seat somewhere near the raised dais in the center of the room.

After all the chaos that occurred the day before at Toad's Corner, Megan seemed to be holding up well enough. Aiden watched her as she sat waiting for the sessions to begin, and looking at her, one might not think that she'd been viciously attacked and almost killed twice just the day before.

As usual, Lord Fendiloch opened the day's sessions. And after several other proposals had been discussed, Aiden's ears perked up when he heard Senator Regis being called the podium. Regis began by restating much of the proposal, as well as his statistics from the week before. Nothing much had changed.

"The tragic incident yesterday," the Senator added, his tone solemn. "Involving the violent assault of one of our own," he said, gesturing to Megan, who was at her table. "Miss Rohan—demonstrates our collective need for a unified law enforcement."

Aiden rolled his eyes. *Seriously?* Aiden thought. How did he even know?

Megan turned vaguely pink as all eyes in the room fell on her.

"Surely, D'Tari were dispatched to deal with the situation," Regis continued, looking solemnly around the room. "But after the fact. If Miss Rohan's friend Dorimar nac Heartwood hadn't intervened... Well, I don't want to think of what a loss that would've been."

Aiden's fists clenched. He bit his bottom lip, coming close to severing it. But he stopped, only feeling shame when he thought of how things might have gone differently had he stayed with Megan while Dorimar pursued the second attacker.

"But this seems to prove my point," Regis continued, his dark eyes finding Aiden's convulsed expression from across the room. "We need a fast-acting force that can be summoned at a moment's notice."

Regis surveyed the audience. "Now that each voting member of the Congress has had a chance to peruse a copy of the proposal, and you've all seen the desperate need for a unified defense force, I trust you'll all make the wisest, most informed decision. How much longer can we afford to turn a blind eye to the violence and crime of the Agnec world? If the situation were different, Miss Rohan might've been murdered," The crowd murmured slightly.

"And would her murderers have been brought to justice?'

"Now I know there's been talk of the dangers of uniting the N'Iatari and the D'Tari," Regis continued, as if getting a second wind. "But having worked alongside them for so many years, I can assure you, the N'Iatari are a small minority. They have also worked tirelessly to step away from the ugly reputation that proceeded them. We all have things in our past we aren't proud of, and some of us have to work harder than others to get away from those things and start over. Many of the N'Iatari are still in hiding, misunderstood, and just trying to make a decent living like everyone else. They want all the same things the D'Tari do. They want all the same things most Agnecs do.'

"I know we all strive for similar things. Similar goals. Most of us have similar values as well. There's no need to fear the coming together of great minds and abilities, especially when they will be utilized for a greater purpose: The common good of the Agnec world. Thank you."

The crowd applauded as the Senator left the stage and Lord Fendiloch resumed the podium.

"Thank you, Senator," the old Faun said. "Now, as Miss Rohan is still a bit under the weather—though we're glad she's graced us with her presence," He smiled at Megan. "In her place, Dorimar will present their co-opposition to the Senator's proposal."

Dorimar took the podium, a dire and serious look on his face. He placed a thick folder before him, and thanked Lord Fendiloch. "Now," Dorimar began. "Let me explain our reasons for opposition.

If you've even glanced at the budget for this proposal, you will certainly see some serious issues—ones which need an entire overhaul before this could ever work.'

"Furthermore," Dorimar carried on. "As my partner, Miss Rohan, has pointed out, there is a history of violence among the N'Iatari. One which may, or may not, be substantiated by current events—as the current attempts on her life seem to have been the work of men who claimed to be followers of Lilit."

The crowd murmured ever so slightly.

"But, these may have simply been rogue extremists," Dorimar continued. "Should there be more investigation? Certainly. Perhaps this is something we can accomplish should Regis' proposal ever see daylight—so whereas I cannot stress the use of caution, I also further stress the need to create a much more stable model for a unified defense force."

Aiden's brow knit. What was Dorimar saying?

"I also propose the need to turn Senator Regis' independent council into a body governed by members of both the N'Iatari and D'Tari governing councils—as well as members of this Congress—so as to insure a fair cooperation between the Agnec leaders and the defense force."

Dorimar carried on about the need to have more specific rules about training the recruits, as well as restructuring the budget so that it didn't put money from each Guild into a common fund—but rather would allocate money to the Guilds in most need first. Aiden agreed with much of it, but there was something about

Dorimar's lack of detail that bothered him. Not to mention that the Elf had failed to push Megan's agenda at all. Other than his initial comment about using caution, Dorimar did not once mention the statistics and eyewitness accounts that Megan had spent the week researching.

When Dorimar was done, Lord Fendiloch seemed relatively impressed. "We have some time for discussion, will Miss Rohan come to the stage? Perhaps she'll be answer at least a few questions," he said as he took the stage next to the Elf.

Dorimar seemed suddenly awkward as Megan finally appeared by his side. Their height difference was more obvious now, and the Elf—though his presence was notable—stood at least a foot and a half shorter than her. Aiden watched, knowing he should have been paying more attention to other security-related things, but he couldn't take his focus off of Megan. He couldn't help but admire her, but now he realized he worried. Like any political press conference, question time was usually when things turned ugly.

"You have said the N'Iatari have a history of violence," a tall, smartly-dressed woman held her hand high and began, addressing Megan. "But you've said nothing of the history of violence among the D'Tari."

Megan made to answer, but Dorimar gestured. "I'll take this," he said. "It can be said that much of the violence you speak of is only reactionary. That is what they say. I have not met many D'Tari, but I know that their purpose is to help people—not hurt. Am I right?"

Megan nodded, looking nervous suddenly.

"Miss Rohan," a short balding Faun called from the audience and stood. "Isn't it true that both D'Tari and N'Iatari have the same powers?"

Megan nodded. "Uh, yes. Of course," she replied, trying to project her raspy voice.

"Isn't it true that your companion," the Faun continued, looking at the back of the room toward Aiden. "Who I'm told is your D'Tari bodyguard, once wrote an article on the similarities of both D'Tari and N'Iatari powers?"

Before Megan could answer, the Faun went on, "Didn't he also state that both powers must draw from some neutral source? This seems to go against the traditional D'Tari idea that the powers are from Shai—and that no evil can come from it. But he says that practicing one wasn't much different than practicing the other. This seems to contradict your point that the N'Iatari are practicing some dark version of the properties. You two seem fairly close. What do you say about his ideas?"

Megan stopped, caught unaware. "I..." she began, but wasn't sure how to respond.

Aiden's heart felt as though it had slid into his stomach. The silence in the room was palpable.

"Um, no," Megan finally said, her voice cracking. "Just because he is my friend and my colleague—does not mean we share the same views on everything. I also fail to see how his beliefs reflect on me. If the N'Iatari are involved in dark doings, then they should be investigated... Plain and simple."

The Faun shrugged, looking somewhat defeated. Megan coughed as several more hands rose, but Lord Fendiloch stifled any further questions.

"We're running short on time, as more proposals need to be discussed," said the old Faun, looking to his pocket watch. "Now, if everyone's ready, let's vote, shall we?"

When everyone had returned to their seats, Megan glanced back to Aiden. She looked somewhat upset, but also unsure. Over the next few minutes, there was an unsteady silence as each voting member of the Congress focused on the table before them and put their vote into writing.

When they were done and the votes had been collected and counted, Lord Fendiloch took the podium again. "It was somewhat close, but the majority has spoken..." he said, looking into the crowd. "Regis' proposal will go on to be considered for legislation in the Peacekeeping and Security Council."

***

As the session ended for the evening, Aiden watched small amiable crowds forming around Senator Regis and Tilli Rosen. The Senator's use of the attempts on Megan's life as a way to promote his proposal was still hanging heavily in Aiden's mind. Furthermore, he watched as Dorimar passed by Regis, and in that split second, Aiden could have sworn the Elf and the Senator had locked eyes in some sort of knowing glance.

Or had he just imagined it?

As the crowds began to disperse, Aiden did not immediately go to escort Megan down the aisle. His vision narrowed in on Dorimar, who had just been talking with Megan. He marched through the shifting faces, not bearing to look at anyone as he could think of nothing else. When finally he arrived, he stopped and glared at the Elf.

"Yes...?" Dorimar said in an upturned drawl.

"Let's talk, just you and me," said Aiden forcefully.

"I assume you mean to give your opinion on what happened tonight?"

"Something like that," said Aiden, looking over to see that Megan was engaged in conversation with Lord Fendiloch. "Let's go... It'll only be a moment."

"Oh you mean in private?" said Dorimar, feigning indifference. "I suppose..."

Seeing that Megan was still busy in conversation, Aiden led Dorimar to the end of the room and out into an empty corridor off the main hall. They stepped into the space surrounded by ancient paintings of Centaurs, Fauns, and wise old Elves, and Aiden kept silent until the door had finally shut behind them.

"So what the hell was going on out there?" Aiden asked, no longer able to hide his anger.

"Whatever do you mean?"

"You know what I mean," snapped Aiden. "You're purposely screwing things up here. First you lose us votes yesterday because of that thing with the Dwarf, and now you're practically promoting

Regis' idea? I mean, c'mon! What happened to all of Megan's hard work and research? You mentioned none of it."

"Frankly, I wasn't all that enthralled with her work, nor did I believe it was necessary to mention."

"Then why the hell did you agree to help her? Why even give the speech in her place?"

"You've heard me explain it before," said Dorimar sharply. "I have my reasons, and whereas she is young, naive, and none too bright, she has the kind of beauty and passion that one can certainly run a campaign with. It's only a shame that not enough people see it as I do."

Aiden wasn't sure how to respond.

"Furthermore, despite today's turn of events, there's still a chance we can garner a bigger following in the Peacekeeping and Security Council... So why are you so upset?"

The Elf had a point, but Aiden shook his head. "I'm upset because—well, first of all," he spluttered, struggling to form the words. "You're either a complete asshole for being such a jerk to the representatives yesterday—especially when you knew we were trying to win their vote... Or you purposely sabotaged the whole thing.'

"And what's more..." Aiden could feel himself starting to peter out. He shook his head. "You talk about Megan like that again, and you'll have me to answer to."

"Surely you did not just threaten me," said Dorimar, locking eyes with Aiden. "My kind do not respond well to threats, as I'm

484

sure you've heard."

"Elves don't get sarcasm either," said Aiden, returning the Elf's gaze. "It's okay to admit you're—none too bright—is how you put it..."

A fist flashed across Aiden's face. He staggered, his nose bloody, and in moments, he drew his rapier.

"Oh so Elves do like to use their tiny little fists sometimes..." Aiden said, wiping the blood with the back of his hand.

"You don't want to cross me," said Dorimar confidently, reaching into his cloak and gripping the handle of his sword. "I don't know why you feel so threatened, is it because you were hired to do a job, and so far I've done it for you?"

Dorimar drew his sword and held it aloft as a challenge.

"Is it because you see the way Megan looks at me," he continued, glaring into Aiden's eyes. "There's nothing more enrapturing to an inexperienced woman than an exotic virile he-Elf. I've saved her life, twice now."

"You killed people needlessly," Aiden spat, trying to ignore the Elf's comments about Megan. "We could've questioned them. You knew that was the proof we needed. People have been trying kill us ever since it got out that we're opposing Regis... Don't you think that's a little too coincidental?"

"I've done my research on you, Aiden Gailhart," said Dorimar. "And given your history, there's bound to be other reasons men might want to kill you..."

Aiden raised an eyebrow.

Just before either of them could move, Megan entered into the corridor, holding the door open behind her.

"What are you doing?" she shouted at the sight of Aiden's bloody face, but clutched her throat in the pain she'd suddenly caused herself.

"Get back!" Aiden warned.

He stared straight ahead at Dorimar, who glared as if calculating what he should do.

"What's happening?" Megan asked, quietly this time. "Please stop."

Senator Regis' face appeared behind Megan suddenly, making her jump. He nodded to her, then stepped beside Aiden calmly. "Now what's this?" he said, looking to Aiden with a less than genuine expression of shock.

"This is between me and Dorimar..." Aiden said to the Senator, with eyes still focused straight on the Elf.

"Surely, we can work this out," Regis said, trying to sound as diplomatic as possible. "There's no need for violence."

"You started this," Aiden said to Dorimar, ignoring the Senator. "You going to finish it?"

Megan tried to grab Aiden's arm, but he pulled away. "No! Don't do this. Why are you doing this?" she asked, in a half-whisper.

"You saw what he did yesterday," Aiden said, his blade still trained on the Elf. "He's acting like he's helping you, but he's not. He even said so himself, just now, that he didn't care for your research, so he didn't present it tonight..."

Megan didn't say anything, obviously shocked. The Elf returned an indifferent look.

"You have no proof I said such things," Dorimar said, no longer looking so angry.

"I guess it's my word against yours..."

The Elf's brow furled again.

"Then you had to step in, didn't you?' Aiden added. "Somehow we all forgot that if it weren't for *my* blood, Megan wouldn't be here right now... And somehow," Aiden suddenly looked to Regis with an unnerving glare. "*You* forgot that I had anything to do with it. How convenient." Aiden set Dorimar back in his sights. "Just doing my job, but whatever..."

"I don't like what you're implying, Son," Regis said, looking confused.

"Not surprised."

Regis made a half-smile, half-confused expression, which Aiden didn't buy for a moment.

"So I'm just a job to you?" said Megan quietly, though everyone heard.

"No," Aiden responded quickly, now flustered. "That's not what I meant-"

"I see how it is now," the Elf chimed in, capitalizing on the opportunity. "Doing the bare minimum for the most money are you? I stepped in and you lost some of your paycheck, didn't you?"

Aiden could only see red now. "No— C'mon!" Aiden finally

shouted. "Do something! You struck me first."

"Of course that's what you'd say," Dorimar said nonchalantly, his eyes searching the corridor.

"'Cause it happened," Aiden said with an incredulous laugh. "You can't play that card here. This is about you purposely ruining Megan's hard work. Now let's do this, since you seemed so intent on fighting before these two stepped in."

"You, Sir," Regis began with a small smile forming. "Are as formidable as you are stupid. Perhaps I'm just an Ambler, but I've never heard of any human surviving a fight with an Elf."

"Then stick around," said Aiden.

Megan and the Senator jumped away in both directions as a wild array of sparks burst into the air. Both Dorimar and Aiden's swords had collided. The Elf had lunged so quickly that Aiden had almost been caught off guard.

They charged each other again, forcing Megan and Regis to take refuge against the walls. Aiden thrust and parried, his buckler at the ready. Dorimar balanced himself against the wall, countering the blow while his emerald robes billowed around him. Aiden stepped aside just as the Elf sent a blue fire ball through the air. The blast narrowly missed and destroyed a painting on the wall, sending flaming pieces of canvass and wood flying.

Aiden likewise launched his own ball of flaming energy with both hands, but Dorimar lobbed it back with his blade. Aiden jumped aside, and the rebounding ball knocked a jagged hole in the wall just behind him. He could see into the adjoining room where several chairs had been destroyed.

"You didn't know Elf-wrought blades could withstand the heat, did you?" Dorimar said with a smug glance at Aiden's surprised face.

"That's alright," Aiden said with a sudden change of pace. "I've got other tricks up my sleeve."

Almost as if it had always been there, white-alloyed metal appeared on Aiden's body. His armor gleamed in the glow of the overhead lights, and the helmet created an almost bat-like shape out of Aiden's face. His eyes were now the only thing visible, through narrow but versatile slits.

For a moment, Aiden could have sworn he saw the slightest flicker of fear in Dorimar's eyes, but then it vanished. The Elf's face twisted into something frightening.

"I tried to explain that I'm here to help Megan," Dorimar said, his blade dancing around Aiden's as the two stalked each other in a slow circle. "But I can see that you can't listen to reason..."

"Reason? Sounds more like lies to me."

Before Dorimar could move, Aiden launched fire from his blade. In that moment, Aiden heard the Elf shout something inaudible. Dorimar vanished in the swath of flame and smoke, and when the flames died, Megan gasped.

Aiden knew the Elf hadn't given up.

The corridor grew silent—although Aiden could hear a small crowd gathering just outside the door—and he scanned everything. Aiden kept his armor and sword ready, but decided to make his way back into the main hall. The huge room was mostly empty now and many of the lights were already extinguished, save for the central chandelier. A crowd of curious and fearful faces met him at the door behind Megan and Regis. Questions began to bombard the three of them.

"Listen," Regis called them to order. "Everything is being taken care of. Please just go home. There's nothing to worry about..."

Someone shouted in shock, pointing up to the ancient chandelier. Aiden looked up, but saw no sign of Dorimar. The chandelier was swinging from side to side, but didn't seem to be falling. Then he caught sight of an emerald-robed figure up in the balcony.

"So this is your idea of proving yourself, huh? Cowardice?" Aiden bellowed up to Dorimar and began to run toward the balcony.

Dorimar lifted a hand, muttering something under his breath, and Aiden could see the chandelier shifting and moving as if it were under the Elf's command. He felt something twinge in his stomach and lifted his buckler up in front of his heart. It was all he had time for, as he heard the crackling of a hundred candle-shaped lights overhead. A thousand shards of glass rained down on him like daggers, all of them bent at a lethal angle.

Aiden's ears ached from the onslaught of glass. Everything struck him with such force that soon he was on his back and he realized that much of his armor was either gone or shattered. In moments, even his buckler had split in two and began to unravel into white mist. When the shattering and the breaking had finally subsided, the pain overcrowded Aiden's senses, like a violent noise in itself.

As his broken armor began to fade from him, the white mist mixed with red. He could feel the warmth of his own blood beginning to flow around his body. Before he would allow himself to lose consciousness, Aiden's last shred of strength was reawakened by the sight of Dorimar smirking from atop the balcony.

He lifted his head, though it was no easy task, and saw that he had a clear shot. Despite the shards sticking in his arms and chest—which jolted him painfully with every slight movement—he sat up and braced himself. Thinking of only the pain and the deceit and the things that Dorimar had said, Aiden blasted a wooden beam directly beneath the balcony.

With a loud crack and a burst of energy, the balcony on which Dorimar had been standing, began to topple. The Elf had been caught unaware and cascaded through the wreckage as the structure collapsed to the lower level, sending the small crowd running for cover and the room filling with dust.

The room fell silent again. Everyone seemed dumbstruck by the events. When the dust cleared, one figure began to emerge. It was clearly a Faun.

"Master Jardun," Aiden heard Megan's voice emerge from behind him.

Jardun approached the small crowd, and all eyes were on him. Megan stepped forward to greet him, though shaken, but the Faun gently dismissed her gesture and stopped to look down on Aiden's battered body.

"I think this time you bit off a bit more than you could chew..." Jardun said, looking troubled.

Aiden winced, his breathing labored. He could not respond.

"What are you doing here?" Megan asked.

"After the last incident," Jardun began. "I've not been far away... Just in case."

From out of the pile of rubble that had once been the balcony, Dorimar crept, coughing. When he finally got to his feet, he looked bewildered for a moment, his face bloodied and dusty.

Jardun frowned at the Elf, then turned back to look at Aiden. He waved his hand over Aiden's fallen body, and a new warmth fell over him. Aiden no longer felt the pain, but shock had set in. He felt almost stable, even if it seemed only temporary. He still could not move anything other than his head, but he tried to pay attention to the events unfolding.

Dorimar looked as though he struggled to compose himself. "Then let this be a warning to you, Aiden," the Elf said, staring down at the bloodied man. "Never contradict an Elf."

Jardun faced Dorimar. "What is the meaning of all this?" he asked sincerely. "You've nearly killed him!"

"I was teaching him a lesson, you foul Faun. You of all people should understand-"

"What lesson?" Jardun interjected, turning to look at Aiden's sad state as Megan now knelt over him in concern. "D'Tari powers were not given to keep the Agnecs at bay—if that's what you mean.

And why me, of all people?" He looked back into Dorimar's dark face. "Because I'm not human?"

Dorimar simply scowled..

"I understand a lot of things, but senseless violence is not one of them," Jardun added before Dorimar could say what he was surely about to say.

"He accused me of intentionally ruining their opposition," said the Elf in a much smaller voice than Aiden had previously heard. "Then I was simply defending myself. If I hadn't put a stop to it, he would have killed me, certainly."

Jardun turned on the spot and looked back at Aiden with pity. "Wouldn't an Elf of your standing know better?" he said. "Aiden, you're an idiot, no doubt. But Dorimar—is it?—you took up the challenge? If this is true, why didn't you walk away? Then you are equally guilty."

Dorimar's face burned with anger, but he did nothing. The crowd seemed to murmur in hushed tones, and it seemed that people were trying to make sense of what they had witnessed. Jardun dismissed Dorimar with a simple gesture, upsetting the Elf even further. Senator Regis turned to Jardun as if about to say something, but the crowd parted and another Faun entered into the circle by the wreckage.

It was Lord Fendiloch. He looked as though he had barely wrapped his cloak around him, and his eyes drooping as if he'd been attempting to get some sleep.

"What is the meaning of this?" the old Faun cried, but seemed to lose steam as he laid eyes on Master Jardun. "I've just been informed... We had to placate the neighbors. What's- what's happened?"

"There's been a little scuffle. Nothing we can't fix," Jardun said with an unusual calm. "I would like to launch an investigation into what happened tonight," he added. "And suggest that Dorimar here be suspended from the Congressional sessions until the investigation is over."

Fendiloch seemed tired and a bit overwhelmed as he looked around at the small crowd, the wreckage, and the blood all around Aiden. "Did he do all this?" he blurted in surprise. "To this man? ...Y-yes, I suppose that sounds good. You'll have to catch me up on what exactly happened."

"Good," Jardun said. There was no happiness in his voice. "Megan, please get Aiden to the healer's hospice," he turned and addressed the woman. "I have some work to do."

With that, Aiden felt his head fall back into Megan's waiting hand, as if whatever had suspended his consciousness finally broke.

Chapter 19
RobThumb Healer's Hospice

The darkness was beginning to subside, and a ringing finally roused Aiden. In those last moments of blackness, before his eyes opened to greet the light that invited them from beyond his eyelids, he heard a shrill screaming. It vanished as his eyes fluttered open, and his body suddenly ached.

"Hey..." a gentle voice said from above.

Aiden could feel a soft hand caress his hair, and as his eyes began to focus, he realized that Megan was looking down at him. Her face was stricken with worry, despite the hopeful smile that had formed on her lips.

When he realized it hurt to move his head, Aiden's eyes scanned the room. He was in a small, white room, laying on a bed in the corner near a table. Megan was sitting next to him, balanced on the edge of the bed.

"We're at a healers hospice," Megan told him, obviously having read his confused expression correctly. "In the Underground."

"Wow..." Aiden finally spoke, his voice cracking. "Very artistic decor... If you like minimalism."

Megan smiled again, though seemed slightly off-put by his

comment. "Yeah... They don't have too much here," she admitted, no longer running her fingers through his hair. "But they do good work here. They saved you."

"How long have I been here?" Aiden asked, the thought suddenly striking him.

"Three days," Megan said as she shifted her weight on the bed, making the entire thing creak horribly.

Aiden finally made to lift his arms from beneath his wool blanket. Where there should have been severe gashes from the shards of glass, there were only small, mostly healed cuts.

Then it all returned, the memory slamming violently into his mind like a brutal ocean wave. Dorimar had nearly killed him.

"Where's Dorimar?" Aiden cried angrily, trying to sit up but feeling his body quake suddenly. A wave of sudden nausea began to grip him.

"Lay down," Megan said, placing a hand on Aiden's shoulder. "Lay down! He's not here. He's been dealt with..."

Aiden struggled, but finally acquiesced to Megan's hand. His head hit the pillow with a lumpy thud, and he could feel his heart pounding with adrenaline.

"You're so hot-headed sometimes," Megan said, sitting back and shaking her head.

"But-"

"Just listen," Megan said, her tone firm. "For once, you're going to listen to me."

Aiden looked back at her in surprise.

"You wouldn't be here if you hadn't challenged Dorimar," Megan said, unable to hold back the frustration in her tone. "So don't go trying to get revenge on him. It's your fault. And what the hell is that about? I've heard that Headmaster Turlin is furious with you right now. And I've never seen Jardun so mad. At anyone."

Aiden remained quiet, though his mind began to race with a rebuttal.

"...I'm mad at you," Megan continued, another emotion beginning to cloud her tone. "I guess I thought, somewhere along the way, that I could trust you. That you were on my side. That this wasn't just about the money for you. Somehow, that maybe you and I were friends, and you cared about our cause... Am I crazy to think that?"

Aiden shook his head slowly, a somber look on his face. He felt his defenses beginning to weaken.

"I don't even know what to think anymore..." Megan continued, a mixture of anger and sadness making her face red. "Sometimes you're more like *them* than you realize..."

Megan was silent for a moment, wiping some tears on her sleeve.

"*Them?*" Aiden finally asked, confused.

"The N'Iatari..." Megan whispered, trailing off on the last syllable as if not really wanting to have said it.

All at once, Aiden felt a white hot anger burn in his chest, but very quickly it subsided and he wondered if perhaps she was right. It was something he'd never thought of.

498

"The healers found your scars by the way... Well, they thought they were scars at first," Megan added, splitting Aiden's thoughts in two.

Aiden went cold inside.

"They asked me about them. Showed them to me," Megan continued, as if not knowing what to feel. "They wondered if I knew what happened. But then I realized they weren't scars... They're not, are they?"

"...No."

"The healers were afraid that you had dark magic in you. They thought it was something that happened in the fight..."

"Um... No," Aiden answered. "I guess I should tell you... They're life-extending formulas. I, uh, *was* twenty-one when I did it. Not something I'm proud of... After a few years of exile, I had a scrape with N'Iatari that made me feel... so..."

"Vulnerable?" said Megan.

"Something like that," he admitted, unable to look into her eyes. "I know it's not allowed by D'Tari standards. I was just afraid..."

"So," Megan began slowly, her forehead lined with obvious concern. "Tell me... Tell me what happened all those years ago. I want to understand. I want to know why you're so difficult sometimes, because I don't like feeling this way... I want to know what happened to you."

Aiden was silent, trying to make sense of what way Megan could possibly be feeling. He sighed, pain emerging in his chest when he exhaled.

499

"Okay," Aiden finally said, trying to gauge whether Megan was concerned, angry, or sad, because at the moment it was hard to tell. "The N'Iatari are after me, for something that I have. Vodin gave me a mission... And Grant—er, Griftwalker—found out about it. I had no idea that it would matter so much, or that he was connected with the N'Iatari..."

Megan watched intently now.

"When I was at the Guild... I mean, I was just a kid, I didn't know about all this political bull-" Aiden stopped himself short when he saw Megan's face. "Stuff, that goes on in the Agnec world. Anyway, I guess I was in my head a lot and other kids didn't really get me—and I sort of think that Griftwalker told people to stay away from me. I was a loner... Always have been.'

"But anyway, so long story short, I was stupid. I used to mess with the local gang members in my neighborhood, just to sort of practice my skills..."

Megan gave him a half-shocked, half-reprimanding look.

"I know it was bad, but on winter break my second year, I was messing with a kid and Griftwalker showed up... Him and a bunch of N'Iatari... Full-grown men. And he was sort of leading them. They tried to kill me... They chased me to my apartment..." Aiden sighed, a tear now falling from his eye. "I couldn't shake them, and I knew I had to get my mom to Menlir's house. I knew she'd be protected there..."

Megan's eyes were no longer dry. She placed a soft hand on Aiden's shoulder.

"But she wasn't... I did everything I could. At least I thought I did. But it wasn't good enough..." he tried to continue, but the tears were falling freely now. "N'Iatari killed her, right there in the snow. Griftwalker tried to take the locket, but Turlin and Menlir arrived and everyone had disappeared without a trace."

Megan was speechless, and tears began to run down her cheeks.

"Dead," Aiden finally said, his voice cracked with emotion. "I could've saved her. I know I could've... I still hear her scream every time I wake."

Aiden painfully turned his head to the side, staring into the blank wall to avoid Megan's gaze. She shifted too, and looked in the opposite direction. It was quiet for several moments, aside from the muffled sound of Aiden sniffling. He wished he could just *not* feel this way. He tried to compose himself, but for every bit of progress he seemed to make, a new wave of horror would arrive with the recalled memories. Finally, he seemed to master himself.

"The Council didn't even let me speak at my own trial," Aiden finally continued. "They accused me of accidentally killing her. Fentl led the witnesses and Monadias watched the whole thing... Vodin wasn't much help," he added bitterly. "They tried to leave me with my aunt, but then N'Iatari killed her too..."

Megan gasped and sniffed, covering her face with her hands.

"I was left to the streets, with only D'Natis... Well, I guess now you know..." he concluded, turning back to look at Megan, who was rubbing her red eyes.

"Because I want to know," she said, returning his gaze.

Aiden stared blankly into the ceiling.

"I'm... so sorry," she finally said. "I don't know what to say."

"You and me both," Aiden said bitterly.

"I can't believe that they did that," Megan thought aloud. "There must be more to the story-"

"Well, whatever it is," Aiden cut her off, anticipating her thought. "I haven't found it, not after fourteen years..."

Megan sighed, composing herself. She bit her lip suddenly, deep in thought.

"Look, I like you," she said, almost awkwardly but with determination.

Aiden blushed suddenly, though he was confused. "Um, thanks?"

"But I realize that can complicate things," said Megan. "And more than anything right now, I need you to be my friend and my protector."

"Why are you telling me this?" Aiden wondered aloud.

"Because I'm not stupid, and I know you like me, and I know you're jealous of Dorimar."

Aiden froze for a moment. "Not jealous-"

"You're jealous," said Megan. "Even if he is a... a-"

"Douche bag?"

"Yes, which I think you might be right," Megan conceded. "He still might be the key to keeping the Elf vote, and I might still have to work with him. Plus he's an Elf; Elves don't usually get with humans..."

"Tell that Turlin's parents..." said Aiden.

"Regardless," Megan cut back in. "You'll just have to trust me and respect my decisions. I know what I'm doing. But also, I'm not yours. I'm not some object you can keep. And if you want us to be anything eventually, you need to sort out your issues..."

Aiden wanted to be offended. He wanted to snap back, but he couldn't. She was right, and he did like her. But at the moment, he could still feel his hate for the N'Iatari burning, and a deep, unsettling sadness for his mother. He had never realized that the grief had never left him. It stalked him like a shadow.

"I don't care about your past. I want to know you, for the *you* right now," Megan continued. "And right now, I just want you to get some rest and heal..."

Aiden nodded slowly. "But who's going to protect you?"

"Jardun will stick around for a while," she responded. "Plus we're going into a week off, then the Peacekeeping and Security Council will begin meeting..."

"Yay," said Aiden sardonically. "But," he began, a new line of thought striking him. "Dorimar did actually admit that he was just using you. He also hit me first. I wasn't lying about that."

Megan looked troubled. "Well... I want to believe you," she said, sighing. "You may be right, but Jardun suggests I carry on—just cautiously."

Aiden groaned. "What? How could he ask you to-"

"I knew that getting into this would be difficult," she admitted.

"I'm aware of the risk, okay? Jardun will be by my side, so please don't worry about it."

Aiden clenched his teeth, then finally sighed. "Alright..." he said. "A couple of things..."

"Yes?"

"When I said earlier that I just wanted it to seem like I was in this for the money... I was only half telling the truth—but now I'm telling the full truth: It's not about the money. Now that you've heard my story, I hope you see that. Also... Um, well, you're right-"

"About what?"

"I'm more like the N'Iatari than I mean to be," he admitted. "I guess isolation and bitterness has kind of changed me... And I don't want that anymore. I think you've helped me to see that."

Megan smiled. There came a wonderful, awkward, quiet moment, and they stared into each other's eyes.

"Thank you," said Megan. "Also..." her tone shifted, her brain suddenly multitasking and her expression changing. "This is sort of strange, but I should tell you that Vodin has sent you a message..."

***

Aiden had heard of lettercasting of course, several times, but had never seen it occur. He sat on his bed for a good hour, staring at the piece of parchment under the dim lamp light. When Megan had given him the letter, much like when traveling by door, she had drawn it with runes, but instead of a door, a parchment letter had materialized.

For the time being, he had some things to ponder, and he kept the parchment just at arm's length.

After Megan had left, Aiden had spent some time thinking about their conversation. He was amazed at her forthrightness. It should have made him happy to know that she liked him, but he knew he had to deal with himself first. Furthermore, he knew they all had to focus on the Congress... And still, Regis and Rosen were too much of a mystery.

Before long, his thoughts returned to the letter. Soon he was forced to look at it. Still aching, Aiden smoothed out the paper and held it taut under the lamp light.

The letter seemed straightforward:

"Aiden, I'm sorry it took me this long to find you. I had no idea where to look, but I was informed that you were working with the Guild. I can only hope you receive this letter sooner than later. I can only hope that you've been able to re-acclimate to the Agnec world without much friction. It's a very long story as to what's happened to me since your time as a student at the Guild, and I don't have time to explain everything. I can only hope life is treating you well.'

"I can't explain exactly what I'm up to at the moment, or exactly where I am. I did want to warn you of something. I was a foolish man when I served you as a mentor, and hope that I have not steered you incorrectly. As I'm sure you now know, we all go through periods of doubt in our lives, and these only serve to make us stronger, if we let them. I have always prided myself on letting my students make up their own minds, and I don't regret letting you make up yours. I'm sorry if I led you down pathways of doubt that perhaps you were not ready for. There are so many things you should know—but all in due time. For now, I must tell you with great surety: Lilit is alive and well, and more fearsome than I ever realized."

Aiden stopped when he read this. He took a deep breath and continued.

"She is very real and her followers are amassing in other parts of the world. Word has it that she is over in the States now, trying to gather followers there. Use caution, as you may be dealing with dark properties yet unseen in this world.'

"I have so much more to tell you, but I can't go into everything now. If you reply with a verified tracer rune, I'll know you've received this, and I'll explain more. But hurry if you can, time is of the essence. Until then, stay well and stay safe. Vodin."

Aiden read it and re-read it many times. He wasn't sure what to think. It did sound like Vodin, but then the information about Lilit was very disconcerting. Aiden thought about whether or not he should send some sort of reply, but he also had no idea what a tracer rune was.

When finally he'd grown tired, he placed the letter on the table by his bed. He had no plans for looking at it again.

***

Over the next week, Aiden had several visits from Megan, and every time she left, Aiden had a strange feeling in his stomach—like a twinge that stretched from his bowels to his heart. Aside from the physical pain he still felt, he knew this wasn't a physical problem. This was something new.

Ever since Aiden had opened up about his mother, more memories began to filter in through his mind. He fought them at first, but then they returned in dreams. At that point, it was much harder to escape. It was everything he'd been running from for so long, and now it held him captive. The healers wouldn't let him leave just yet, thus Aiden was left to deal with his own thoughts, without distraction.

At one point, Headmaster Turlin appeared, after knocking on Aiden's door. Aiden nodded and the Half-Elf walked in with a grim expression. Aiden had not looked forward to this moment.

"So... Aiden," Turlin began, after he had closed the door behind him and faced Aiden's bed. "Let me first say that I'm glad you're doing well."

"But...?" Aiden prodded, not wanting to prolong the inevitable.

Turlin glared at Aiden for his lack of patience. "Well, frankly, I'm disappointed," Turlin said with a sigh, pulling up an old wooden chair beside the bed. "I suspect that your actions lost the Guild's position a lot of respect."

"It wasn't all my fault— and is that all you care about?" Aiden said, feeling defensive.

"Of course not," Turlin said, holding out a calming hand. "You were trying to defend Megan—as I understand it—not from physical threat, but from ideological. You should know that she's capable of doing that on her own."

Aiden was silenced, his head falling back on his pillow.

"If it helps... at all," Aiden began, looking into Turlin's eyes. "I-I'm sorry. I know I screwed up."

"Vodin always trusted you. He saw your potential. I was also sure you were the man for the job," Turlin said, but this time with a smile forming.

"I still am the man for the job," Aiden's voice cracked, almost forcing him to sit up, but the pain still kept him on his back.

Turlin nodded. "Then prove it."

Aiden paused, thinking about Vodin's letter.

"The N'Iatari have a certain attraction to you," Turlin added, looking thoughtful. "Perhaps you can use it to your advantage..."

Aiden looked down and realized that the locket around his neck, which was usually tucked down into his shirt, happened to be laying across his chest, fully visible. Turlin was staring at it, almost unconsciously. Aiden reached up and tucked it back into his shirt, and shot Turlin a suspicious glare. The Half-Elf only returned a knowing smile.

"Perhaps it's hard for you to believe, Aiden," Turlin said, breaking through Aiden's paranoia. "But there are people out there who care for you. You're very lucky, because Vodin is one of them. But then, so is Megan. Believe it or not, even Jardun has taken a liking to you..."

Turlin smiled and Aiden felt a sudden warmth inside. It was not anger, but peace.

"Speaking of Jardun, he mentioned that you struggled with some of your abilities. There's no better time like the present to continue in a discipline... I suggest you use this time wisely..."

***

For the first few days, it was almost as though Aiden couldn't quite make sense of his surroundings. Of course he knew he was in the healers hospice, but sometimes the room seemed very nondescript. He mostly noticed things in his very near vicinity, such as the lamp, the table, and his bed. When he first woke, he had thought there was next to nothing in the room, and at the moment, he only had eyes for Megan. After that, his mind was still so focused on his thoughts, and on Vodin's letter, that he had not noticed much else.

Over time, it seemed as though his eyes readjusted. Slowly, he began to notice that the walls, while still very white, were sort of a dull gray in some places, as though the paint was wearing thin. There were some stains, smudges, and other things Aiden wasn't sure he wanted to identify. The floor was tiled, and covered with an eons-old enamel. None of this would matter so much to Aiden, but it struck him as odd that he hadn't noticed it all from the moment he awoke.

There was also a window in the room, and though it did not let in much light, it must have let in fresh air, because though the room smelled somewhat musty, the air circulated somehow. The assistant healers would come in and open it sometimes. At night,

Aiden would occasionally hear what sounded like voices a long ways off. Once, he thought he was dreaming, because he could swear that he actually *saw* the people talking, despite how he lay in bed in his room.

He began to wonder if he'd been scrying. Nearing the end of his week stay, he began to put it to use, trying hard to concentrate on faint traces of noise he heard at night.

While laying in bed, he knew that the voice he heard was a healer talking.. He concentrated on the sound's source until he could get a very small glimmer, a blurry image, of what that source looked like as it made the sound. Aiden wondered if this was anything like the images bats saw when they used echolocation.

Soon he realized he was seeing more complete images around each sound, like catching a piece of the scene through a fish eye lens. "Did you check Miss Darple's vitals yet?" Aiden heard a female healer say, and he could suddenly see her talking to another white-robed healer, who nodded in reply.

An animal wailed somewhere down in the village streets, and Aiden watched as a withered alley cat ran across the old cobblestones while pursued by another feline, the two of them whipping around the corner wall of an ancient brick building.

It was odd. Aiden's senses seemed keener somehow, despite how he had to let his ears do the work and let go of what his eyes currently saw. In many ways, his thoughts grew slightly more clear.

Suddenly he pulled himself away from the sounds and looked

around at the dark room. He concentrated and stretched out his hands, realizing that his arms were no longer in much pain at all. An image appeared just feet from him. It was tall, feminine, and emitting a gentle glow. It looked like Megan, but still, it was not exactly perfect. Aiden let the illusion fade.

He fashioned another one, this time no longer daring to duplicate Megan, but instead a translucent rose appeared there, stem and all. It glided toward him, his mind still focused on Megan, and when it was near, he observed his craftsmanship. It was so near perfect, he wondered if it was possible... Slowly, he reached out. It was solid.

Aiden's heart leaped, but an instant after he had touched it, the rose faded.

***

Aiden had spent the second-to-last day of his stay at the hospice working on his wristwatch. He woke up with a sudden urgency in his mind, and began experimenting throughout the morning. At first, not much seemed to change, but he continued to capture small bits of footage of himself talking until finally the sound would also play back, along with the image. He tried it several times just to make sure.

After a hospice worker had brought in his meal and checked his vitals, Aiden placed the watch back on the table. He was now very eager to leave, but had been told that he had one more day. Carelessly he felt something wood gently scrape his knuckle. It was a little wooden box on the table.

"Huh..." Aiden thought aloud. "Has that always been there?"

He opened the box, and inside there was a copy of *The Agnec Chronicle*, just waiting to be read. Aiden's face scrunched in confusion as he perused the headlines. The news seemed fairly run of the mill for an Agnec paper. It was the mention of Lord G'nehon that caught his eye.

"Wild Scene in Alleyway Connected to Lord G'nehon?" the headline read. It looked like an opinion piece, and Aiden continued to the article: "An incident that occurred earlier this month, in an alley in Washington D.C., still has local Ambler authorities confused. On the night in question, Ambler police claim that someone vandalized the alley, perhaps attempting to break into the paint supply warehouse adjacent to it, and fought with security.'

"Philadelphia Senator Philip Regis, an Agnec-friendly Ambler, believes it was a stalker. I would suggest that the Senator not flatter himself. Despite the lack of evidence gathered by Ambler police—but why should we be surprised?—two Agnec individuals have come forward as witnesses to the incident. Neither of them have been allowed an interview by the *Chronicle*, and I hope my own investigation can change that.'

"The names have been withheld for their own protection, but each of them witnessed the presence of an infamous N'Iatari known to most as Griftwalker."

Aiden's heart launched into his throat when he read the name.

"It's been said that Griftwalker is Lord G'nehon's right-hand man. And if you're unfamiliar with G'nehon, please refer to several older editions of the *Chronicle*, as they have covered his exploits in the past. Perhaps that was a long time ago, but nothing has changed. I will say that G'nehon is a force that must be dealt with, as his crimes against both Agnec and Amblers alike have made him an outlaw even among those who support the idea of peaceful N'Iatari sects.'

"If you're unfamiliar with Griftwalker, you should know that he's the son of Monadias Griftwalker, head of the D'Tari Council. I have tried to contact her, but she has not replied to any of my letters. Should we be concerned?'

"The man who battled with Griftwalker is still an unknown. But he had powers similar, if not greater than, the N'Iatari. Rumor has it that he may be a vigilante known as *demiGod*, who is mostly known by Agnec and Ambler locals in the Philadelphia area. There were other N'Iatari in the alley with Griftwalker, and the body that Ambler police claimed to be a security guard was, in fact, a fallen N'Iatari man. A battle certainly occurred, there's no doubting that. Both witnesses can attest to that.'

"Perhaps we're seeing history repeat itself? Are the N'Iatari and the D'Tari gearing up for another war? For those of you who don't know your history, the D'Tari and N'Iatari last clashed in 1966. After years of fighting—often unbeknownst to the Ambler world at large—the D'Tari, led by former Mount Katahdin Guild Headmaster Vodin, raided the N'Iatari Guild in California's Big Sur. Some of the details are certainly lost to history, but it was the turning point for the N'Iatari. They no longer publicly opposed the D'Tari."

Aiden paused after reading Vodin's name. He would have to revisit that thought later.

He continued reading, "Or was this present incident simply a case of N'Iatari-on-N'Iatari violence? I plan to investigate more, but I hope that I have stirred some of you, my readers, to seek the truth for yourselves. I also hope that the *Chronicle* will see to it to send a more heavily-resourced field investigator into this arena, rather than gloss it over. By all means, we need the truth. — Opinion by Charles Glozzman."

When Aiden had realized he was finally reading something that wanted to expose the N'Iatari for what they were, he'd been reading with great enthusiasm. His mind made a sudden cognitive jolt when he read the name of the article's author.

"Charles Glozzman?" Aiden said aloud. "Charlie Glozzman?"

Aiden shrugged, now thinking of the boy who, along with Chad and Grant Griftwalker, had led him into the woods all those years ago. He had really thought they were his friends. But Charlie... Charlie had at least made some attempt to help in the end.

Aiden couldn't be sure if this was that Charlie, but nevertheless, he was glad to see that maybe there were some people on his side after all. Some people out there, who felt like he did, and had probably witnessed horrors at the hands of the N'Iatari. And maybe... people *could* change.

After having exhausted his use of the paper, Aiden placed it back in the old wooden box.

***

The next day, just as Aiden prepared to leave the hospice, Megan entered the room.

"You're doing so much better," she said enthusiastically.

"Well, ya know," Aiden said, feeling good about being able to pull on his own hooded sweatshirt for a change. "They are using magic to heal, and thanks to you guys I didn't have to worry about insurance premiums..."

Megan smiled, though Aiden wasn't sure if she had understood the joke—considering she had never lived as an adult Ambler—but it didn't matter. He smiled back.

"There is one more thing I've been wondering about," said Megan, sitting on the bed.

"What's that?"

"What's this thing that Griftwalker wants from you?"

Aiden sat next to her. "What?" he asked, wondering if he had heard her correctly.

"You said that Vodin gave you a mission," Megan said, looking pensive. "I think at some point you mentioned a locket?"

Aiden placed a palm to his forehead, sighing. "Yes, I did say that, didn't I?"

Megan eyeballed him, looking confused by his reaction.

"Well, I'm really not supposed to say anything about it," he finally said. "But I guess since we're being honest these days, I can tell you."

Aiden reached into his shirt and pulled the locket to the surface.

He held it up by the chain, gazing at the familiar designs on its exterior. Megan stared in awe, her face alive with questions.

"It's a for-"

"A forca locus," said Megan, an excitement in her tone. "Sorry, I've just never seen one."

"Almost no one has," said Aiden. "This may be the only one left... But don't be too happy about it. My research is not..." Aiden sighed. "Well, it sucks, really."

Megan raised an eyebrow.

"Vodin thought it might contain a very dangerous sort of place, and my research leans that way as well," continued Aiden, finally sticking the locket back inside his shirt. "If it's all true, if everything is real... Then this is something the N'Iatari really want their hands on. We're talking..."

"You mean they want to kill you for it..."

Aiden nodded. "If it's true, then this could be the worst weapon of them all. Which is why I must keep it safe, but it also complicates everything I do—even protecting you."

"Vodin wanted you for the job," concluded Megan. "There must be a reason."

Aiden sighed, looking around the room. "Well, until we can figure it out, I guess we can get out of here..." His eyes fell upon the wooden box on the bedside table. "Hold on a sec."

He checked the box again, wondering if he had missed something in the article he'd read the day before. Instead of the same paper he'd seen previously, the current day's edition was sitting there, crisp and waiting to be read. After a few moments of Aiden's amazement, Megan chuckled slightly.

"It's a replenishing box," she said, amused.

Aiden picked up the newspaper and began skimming headlines, and though there was a short blip on the state of the Shadow Congress, he didn't see much that caught his eye. Finally, he wondered if Charlie had written more on the N'Iatari, but there was no such article.

Instead, there was a retraction: "We formally retract an article entitled '*Wild Scene in Alleyway Connected to Lord G'nehon?*', run as an opinion piece yesterday. We do this at the request of the D'Tari High Council and their current head of council Monadias Griftwalker. We do formally apologize to her and our readers if the article presented what may have appeared to be slander or libel against either the D'Tari Council or Mistress Monadias herself.'

"Due to this complaint and several others submitted by patrons, we will no longer be accepting pieces by the article's author. The opinions stated therein do not reflect the *Chronicle*, nor do they reflect the Agnec community at large, or anything we stand for as a community source for news and entertainment. We hope and will ensure that nothing of this sort happens in the future. — The Editors."

Aiden stared blankly at the printed words. Had Charlie just been censored?

Chapter 20
Dwarvahall

Aiden had rolled Megan's words over and over in his mind. She liked him.

He knew that he couldn't focus on that now, but he wanted to. But he couldn't. The thought reappeared often, disrupting the more pressing issues.

He also thought about Vodin's letter, and then about Charlie's article, and Grant Griftwalker...

Aiden and Megan entered their hotel room, only to see Jardun waiting for them. He never thought he would admit it, but he was glad to see the Faun there.

"Doing much better I see," said Jardun as he stood to greet Aiden.

"Thanks to you," said Aiden, dropping his things on his bed. "It's been a rough week, but I think I figured out some things..."

"And what would those things be?" D'Natis' voice arose from the window at the end of the room.

Aiden smiled. "Hey, long time no see," he said, walking over to the windowsill where the raven perched. "Where were you this whole time?"

After Aiden sunk into the cozy chair by the window, D'Natis hopped to the table, as if feeling a sudden breeze at his tail feathers.

"They wouldn't let me in, despite how they knew I was not a common beast..." the raven said in an annoyed tone. "I suppose I don't blame them. My lesser *brethren* are not known for their excellent hygienic qualities."

"Well, I'm glad to be out," Aiden said, smiling. "I have far too much on my mind, and way too much to do."

Jardun and Megan now joined Aiden and D'Natis at the small table at the end of the room. D'Natis instinctively inched away from the Faun.

"What do you mean?" Megan said, a look of surprise crossing her face.

"I've been doing a lot of thinking," Aiden began. "And I have a plan to help us get the evidence we need."

"For what?" asked Megan.

"I saw Senator Regis use D'Tari properties in the alley," said Aiden in a firm tone. "Griftwalker is at his disposal somehow—and frankly, at the risk of making an accusation here—what if Monadias was also in on it?"

"That is quite an accusation," said Jardun, frowning. "One that would be hard to prove."

"I know, I know," said Aiden. "I need more information first, but if I were able to get into the Griftwalker Estate-"

"Their Estate?" Jardun asked incredulously. "You do know that Monadias is very skilled in D'Tari swordskill, don't you? Also, this seems like an awfully big risk for something you only seem to have a hunch about."

"It might be more than a hunch, but first I need to make contact with someone..."

"Who?"

"Someone who knew the Griftwalkers pretty well when we were at the Guild together... Charlie Glozzman."

***

It was already the beginning of November, and the Peacekeeping and Security Council had been meeting for only a week. Aiden was glad that Jardun was still around, because it gave him time to work on a strategy.

As Aiden sat at the agreed-upon table, the cold crept into his bones, but he knew he had to stay outside and visible. He'd long since given up trying to blend in with the Ambler patrons sitting outside the generic coffee shop, as the passersby gawked and stared at the large raven sitting on the table just across from Aiden.

Aiden's eyes darted back and forth, wildly surveying the shops and streets. He was feeling somewhat anxious.

"Where is he?" Aiden mumbled through gritted teeth.

"Perhaps he... likes to write fiction..." D'Natis said, hesitating as if realizing what he was saying.

"That's reassuring," Aiden quipped, looking at his hand as if expecting to have a coffee there, but then realizing he'd never ordered anything.

"Are you *demiGod*?" a man's voice half-whispered from Aiden's left.

Aiden turned with a jerk, and there stood Charlie Glozzman, tall and dark-haired. He looked tired and older than he should be, but Aiden could see that it was the same Charlie he had known. For a moment, it was very hard to see his face without thinking of what had happened between them as boys. It was an odd moment; one that Aiden could only hope would end well.

He forced himself to stand and shake Charlie's hand, which was something he didn't often do with just anyone.

"Aiden?" Charlie gawked, shock spreading in his eyes. "Are you Aiden Gail-"

"Yes," Aiden said quickly, shushing the man. "Yes... Yeah. I'm demiGod. Please sit down." Aiden gestured to the table, and D'Natis inched away to accommodate. "Sit down," he said again after seeing Charlie's blank, unsure expression.

Charlie refused. "So... Did you send that letter just to get me here and take revenge, is that it? You know it wasn't my idea-"

"This is a public place," Aiden scoffed. "Do you really think I would try anything here?"

Charlie shrugged and finally sat down. As he took a seat, he eyed D'Natis suspiciously, then looked to Aiden, unable to take his eyes off him.

Aiden lowered his voice and focused in on Charlie. "Look, I meant what I wrote in that letter," he said. "I read your op-piece in the *Chronicle*, and I think you can help me."

"When I received a lettercast from the infamous *demiGod*... I never knew it was you," Charlie finally said, still in thought.

"I'm really that well-known?" Aiden wondered aloud, feeling

doubtful.

"Some of the N'Iatari talk about you," Charlie said in a very straightforward tone. "They don't like you. And the one reference of you in the *Chronicle*—denied your existence."

"I'm starting to think they deny a lot of things," Aiden said, choosing not to think of his *title* at the moment. "But how do the N'Iatari know about demiGod? And how do you know what they talk about?"

Charlie sighed. "I've been researching them for years—ever since—well, ever since what happened to you. I knew something was wrong when Griftwalker left the Guild. It hasn't been easy, but let's just say that Chad has been infiltrating the N'Iatari ranks for some time now."

"Chad?"

"Yeah, he's found out a lot of helpful things. I know that Griftwalker's working directly for Lord G'nehon now, and Chad is pretending to. I also know that ever since you escaped them, and *Aiden Gailhart* disappeared, they've been after you—but obviously unable to find you. They have also kept close tabs on demiGod ever since the incident with the airplane and all the Ambler witnesses."

"Yeah," Aiden muttered. "That's when I first saw the name demiGod in print too... Stupid Menlir..."

"Lord G'nehon began looking for demiGod right after that. Maybe he knew there was a connection, or something? So... Why are you here?"

Aiden gathered his thoughts. "I knew when I saw the *Chronicle*'s update on your piece, that you could help me. They don't usually censor people who aren't a threat, and the D'Tari Council's involvement has me concerned. I need to know what you know."

"Why? How can I be sure to trust you?"

"Fair enough," Aiden admitted and lowered his voice. "Because I'm working with the Guild now—Headmaster Turlin is convinced that Senator Philip Regis—who's presenting in the Shadow Congress—is connected to Lord G'nehon, trying to legalize a way to fund and form an army... One that would mostly consist of N'Iatari."

Charlie looked pensive, as if calculating his expression. He remained silent.

"Since the N'Iatari have tried to kill me a few times since I've been openly opposing Regis... I'm pretty convinced that something's seriously wrong here."

Charlie looked almost happy for a moment, then looked to D'Natis. "Okay, let's talk—but is he safe?"

"What do you mean?" D'Natis snorted, his wings rustling. "Like I'm some common bird?"

"I know you're a Raven Lord. It's sort of obvious," Charlie quipped. "Can we trust you?"

"Yes. Of course, yes," Aiden held a hand out to calm them both. "Yes. I'm sorry. This is D'Natis, my *associate*."

D'Natis bowed his head as if appeased by Aiden's gesture, then he settled down onto the table, acting as though Charlie hadn't spoken at all. Charlie seemed to be making up his mind.

"Alright," Charlie finally said. "At least fill me in first. I suspect you know a great deal about what happened that night in the alley with Griftwalker."

Aiden almost laughed. "I was there," he said. "It was demiGod—me—who fought with Griftwalker. I was..." Aiden looked around, and then finally committed. "I *was* tailing Senator Regis. So, in some sense, he was right. He has a stalker. Griftwalker and his men caught me in the alley, and I fought them until the cops showed up."

"Okay, so I was right about one thing..." Charlie mused. "Chad and I saw something going on—and Griftwalker was there..."

Aiden raised an eyebrow. "Were you the two eye-witnesses? What were you doing there?"

"Yes, we were the witnesses," Charlie admitted. "But technically, Chad was supposed to be there because he's been working with Griftwalker, and I had followed him to see the location of the operation."

"Operation?" Aiden asked, eyeing Charlie.

"Okay..." Charlie paused and looked around. "That warehouse is a front for a training facility. G'nehon's been recruiting and fast-tracking N'Iatari training for some time now."

"So he is already building... But why? What's he want?"

"From all I know, he seems pretty bent on planning a full scale assault."

"On who?" Aiden asked, feeling his stomach lurch.

"Well... On Amblers. I mean, the plans are unclear to people at Chad's level, but from what I gather, aside from gaining some sort of political support and funding, I think G'nehon plans on overrunning the Ambler President..."

"But that's insane," said Aiden. "I mean... Isn't it?"

Charlie sighed. "Yes, but not impossible—but I think you're on the right track with opposing Regis—because if Regis is helping support G'nehon..."

"Then G'nehon gets his army, and the Feds can't really stop him—but the Agnec world will practically be supporting it," Aiden concluded.

"More or less," agreed Charlie. "You know how muddled politics can get. What's worse is that G'nehon claims to be operating directly under Lilit, at her command... I never believed in her... But I have multiple sources, eye-witness accounts... If anything, we have to be alert. You know?"

Aiden could only nod, though he hadn't made up his mind about it.

"I have also heard that G'nehon has already built an army in Europe... I hear that they're trying to recruit Dwarves and Elves, and have made an effort to round up any Centaur tribes... and stamp them out..."

Charlie could hardly finish the last sentence, and his eyes fell.

"I wasn't aware there were even Centaurs left..." said Aiden, feeling suddenly sad.

A mixture of anger and hurt filled Aiden when he saw Charlie's face. Innocent people and creatures were dying, and no one seemed to be aware of it here in the States.

"And there's one more thing, now that I know you're here to help..." Charlie added, then grew solemn all the sudden. "They took Chad."

"What do you mean... Took him? I thought he was working with them?" Aiden asked, staring in confusion.

Charlie's eyes fell to the table. "Captive," he said, obviously holding back his emotion. "Right after that article ran in the *Chronicle*, it was as if they suspected Chad's involvement and they've been holding him prisoner. I should've never signed my real name to any of those articles... I was just trying to take a stand. I'm such an idiot." He slammed his hands violently on his forehead and stared at the table, a tear falling from his eye.

Aiden stared blankly at the man. He was speechless, and as much as he wanted to say something understanding, he could only manage silence.

Charlie simply shook his head and shrugged. "I know," he said in a forcibly emotionless way.

Aiden could only shrug.

"So..." Charlie began again, mustering himself. "I think I have some information on G'nehon's past, and where his base of operations may currently be. If you're serious about this, then I would be willing to help you."

"Of course I'm serious," Aiden said, almost protesting the statement. "Look, I know we had some bad blood when we were kids..."

"To be fair," Charlie cut him off. "I... I never wanted to... I just went along with people. I was stupid. And weak."

"Forget about it," Aiden said, finding a reason to smile. "This more than makes up for it. I think we're all still figuring out how to do the right thing—especially when it's not always clear."

"Ahem," D'Natis said, utilizing a very human expression to rouse Aiden's attention. "Focus," he hissed.

Aiden's mind shifted back into gear. He leaned forward to gaze at Charlie across the table.

"Okay..." he said, popping the knuckles in his hands. "I have at least a week and a half. I need a plan. I need proof that G'nehon and Regis are somehow linked, and I need to prove it to the Shadow Congress... And I can help you get your brother back."

Charlie gazed back with a determined expression. He smiled as though Aiden had granted him a second chance at life.

***

A knock came at the hotel room door, and Aiden quickly opened it. There stood Charlie, looking prepared for fall weather in a long coat.

"Just a sec," said Aiden as he gestured for Charlie to come in.

As Aiden put on his coat, he noticed that Charlie observed the room. Things were still dark as it was early morning, and after a long day at the congressional sessions, both Megan and Jardun were still sound asleep in their own respective beds. Charlie gawked at the Faun asleep on his cot.

"Who's that?" whispered Charlie, pointing to where Jardun lay.

"Master Jardun," said Aiden quietly as he slipped his arm in his sleeve. "He's guarding Megan, sort of taking over for me while I work with you."

Charlie nodded, and the two of them silently left the room, closing the door behind them.

"Guess I didn't realize there was a D'Tari master with you," said Charlie.

"He's just hangin' out," said Aiden, eying Charlie suspiciously. "But what's that matter?"

"It doesn't, really," said Charlie as they walked down the hallway. "I was just thinking that it's good to have backup... just in case."

After a moment of thought, Aiden spoke again, stopping mid-stride, "Okay now you've gotta stop keeping me in the dark, who's this guy you know, and how can he help us get into the Griftwalker Estate?"

Charlie kept his voice low. "Well," he began with a heavy-hearted sigh. "It's complicated. He's my half-brother, and he lives in Philadelphia-"

"Oh so he's from my neck of the woods."

"I don't know how close... Do you know where the Gryphon Claw is? Because that's the best place to find him... usually."

Aiden shook his head for a very brief moment of surprise. "Do I know it?" He laughed. "All too well," he said, smiling. "So, do we take the Underground, or go by door?"

"Let's just jump, it's fastest," said Charlie, looking enthusiastic.

"Never really done that," admitted Aiden. "Guess I kind of missed that stuff..."

"Don't worry about it," said Charlie. "Just hang on."

With that, Charlie grabbed Aiden's arm and the world grew fuzzy. In seconds, it seemed as though everything had imploded around the two of them, and then a new sensation engulfed Aiden. It was as if he had been been fired from a canon and launched forward through an intense blackness.

In another second, the two of them appeared in a dark alley. No longer were they in the hotel corridor inhaling the stale air full of dormant cleaning chemicals and cigarette fumes. They were now surrounded by old boxes and barrels, feeling the morning air chill them through their coats.

Charlie looked around and exhaled as if relieved. He slowly walked to a door on the side of one of the brick buildings, and after observing it, he smiled. He traced a rune and the door creaked open. He gestured for Aiden to follow.

Aiden was still trying to gather his bearings. The jump had been such a strange sensation. Finally he followed Charlie inside where the sights and sounds of the Gryphon Claw's back room came alive.

It was still early yet, and Aiden didn't see any of the usual faces anywhere.

"You two are a little late for the night crowd, aren't you?" the bar keeper said with a smirk.

"Just looking for someone," said Aiden.

"Oh yeah, who?"

"Him," said Charlie suddenly, his eyes glued to the squat creature at one of the tables just feet from them.

Aiden nodded to the bartender and followed Charlie to the table, unable to see who it was they sought, because Charlie had blocked Aiden's line of sight.

"Regnir?" Aiden said, shocked as he and Charlie stood around the table and caught the Half-Dwarf by surprise.

"I thought you were off on some fancy Guild business," Regnir said, putting down his paper and raising an eyebrow at Aiden. "And you," he said, glaring at Charlie. "What the hell are you doing here?"

"Um," Charlie began, looking nervous. "You two know each other?"

Aiden and Regnir both nodded, though without enthusiasm.

"So," Aiden began, unsure what to say. "He's your..."

"Half-brother," admitted Charlie sheepishly.

"Yeah, we don't talk about that," said Regnir, lighting up a cigarette and taking a drag. "You never write, you never visit..."

Charlie sat down at the table, and Aiden followed suit. "Look," began Charlie. "I would do those things more if I knew where to find you half the time... It's not my fault that-"

"What? That Chad, Mother... Father... Everybody abandoned me? No, I'm good. I am over it."

Aiden sat back, never realizing just how much he could relate to the Half-Dwarf. He suddenly remembered Megan's words about the way he had treated Regnir just before they left for the Guild, and shame began to crawl through him.

"Do we have to bring this up every time we see each other?" said Charlie, looking flustered already. "I've kept in touch when I can, you know that."

Regnir finally assented with a nod. "So... Then tell me why you're here," he said with some finality. "Why are the two of you here?"

"Well," began Charlie uneasily. "We need your expertise about getting through Dwarvahall."

"Alive?" said Regnir, laughing.

"Preferably," replied Aiden, giving the Half-Dwarf a knowing glance.

"What's in it for me?" asked Regnir, taking another puff of his cigarette.

"If all goes well, you'd be helping us stop Lord G'nehon," said Charlie. "You know, the N'Iatari?"

"Oh that whole thing? Why do I care?"

"Because part of you is still human, and no matter what, you're still family to me," said Charlie in a sincere tone. "Plus, if things really do get bad around here for Agnecs, it still affects you, doesn't it?"

"Meh," the Half-Dwarf grunted with a shrug. "Sure? ...So you're asking me to risk my life? What else is in it for me?"

"Look," Charlie began, but Aiden raised a hand.

"If you're going to play it that way," said Aiden, reaching into the pocket of his coat. "You'll be doing this on the Guild's ticket..." He threw several Agnec gold coins onto the table in front of Regnir. "That'll buy you all the smokes you want."

***

The hotel room seemed a little more packed than usual over the course of the week, aside from the times that Aiden and Charlie had to go somewhere to gather research. At the moment, the two men and the Half-Dwarf crowded around the small table, while D'Natis perched on the windowsill nearby. Jardun and Megan also sat just a little ways off with curious expressions.

"There's a passage here," Charlie said, tracing a line on the map with his finger. "But I don't know if that connects..."

They all stared, fixated on the map sprawling out before them. It was an ancient document detailing the routes, passages, and railways of a section of the Agnec Underground. Aiden was concentrating, trying to fix as much of the information in his mind as possible. He had been nothing short of amazed when Regnir had brought the map earlier in the week. Aiden had never known about maps like this.

"And you're absolutely sure that G'nehon won't be there that night?" said Aiden, looking back to Charlie.

"Not according to Chad's final lettercast before he was taken— G'nehon will be at the training facility. Should give us plenty of time to get in and take a look around."

"So what if they're not documenting this recruiting process right now?" said Jardun from behind them. "What happens then?"

"Then... I guess we get the hell out and figure out another plan," said Aiden. "But guaranteed, I can gather evidence to show Griftwalker's involvement—and Monadias as well."

"I suppose it's a start," said Jardun, stroking his beard. "I'm just afraid you might be walking into the belly of the beast. You know that once you're inside, there's no quick escape—being that Monadias is the head of the D'Tari Council, they're bound to have multiple protections..."

The room grew still for a moment.

"That's true," admitted Charlie. "But according to Chad, they only repel Amblers and Dwarves and Orcs—they're apparently not expecting any D'Tari to try anything... Also, this is why we have to go the Underground route."

"But does Chad really know?" chimed in Megan, looking slightly worried. "I mean, what if his information is-"

"Chad knows!" said Charlie with a defensive tone. He composed himself quickly with an apologetic look. "Him and Griftwalker work closely together, and he gets info that others at his level don't... Plus, this is what I have to go on. If I can't trust my own brother..."

"Well, then we're all screwed," said Aiden, having flashbacks of Chad as a taunting teenager. "But it's our best hope yet—to get any bit of info we can out of the Griftwalker Estate while G'nehon's away."

Dwarvahall

"The upside is that some of the delegates are coming around," said Megan with a hopeful expression. "So anything helps... I think that Jhon of Agnec Nation has at least been spreading the word. Dorimar has actually done his part this week, and at least one Elf group has decided to openly object..."

Aiden sneered without realizing it, then caught himself. "Well, that's good," he said, trying to sound upbeat. "At least someone's seeing the light. You have another debate, right?"

Megan sighed. "Tomorrow, while you guys are doing this, I'll be debating Regis," she said, looking at the floor. "Then the final vote is Thursday..."

"Cheer up," said Aiden, stepping closer to her. "You'll be fine. You know your stuff. That, and I know that Turlin's proud of the work you've done."

Megan smiled and Aiden returned it. He felt somewhat awkward suddenly, as he often had since they had admitted their feelings in the healer's hospice. But Aiden knew that he couldn't think about these things now, and he turned back to the table, focusing on the map again.

He observed the route they had been studying. It wasn't too far from the nearest railstation.

"You're sure that it's not guarded?" Aiden asked. "It seems close to the public sector."

"You're forgetting that this is a private map. And these lines here," Regnir said, tracing a blue route along the map with his finger. "Are unmarked passages. They don't connect to the public walkways or rails."

Aiden scrunched his face in thought. "Hmm... Well, alright then, but let's map a second route, just in case."

"I guess it's settled then..." Charlie said, with a look of anxiety, though he smiled.

"Yes," Aiden said, embellishing the excitement he felt, pushing away his own worries. "Tomorrow afternoon, we're breakin' in."

***

On Wednesday morning, Megan and Jardun met Aiden and D'Natis just outside their hotel. Jardun wore a wool cap to cover his horns and ears, his long coat and dark pants seemed to do the job of disguising his legs well enough. Megan looked beautiful, despite how she wore a simple business suit. Aiden smiled at her, unable to take his eyes away.

"Okay, we're taking off," said Megan.

"Yeah, us too," returned Aiden.

"Wish me luck," she said, trying to sound confident.

"You'll do great. No worries."

Megan smiled, looking less than convinced. "Stay safe, okay?" she said, then kissed his cheek.

Aiden had almost begun to lean in for more, but he stopped himself, seeing a reproachful look from both Jardun *and* D'Natis. He had to be content with watching Megan walk away.

"Killjoy..." Aiden muttered to D'Natis, while watching Megan and Jardun disappear around a corner.

When the sun began to warm the air and Aiden had eaten some

lunch, he set out, with D'Natis on his shoulder, and met Charlie at a nearby coffee shop. They wandered down the street as though they were tourists taking in the sights.

They made their way into the Agnec Market Street. The market was rather busy, and many of the shops were alive with customers, which did not surprise Aiden, considering it was only mid-week. It was here that Regnir appeared, and the small group made their way through the old cobblestone square and down a familiar alleyway. Aiden glanced in as he passed the Toad's Corner pub where Megan had been attacked. The memory was still too fresh, along with the scar he'd gained while healing her.

They entered the long corridor, and though they picked up the pace, it seemed to drag relentlessly on into the darkness. At some point, Aiden noticed how it had turned into a tunnel, lit only by dim torches. Aiden passed the place where Megan's first attacker had fallen. There was no sign of a struggle, not that he had expected there to be a trace left.

Their decline grew steeper until it seemed as though they hadd been walking for over forty-five minutes. Aiden was growing concerned, but Charlie actually seemed confident. Finally, they reached another door, lit only by a flickering torch on the wall. This door was also locked with three enchantments, just like the door that opened into Market Street. Regnir knew the various passwords to get in.

Once over the threshold, Aiden noticed how the corridor was well-lit and supported by ornate stone pillars. The path widened and they found themselves walking along a broad avenue surrounded by ancient shops and medieval smithies. The old cobblestone street was empty, but the two men, the Half-Dwarf, and the raven could hear the sounds of village life not far off.

Heading east, they followed signs for the nearest railstation. In no time at all, it seemed that the Underground had suddenly come alive. Long lines of people—mostly humans, Dwarves, and the occasional Faun—were queued up at the ticket counters near a large round house.

Aiden's eyes scanned the crowds suspiciously, but nothing seemed too out of place. He, with D'Natis still on his shoulder, got in line, followed by Charlie and Regnir. In no time at all, they got their tickets and waited to board a railcar.

"This is why I really wish we could just jump or something..." whispered Aiden to Charlie as they huddled into a glass vestibule, pressed up against the crowd.

Soon the railcar appeared and everyone bustled inside. In moments, they were off down the tracks, whirling and speeding. This brought back memories of Vodin, and Aiden realized that he hadn't written him back—though he'd seriously considered it.

***

Once they left the railcar only fifteen minutes later, they found themselves near another village. Aiden continued to recall the map in his mind. All was silent as they stopped, Aiden examining the nearby walls and seeing the distant glow of giant mushrooms.

His thoughts were interrupted by the familiar uneasy nestling of

D'Natis' talons in his shoulder.

"It's just beyond here, and there's our pathway to the village," said Regnir.

Aiden looked over, realizing that this was the first thing Regnir had said since they'd met up with him today. He nodded to the Half-Dwarf and they resumed walking. Soon the way grew silent, the sounds of life fading behind them. They passed a large stone pillar and found themselves walking along a narrow corridor lit by torches.

They followed the path for some time until Regnir stopped, stroking his long beard. "I know it's been far too long, but a Dwarf never forgets..." he muttered to himself, resting his palm on a slab of stone. He whispered something quietly to the wall.

Without warning, the stone wall began to slide away. Aiden shaded his eyes, almost blinded by the sudden light from within. D'Natis had nearly fallen off of Aiden's shoulder.

Regnir stepped inside, giving the two men and the raven a look of caution. In moments, Aiden realized that they were looking at another stone corridor, but instead of just one or two torches to light the way, the ceiling was aglow with what looked like flickering fire. The fire wasn't really burning, and there wasn't any smoke, despite how it seemed so alive and bright.

"Dwarves like a little extra light sometimes..." whispered Regnir, seeing Aiden's surprise.

Aiden, with D'Natis gripping his shoulder and Charlie at his side, took a few steps into the corridor behind Regnir. The stone door slid shut just behind them, making Charlie jump. Aiden shushed him.

"This way," Regnir whispered, his eyes scanning the narrow expanse before them. "And shut up."

They wandered along the corridor, every step illuminated by the enchanted artificial fire above them. The passage was ancient, and the stone walkway sat under centuries of dust, despite how well worn it was. The walls were hewn of thick stone, giving Aiden the impression that they were nearing some sort of dungeon.

Finally, they came to a split in the passage, and three arched passages lay before them. Each one looked identical to the next. Regnir gestured that they take the passage to their right.

As they neared the end of the curving passageway, they began to hear the gentle sounds of water lapping, and the occasional voice carrying on a gentle breeze. Aiden looked to Charlie, then to Regnir, and they slowed their pace, creeping along the walls until they began to see out the end of the passage.

They stepped out onto a rocky outcropping and found themselves staring out over a huge underground lake. The cave's ceiling stood nearly fifty feet above the water's surface. The water smelled fresh and lapped across the shoreline in gentle waves, leaving Aiden to wonder if the lake's source had come from outside, somewhere beyond the furthest end of the cavern, shrouded in darkness.

Aiden had not expected the lake. It certainly wasn't written on the map.

He finally noticed that a stone-carved sign stood before them displaying ornate words in Dwarvish. There were also English words, which read, in less ornate letters, "Dwarvahall". Aiden took a deep breath, steeling himself as he realized they stood at the top of a winding path which led down into a stone-housed Dwarven village.

"Okay..." Aiden said, pulling his hood over his head. "We ready?"

Charlie nodded, and Regnir mirrored the gesture.

"Let's get out of sight."

Cautiously, they descended along the path, which at first consisted of uneven stone, then became a winding stair. Charlie almost lost his balance on every other step, and Aiden was beginning to worry that the man was losing his nerve. Regnir on the other hand, seemed to have no trouble at all. Aiden kept one eye on the village at every turn, hoping that the inhabitants were too busy to notice the newcomers. It was hard to tell from this vantage, but he couldn't help feeling as though they were all on display, this far above the village.

Finally Aiden and Charlie managed to clumsily make their way down to level ground, following Regnir's casual gait. The village was bright as if daylight had been shining through, and it dawned on Aiden that the ceiling was enchanted with the same bright fire as the corridor had been.

Regnir pulled Aiden and Charlie off the beaten path and into a niche between two old stone huts.

"Just standing there; That's real smart," chided the Half-Dwarf.

"Right, sorry," said Aiden, bracing himself against a wall. "Okay, D'Natis, it's your turn..."

"I thought you'd never ask," the raven sighed and hopped onto a short stone wall just in front of Aiden.

In moments, the raven had disappeared.

***

Aiden was beginning to grow worried.

"What's taking him so long?" muttered Regnir.

"Don't know..." was all that Aiden could manage.

It had been almost two hours since they'd first entered the huge cavern, and they were growing weary of waiting, huddled in the cramped corner between stone huts. The village had been relatively quiet, but Aiden could hear plenty of activity down somewhere in the village center. In the time D'Natis had been gone, the cave's ceiling had also begun to dim, which made Aiden wonder if the sky on the surface was also growing darker. Winter was nearing after all.

With a quiet flutter, D'Natis appeared just from over the wall, making Charlie jump. Aiden looked at his watch, it was nearing 4:30 already. He sighed, but could see D'Natis' glaring eye. It was a look that told Aiden he'd better not complain.

"There is a parallel path through the village we could take," began D'Natis.

"I could've told them that," said Regnir.

"Yes, but I will also report that the central square is quite busy. It seems as though they're all worked up about something," the raven finished, glaring at the Half-Dwarf.

"What's that supposed to mean?" Regnir asked defensively.

"I must warn you," D'Natis added, ignoring Regnir and looking to Aiden. "Even a casual glance tells me that the smithies here are making weapons and armor in vast quantities. And..." he paused. "Judging by the row of wooden huts at the end of the village, and the dried blood stains on the doorposts, there's Orcs stationed here."

"Stationed?" Charlie asked in disbelief.

"If someone is building an army, why not start right here?" D'Natis said in his knowing tone. "That's what took me so long, I was trapped for a good hour near one of the smithies... I was almost seen, and I had to hide somewhere didn't I? One of the Dwarves just seemed content to sit there working, not knowing of my presence just feet from him..." The raven sighed, irritated.

"Okay," Aiden said, summoning himself. "D'Natis, I need you to spot us. We have no choice but to sneak through town through the alternative route. We'll find as much cover as we can, but if something or someone suspects us, I need you to act as decoy. Alright?"

D'Natis nodded solemnly and took to the air again. Slowly, Aiden, Charlie, and Regnir made their way back down the path into the village. They took great pains to keep their steps silent on the old cobblestones—a feat which Regnir seemed to have no trouble with. Aiden didn't want to think of what could happen if their presence was known in *this* village.

They crept along, keeping an eye on anything and everything, if possible. The village was growing darker, as reflected by the ceiling overhead. Aiden knew they could use this to their advantage. With each change in the darkness, he noticed that the lamp posts along the path grew just a bit brighter, as if by magic. Aiden grunted, feeling cheated out of the darkness they desperately needed. So they kept to the shadows, following a path between stone huts and gardens.

They were nearing the small village square, and could hear activity not far off. Aiden heard a couple of Dwarves chatting, and he pulled Charlie into a tight space between a pub and an old hut. Regnir joined them momentarily. In moments, the Dwarves had passed without notice.

The two humans and the Half-Dwarf continued back onto the path, walking slowly between more stone huts and gardens. Here, they heard some of the Dwarven families still chatting around their dinner tables. Aiden kept low to the ground and tried to stay out of any line of sight, behind tall mushrooms or stone brick walls.

At one point, Charlie tripped over a stone near the road, and as he caught himself, it echoed. Regnir glared at him, but motioned for him to lay low.

"What was that?" Aiden heard a growling voice come from behind him.

Aiden had been creeping low near a giant mushroom in a garden near one of the stone huts. He didn't dare move, though he felt his heartbeat shaking him. He could hear the sound of someone rustling and opening a wooden door. Charlie, who remained still on the ground some feet away, looked petrified. Regnir was in plain sight, and remained frozen.

Aiden's mind raced. His usual set of reactions would not apply here. If he did anything, it would likely set an entire village after them. Their mission would be completely ruined, and, worst of all, they would be captured...

The footsteps grew louder behind Aiden, and he didn't dare look. He wondered if the Dwarf could see Charlie or Regnir yet. Despite the sounds of walking and grunting, the Dwarf was silent, so he must not have. It was only a matter of time.

Aiden suddenly heard something he did not expect.

"How'd that bird get in here?" Regnir yelled suddenly.

A loud crowing echoed down the street, and Aiden turned just in time to see D'Natis swooping down in front of the Dwarf. Aiden burst into a run and grabbed Charlie by the arm. Regnir, acting as though he was one of the villagers, pointed other passing Dwarves toward the wild antics of the raven, then when the villagers were distracted, he ran.

Joined by Regnir, Aiden and Charlie rushed as far away as they could while the distraction continued. Aiden was almost giddy when he heard the confused Dwarves swearing at the raven.

In minutes, the noise died down. D'Natis had fluttered to safety, and Aiden, Charlie, and Regnir had made their way to the outskirts of the village. The two men and the Half-Dwarf walked past the odd wooden huts that D'Natis had mentioned earlier, and it seemed that the Raven Lord was correct. From all that Aiden knew about Orcs, which wasn't much, these were clearly tell-tale signs.

So much for peace treaties and political correctness... Aiden thought, even though he knew Megan might have some things to say in protest.

Now that they'd passed the village, Aiden could see the path winding and building upward, until it formed an ominous stone stair. The stairway stretched upward into the darkness, climbing and climbing until it lost itself in a dark, twisted mass of roots and stone jutting out from the ceiling of the cavern. The stair itself hung precariously, as if supported by nothing.

"You kiddin' me?" Aiden said without realizing how loudly he'd said it. "I don't remember the map saying anything about this..."

He had just realized that the incredible mass of roots and stone almost fifty feet overhead was, in fact, the undercarriage of a house; It could only be the Griftwalker Estate.

"You'd better get going," D'Natis piped up as he fluttered past Aiden's head.

Aiden shot him a look, but then turned to see that Charlie was sweating and Regnir was prodding them along. Aiden sighed, steeling himself, and without another word, walked up the incline in the path. Charlie seemed reluctant at first, but then followed.

At first, it wasn't such a bad climb, but soon the way grew steep. The stones wobbled, and some of them fell loose, toppling to the dark lake below. Aiden didn't dare look down, and he found himself constantly encouraging Charlie to look up. He soon realized it wasn't just Charlie he was trying to encourage. Regnir, of course, did not seem worried at all.

As the stair continued to wind, Aiden wondered what time it was, knowing he wouldn't be able to look at his watch in this darkness. As they rose higher and higher, the darkness grew thicker, and Aiden could only sometimes guess at which steps his feet were taking. He clutched tightly to the thin rod that served as a railing, and he urged Charlie to do the same with nearly every step.

"Still with me?" Aiden asked at one point.

"Here," said Charlie through heavy breaths. "Still here..."

"Regnir?"

"No problems here," came the Half-Dwarf's graveled tone. "For being D'Tari, you both are in poor shape..."

Mostly, Aiden had wanted to make sure Charlie hadn't fallen, but now he tried hard to ignore Regnir's comment.

The temperature had begun to drop, and the deep smell of soil entered Aiden's nostrils. By now, his arms were burning from how tightly he'd been hanging on to the rod. He no longer trusted the stairs, as each foot had slipped on nearly every step for the last ten feet. He knew they must be nearing the end, and his shoulders were on fire.

Charlie seemed to be doing fine, or at least as fine as Aiden was, but there were moments, amid Aiden's own loud thoughts and the piercing silence of the climb, that he could have sworn he heard the man quietly weeping. He wanted to tell him to pull it together, but decided to let Charlie keep it to himself.

"C'mon, ya nancy!" Regnir chided Charlie from somewhere behind him. "We're almost there."

"Hey," Aiden cut in. "Shut it. Your brother's been kidnapped. Don't you care at all?"

Before Regnir could reply, Aiden stopped for a moment and blinked, wondering if his eyes were tricking him. Just a few feet above them, he could see the tiniest sliver of a light. He craned his neck to see it, and as he did so, he realized that even that tiny light, by contrast, revealed a massive and tangled dark shape looming before them. The huge underside of the house hung there, held solidly in the stone ceiling, and dwarfed the three of them considerably. Aiden marveled at the size of the roots and clumps of earth attached to the stone edifices.

He craned to look back at the light, and started off again, focusing on that light. He could hear Charlie clambering up behind him, followed by Regnir. There was no time to lose.

Aiden finally reached the top, his arms and shoulders aching, and his legs quivering. He waited for Charlie and Regnir to arrive and helped them to their feet on the last stair. The sliver of light seemed much brighter here, as it arched around the door, and Aiden slowly placed his hand on the doorknob. At the moment, he'd just been happy to stop climbing the stair.

The door was locked, and Aiden drew an unlocking rune on the old door. The letters settled, blackened, then began to glow. He heard the knob click, and he drew a deep breath. He slowly pulled the door open, revealing a bright light from inside.

"Better get your sword out, just in ca-" Aiden began, looking from Charlie to see what lay beyond the door's threshold.

He never finished the sentence.

Chapter 21
The Griftwalker Estate

"But please don't hurt him..." Charlie's feeble voice entered Aiden's mind, as if spoken from some far off place.

"Don't worry about that," another voice said unenthusiastically. "If it were up to me, I'd slice him up right now and sell him on the black market... But Lord G'nehon's got plans for 'im."

Finally, Aiden began to see fuzzy shadows embellished against the brightness of the room. An annoying pain throbbed in his temples. He stayed still, not letting his eyes open any further than he had to. His vision remained blurry through his eyelashes.

"Grant!" came an older woman's voice. "You know better than that. Or have you forgotten the Griftwalker honor? Never attack someone who is unarmed. Never attack someone who-"

"Mother!" the man's voice yelled back in irritation. "I know. I know. But the rules have changed."

Aiden found it harder to lay still, now realizing that both Grant Griftwalker and Monadias were in the room, and by the sound of it, they were only feet away.

"Never," said Monadias. "If only your father were still alive."

"Get him off that pedestal, you meddling old whore..." Griftwalker muttered.

Aiden could not see clearly whether Grant's mother had

responded. There was a tense silence in the air, but Aiden waited to see what else he could hear.

"When will I see my brother?" Charlie asked, his voice quivering. Aiden wondered if Charlie was bound in a chair somewhere.

"When we're good and ready to release him," Griftwalker grunted. "We can't do much until sleeping beauty awakes, and G'nehon deals with him."

"Deals... with him?" Charlie asked.

"I already told you," Griftwalker growled, an impatient tone rising in his throat. "Now shut up. Between you and Chad, I always thought *you* were the weakling. The annoying one. After all these years, it looks like I'm still right."

Aiden turned his head ever so slightly, still feigning something like sleep or unconsciousness. Finally he could see Griftwalker's fuzzy outline. The man was visibly irritated, and he momentarily looked away, rubbing his temples as if a headache was coming on.

Aiden took his chance. He sat up with eyes wide open, and held both hands out to launch a ball of energy. Aiden's hands exploded with blue fire, but the burst exploded back onto himself. He flew back to the ground, the floorboards cracking loudly as he landed. He groaned as intense pain wracked his body.

Charlie gasped, but Griftwalker laughed uncontrollably. Aiden moaned again, lifting an aching hand to feel his singed face. The laughing continued, and Aiden sat up, glaring at Griftwalker. He realized that he was in a lavish parlor room lit by bright lamps and candles, and that he sat inside an odd cage as tall and wide as a man. His feet were shackled by long chains to each side. There was floor—not bars—beneath him, and he wondered why no one imagined a prisoner to simply tip the cage over and get out... But his energy rebounding might have had something to do with it.

Aiden stood, getting his bearings. His legs still felt weak, and his body ached. Griftwalker continued to laugh and point until he seemed to agonize from a stitch in his side.

"Hysterical," Aiden said, glaring at Griftwalker again.

Aiden reached to his side and felt for his blade, expecting it to appear in his hand. Nothing happened. Aiden felt his heart skip a beat in sheer panic.

"Not going to work," Griftwalker finally stopped chuckling long enough to speak. He sighed, catching his breath and wiping his eye. "You made my day. I guess you're looking for this."

Griftwalker walked over to an antique armchair and lifted Aiden's swept-hilt rapier into the air. Aiden's jaw fell open. Griftwalker laughed triumphantly and tossed the blade aside as though it were a toy.

"Shield's over there," the man said, pointing to another chair nearby. "Oh, and don't bother trying anything else," Griftwalker warned. "That's a rebounding box. Anything you do in there will come back to you. Call your armor, it'll crush your body. Call your helmet, it'll crush your skull. Try to break those chains or tip the cage, it'll crush your ankles..."

"I get the point," Aiden said finally.

Monadias, who Aiden noticed was greying yet still quite refined, sat quietly across from him at a small ornate table sipping from a teacup. She seemed to be trying her hardest to ignore the situation.

"So you're in on this too?" Aiden asked her, knowing the answer.

"As if you hadn't already suspected," she replied airily.

"What about leading the D'Tari? What about setting an example?" Aiden said, hoping to get a sincere response, if at all possible.

"The Council has been broken for some time," Monadias said, looking at him now. "This is the new path. I seem to be helpless to stop it."

Aiden gaped at her as she calmly returned to her paper and tea.

His mind quickly returned to Charlie and he realized something else was wrong. Charlie was standing just feet from him, but was unchained. Unbound. Aiden threw Charlie a confused look, demanding an explanation without wanting to verbalize it.

"Charlie..." Aiden finally said. "What's going on?"

Griftwalker started laughing again. "Looks like we got you again," he cackled, despite the fact that Charlie looked miserable. "This time, we're going to break more than just your leg."

It was as though Aiden was back at the Guild. Fourteen years had apparently changed nothing for Grant. Despite his rough, bearded exterior, behind his eyes shined the cheap joy of a pitiful child who had never moved on. Aiden straightened up and looked determinedly into the man's face.

"I don't know if you've realized this or not, but we're not at the Guild anymore," said Aiden, trying to remain calm. "We're not teenagers anymore. Why the hell are you still acting like some attention-starved, hormonally-imbalanced punk kid?"

The moment the words had left Aiden's mouth, he realized that not long ago, he could've asked himself the same question. But, he reasoned, perhaps he had changed slightly more than he realized. At least he could hope.

Griftwalker was no longer laughing. In fact, he sneered and bared his teeth. His fists clenched.

Aiden could see a small, but hesitant smile forming on Charlie's lips.

"And I've gott'a say..." Aiden continued, before Grant could interject. "I know you're supposed to be G'nehon's top guy and all—but c'mon—he won't even let you deal with me? I guess he's still pretty sore over the way you botched your chance back in the alley. Botched it all up..." Aiden sighed and clicked from the side of his mouth. "That's really going to hurt your reputation, *Granty*."

Griftwalker drew his own blade and rushed at the cage, his face red. Sparks exploded off the bars and blew into his face, knocking him backward onto the floor. His curved blade clanged loudly on the floorboards and began to unravel into a white mist. He swore loudly, only to be chastised by his mother from just across the room.

"Interesting..." Aiden said with a smile.

The cage also rebounded everything from the outside. Aiden had been wondering about that. He took a strange solace in knowing this.

Now he wondered about Charlie. He looked to him, silently begging him to explain.

"It's not like it seems," Charlie finally spouted. "They told me they'd kill Chad if I didn't... deliver you."

Griftwalker had finally gotten to his feet, his beard and long hair were slightly singed, but he was mostly unharmed. He shook his head.

"Joke's on you, Aiden," Griftwalker said, smiling again.

Aiden still looked to Charlie, whose expression remained grim. Even though he felt betrayed, Aiden had sympathy for him. He wanted to be angry at him, and in truth, he was. He hadn't yet made up his mind what he should feel.

"I'm... sorry," Charlie finally said, his voice weak. He could no longer bear to look at Aiden.

"Forget this," Griftwalker growled. "You two lovebirds are going to get what's coming to you."

Griftwalker snapped his fingers, and in moments, Regnir appeared, as if from nowhere. The Half-Dwarf looked at Aiden in amusement, then turned to Griftwalker.

"Regnir?" Aiden asked in shock. "What're you doing?"

Regnir laughed callously. "Your offer was good, it's just that G'nehon's was better..." he said, looking to Aiden. "Nothing personal-"

"But what about your half-brothers?" Aiden asked, seeing the hurt look of betrayal cropping up on Charlie's face.

"Gold's thicker than blood," the Half-Dwarf said, then faced Griftwalker again. "Yes? You rang, your royal highness?"

Grant sneered at Regnir's sarcasm. "Go get Chadwick," he commanded.

"I'm sure I heard Lord G'nehon order something else," said Regnir obstinately.

"Do it!"

"Alright, alright," Regnir growled, and in seconds, he had disappeared.

Aiden sighed. This was all too much to process at the moment. Suddenly remembering something else, he reached up to his chest and felt inside his shirt through his coat. He began to panic.

"Looking for something?" said Griftwalker.

Aiden paused and glanced up, only to see the man dangling the locket from its chain.

"I guess it was worth it then," said Griftwalker. "After all these years, we finally got this from you... Only to have to wait until G'nehon summons Lilit so she can open it..." he added with a rising impatience and a slight hint of bitterness. "Of course I'll be rewarded."

"How nice for you..." said Aiden, unable to say much else. The moment he'd feared had arrived, and he was helpless to stop it.

Grant chuckled and placed the locket on the chair with Aiden's sword. Another moment had passed, and Regnir materialized again, this time alongside a human. It was Chad. There was no denying he was Charlie's twin, but he seemed a bit taller, and more muscular. Aiden would have suspected something other than Chad's confident expression.

As Regnir vanished, Charlie smiled, relieved. "Chad!" he said, moving closer to his brother. "I couldn't be sure you were still-"

"Very much so, Charles," Chad interjected, refusing to hug him. "In fact, I was never captive at all."

Charlie's face twisted in confusion.

Chad grabbed his brother's coat around the collar. "I thought you might've suspected it by now," Chad said, his face close to Charlie's. "I haven't been spying for the D'Tari... In fact, just the opposite."

"But why?" Charlie asked, grabbing Chad's wrists, trying to get free. "They're killing people, Chad! They're-"

Chad backhanded Charlie, but maintained his grip on the flailing man. "Of course we are!" he returned passionately. "It's a small cost to win a righteous war. I've seen the immortal light of Lilit's glory, and she will lead the Agnec world to enlightenment and peace... But peace comes at a price."

Charlie fell out of Chad's grip and stumbled back onto the floor, still flailing. His face was a mess of blood and troubled emotion. Tears streaked his cheeks, and he was at a loss for words.

Chad seemed to have little sympathy. "I'm sorry, Charles," he said in a stoic tone. "You know how passionate I can be. Clearly I want you to be on the winning side. Our side. G'nehon's side."

"What makes you so sure it's the winning side?" Aiden spoke up finally, unable to stand the sight of Charlie wallowing on the floor.

"Shut up!" Griftwalker snapped, walking to Aiden's cage and glaring at him. "How can you even ask that from inside a cage?"

"It's a lot easier for you to be confident when you're outside of one," Aiden replied, keeping his voice as calm as possible. "And I don't claim to believe in many things, but I do believe *you* are on the losing side."

"Again, how can you say that?" Griftwalker asked, bemused.

"It doesn't take a rocket scientist," Aiden quipped. "I see someone beating down their own brother, and I'm pretty sure I don't want to be a part of that."

"You sound just like Vodin," Griftwalker laughed. "He also didn't believe in using force to quell the dissenters..."

"Spoken like a true bandwagoner," Aiden said. "Did you read that in a pamphlet, or did you sit through a brainwashing session?"

"Idiot," Griftwalker muttered, but stayed where he was.

"You're obviously intelligent," Chad told Aiden, sizing him up behind the bars. "You'd be a fool not to share G'nchon's vision for Agnecs. Sometimes... the weak have to be done away with, for the strong to survive. Survival of the fittest, right? We all must adapt. I follow the Shadow Congress. I heard about your little article. You said it yourself that the N'Iatari and the D'Tari are not so very different..."

Aiden was about to say something, but stopped himself. He looked into the angered and passionate eyes of Chadwick Glozzman, and he knew that he could no longer agree.

"No..." said Charlie, wiping the blood from his nose and forcing himself to stand.

All eyes in the room turned to Charlie.

"Though animals we may be," Charlie said, his voice still feeble. "We're better than *that*. Even dogs make friends with cats. Life can be a symbiotic relationship. The only way *we* win, is if *everyone* wins."

Aiden looked at Charlie, impressed, and surprised. The others did not share Aiden's opinion.

"So you refuse to join us?" Chad asked, his eyes ablaze.

Charlie hesitated, then puffed out his chest. "I will never join you," he said, closing his eyes proudly.

"Then I'm sorry, Brother," Chad said, drawing his blade.

In one swift motion, Chad had thrust his blade into Charlie's chest and let the man fall to the floor. In moments, all was silent. Aiden could not believe what he'd just seen. Griftwalker's mother gasped while Aiden screamed, but no one else seemed to care. Griftwalker smiled lustily, but Chad simply put away his blade with a solemn expression. He looked away, as if disgusted by the dissenter on the floor.

"Those who will not join us, will die," Chad said without any emotion whatsoever.

Though his insides raged, Aiden kept himself still. He was glad, for the sake of Griftwalker and Chad, that this cage was protecting *them* from *him*.

***

Aiden found himself waiting silently. Chad and Griftwalker had removed Charlie's body right away, despite Aiden's protests. Aiden was hoping he'd be able to bring it back to the Guild, or something... He wasn't entirely sure. He just knew he had no desire to see what those two would do with Charlie.

What made matters worse, is that he was powerless to stop them.

Monadias had chastised the two men for their brashness. "How dare you kill a man in cold blood in our parlor room?" she screamed. "That is what streets are for!"

While Aiden waited, once again plopped on the floor in the center of his cage, he thought about Charlie. The shock of the incident still rippled through his being. He had started to like Charlie. The revelation that Charlie had been forced to betray him began to make the most sense. Regnir's betrayal made even more sense, but Aiden had gone against his own suspicions because Charlie seemed so sincere and trusting of the Half-Dwarf—more sincere than any street thug or con man Aiden had before met.

He shook his head when he realized how much he'd begun to sympathize with Regnir, but now he only felt hatred for him.

Even still, he could not feel any hatred for Charlie. The man had been desperate, and himself had been betrayed...

In the solemnity, Aiden had also been reminded of his mother.

It was all he thought of when he remembered Griftwalker holding up the forca locus. Strangely enough, he remembered the shadow that seemed to follow him throughout his life. It was there when he'd been attacked by the Windigo. It was there when he stumbled upon Cardibran and Barty talking in the library. Had it been there when Aiden's mother had died?

He felt that perhaps it had been. All these things had to mean something. Vodin had suggested the shadow may be connected to the unKing—though the thought was baffling right now.

The shadow had even been there when D'Natis was attacked—

Where is D'Natis? thought Aden. And Megan? How was she doing at the moment?

Suddenly, Aiden felt that everything was spiraling out of control. The very structure of reality seemed to be imploding, and he panicked. He was alone, and for the first time, he realized just how much.

"Sometimes a terrible mistake can be redeemed," his mother's words suddenly echoed in his mind, as though she were visiting with him in their tiny kitchen all those years ago. "You were my redemption," she had told him, looking into his eyes.

This memory alone began to shake him inwardly.

Again, more of his mother's words returned, "The past is past, and we all need to move on."

While Aiden sobered from these thoughts, he fiddled with his watch, suddenly remembering that it was fully functioning now. Monadias was still in the room, but as usual, she seemed glued to her newspaper and her tea. Aiden wondered if the rebounding box would react to the watch's powers, but what could possibly happen?

Making sure the older lady wasn't watching, Aiden clicked the button on the side of the wristwatch. Nothing seemed to happen, so he had to trust that it must be working.

Finally, while Chad and Griftwalker were gone, having taken Charlie's body away, Aiden heard voices from the other room. Monadias stirred, looked to the door just feet behind her, but then shook her head and returned to her paper. Aiden's stomach growled and the house creaked. Noises became more detailed. It sounded as though people were in the other room, chatting quietly and looking in cabinets of some sort.

Aiden focused intently on those sounds, blocking out everything else. He closed his eyes, listening for the distinctive voices. There were two people in the room: A man and a woman. The scene came into focus, and Aiden realized he was able to see what he heard with great clarity.

Senator Regis stood up against a cabinet in the kitchen, still donning his usual suit and looking across at Tilli Rosen. The wood panels, floor tiles, and ceiling were all very ornate and looked centuries old. The room was wide and somewhat dark, although tidy. Regis was casual in his stance, although he seemed to show a sort of reverence for Rosen not often seen at the Congressional sessions.

"Are you sure?" Rosen said, her voice soft but authoritative.

"Quite sure," Regis said, his eyes looking dejectedly at the floor. "He is my son after all. Even Vodin has confirmed it. I was young, and I was ashamed. Please forgive me, my Lord."

Rosen's beautiful eyes scanned the room, but then a smile began to form on her lips. "All is well," she said. "We can use this to our advantage, after all, we will need him in the end."

"How so?" Regis asked, suddenly looking up. There was a flicker of fear in his eyes.

"Don't tell me you care about him? Not when you have others..." Rosen asked, her tone incredulous.

"No. Of course not," Regis piped up. "The whole thing is just... a bit surprising."

"Of course it is," Rosen said, smiling again. "But we can leverage this. For now, he must not know. And we must not kill him yet, of course."

"What *will* we do?"

"You must reveal yourself to him."

"Forgive me, my Lord, but... What?" Regis asked, his voice alive with shock.

"We have him exactly where we want him. If you reveal yourself and the plan for the girl..." Rosen said, her smile twisting cruelly. "His own love for her will betray him."

"How can we know for sure?" Regis asked, his eyes returning to the floor again. "Does he really love her?"

"You see now that the Dwarves in our alliance have already more than exceeded our expectations as worthy sources of information,"

Rosen said, sounding more like the commander of an army than a politician's aide. "Our dear friend Regnir has reported everything, Cardibran too. Of course, there's others as well. We *know* that he will do the *right* thing..."

Rosen chuckled to herself confidently.

Regis looked up finally and took a deep breath. "Yes. You're right. Forgive me for doubting," he said, standing straight. "But he will not know all my secrets..."

"Naturally," Rosen said, still smiling. "Let us go meet the prisoner, shall we?"

Aiden felt himself begin to panic as he heard the kitchen door creak open. As though he had just pulled his head out from under water, the present room filled his senses and overwhelmed him like lungs full of fresh air. He shook his head and looked around, realizing that Monadias had stood to greet the newcomers, making a furtive curtsy to Tilli Rosen.

***

Aiden steeled himself against the arrival of the Senator and his aide, and he stood as they walked towards his cage. Regis looked as bold and confident as ever, much like he had on so many occasions when approaching the podium to speak. Aiden watched calculatingly.

"Ah yes... Aiden," Regis said with a calm smile. "I don't suppose you're surprised to see me here. I knew that was you in the alleyway last month. So very uncouth."

Aiden worked hard to keep his expression the same.

565

Tilli Rosen leaned up against the armchairs where Aiden's blade and shield rested. She seemed very focused suddenly on the locket, and Aiden frowned, though he tried to stay trained on Regis.

"I don't understand why you don't like me, Aiden," Regis said, feigning a disappointed look. "You and I are much the same. You don't like Amblers very much, even though you've worked and lived among them most of your life. You don't even like D'Tari very much, and let's face it, many of them have very little love for you..."

Aiden steadied himself and maintained a stoic expression. He refused to speak.

"You even know some of the properties unique to the N'Iatari... You've extended your life," Regis added, and Aiden's jaw dropped just for the moment. "You've broken a cardinal rule of the D'Tari: Never alter time or aging."

Aiden still did not speak. He was admittedly shocked that news of this had gotten to Regis.

"And who do you suppose taught you that? Why Vodin of course. Vodin knows all about the N'Iatari," Regis laughed, and then began pacing around the room. "But perhaps one of these days, you'll have to ask him about that yourself. That is, *if* he's still alive.'

"Your mother was an Ambler," Regis said, shifting his tone. "Well-meaning woman; a little plain; a little slow perhaps."

Aiden felt heat begin to burn inside his chest, and he grit his teeth just to keep himself from saying anything. He thought back on what he heard Regis say in the kitchen.

"Your father..." Regis began, smiling. "Well, he was just an idiot, wasn't he?'

Aiden's fists clenched.

"What sort of Agnec gets an Ambler in trouble and then just leaves her with a talented son like you?"

Aiden was confused. What had begun as an insult almost sounded as though it was supposed to be a compliment.

"How would you know anything about my father, or my mom?" Aiden blurted, unable to stop his curiosity.

"Oh you'd be surprised what I know, and who I knew for that matter," said Regis smugly. "I've followed your career for some time, demiGod—and I personally feel like you were cheated out of a better life."

Aiden's face softened.

"When any self-respecting Agnec would have introduced you to the Agnec world and the superior things it has to offer, your father didn't. No, he simply ran away... He should have raised you himself," Regis continued with an expression Aiden found hard to gauge. "But, as it is, you're just a bastard. And that's a shame."

Aiden glared at Regis, but forced himself to stay silent. Regis looked back and gave him a querying look.

"It looks like you have something to say," Regis said in a tone so diplomatic that Aiden couldn't tell if it was serious concern or pure mockery.

Aiden remained silent.

"I know your secrets, Aiden," Regis said, after a pause. "Why not join us? You'd make much a better N'Iatari anyway." He walked to the chair and picked up the locket, smiling as he held it in his hand. "You can be the one to unleash this upon the world. After all, there's no escaping the fact that you've kept it safe all these years, only to bring it to us now. I mean, surely, we would've gotten it in the end, one way or the other..."

"Stolen it, you mean," said Aiden. "It doesn't belong to you."

Regis laughed. "True, but it's not yours either—if anything, I know exactly who this belongs to," he said, his eyes wandering in Tilli's direction. "So come join us, Aiden, and save yourself the humiliation. Not to mention the pain."

Aiden held his head up straight and finally spoke, "Never."

Regis sighed, and began pacing the room again while Monadias—from her table—and Rosen—from just feet away—both watched intently. "Well, that leaves us little choice then, but to kill you," Regis said casually. "What a waste of talent. Good talent's hard to find."

"I've seen what you call talent..." Aiden said in a mocking tone.

"Yes, they are miserable, aren't they? Mostly arrogant. I suppose that's my fault," Regis said, still pacing. "That's why I could use someone like you. Your skill and potential outmatch even my top men. Even my highest commander, *Griftwalker*," Regis paused and shook his head in disappointment, then continued, "Couldn't defeat you, while being aided by others..."

Aiden shook his head in refusal. At this point, he was trying to tune the Senator out. All he could do was kill time until he could think of any other options.

"And if power and potential cannot persuade you, well... I don't know what can," Regis added. "Certainly you're not easily persuaded by money. Because at least by joining my forces, you'd be very well paid."

His attempts at tuning Regis out suddenly failed. Regis smiled, seeing that Aiden was listening, though Aiden realized this too late.

"No," Aiden resolved.

"You think the family fortune is enough to keep this... wonderful estate up and running?" Regis asked, his hands out in a wide gesture to the room.

Monadias huffed and threw Regis an unpleasant look, but finally conceded with a terse nod. She returned to her paper.

Aiden shook his head. He thought of Charlie, and the attempts on Megan's life...

"Kill me," Aiden said in a low voice. "I'd sooner do that than join you."

Regis smirked and released a single, mirthless chuckle, as if reflective. "Such a hero. I know it may seem a wonderful escape right now," he said. "But I assure you, when Amblers know our power, they will desire to unite with us. Naturally, we will take our rightful place as first-class citizens of the world. We will flip this world upside down. Let the Amblers live underground! Let them hide away for a while. Eventually, order will be restored."

"And your method is blood shed..." Aiden added.

"Sometimes it is a necessary evil."

Something struck Aiden. "You talk about this as if it's *your* army, and these plans as if they're *your* plans... What about G'nehon? I know you're working with him..."

Regis sighed, then laughed. "Perhaps I pegged you as smarter than I should have. I would have thought you'd have figured it out by now. I *am* Lord G'nehon," he said, his hands out.

Aiden stood back. Of course, why hadn't he figured it out sooner?

"It's so obvious," Aiden muttered in bitter agreement. "You had to keep a public identity to stay active in both congresses, but you needed another public alias to lead the N'Iatari..."

Regis nodded in agreement, smiling as if proud of himself.

"Mostly for my own amusement," Regis began, a smile forming on his lips. "I don't mind telling you that I have spies everywhere, and one of them tonight will also act as an assassin... In fact, he may have already done the deed by now."

Aiden was growing sick of Regis' wide grin. "What're you talking about?" he asked.

"Your friend Megan... Well, she knows too much. I never dreamed that people would actually be taking her side against my proposal. Frankly, your suspicions are right on the money. As I'm sure you've noticed, we are planning an army, and a hostile takeover of any D'Tari forces that might join. I suppose it pays to be a little paranoid sometimes."

"What are you doing with Megan?" Aiden asked, feeling his stomach lurch.

"Very soon, if not already, she will be just another statistical reason we need a united militia to fight against the horrible wave of crime sweeping across the Agnec communities..." Regis said, his tone mocking.

Aiden stopped to think. In the kitchen, Rosen had mentioned something about their plans for the girl—they must have meant Megan. Certainly Regis was trying to get into Aiden's head, wasn't he?

"Of course..." Regis said as he watched Aiden's face calculatingly. "It may not be too late to stop the incident, if you think she's worth saving... But it will come at a price."

Aiden took a deep breath, his mind racing.

"What sort of price?" Aiden said, shifting uncomfortably in the cage.

"The girl lives, but you must do us a favor..."

"What sort of favor?"

"You must help us get into the Guild, and you must be the one to kill Turlin the Half-Elf..." Regis smiled, his face twisting. "My spies have tried for years... But Turlin trusts you, and will not be on his guard against you."

"So... You'll just roll through there, slaughter everyone and call it a day?" Aiden asked, trying to keep the fear away from his tone.

"Essentially."

"But Megan will live?" Aiden asked.

"Yes, she'll be free to go with you, and you two can live happily ever after," Regis replied, his tone condescending.

Aiden thought about all that he'd heard when scrying. He also wondered why Rosen had been silent this whole time.

"Hmm..." Aiden said, appearing to be in some serious thought. "I guess I have no choice," he finally said. "But to say no. You're bluffing."

"You do realize many people will die, including the woman you love?" Regis said, looking intently into Aiden's eyes.

"You don't know if I love her, you even admitted that yourself," Aiden said, his face like steel.

Regis' face changed in surprise. "You've been eavesdropping, haven't you?"

"Possibly," said Aiden coyly. "Things are finally making sense now. I've been working it out."

"Oh really?"

"You don't need me to get into the Guild; If Monadias is in on this, then Fentl definitely is—he's your link to the Guild, and likely your spy. Sure, maybe Turlin is on guard against Fentl, but you must know by now that I'd never turn on someone like that— plus, c'mon, Turlin's too powerful—even for you."

Regis smiled, though Aiden could see the slightest bit of irritation in his eyes.

"There's got to be some other reason you want me out of this cage—and I'll bet it has to do with the forca locus," Aiden added, looking at the locket, still in Regis' hand. "There has to be some other reason you need me to join you..." He stopped and swallowed, preparing for what he was about to say. "But I also think... It's personal... because I think, you're my father."

The room was silent, and Regis actually looked nervous for a few moments.

Before there could be a response, Aiden continued, "And though I didn't want to believe it, she must be Lilit." He pointed to Rosen. "Don't know why I didn't think of it before. 'Tilli' is an anagram for 'Lilit' after all."

"They told me early on that you were clever," Regis sighed. "I suppose I should've known better."

"This is nonsense," said Tilli.

"Don't think this means that I have any sympathy for you, or any desire to get to know you," Aiden told Regis, though unsure how true his own statement was. "Now you're the asshole who abandoned my mom and left me in the Ambler world for fifteen years..." Aiden paused, looking around. "But maybe I should be thanking you."

Regis, looking defensive, shook his head. "You have no proof that I'm father. That's simply ridiculous," he said, although not with any extreme confidence. "Although I still believe you'll make a great N'Iatari once you accept certain realities."

"I don't know about certain realities..." Aiden said defiantly. "But I know I'd never forgive myself if I became just like you."

Regis glared back at Aiden.

At just that moment, a small scroll appeared in the air before Senator Rosen, materializing in a puff of black smoke. She caught the scroll before it hit the ground and opened it to read. Regis watched, concerned.

"There is something that needs my attention," Rosen said, rolling up the parchment. "Carry on, G'nehon, and I'll return later tonight."

"Very well, my Lord," Regis agreed with a nod.

While Regis and Rosen looked away, Aiden knew he had only one chance. He cast an illusion—a solid copy of himself—in the center of the cage, and as he'd suspected, it suddenly appeared outside the cage. The rebounding box could work in reverse, at least with illusions.

Regis and Rosen stared with wide eyes at the phenomena. They looked back and forth from the cage to the illusion, trying to make sense of things. In mere moments, the solid illusion picked up Aiden's rapier from the armchair and raced back to the cage. With a loud metal clank, the illusion had cut the lock off the cage by jamming the blade into the ancient keyhole.

As the illusion faded, the lock clattered to the floor and Aiden could feel the chains fall off his ankles. The gates swung open, but as they did, Regis drew his blade, a rune-laden broadsword, and held it in front of him.

A giant blast of energy consumed Regis, slamming him against the far wall of the parlor room. As the blast hit him, the locket flew from his hands and Aiden jumped to catch it. The chandelier above him rattled and shook violently while some of the old wall paneling behind Regis had broken away.

"Not in *my* parlor room!" Aiden heard a voice cry from his left as he placed the locket back around his neck, stuffing it into his shirt.

He had nearly forgotten that Griftwalker's mother was still in the room. Monadias stood and took a surprising stance, her face twisted in outrageous fury. Twin blades appeared in her hands while a glistening black armor covered her from head to toe. Aiden grabbed his rapier from the floor, tracing a rune and returning it to his arsenal.

Just then, Tilli stepped forward and burst into flames. These were strange blue and black flames that did not seem to burn anything, yet they remained alive and dancing in mid-air. In a moment, her face emerged from the fire, but it looked different. It was less human than her appearance as Tilli, and more menacing. Her blonde hair had been replaced by long black locks that seemed to lick the air like flaming tongues, and her armor was also a glistening black covered in sharp studs.

"Perhaps we couldn't outsmart you, but we can certainly silence you," said Lilit in a very unearthly voice—one very different from Tilli's.

Aiden suddenly felt his tongue roll up in his mouth. He gasped, but realized he could still breath. He could just no longer talk.

Monadias made to attack Aiden, but Lilit, still floating eerily in the air before them, gestured for the older woman to stand down.

"Let G'nehon handle it," she said, looking to where Regis stood, pulling himself up.

Aiden launched a ball of energy at Lilit, but she lobbied it back to him with the sudden appearance of her massive black blade. The rebounding energy exploded behind Aiden, and he crashed to the floor, cracking one of the floorboards beneath his shoulder. Plaster and paneling rained down on him as he struggled to his feet.

A strong arm rushed around Aiden's neck, and the sudden grip almost forced him to fall forward. Regis was behind him, and Aiden was winded. He struggled, trying to grip the man's arm just long enough to get some air back into his windpipe, but it was futile. He no longer even had the strength to form an energy ball...

The world was beginning to grow fuzzy and dark.

A loud crack at the end of the room forced everyone to stop. Aiden felt himself crashing back into the floorboards, and he gasped for air while spinning on the spot.

From where he sat in Regis' shadow, he could see that two figures had emerged after having blown open the back door. One of them was a Faun, and the other a woman.

Chapter 22
Casting the Beast

Aiden had no time to think. While Regis and the others were distracted, Aiden got to his haunches and launched himself at the old armchair where his buckler sat. He heard several things happening in about the span of three seconds, and he couldn't really process what everything was. All he knew was that he'd reached the chair, and he traced a rune on the side of the buckler, returning it to his arsenal.

When he stood up, he saw that Megan and Jardun stood at the back door, glaring intently at the others in the room. None of them seemed to be focused on Aiden. He also noticed that Lilit was still nearby, her strange fire no longer burning, and her focus on the newcomers.

Jardun stood fully clad in armor, clutching his longsword, whereas Megan also had armor, but in her hands Aiden saw a strange instrument. They continued staring at Regis and Lilit with determined faces. Regis' blade was also in hand, although he had not called his armor. The room had fallen strangely silent.

"Miss Rohan," Regis said, sounding much like his usual Senator self as he looked to Megan. "I see that after all my arguments you're still on the wrong side of the issue..."

"Save your *rhetoric*," Jardun said, his eyes ablaze. "You can tell it the rest of the D'Tari Council and the Congressional heads when we expose you for what you are."

"And what am I?" Regis said, smirking, his blade still aloft.

Clenching his teeth, still feeling his tongue wrapped up inside his mouth, Aiden drew his rapier and plunged it into Lilit's thigh between the plates of armor. She screamed as he drew it out, and instantly his tongue returned to normal.

"He's Lord G'nehon!" Aiden shouted, stepping several feet back as Lilit reeled around.

"G'nehon's son or not," she growled. "You'll pay dearly..."

Lilit's massive sword materialized again and she easily lifted it to strike. Aiden made to block, but had a feeling that the immortal blade would likely leave his rapier in pieces. He rolled out of the way instead, just in time to see the black blade slicing through one of the armchairs. The armchair fell in two pieces as though it were butter.

The room erupted into violence.

Jardun and Regis locked blades, while Monadias rushed across the room toward Megan. A sharp blast from Megan's instrument sent Monadias flying backward into a table, knocking her unconscious. Aiden scrambled at every turn to avoid the reach of Lilit's blade.

"It's time to give it up, Philip," Jardun said, staring into Regis' eyes across their blades. "Come with us!"

"Never!" Regis bellowed, his blade clanging loudly against Jardun's.

Aiden called his armor to himself, and fell backward as Lilit's blade swung past. He scrambled to his feet again and blasted her with an energy ball, but she sent it flying back. He narrowly avoided it, managing to launch another, and this time Lilit had not been prepared.

She wailed and reeled back, clutching her side, her blade slamming to the floor and cracking some more floorboards. Aiden rushed over to the massive sword and wrapped both hands around the thick handle. In that moment, a hand violently gripped his neck.

"Idiot!" Lilit yelled, pressing her black, claw-like finger nails further into Aiden's neck. "You've lost. Just give up. You're wasting your time."

The air was quickly escaping from Aiden's lungs with no chance of returning. He squeaked, feeling something pop in his neck, but he didn't dare move. Lilit was face to face with him now, her strange eyes simply shadows of her formerly human alias.

Amidst the chaos and the clatter in the room, Aiden could see shadows shifting in a frenzied dance all along the walls. In those moments, where he struggled to hold onto his last bit of breath, he saw one shadow stand out. There was something strangely familiar about it. Perhaps he was just growing fuzzy, but he realized it was his own shadow he'd been looking at. He could see his silhouette, hanging there in Lilit's grip, still struggling to hold the sword in two hands, despite how the blood seemed to have drained from his body.

As he watched, his shadow—independently of himself—lifted the massive shadow sword and cut the arm off Lilit's silhouette. Instantly, the shadows returned, as if nothing had happened. Lilit took notice of Aiden's wide eyes and glanced at the wall, but there was nothing to see but their shadows acting as shadows should.

Lilit's grip had loosened, and Aiden could feel energy pumping back in a wave of realization. He pulled the sword up and mustered the strength to swing. With a spurt of black blood, Aiden fell to the floor, struggling to keep the heavy blade within his grip. Lilit screamed, watching her severed arm fall to the floor beside Aiden. The limb quickly shriveled and then vanished in black smoke.

The room grew quiet, staring in fear and awe. Lilit released something like a roar and lunged at Aiden. He scrambled backward on the floor, struggling to pull the sword upright. As Lilit went into a rage, Aiden felt her heavy boot trample his foot. Inadvertently, she fell forward, toppling onto Aiden. In one blood-curdling shriek, everything was quiet.

"My Lord!" cried Regis from just feet away.

Aiden groaned and rolled aside. Lilit lay on the old flooring, glaring at him, her own blade protruding from her back. She struggled to get up, and when she did, black blood began seeping to the floor—steaming, and burning holes in the old carpet where it fell.

Regis now stood not far away, speechless and shocked.

Lilit crawled, grasping with an empty hand toward Aiden, who scrambled back even further, attempting to stand.

"Immortals can never die," Lilit said weakly, her teeth dark with blood. "Fear my return. My revenge is swift."

With that, she burst into the same strange fire, and vanished in black smoke.

All eyes were on Regis now, and he glanced around the room, looking more fierce than ever.

Aiden brushed himself off and ran to where Monadias lay. He pulled her up and over his shoulder, realizing that all of her armor and weapons had now faded, and with all his might, he thrust the woman into the rebounding box.

Aiden could see that Regis was still staring down Megan and Jardun, and he knew no incantations that would permanently lock the cage. Still he had managed to place the lock back on the door and secure it. Monadias, though still unconscious, writhed on the floor inside the cage, chains now appearing on her ankles. This would have to hold her for now.

"Look at your precious parlor room now," Aiden said to her, thinking it ironic.

"This is far from over," said Regis, now eyeing Aiden, getting his attention.

Regis called his armor to him. Black glistening metal spread over his body, dark spikes protruding from his helmet, his shoulders, his gauntlets, and from the sides and tips of his boots. A crimson cloak had also appeared, flowing behind him.

The sight had given everyone a moment of pause. None of the D'Tari currently wore armor so impressive, nor so intimidating.

Regis really had gone from being a well-kept man in a nice suit, to being Lord G'nehon.

"Now certainly," Regis began, his dark eyes gazing at Aiden through the menacing slits in his helmet. "Three against one is not a fair fight."

"Then give yourself up," insisted Jardun, his blade still trained on Regis.

Regis sighed and looked around the room, as if observing the damage done by Aiden's duel with Lilit. "You know I can't do that."

Without another word, Regis burst forward at full speed. Aiden reared back, his blade out, but Regis never came at him. The man had flown out of the room and into the kitchen, knocking the door off its hinges.

Aiden shuttered in pure confusion, and exchanged glances with the others.

"After him!" Jardun yelled with a hint of incredulity at what he'd just seen.

Aiden, Megan, and Jardun raced into the kitchen as pots and pans rattled from the ceiling. The trio's armor jingled lightly with each step, but Aiden could hear Regis racing ahead of them into the next room.

With a loud crack, a horizontal pillar of flame burst into the kitchen, shredding the wall and burning the old wooden door frame. Aiden ducked just in time, pulling the others down behind him. Pots and pans rained down on them from overhead, while bits of wood and paneling splintered. Aiden held out his blade and doused the flames with a watercast.

He sped over the blackened threshold, only to find himself in a wide circular room with high ceilings and ornately tiled floors. A chandelier hung above him, lighting the room with a reddish glow. The furniture looked ancient and very ornate, but it was strange that there were no windows.

Aiden's nostrils burned as he passed through a cloud of dissipating smoke. Regis was nowhere to be seen. Aiden would never have suspected the man to run like that.

Jardun and Megan walked in behind Aiden, surveying the room. The red glow seemed to be playing tricks on Aiden's mind, and he walked into the center of the room, directly beneath the glowing chandelier. The silence was unnerving.

"Aiden?"

Aiden turned around, wondering where the voice had come from. He looked to both Megan and Jardun, but they shook their heads, as if to answer his unspoken query. They had not spoken.

"Aiden?" the voice came again.

Aiden knew it was Regis, and he spun around. Still there was no sign of the N'Iatari lord.

"Megan? Jardun?" the voice continued.

The trio was now scanning the room hopelessly, desperately seeking the source of the voice. The voice continued calling them by their names, eerily beginning to chant. Soon it sounded as though multiple voices had come into being, though they all held the same timbre and tone as the first. The voices multiplied rapidly, and from all directions of the room, like some great echo chamber.

"Megan? Jardun? Aiden?"

The three of them were soon wandering in circles, wondering if they weren't going insane. Aiden could no longer think straight.

"Regis!!" Aiden finally shouted over the cacophony. "Shut up!"

The voices echoed on, but Aiden refused to drop his sword. Megan fell to her knees, clutching her ears as if in pain. Aiden ran to her side in order to catch her before she landed face first on the tiles. The sound was deafening now. He could no longer manage a single thought.

"Aiden?... Join me..." the voice said softly, but Aiden shook his head.

There was a strange emptiness slowly beginning to rise inside him, but he refused to listen to the voice.

"Jardun? Aiden? Megan?" The voices droned on.

A low tone suddenly appeared, and began to creep into the wild cyclone of sound that filled the room. The tone grew until it began to clash, as though doing battle with the vocal chaos that churned the air, voicing their names. The sound grew louder until Aiden realized several notes were forming. It was music.

He looked up, now clutching his own ears, pressed against Megan's kneeling form. Jardun no longer held a blade, but a strange musical instrument—the same kind that Megan had wielded earlier.

It was a very bizarre thing, being somewhere between a harp and a double-headed horn. Jardun plucked the strings, which seemed to manipulate the sounds he blew through the mouthpiece.

The notes grew louder, taking on a solemn melody, battling the unholy noise that had once filled Aiden's mind. He stood, finally realizing he could think again. He helped Megan to her feet and looked around, realizing that Jardun's music was now filling the room, and itself growing boisterous with victorious tones. They were tones that gave Aiden a sense of renewal.

The chandelier overhead suddenly rocked back and forth to Jardun's rhythm, each bulb on the golden ring bursting in step. As glass rained down into the center of the room, the red glow disappeared and the chandelier manifested its original candles, which set the room newly aglow.

At that moment, the spell broke. The noises and the voices were completely gone.

A small energy ball, shaped like a bullet, raced out of thin air and trained itself on Megan's heart. Aiden's blade caught the ball, splitting it in two. It exploded, sending sparks in all directions. Megan fell back in surprise. The music stopped, and Jardun replaced his instrument with his longsword.

"Well played..." Regis' voice echoed throughout the room. "Pun intended."

Regis appeared before them in a burst of black mist, his blade at the ready.

"Let's do this!" said Aiden with a deep breath.

Aiden attacked with all his might, catching Regis' blade with his. Jardun ran into the melee as well. Regis countered, and with his other hand, launched an energy ball at Jardun. The Faun dodged, but fell back.

"It's not worth it," yelled Aiden as he swung, nearly catching Regis' hand.

"You don't understand," Regis said, blocking Aiden's blow and calling his shield to protect his left side from Jardun's returned onslaught. "My way is the better way, if you could just see that-"

"Better for you," Aiden quipped, falling back and letting Jardun attack.

Regis narrowly dodged Jardun's blade, while blocking Aiden's next attack. "Better for all of us!" he said, sprinting away from them, blade out and ready again. "The Agnec communities will be destroyed if we don't do something..."

Aiden stepped forward, his blade trained on Regis' armored face.

"I refuse to believe there isn't some other way," Aiden said, now glaring into Regis' dark eyes. "I'm not going to let you justify killing innocent Amblers for some power trip. Don't think I don't know that you intend to lead this new army. Isn't that true? You want to lead some glorious revolution? Is that it? And at what cost?"

Regis' brow furled and his eyes gleamed menacingly. "You miserable little fool," Regis said, spitting from beneath his helmet with each furious inflection. "How can you care about them?

Those damnable ignorant bastards that would rather kill us than talk with us! You're just a traitor like Turlin and Vodin... And all the others who dared debate me! Perhaps I should've killed you when you were a baby, and your whore of a mother too."

Aiden could only see red, and what he remembered next was a blur. Blood flew into the air, and whether or not it was his own, he could not tell. In a moment, he was on the floor, watching Jardun duel with Regis. The lord's helmet was gone, along with his left shoulder armor, and crimson streamed from his upper left arm.

Aiden sat up and realized his gauntlets were gone, along with his sword and buckler. He tried calling his sword to him, but it would not return. It must have been damaged, which meant it would take longer to come when he called. He stood up, and lobbed small energy balls at Regis' feet from behind.

Regis collapsed backwards. His sword and shield clattered out of range behind him on the tiles, echoing throughout the room. Before Regis could get to his feet, Jardun was looming over him with the tip of his longsword resting gently on the man's neck.

Regis looked up at Jardun calculatingly. There was no trace of surrender in his eyes, despite how the blade rested on his throat. Aiden stood back, still unable to call his blade.

"Surrender, Philip," Jardun said, breathing heavily.

Regis returned Jardun's gaze without a hint of fear. Aiden realized that Megan stood a ways off to the side of the room, watching, looking slightly terrified. Regis appeared to notice this as well.

"I just can't do that," Regis said softly. The conviction in his voice shook Aiden inwardly. "If I were truly wrong, then I would have reason to. But not now. Not when the Dark Goddess has shown me the future..."

Regis looked as though he were reliving a horrifying memory, but then he regained his resolve, putting it aside.

"I cannot. I will not surrender," he gasped. "You'll all die for your ignorance."

Jardun braced himself as Regis jostled beneath his blades. The lord grabbed his left arm and flinched from the pain. In a swift motion, Regis knocked the blade away with the spikes on his gauntlets.

He disappeared in a cloud of black mist.

"Dammit!" Aiden growled, rushing to the spot where Regis had been. "Can he even do that in here?"

Megan froze, looking around. Jardun gestured for them to be silent, his pointed ears twitching.

"Get down," Jardun ordered.

All three of them hit the tiles as a volley of bullet-sized energy balls tore through the far wall and ricocheted across the circular room. The air was ablaze with red and blue light, the balls buzzing like mosquitos just over their heads. The wall paneling splintered in all directions, floor tiles erupted, and furniture exploded and caught on fire. Aiden was sure that several N'Iatari must have been in the next room, opening fire.

In moments, the room was silent again. Jardun motioned for

Aiden and Megan to follow him. The trio crawled along the floor, and in moments, they had reached the door at the far end of the room. Jardun and Megan stood to each side of the splintered frame, and Aiden crouched, waiting.

Nothing happened.

A flurry of armored footfalls echoed from the next room. Aiden realized that someone was racing up a flight of stairs. He reached down and his blade appeared. Overjoyed, he called the rest of his armor back to him and raced over the threshold, followed by the others.

"Shields out!" Aiden warned, calling his buckler to his side.

As they entered a small downstairs landing, Regis stood at the next level, opening fire on them. This time, the three of them were prepared and successfully dodged what they could not block or lob back. Megan kept herself as far back as possible, avoiding the onslaught.

"You should go!" Jardun told her. "Find somewhere safe."

"Is any place safe?" Megan asked, incredulous. "I'm staying with you," she insisted.

"Then stay out of the way!" Aiden told her.

The wooden railing began to splinter and a couple of the stairs erupted. Aiden ran forward and launched a massive energy ball up the stairs and into Regis' face. Regis narrowly escaped, crashing to his side, and then scrambling up the next flight. Aiden followed with blade out.

Another explosive volley of bullets began to destroy the narrow stairway, but Aiden pushed through them, followed by the others. They forced Regis up three flights until the man was suddenly gone. Aiden and the others stepped off the landing and found themselves in a massive formal dining room.

It was nearly pristine. An ancient oak table stretched out before them, surrounded by chairs. Wide windows adorned three sides of the room, looking out over a breathtaking stretch of hills and mansions darkened by the night sky. Deer heads, antlers, and ancient portraits raced across the walls around the room.

Aiden could not be sure if Regis had left for good, or was simply baiting them. The silence only made the immensity of the room seem more daunting. He kept his sword out as he walked slowly across, observing everything he passed. Jardun did the same on the other side of the room, with Megan by his side. Despite the wide open space, it would be easy to get lost in here, strange as that would seem.

A couple of lanterns were burning at each end of the room, and in a room only lit by two lanterns and the night sky, many objects were difficult to see. Aiden softly wandered alongside the table, observing several of the paintings and the deer heads. He stopped. The sight that met his eyes nauseated him and sent him into a rage all at once.

On the wall, mounted there like all the other hunting trophies, was a person's head. As Aiden drew closer, he realized it wasn't a human's head. Although it might as well have been, it was so human-like. Judging by the long, pointed ears and the lack of small horns... it had been a Centaur.

The creature's expression was one of shock and horror. Aiden stood back, willing himself to look away, though the sight was so awful that he found it hard to.

"Magnificent, isn't it?"

Aiden spun around, his blade out and gleaming in the light of the lanterns. Regis stood silhouetted against the large window pain just near the end of the table. All of his armor and weapons had also returned.

"I believe he was the last of his kind on the North American continent," Regis said, a smug tone back in his voice after having been absent for some time. "I let Griftwalker do the honor."

"You really are sick," Aiden said, not daring to look at the grotesque trophy on the wall to his right.

"Well," Regis began calmly. "We can't have them running around here, can we? They certainly didn't like the N'Iatari..." He sighed. "Just kept getting in our way, so we handled it."

Aiden grimaced. Although he wondered where Jardun and Megan had gone, he carried on, "I uh, saw you lost your temper back there..."

Regis was still and silent, the darkness of his helmet masking his eyes from Aiden's gaze.

"Some things were said. *Your* feelings were hurt." Aiden stepped a little closer. "You don't like being contradicted, do you?"

"Only when I am not wrong," Regis' voice finally arrived, determinedly. "I'm trying to give you a chance to see your error.

You would be smart to use some reasoning and join those of us on the right side of things."

"I think reasoning went out the window a long time ago..." Aiden said, taking yet another step. "But alright. There's some *reason* you're keeping me alive... Although just barely. Isn't that right, Father?"

"I have other children," said Regis after a moment's pause. "I suppose losing one will be no great loss. Especially one as ignorant and arrogant as you."

A burst of blue light burnt the side of Aiden's face and he crashed into a wooden chair on his way to the floor.

***

When things came back into focus, Aiden saw that the world was covered in silver moonlight and the dim orange glow of lanterns. His head ached, and he forced himself to stand, the sound of blades clashing rang like bells inside his head. Just on the other side of the room, Jardun was locked in combat with Regis.

Aiden's helmet was gone and the side of his face had been singed. Everything seemed fuzzy, and he couldn't seem to focus. His blade was also nowhere to be found, and he couldn't seem to call the item back yet either. He sighed, but then decided to stay low, realizing that Regis was unaware that he had awakened.

Aiden crept low alongside the table, tracking the movements of Regis and Jardun as they scuttled about the room in a violent dance. Megan looked frazzled as she sat several feet away; Her helmet was gone, revealing hair that was undone and a face glistening with sweat. Jardun likewise seemed out of sorts with random pieces of armor missing. Both of them sported bleeding cuts and slashes. Regis' helmet was once again gone, along with some of his armor.

Jardun grunted, his sword catching Regis' with such force that Aiden was surprised to see the N'Iatari lord hold his ground.

"Won't you just die already?" Regis yelled, forcing the Faun back.

Megan ran forward, her instrument in hand, but Regis caught her unaware. She let out a stifled scream and fell back, clutching her arm.

"You see what you're doing to her!" Regis said, forcing Jardun back toward the far wall. "She's still young, and you're putting her through all this. I thought D'Tari masters were meant to empower their pupils, not endanger them."

Jardun growled, blocking blow after blow.

Aiden jumped up onto the table and blasted Regis with an energy ball. Megan looked up with surprise and a sudden hint of a smile. Her expression changed as Regis dodged the explosion and fired back at Aiden, narrowly missing him.

Jardun took that moment to attack while Regis was distracted. He swung and hit the man's other shoulder in a spurt of blood. Regis screamed and retaliated, his blade glinting in the dim light. Jardun ducked low, dodging Regis' blade, and with a quick snap, the Faun jumped up, bounced himself off the wall, and landed an armor-clad hoof directly into Regis' mouth. As the man began to fall back, Jardun whipped his tail up around Regis' neck, pulling him to the floor with a crash.

Jardun released an inhuman shriek that echoed across the huge room. Aiden jumped from the table to see what had happened, he realized that Jardun was on his back, clutching something behind him. He was writhing in a dark puddle of what appeared to be his own blood.

Regis stood, wiping his bloody face. He held up the end of Jardun's tail, growled, then discarded it as though it were trash. Megan was still several feet away, clutching her wounded arm, a look of shock twisting her tired features. Jardun moaned, but finally rolled over to his hooves. Most of his armor was completely gone now.

He stood weakly, and glared into Regis' dark eyes.

Aiden raised his hands, readying another energy ball. It began to pulsate through him.

"You will not win this," the Faun said, his tone determined despite the underlying shaking. "Mark me. Even if you defeat me, you will never win. You will be your own worst enemy."

Regis smirked. Jardun ignored this and called the musical instrument to his side once again. Regis' smile turned to twisted anger and he raced forward, cutting the instrument loose from Jardun's hands with a burst of blood.

"Jardun!" Megan cried.

The Faun collapsed against the wall at the end of the room, and his instrument began to fade. Aiden felt himself go cold. Regis turned to face Aiden, but then his eyes turned to the woman, his features ferocious in the shadows. Aiden could feel his own heart pounding.

His armor and sword were still not returning, which seemed unusual. He let another energy ball fly, but Regis blocked it.

"I only had seconds to draw it," said Regis with a laugh, stepping over Jardun's fallen form. "But thanks to that new rune on your skin, you won't be able to recall your weapons..."

Aiden tried to look unimpressed, but he knew the man wasn't bluffing. He glanced to his wrist, seeing a rune—much like a tattoo—written there.

"Do what you will, but you're not all that impressive without your sword, are you?" Regis taunted, walking slowly closer. "So much faith in one measly tool... Of course you are Vodin's pupil after all, so let's not even call it real swordskill..."

Aiden cursed and shook his head quietly. He'd been so focused on getting the sword and armor back, that he'd forgotten his options.

He realized that he was shaking, and for the first time in a long time, he felt himself beginning to blink uncontrollably. Regis raised an eyebrow, stepping closer. Aiden filled with panic, unlike any he'd ever known.

"I'll deal with you in a moment," Regis grunted, suddenly passing Aiden in a casual manner.

"No!" Aiden managed to yell, but he felt no longer in control of himself.

Regis swung back around and Aiden felt a metal fist smash into the side of his face. As he met the hard floor, he heard Megan gasp. Aiden's body trembled, and he struggled to sit up. Everything ached.

Regis pulled Megan to her feet and thrust her against the wall, knocking one of the paintings down. She shrieked, but didn't retaliate. All she could do was stare down her nose at the wide blade of Regis' sword.

"I could've killed you at any time, you know," said Regis, lifting the blade to Megan's throat. "At any of those moments, at my word, my assassins could have finished you quickly—but I told them only to wound, and make it look like a failed attempt."

Aiden strained his neck, but felt as though a seizure was overtaking him. He struggled to maintain consciousness. Was this fear? He couldn't make sense of what was happening to him, but he fought it, whatever it was. The horrified look on Megan's face was all he could think of to keep him fighting.

"I asked Dorimar to get close to you," Regis continued, looking into Megan's eyes. "To ruin your efforts, but to save you, to gain your trust. It was his idea to kill my assassins—that Elf loves killing even more than myself, I suppose. Of course it was all to stop you, but now that I have him," He looked at Aiden. "I have a weapon I can use," he said in a quieter voice, as if thinking Aiden could not hear him. "And I'm no longer in need of your services..."

A dark shadow raced across the room. When Aiden laid eyes on it, the blinking and the trembling stopped. He could see clearly now, even in the darkest places. He followed the shadow with his eyes, and it directed his gaze toward Regis and Megan, then vanished.

Aiden watched as Regis draw back, his sword just moments away from striking Megan.

A sudden burst of energy roiled inside of Aiden and he lept to his feet with hands out. A semi-transparent beast with powerful claws and gaping jowls now stood bellowing before Regis. The man almost fell back in surprise. The beast stood where Megan should have been, and was the size of a small car. It slowly approached Regis, its yellow eyes transfixed on him.

Looking from Aiden to the beast, the man backed away. "Where did she go?" he growled, looking around for Megan who seemed to have disappeared.

Aiden did not answer, but simply concentrated.

Regis held his blade out, but one swipe of the creature's claw sent the blade skittering across the floor and away from him. The beast roared, its hot breath ruffling Regis' hair. It was sizing the man up.

"Just an illusion..." scoffed Regis. "Good trick, Aiden—but even the most solid illusions can only do so-"

With another bellow, the creature slashed across Regis' face, leaving three red lines that soon began to drip darkly. Regis puffed out his chest and raised his hands as if to summon an energy ball. The beast reared on its hind legs and pounced.

The energy ball launched off-course and exploded into the

ceiling, sending paneling and wood raining down on them. Regis screamed as the beast sunk its teeth into his leg. The creature stepped back, blood dripping from its lips, and Regis clutched his leg, scrambling toward the long table.

The beast vanished, and Megan stood in its place. Her face was white and she covered her mouth with both hands, staring down at Regis' bloody, struggling figure. Aiden raced to Megan's side, then stepped between her and Regis.

"You'll have to kill me before you can ever touch her," he said, "And it won't accomplish anything anyway..."

Regis' face twisted in a blind fury, then he composed himself. "You're trying to be clever, but it's useless."

"Hear me out," Aiden added with a slight smirk. "You should know that Megan's death would not have gained you any followers, it would have made her a martyr. Just like Charlie's a martyr, and anyone else you've silenced. You should know this stuff. By now, Turlin's already spreading the news, we've sent lettercasts, I've got footage..."

At this, Regis' face went blank, and he no longer looked as though he might spare Aiden.

Regis sped forward blindly with blade out, a strange look in his eyes. Aiden pushed Megan away and he jumped atop the table beside him, launching an energy ball at Regis. The blast erupted the floor behind the lord. The man turned around, his face still wild, and with a loud crack, he had sliced the ancient table in two.

The tabletop began to shift and totter, and Aiden raced to the far end, keeping the giant window in his sight. Regis flew alongside the table, slicing chunks of tabletop off every so many feet, until the long table's structure was beginning to collapse all along its expanse.

Aiden heard an explosion tear up the wood behind him and he dove to the floor just as the splinters rained down. He had landed just feet away from the large window. He turned his back to the glass, to face Regis.

Regis' face twisted with in almost inhuman look of rage. He panted, blood dripping from his face, glaring into Aiden's eyes.

Aiden tried to keep himself calm. "If you'd really wanted to kill me, you would have done it by now."

"Then stop running," Regis growled. "Take it like a man."

"Alright, okay. Here I am," Aiden said, his eyes watching Regis' every movement with precision.

Megan stood at the far end of the room in the opposite direction, still looking pale and worried. Aiden stood his ground, despite her glances of desperate concern.

Regis finally lunged forward, his blade coming within inches of Aiden's chest. Aiden sidestepped him and clutched the man's sword arm, forcing the blade through the glass window. Patches of glass shattered around Regis' unprotected hand, forcing him to drop the blade. The noise was deafening, but Aiden kept his grip on the man, letting him hang half way out of the window.

Pieces of glass and pane shattered and trickled down to the streets and hills far below them. Freezing air began to fill the room, swept in by a small breeze. The world below seemed so quiet and still.

Regis roared and found his balance, backhanding Aiden with his free hand.

Aiden staggered backward to the table, now facing Regis. The Senator's back now faced the open air where the window had shattered.

Regis took a deep breath. "Son or no, you're dead to me now."

A large dark shape swept in suddenly over Regis' face, setting him off balance. A violent fluttering and flapping surrounded his face, and he screamed while black talons and a razor beak terrorized him.

Regis stumbled back to the edge where glass had once been, and turned on his heel, losing balance. In an instant that made Megan gasp, Regis fell.

Aiden rushed to the edge, careful not to slip. It was too dark to see the details down below, but he had not heard anyone land. D'Natis' dark shape fluttered inside, the occasional feather floating to the floor, and landed on the remains of the ancient table. The bird looked exhausted.

Megan walked forward, clutching her arm again, and arrived next to Aiden and the raven.

"How did you know D'Natis was just outside?" she asked, her voice cracking.

"I saw his shadow through the glass," Aiden replied, panting.

"Lucky you," said D'Natis grumpily.

Realization struck and Aiden rushed to the other end of the room.

Jardun lay there, quite still. He was an awful mess, and Aiden almost turned away at the sight. Megan and D'Natis were by his side in a moment, and they too were horrified at what they saw. Megan checked for a pulse and exhaled a shriek of excitement and fear.

"He's alive," she said, her eyes lighting up. "Can you heal him?"

"I don't know," Aiden admitted, feeling little confidence left after such a long fight. "It could kill us both."

"Let's get back to the Guild," Megan said, bending on one knee to hold Jardun's bloody hand.

"We can't jump from here, can we?"

"Believe me, we've shattered the protections from this place. Let's jump."

Megan grabbed Aiden's hand, while still holding Jardun's. "D'Natis, land on my shoulder!" she ordered, and the raven didn't ask questions.

"You're sure?"

"Trust me," Megan said with a commanding tone in her voice that silenced Aiden immediately.

As if spreading out across the four of them, Aiden felt a sensation bursting through his body, beginning at the touch of Megan's fingers. The world grew fuzzy, and the room seemed to implode and contract around them. With a sickening lurch, as if being fired from a canon, everything went black. The room was gone.

Chapter 23
The Lockdown Before the Storm

In seconds, the two weary humans, the raven, and Jardun's near-lifeless body had reappeared, as if time and space had unraveled around them, spreading out to its normal dimensions. They were no longer in the devastated dining hall of the Griftwalker Estate, but were surrounded by snow-topped evergreens.

Aiden let go of Megan's hand and stumbled back, his stomach feeling queasy. Gentle snowflakes fell around them, floating through a white world speckled with moonlight. The wood was so silent and still that Aiden wondered if he'd lost his hearing. When he finally stopped staggering, he realized they were in the woods near the Guild, and he turned to see that Megan was trying to lift Jardun's battered body.

"Let me help," Aiden said, rushing to her side and hoisting the Faun over his shoulders as gently as he could.

Jardun's breath was shallow, and he was covered in blood. Aiden took a deep breath and watched as Megan instinctively clutched her own wounded arm, now shivering from the intense cold, and began to trudge through the deep snow. Aiden followed. D'Natis flew on ahead of them, as if catching a second wind.

After a few moments of watching Megan shiver, Aiden stopped and slid his own coat off his shoulders. This was no easy task while he managed to hang onto Jardun's limp body. He placed the coat on Megan's shoulders, and before she could thank him, he carried on ahead of her, forcing his way through the frozen branches.

A solemn silence seemed to carry them through the wood. Aiden had wanted to say something. In fact, there were several things weighing heavily on his mind.

His heart hurt for Charlie, and he wondered what the others had done with the body. And just where had Griftwalker and Chad gone to? If anybody could have entered the battle to help Regis, it would have been those two. Aiden was glad they had disappeared though.

He thought about Megan. Her face was stained with tears and blood as she trudged determinedly against the thick snow.

He thought about the fact that Tilli Rosen was indeed Lilit. It was almost unreal, but he had seen it, and he had battled her. What seemed even more unreal, was the apparent fact that Regis was his father. He wondered how it could be possible, but Regis had admitted it, hadn't he?

They passed through the Otter Gate and into the Guild. The grounds were very quiet as it was nearing midnight, but everything looked much the same as it had when Aiden left, despite being covered in snow. Megan and Aiden, now tiring from the journey, struggled to get Jardun inside the main hall.

They pushed through the doors into the wide circular room where tables were arranged all around the center point, and a distant fireplace brought welcomed warmth to their shivering bodies. Even D'Natis fluttered through the open doors and alighted upon one of the tables as the others passed through. Aiden and Megan placed Jardun gently on his back upon the long central table where the masters normally dined.

The Faun's pulse was weak.

"I'll go get the Headmaster-" Megan said, beginning to turn.

"There's no need," a voice broke the silence from the direction of the doors.

Headmaster Turlin rushed in, wading through the tables until he stood by Megan's side, staring at Jardun's limp form. The Half-Elf looked warily to Aiden. He rested a pointed ear to the Faun's chest.

Turlin placed his hands upon Jardun's colorless neck and began muttering various incantations in Elvish. Nothing seemed to happen for some time, and Aiden and Megan stood back, exchanging worried looks. D'Natis seemed on edge as well.

Finally some color began to return to Jardun's skin, and his fingers began to twitch. Megan had been holding back sobs, as if hoping not to distract Turlin, but she soon noticed that Jardun was moving. The Faun began to stir and his dark-furred legs stretched as if he'd just been sleeping. Turlin continued whispering Elven words, and with each phrase, Jardun seemed to wake up just a bit more.

Megan's face began to light up, and she wiped her tears.

Jardun moaned, his eyes slowly opening. Turlin finally stopped speaking incantations, but as soon as he did, he half-stumbled, half-sat on the closest chair, looking weak and breathing heavily.

"What's the matter?" Megan asked the Headmaster, nearing him.

"Oh nothing," Turlin replied, trying to catch his breath. "This sort of magic simply takes a lot of energy... I'll be fine," he said, forcing a smile, but steadying himself on the seat as if he thought he might fall off.

Megan nodded, still looking unsure, but then looked to Jardun. She gently leaned over and looked into the Faun's eyes.

"Master Jardun... I was so afraid..."

"Everything's alright," Jardun said after a quick sputter. "I have all of you to thank," he coughed, a small smile showing through his beard.

"Even me?" D'Natis piped up from his table across from them.

For a moment, Jardun glared, but wasn't able to hold that expression for long.

"Especially you," Aiden told the raven. "We'll tell you why later," Aiden said to Jardun, turning back and smiling.

Turlin finally stood up and looked to where Jardun lay, still weak and pale. "Tell me, what happened?"

"Put the Guild on lockdown," Jardun said. "We have to lock it down now."

***

The Guild masters had rushed to every corner of the grounds, setting up new charms, enchantments, and D'Tari protections over the property. They checked and double checked every student's dorm room and every teacher's quarters to make sure everyone was still present. So far it seemed that all was well, except for one thing...

Master Fentl was missing, and he had left no message.

When Aiden relayed all that he had learned to the Headmaster, Turlin announced that they must not let Fentl return to the Guild. After all the ruckus had died down, their wounds tended, and their stomachs fed, Jardun, Aiden, and Megan were told to go off to bed. Aiden was reluctant, but Turlin insisted.

Aiden wasn't sure his mind would let him sleep, though his body desperately wanted to. When he finally calmed himself down, resting in the same old bed in the same stone hut he'd lived in at the end of summer, he fell into a restless sleep.

Images floated disturbingly in his mind: Charlie's death; the horrified face of the Centaur on the wall; Griftwalker's smug look; Chad's obsessive devotion to an ideal; Regis' wild look when he raced toward Aiden...

He could still hear the shouts, grunts, and struggling screams of both Jardun and Megan as the violence ensued. He recalled the trembling and the strange seizure that had almost overtaken his nervous system, but then stopped at the sight of the familiar shadow.

Was it really the unKing, as Vodin had suspected?

When Aiden awoke, he didn't feel rested, but he knew he had

too much to do. He forced himself up, bathed for the first time in too long, and went looking for Megan. It was still very early in the morning, and the main hall was empty when Aiden arrived. He found Megan, wrapped in a blanket, drinking hot chocolate by the fireplace at the end of the room.

Aiden approached slowly. She nodded, but never faced him directly. Her face was tear-stained and her eyes red. He cautiously sat next to her on the wooden bench by the hearth.

"Is Jardun okay?" Aiden asked, wading slowly into his words.

Megan nodded, then took another sip of her chocolate.

"A-are you okay?"

Megan shook her head and put the mug down next to her on the bench.

"I just wanted to thank you," Aiden said, looking at her, though she still stared into the writhing flames.

"For what?"

"For dragging me back into the Agnec world—back to the Guild..." Aiden said.

"It was Turlin," Megan began.

"I know," Aiden said softly. "But it was you I agreed to protect, and it was you that ended up helping me."

Megan was quiet, aside from the occasional sniffle. Aiden sighed. He wanted to say so much more, but wasn't sure of all he felt.

"Can you please tell me what happened last night?" Aiden finally asked. "There's so much that I can't figure out."

Megan finally looked at him. She seemed to be reining herself in, and mustered up the courage to say something, "You were right about Dorimar."

Aiden nodded, although he realized how unfortunate it was that he'd been right to suspect the Elf.

"I mean," Megan continued, holding back tears. "I guess I thought, in the end, we could still work together... But yesterday was the worst. I began to see what you were talking about. I wanted to give the debate—and technically he couldn't because he's still suspended—and I wanted to present some new evidence I found, and he refused to help. He didn't want me to present it. I just couldn't see why..."

She paused, and Aiden withheld his comments.

"He seemed more upset every time I mentioned how much the people were starting to believe us..." Megan continued. "He became like another person. He started telling me I was delusional, and that I would just ruin all his hard work... Jardun was gone for only a minute..."

Megan stopped and wiped her face with her arm. She seemed to be losing control of herself, if just for the moment.

"He tried to..." she said through a sob. "He tried to force himself on me."

Aiden clenched his fists. He had almost stopped listening because the blood had rushed to his head. He took a deep breath, and forced himself to stay silent.

"I fought back, and Jardun returned and fought him," Megan said, her tears still flowing. "The hotel room was totally destroyed..." Megan laughed slightly between sobs. "Then D'Natis showed up.'

"He told us you and Charlie and Regnir were captured," Megan said, reining in her tears once more. "Jardun called for Turlin and he arrived almost instantly—I guess Elf magic makes that easier or something—and began fighting Dorimar. Jardun and I jumped to the Griftwalker Estate, avoiding the Underground..."

Megan wiped her face again, and sighed. "Then we saw Charlie on the street..." Megan's tears fell afresh at the words. "Charlie... He was a good guy..."

Aiden finally put a comforting arm around her shoulder. They rocked for a moment, and Megan seemed to catch her breath.

"Jardun fought Griftwalker and Charlie's twin... And we took Charlie's body back to the Guild..."

"Charlie's here?" Aiden asked, his face alive with surprise.

"Yes," Megan said, nodding and sniffing. "I think we're going to have a funeral, or something, for him soon."

Aiden couldn't help but smile as if feeling that some small victory had been won. Then it struck him, "What did you do with Griftwalker and Chad?"

"We snuck around the house for a few moments before we found you, and Jardun discovered the basement door that opens into the Underground... So he left the two of them hanging upside down in the cavern, high up from underneath the outside stairway... Still alive of course."

611

Aiden chuckled. He couldn't help himself. The image of those two upside down and staring fifty feet below into the freezing lake was simply too funny. Megan looked up and realized that she could laugh too. Aiden smiled, it was good to see her laughing.

"It was kind of inspired..." Megan said, chuckling. "So, then we found you," Megan finished.

"Wow," Aiden sighed, sniffing. "Rough night."

"As usual, Turlin seems to be steps ahead; he already knows everything," Megan said, no longer crying but still red-faced. "He told me that after Jardun and I had left, Dorimar escaped, but not without being beaten pretty bad."

"I wonder if it was Dorimar who sent Lilit that message," Aiden wondered aloud.

"What're you talking about?" she asked, looking back to Aiden.

Aiden proceeded to tell her the whole story from the beginning: Of how Regnir had led them through the village and betrayed them, and of how Charlie had been forced to betray Aiden and was himself killed by his own brother.

Megan was in tears again. "I believe you..." she said, though still in shock. "It makes so much sense now... Though how awful..."

Aiden went on to finish describing how Rosen and Regis had arrived, and what he'd heard when scrying. He told of how Regis revealed that he was Lord G'nehon and that he was building an army, and of how Rosen had gotten a message just before Aiden managed to break out of the rebounding box.

"So... Philip is really your... dad?" Megan finally asked, the question burning in her mind.

"I think so..." Aiden sighed. "It sort of makes sense, I guess... There's still some things I have to figure out."

Aiden sighed, feeling as though a weight had been lifted from him. He looked down to where his hand rested on the bench, and realized that Megan's fingers were slowly tangling with his. He looked to her smiling. It was almost awkward, but not as much as he'd imagined it would be. Megan continued to smile back, but then another thought seemed to strike her.

"What happened to you, in the dining hall? I mean, you-"

"The trembling and blinking? It's like a nervous twitch or something that I had when I was a kid..." Aiden sighed. "It almost got me, but I think I beat it."

"We all have our own internal enemies, don't we?" said Megan pensively.

"You seemed pretty shaken yourself," said Aiden.

"I know," she said, shaking her head. "I know I'm not very skilled in combat, and I tried to help, but I froze... I just kept seeing the flames and hearing the voices chant his name..."

"G'nehon's?"

"...I was a little girl again," She sighed. "Praying to Shai that someone would rescue us from the men in white cloaks..."

Aiden grabbed Megan's hand again and held it tight. She composed herself and caught his gaze.

"Are you ready for today?"

Megan pursed her lips. "No, but maybe Regis won't show up... I'm pretty sure Tilli won't be back."

***

As the morning progressed, Aiden and Megan prepared for the day, and agreed that they should say goodbye to Jardun. Soon, they made their way along the winding path in the snow, between buildings and stone huts, until the hospice building came into view. It was small and round, stretching two stories into the air. The ancient wooden door creaked when Aiden entered.

There was no one in the front room, but a small clipboard on the desk listed the room where Jardun was staying. Aiden shrugged, looked around and pressed on through the next door, followed by Megan. A narrow hallway with several closed doors led Megan and Aiden to its very end. It was still so cold in here that Aiden could see their breath in the shadows. He looked to his left and saw a large number '6' on the old wood.

He placed his hand to the door, ready to knock, but suddenly heard voices from within. Megan looked to him confused, but he gestured for her to listen.

"Let it never be said that a Raven Lord can hold a grudge... forever," a voice said in a croaking tone.

It was D'Natis. Aiden pressed his ear closer to the door, followed by Megan.

"You know that I never meant to destroy those eggs..." Jardun's weak voice responded. "I apologize... that I denied responsibility."

"A raven has his pride," D'Natis said with a small cluck. "They were the last Raven Lord eggs in existence after all. My mother had just been killed by a Dingball the week before. What if I had come to your family home, your ancestral grounds, and killed your unborn children?"

There was a pause.

"I am so sorry..." Jardun finally said, a sadness in his voice. "It was so long ago. I was still so young and foolish. I'm also very sorry that the Council never saw it from your perspective... They've been a little too content to let some animal lords just die off. I guess I just didn't want to admit that I made a mistake."

"Thank you," D'Natis said, his tone uplifted. "But there are upsides to my situation. I would have never met Aiden if it hadn't been for our incident. I would have never stayed close to the Guild, nor would Vodin have asked me to stick by Aiden's side all these years."

Aiden felt a warmth in his heart.

"That kid's definitely gotten us into a fine mess," Jardun said, almost laughing. "I don't think I would change things though."

"What about your tail?" D'Natis asked. "I don't mind telling you, from one *animal* to another, that seems to be a shameful thing—to go on living without a tail."

"A greater shame would have been to stand by and watch Lord G'nehon win," Jardun said, very straightforward.

Aiden stepped back, his eyes somewhat glassy, and looked to Megan. She knocked before he'd had the chance. Once inside, they saw Jardun with a smile on his face, sitting upright on a cot in the small room. D'Natis perched nearby on an end table.

"Well, we've come to say goodbye," said Megan with a smile. "Wish us luck?"

"Naturally," said Jardun. "You'll do fine. You've got an excellent friend and helper at your side."

Aiden's face flushed at the compliment, but he shrugged, unsure how to respond.

As Megan bent to hug her mentor, Aiden looked to the raven. "You coming, D'Natis?"

"I think I'll stay behind... with Jardun."

Aiden, not wanting to let on that he fully understood, simply nodded with approval.

In moments, Aiden and Megan were off again. They entered the Great Hall and enjoyed a brief breakfast at the Masters' table. It was a silent occasion, as the entire Guild seemed solemn and pensive about the last night's events.

"Before you leave," said Turlin, catching Aiden and Megan just as they were about to leave the main hall after the meal. "Let's remove that blocking rune."

Aiden raised an eyebrow, then looked to his wrist. "Oh yeah. Forgot I had this..."

Turlin cast a series of runes onto Aiden's wrist, and in moments, the original rune—which Regis had drawn—vanished.

"This is some very complex runework," said Turlin. "But you should have all the properties back. Give it a try."

Aiden drew his rapier and called his buckler to him. They looked as beautiful as ever, and his spirits raised. He thanked Turlin, and in moments, he and Megan were on their way.

As Aiden stepped out through the Otter Gate and into the deep snow, he felt free, if only for the time being. He still felt tired and most of his body ached, but he was somehow lighter, despite knowing what he had to do. Megan smiled at him and then, holding hands, the two of them vanished into nothingness, the fabric of reality imploding around them.

Chapter 24
The Proof

They arrived discreetly in the alleyway just outside of their old hotel, and from there it was only five or six blocks to the entrance to the Underground.

There was certainly a palpable tension inside the main room at Council Hall as everyone shuffled in and found their seats. Everything was much as Aiden had remembered it. The crowd did not seem nearly as noisy as they had been in the past. If anything, there seemed to be whispers and murmurings. Especially at the sight of Aiden escorting Megan to her seat.

He found it hard to translate the looks he was receiving. Had word of his fight with Dorimar gotten out? Had Monadias told people her own version of what happened the night before?

Dorimar was not there, and Aiden smiled. Turlin must have given the Elf the beating of a lifetime. Much to Aiden's chagrin, Regis arrived, looking as refined and pleasant as ever, despite the scars on his face and the limp in his walk. The Senator sneered at Aiden when he caught his gaze from across the room.

When the session began, Lord Fendiloch announced that the President was in attendance, and Aiden glanced around, seeing the secret service agents stationed at all corners of the room. One of the dark-suited men nodded to Aiden as if to warn him about any false moves he may make. The President was in his usual box at the back of the room, sitting patiently.

Aiden glanced around one more time while Lord Fendiloch talked, and he realized that Master Fentl was sitting just seats away from Philip Regis, but Monadias was nowhere to be found. Aiden tried to calm himself, focusing on what lay ahead.

Soon, he told himself. *Soon*.

The first hour or more of the session consisted of the final votes for simple housekeeping issues and minor policy changes. Finally, Lord Fendiloch announced that Regis' proposal would be up for a vote. The room became alive again. The tables and chairs were full of whispers, and soon the entire room was chattering nervously, bringing the tension back in full swing. So much so that Fendiloch could only quiet the room by slamming his cane down on the podium.

When things died down, the President spoke, and even to Aiden's surprise, President Johnson said he was in favor of Regis' proposal. Aiden shook his head.

Of course he'll support something he doesn't even understand, Aiden thought. After all, the President had only been there for half of the sessions. He had hardly heard the opposition, nor acted as if he cared to.

The President personally introduced Senator Regis back to the podium and shook his hand. Regis approached the podium and thanked the President, Lord Fendiloch, and the room, posing as his usual charismatic self—which was hard for Aiden to take, after having seen Lord G'nehon manifest in his battle armor.

"What more can I say?" Regis postured as the room quieted. "I have already laid out many of the fine and logical reasons we need this proposal to be enacted in our Agnec communities. First, here in the US, and soon, the world."

The crowd murmured at this, but Regis ignored it and carried on.

"More than enough has happened to me and my colleagues this past few months to prove my point. More than a few of us have been attacked, and some even, to the point of near-death," Regis said, looking sternly at portions of the crowd. "Someone is out there, not wanting this idea to become law, but I'll say it again, their very actions prove that a united militia is needed. There are forces at work, my friends. Dark forces that would dare to tear communities apart."

Regis paused, looking pensive. Despite trying to keep his tone somewhat stern, there seemed to be a vague sign of desperation in his manner.

"I dare say that some extra tax dollars and funds are worth our protection and our peace of mind, are they not?" Regis said, looking about the room, almost as if expecting an answer. "Are they worth your freedom?"

Aiden bit his tongue, almost painfully.

"I have no further need to go on about this, as I've given you all more than an earful about it for the past many weeks," Regis added, chuckling to himself. "But for the sake of our communities and our continued peace of mind, please consider my proposition. We must unite to build up the Agnec world for the better, and rise to the occasion, rather than crumble from within. I fear that we will simply fade into oblivion if we sit back and let ourselves be overcome by crime and poverty. Thank you," Regis finished with a slight bow and left the stage to a gentle applause.

Aiden could sense the mixed feelings scattering about the room. People glanced to each other with looks of concern, whispering and wondering. Lord Fendiloch took the podium again, looking thoughtful. The old Faun then called Megan to the stage. Aiden watched as Megan slowly took the podium. Her hands were no longer shaking.

Megan thanked the Faun, the room, and even Regis, then began. "Like Senator Regis, I have also said much about my opposition to this act. The Mount Katahdin Guild still opposes. I have given you all plenty of reasons to consider rejecting it: The unprecedented taxation it would bring; the lack of privacy it would give shop owners and local schools; the regulation it would bring to the Guilds; the lack of regulation the militia itself would have... The list has gone on."

Megan sighed gently before her next words. "Tonight I bring before you one last piece of evidence. One that I hope you will consider with an open mind." She swallowed, as if starting to feel a bit nervous again. "The accusation has been brought that Senator Regis is trying to unite both D'Tari and N'Iatari forces, and myself and my colleagues have battled against the notion that the N'Iatari organization has any good intentions—but in fact, has the opposite. In fact, if there's any one N'Iatari representative that we can all look to as a prime example of ill intention, it is the infamous outlaw Lord G'nehon."

The delegates bristled at the name. Several people nodded their heads in full agreement with Megan.

"Tonight, we can prove that Lord G'nehon is fully involved with this proposition, and that he plans on forming an army to conquer the Amblers."

At this, the room broke into a tumult. Several people stood, loudly voicing disbelief, their faces painted with incredulity. Other scattered groups stood to debate with those who disagreed. The remainder of the room chattered and voiced their mixed feelings. Emotions were heavy. Aiden smiled, because Megan was keeping her cool. Regis remained seated, looking almost unsure of what would happen next.

Lord Fendiloch rose to his hooves, just feet away from the stage and shouted, but no one seemed to hear. They certainly couldn't see him, because he was a little Faun after all. The old gray Faun shouted again, slamming the butt of his cane into the floor. A shock wave emanated from the blow, rippling outward and rattling the room, launching delegates off their chairs. Shocked by this, the room fell silent and people quietly returned to their seats.

Fendiloch looked back to Megan, bowing slightly, giving her the floor.

Megan grinned, energized by the reaction. "Thank you," she

told the old Faun. "As my witness," she began, looking back out over the room. "I call Aiden Gailhart."

The walk from the wall to the stage seemed to last forever, and Aiden could sense that all eyes were on him, burning holes in him. Honestly, he no longer cared. It had come down to this.

Regis gazed intensely as Aiden took the podium. After thanking Fendiloch, Megan, and the room at large, Aiden sighed, trying to gather his thoughts. He supposed he should try to be somewhat tactful. After all, he wasn't sure if he had many friends here. In his mind, he recalled the fear of being on trial when his mother had died, but he pushed it aside. This was different. He had proof now.

"Again, thank you..." Aiden began cautiously. "As many of you know, I have been assigned by the Guild to help protect Miss Rohan over the course of her time involved in this Congress. There's been several attempts on her life, all by N'Iatari."

The crowd grew further restless.

"Dorimar killed her attackers, in order to stop us from questioning them. I can sense already that you're unwilling to believe me. But what is the whole truth?" Aiden said, looking out over the crowds. "Is something only truth if it's proven in a court or a trial... Or a Congressional session? Or is truth something that goes beyond the head, and must be known in the heart?"

Various members of the crowd seemed to shift uncomfortably in their seats.

"I can tell you without a doubt the things I know, but you won't believe me until you have proof," Aiden said, thoughtfully. "I can tell you that the N'Iatari are trained to hate D'Tari, and are ingrained with a general disdain for Amblers. You won't believe me until you have proof. Does that mean they are all evil? No. If only this world were so simply black and white.'

"Does that mean that all D'Tari are perfectly good? Of course not," Aiden almost laughed derisively, thinking of Fentl and Monadias. "But according to the principles which were originally laid down to govern Agnecs, D'Tari are usually taught tolerance and charity. Sure I said that D'Tari and N'Iatari powers are similar, but it's the way they choose to use those powers that makes all the difference. I'm not saying they always get it right, but sometimes, even love, peace, and diplomacy are much more preferable than war. Imagine that."

Aiden looked up and reached for a string that hung above his head. He struggled for a moment, but then managed to pull, and down came a white canvas screen. He secured it so that it stretched out on its own, just behind him.

He sighed. "There are things out there beyond knowing with your head. Something I'm learning, I guess," Aiden said, almost forgetting that he stood before the room. As if catching himself, he looked down at his wrist and spoke again, "But tonight, I can give you real proof. Proof that even the smartest of us in this room have been lied to. And almost fooled."

At this, the crowd chattered among themselves.

Aiden took off his wrist watch and studied it for a moment.

"Proof that Senator Regis is not who he claims to be," Aiden said, then paused, winding the watch and placing it gently on the podium before him. "Proof that his agenda for this proposal is destructive and immoral. I'm actually a little surprised that he even dared to show up today... Naturally I'd say he underestimates his opponents. He certainly doesn't think that any of you out there are smart enough to make up your own minds."

While the crowd continued to whisper and shift, Aiden lined up the watch, balanced it so that it aimed at an angle toward the canvas screen, and finally pressed one of the buttons. A semi-transparent image appeared, a near-hologram, glowing and visible from both sides of the canvas. Aiden wound the button until the image grew big enough for the room to clearly see.

The delegates seemed mesmerized by the image, because they soon realized it was moving, and that some noise began broadcasting from the watch to accompany the images. The scene opened from a view inside a cage, staring out into a luxurious parlor room.

"A handful of us went to investigate the connection between Lord G'nehon and the Griftwalkers. They captured me. This is when I was trapped inside a rebounding box at the Griftwalker Estate," Aiden explained, stepping aside so the room could get a better view of the moving images.

Aiden wound one of the buttons so the images sped forward quickly until the desired moment. Nothing seemed to be happening, but then Aiden stopped and let the images play—like a video—at their normal pace. Senator Regis could be seen stepping into the parlor room. Someone else had also walked in with him, but the image looked dark and blurry.

Aiden frowned, knowing that something strange had happened to the images of Tilli Rosen. Aiden could only wonder if it was impossible to record images of immortals...

Aiden pressed another button on the watch, and the footage paused on an image of Regis. He looked and realized that Senator Regis was beginning to stand among the sea of delegates.

"What's the meaning of this?" Regis asked, shouting to the stage. "I did not authorize this sort of thing."

Aiden smirked. "If you've done nothing wrong, then why worry?" he said, staring into Regis' eyes. "Right?"

Regis nodded tersely, fumbling with the top button on his suit coat, and finally sat back down.

"As you can see, and verified by his own reaction, Regis was there," Aden said, looking back to the paused footage on the wall.

Aiden resumed the footage, but fast forwarded some of it. Suddenly, he stopped and simply let it roll.

***

"So come join us, Aiden," said Regis. "And save yourself the humiliation. Not to mention the pain."

Aiden held his head up straight and finally spoke, "Never."

Regis sighed, and began pacing the parlor room. "Well, that leaves us little choice then, but to kill you," Regis said casually.

"What a waste of talent. Good talent's hard to find."

"I've seen what you call talent..." Aiden said in a mocking tone.

"Yes, they are miserable, aren't they? Mostly arrogant. I suppose that's my fault," Regis said, still pacing. "That's why I could use someone like you. Your skill and potential outmatch even my top men. Even my highest commander, *Griftwalker*," Regis paused and shook his head in disappointment, then continued, "Couldn't defeat you, while being aided by others..."

Aiden shook his head in refusal.

"And if power and potential cannot persuade you, well... I don't know what can," Regis added. "Certainly you're not easily persuaded by money. Because at least by joining my forces, you'd be very well paid."

"No," Aiden resolved.

"You think the family fortune is enough to keep this... wonderful estate up and running?" Regis asked, his hands out in a wide gesture to the room.

There came a huffing sound from just outside of the scene.

Aiden shook his head.

"Kill me," Aiden said in a low voice. "I'd sooner do that than join you."

Regis smirked and released a single, mirthless chuckle, as if reflective. "Such a hero. I know it may seem a wonderful escape right now," he said. "But I assure you, when Amblers know our power, they will desire to unite with us. Naturally, we will take our rightful place as first-class citizens of the world. We will flip this world upside down. Let the Amblers live underground! Let them hide away for a while. Eventually, order will be restored."

"And your method is blood shed..." Aiden added.

"Sometimes it is a necessary evil."

"You talk about this as if it's *your* army, and these plans as if they're *your* plans... What about G'nehon? I know you're working with him..."

Regis sighed, then laughed. "Perhaps I pegged you as smarter than I should have. I would have thought you'd have figured it out by now. I *am* Lord G'nehon," he said, his hands out.

"It's so obvious," Aiden muttered in bitter agreement. "You had to keep a public identity to stay active in both congresses, but you needed another public alias to lead the N'Iatari..."

Regis nodded in agreement, smiling.

"Mostly for my own amusement," Regis began, a smile forming on his lips. "I don't mind telling you that I have spies everywhere, and one of them tonight will also act as an assassin... In fact, he may have already done the deed by now."

"What're you talking about?"

"Your friend Megan... Well, she knows too much. I never dreamed that people would actually be taking her side against my proposal. Frankly, your suspicions are right on the money. As I'm sure you've noticed, we are planning an army, and a hostile takeover of any D'Tari forces that might join. I suppose it pays to be a little paranoid sometimes."

***

Aiden paused the footage and stood back. The crowd was silent. Shock had spread across the sea of faces. Aiden looked to Regis, seeing that the man was sweating and on the edge of his seat as if daring to stand up. All eyes turned to the Senator's table, and finally, Regis did stand.

"Lies!" he shouted to the stage. "You've planted this evidence through dark magic!" he said, wiping his forehead.

Aiden couldn't help but laugh, if even a little. "You know as well as I do that I couldn't have done this," Aiden said. "And if you're in doubt, let's ask Lord Fendiloch about it," he added, looking to the old Faun.

Fendiloch, looking suddenly grave, stood to his feet as the crowd grew quiet. "These are memories recorded in the Shai'atic Record, they are not easily changed, especially once set," Fendiloch said, as if having thought well ahead of time that he would be needed for clarification. "These are not illusions, but, judging from the quality of these recordings—and I have seen many like these before—these are true occurrences."

When the Faun bowed and took his seat, the delegates began to talk among themselves. Regis stood speechless for a moment, his face frozen in a perpetual state of feigned confusion, as if masking rage.

"But they *could* be tampering!" Regis shouted, pointing a finger at Aiden. "How do we know that this man is not a powerful dark lord himself, just pulling the wool over our eyes?"

Aiden, feeling himself grow angry but trying to keep his voice calm, said, "Mistress Monadias can vouch for me. I'm a Guild dropout." It was strange hearing himself say it before the room.

Aiden looked down to where Megan sat and could see her smiling from ear to ear. His anger subsided and Megan's smile gave him hope, even as the surrounding crowds grew loud with confusion and discussion.

"I would be willing to go before the D'Tari Council and all the heads of Congress—everybody—and be tested and questioned," Aiden added, yelling above the rising tumult. "I have nothing to hide, Regis! You have everything to hide. Come clean now."

More than half of the crowd had already begun to stand and were moving, like a school of fish, toward where Regis stood. The Senator was frozen there, sweating profusely. Several groups of delegates surrounded the Senator's table, lobbing questions and accusations against Regis. He was speechless.

Lord Fendiloch finally joined Aiden on the stage and yelled, "Silence now!" The roar of the crowd began to fade. "In light of this new evidence, and the fact that someone has just informed me that two accomplices of Lord G'nehon's have admitted that he *is* Philip Regis," Fendiloch bellowed, ignoring Aiden's surprised expression. "We must insist on a postponement of this vote, *and* we must ask Senator Philip Regis to turn himself in to the D'Tari Council for questioning. Mistress Monadias will likewise be questioned in connection with her son-"

Aiden watched as the room rapidly fell into chaos. Several

things all happened at once. The President, looking alarmed, found himself surrounded by his secret service detail and was rushed from the room. Regis jumped away from his table, barrelling through the crowds, knocking delegates over and claiming that he was innocent. Several other delegates in the room stood and ran to confront Regis, many of them brandishing weapons. Still others raced to the outskirts of the room, fearing for their safety.

Aiden had already rushed to Megan's side, now encased in his armor and bearing his blade. They were not far from the circle surrounding Regis. He glared at the man, but the Senator insisted on feigning shock.

"If you're innocent, then why not come quietly?" Aiden yelled over the crowd.

Regis' eyes gave him away. He glanced over and above the crowds.

"Fine then," Regis roared. "I am Lord G'nehon!"

If Aiden had thought the room loud and chaotic before, he couldn't imagine what to call the events that came next. The circle of armed humans, Fauns, Elves, and Dwarves closed in on Regis with a violent crash. A handful of D'Tari also seemed to appear. Aiden had been knocked out of the way by the riotous explosion, and he whirled around, trying to stay on his feet. The noise was deafening in the round room.

Someone caught Aiden's hand and pulled him back on balance. It was Megan. The two of them turned and looked into the chaos, only to realize that Regis was fully armored now, his crimson cloak swinging out behind him as he spun. Swords clattered and shields clanged. Energy explosions blew delegates into the air.

Aiden and Megan couldn't seem to make sense of the mass of bodies swarming the battle, but soon it became evident that it wasn't simply Regis fighting the horde. From the far side of the room, just on the other side of the battle, three other figures had appeared and were attacking people.

Aiden grabbed Megan's arm and they raced around the chaos to get a better look. He grimaced. There were two Elves he had never seen before, but then, there was Master Fentl. The traitor and the two Elves were cutting through the crowds, taking the opposition by surprise. Finally the three broke in and fought alongside Regis, slowly moving, as a unit, back toward the front of the room.

"No!" screamed Aiden. "They're helping him escape."

Aiden raced forward, trying to place himself in their projected path, but it proved difficult as the people around him continued shifting and running, fighting and retreating. Aiden could hardly stand still, let alone see what was happening. One thing was for sure, Regis could have staved off almost the entire room on his own if he'd wanted to. That single thought made Aiden realize how strangely lucky he was to have somehow fought him off back at the Griftwalker Estate.

Many of the D'Tari, Elves, and Dwarves were starting to retreat, as Regis and his companions edged further toward the front of the room. Aiden placed himself in their way, but in the commotion, found himself knocked to the floor by a man escaping a barrage of Elven arrows. By the time Aiden looked up, he realized that the Elves and Fentl were leading Regis out of the room through the door into the main corridor.

Aiden swore and jumped to his feet. He sped through the corridor after the quartet and found himself in the village street before Council Hall, the huge mushrooms in the distance still glowing brightly. Regis was in the street talking to Fentl, while the Elves stood with their backs to the two men, arrows at the ready. Aiden approached them with his blade out. He was surprised that no one else had followed him out through the door.

"Regis!" Aiden yelled. "You're finished. Secret's out."

The Elves stood alert, glaring at Aiden, but they stepped aside as Regis came forward. The Senator's left arm was missing armor, red and bloody, and his head was without a helmet and severely bruised. Nevertheless, he managed to grin as if he had somehow won.

"Call me Lord G'nehon," he said, glaring. "I may have been revealed, but this isn't over."

Aiden rushed forward, and an Elven arrow sped toward him. He caught it with his blade, knocking it aside, launching an energy ball at the Elf. The Elf held up a hand and the ball rebounded, nearly hitting Aiden.

"Farewell, Aiden," G'nehon said. "I realize now that killing you is not in my best interest."

Aiden ignored the man's words and rushed again, this time he didn't see the Elven arrow. A pain tore through his left leg and he collapsed on the cobblestones. The arrow had struck perfectly between the pieces of armor and straight into the flesh beneath. Aiden moaned, but attempted to stand.

"You can't win this one now," G'nehon said. "We'll try again later. Thanks to you, I now have nothing to hide. You were right about that."

Aiden got to his feet, but staggered to a nearby wall where he caught himself. He tried to create an illusion, wondering if he had the strength. Nothing. G'nehon laughed.

"It's more satisfying for me," the man said, starting to turn away. "Knowing that you're aware of our connection, and it will only be a matter of time before you realize you need me. And that you are like me."

Aiden felt the rage mingled with confusion boil over inside, and he raised his blade again, starting to leap forward. His wounded leg collapsed underneath him, and he crumpled to the ground. His rapier fell and clattered away in the opposite direction. He could feel blood running down his face, and for the first time since he'd stepped outside, he felt the stinging cold of a breeze beginning to bite at him. He rolled to his side and glared up at G'nehon, who grinned.

"I trust I've left you plenty to think about."

G'nehon made to turn away, and Master Fentl with him. Aiden grunted and pulled himself up against the wall.

"You can't win," Aiden said, his voice feeling small.

G'nehon turned back, a determined look in his eyes. "Oh don't worry," he said, his voice alarmingly calm. "People will see the truth in the end. They'll come around..."

"So delusional..." Aiden muttered, clutching his leg.

"One man's delusion is another man's motivation," G'nehon said, looking at Aiden's wounded leg and grinning. "I think that should suffice as a reminder, until we meet again."

Aiden growled, seeing only red as he launched small energy balls at G'nehon, but the Elves stepped in to block them. The balls rebounded, and two of them exploded on the stone wall, mere inches from Aiden's head. He coughed as the dust rained down on him. G'nehon laughed and began to walk away under the protection of the Elves.

"Coward," Aiden said, though he suddenly felt very much like giving up.

"A slow suffering is much more enjoyable," G'nehon called back without even bothering to look at Aiden.

"And you, Fentl!" Aiden yelled, watching the group walk away. "You traitor. You... Traitor..."

Fentl did not bother to look back.

As G'nehon, Fentl, and the two Elves walked away, Aiden found himself slumping down against the wall. The pain was tearing at him now, and the cold only made things worse.

The Council Hall's double doors smashed open, and Megan and Lord Fendiloch burst out into the street. Aiden had almost jumped, but he realized he could no longer move his leg. Megan rushed to his side, while Fendiloch stood watching the silhouettes of G'nehon, Fentl, and the Elves in the distance.

"What happened?" Megan said, panic in her voice. "They must've put some sort of spell on the door-"

"He got away..." Aiden said, unable to mask the disappointment in his voice.

Lord Fendiloch turned back to Aiden, both fear and relief seemed to be playing with his ancient features.

"Well..." the old Faun began, sighing deeply. "This cuts through the red tape a bit. I don't think he'll be returning to office any time soon."

***

Aiden was exhausted. A healer attended to his wounds while the crowds of delegates attempted to pick up the mess in the aftermath of battling Lord G'nehon. It was almost surreal, as Aiden watched the crowds pulling together and putting the room back in order. When they were done, things looked almost normal, save for the physical damage to the walls and floors, and the haphazard rows of wounded combatants being treated by healers.

The room grew silent and Lord Fendiloch took the stage again. There were a few moments of solemn silence, and after the chaos that had ensued, this silence was like a palpable peace that had come over them.

"In the wake of this event," the Faun began very solemnly. "Senator Philip Regis is hereby banned from the Shadow Congress. He and every person in connection with him shall be under immediate investigation." At this, the scattered crowds seemed to breath more easily. "The President of the United States has also informed that the Senator is no longer welcome in the Ambler Congress. Rest assured, there will be a full-scale investigation on all fronts."

Aiden could not help but smile.

"After today, we will adjourn sessions for the week," Fendiloch continued. "And will readjourn Monday. I should also add that this vote is postponed until then."

Aiden raised an eyebrow.

"I have called an emergency committee, consisting of delegates from the Mount Katahdin Guild, the D'Tari Council, and the Agnec Court of Justice—to oversee the possibility of reworking and amending Regis' original proposal. We hope to find a middle ground, as well as to keep it strictly in line with traditional Agnec and D'Tari moral standards."

Fendiloch scanned the room, gauging the reactions—which seemed mixed, but considerably more positive—and then he ended on a note of warning: "And in light of this, let us never again be so foolish as to believe with our eyes and not with our hearts. Let us be humble, lest we are overtaken by another, perhaps greater threat. Be alert. Be safe. Go in peace. Thank you."

The crowd did not applaud, but shuffled silently from the hall almost as one entity, their faces solemn. Many people approached Aiden before they left, thanking him for his bravery, while some of them even apologized for not believing him or Megan. Although Aiden was glad for this, he felt awkward just the same. Megan stayed by Aiden's side until the healer allowed him to leave.

Aiden managed to catch Lord Fendiloch before he had gone. Aiden tried to explain how the footage had seemed tampered with, and that the other person in the room was truly Tilli Rosen.

"Mistress Monadias was also there, although the footage didn't show..."

The old Faun looked back at Aiden with honest eyes.

"I want to believe you, and after today, I'm inclined to," the gray Faun said. "But I cannot convince the others just yet. I will keep the footage you have entrusted me with. I will also see if we can locate Miss Rosen. She will be questioned, and perhaps we'll know more. Until more evidence appears, we cannot do much else."

Aiden sighed, having been afraid that Fendiloch would say such a thing, but then another thought struck him: "Who were the two accomplices that you were talking about?"

Lord Fendiloch sighed, as if already tired of dealing with the day's events. "I believe you know both of them, from what I understand. Based on your information, Regnir was captured by Turlin just last night, and this morning, one of our guards caught the keeper of the Gowry Tavern and Inn—he was apparently hired to keep D'Tari delegates from entering the village through his establishment."

Surprised and pleased, Aiden thanked the old Faun. Megan appeared by Aiden's side, and with her help, he limped out of Council Hall and out of the village. Once they found themselves back on the streets above, the two of them jumped back to the woods near the Guild, now dark and heavy with snow.

Once inside the enchanted protection of the Guild, Aiden trudged straight back to his stone hut and collapsed into a deep sleep.

Chapter 25
Moving On

Aiden did not wake until the next day. When he finally opened his eyes, he realized that he was no longer hearing the scream that had haunted so many twilight moments. Instead he saw his mother smiling. He felt refreshed.

He realized that Philip Regis was no longer in a place of public power. Joy flooded his being.

As Aiden dressed, bundling himself up, and stepped out into the cold crisp air, his mind no longer filled with the usual disdain he had once held for the Guild.

He still had questions, but now he knew he would be better able to find answers, rather than run from them.

Along the way to the Great Hall, D'Natis fluttered to Aiden's shoulder, and Aiden felt a familiar warmth. He was actually happy to be here. D'Natis also seemed more chipper than usual.

The two of them met Megan and Jardun in the Great Hall and enjoyed a warm breakfast. Aiden's sudden happiness was cut short when Megan told him that Charlie's funeral was only an hour away. It seemed as though no time at all had passed, and soon they were standing in tight rows beneath a wide, open-air tent covering, surrounded by many others.

The proceedings were brief but solemn. Aiden wasn't sure what to say, and though no one asked him to speak, he almost felt as though he should. He decided against it. He could feel eyes boring into the back of his neck, but he just wanted to remember Charlie right now.

He was surrounded by nearly a hundred students, eleven D'Tari masters, the Headmaster, and others. Everyone was there, even D'Natis had stuck around, despite the cold. Jardun had even hobbled out from the hospice building, under care of one of the healers. The Faun seemed a little off balance, but he managed.

During the procession, somehow all of those memories of Charlie as a kid were painted in a different light. It was true that Charlie had never been the instigator. Sometimes he had even offered to help Aiden, when the others weren't looking. Charlie's greatest victory was finally standing up for something, even against his own brother. Aiden could find something to smile about, just knowing that.

Though everyone was somewhat sad and confused about the events, the inhabitants of the Guild seemed to find hope. Many people spent the rest of their afternoon trying to relax. Several of the students went out to the grounds, playing in the snow, and Aiden saw them from a distance, remembering when times were simpler. He watched Megan's younger sister Dora, bundled in a warm cloak and scarves, having a snowball fight with two other girls.

"Everyone's very proud of you, Aiden," Megan told him, taking his arm. "Don't be so surprised. I am too."

"It's just so strange," said Aiden, scanning the white landscape. "Weird to have people actually congratulating me for once."

Megan laughed, although she stopped when she realized he was serious.

"Also weird to say goodbye to yet another person..."

Megan nodded in agreement, but she perked up. "Despite that, I still think we have reason to hope. I guess we need to really thank Turlin. At the Council's request, he got Regnir and Barty to confess. That was the last bit of evidence for Lord Fendiloch. Turlin sent him a lettercast at the last minute."

Aiden nodded, smiling. "So Monadias didn't object?" he wondered suddenly.

"No one's seen her, so the others took action."

Aiden smiled. Maybe there was hope for the D'Tari after all.

"I was really hoping they would get rid of Regis' proposal altogether..." Aiden said, suddenly remembering Fendiloch's statement.

"Well," Megan mused. "It seems like they're doing it the right way now. Turlin's on the committee, so we know that they're doing something right."

"Yeah," said Aiden, smiling though still pensive. "I guess we'll see."

At that moment, D'Natis alighted on Aiden's shoulder. Silently they all wandered along the snowy pathways between buildings and by white fields as snowflakes floated gently around them. The world felt new and untouched.

At the far end of the grounds, there stood a section of land separated from the rest by an old iron gate. Aiden led them to the gate, pushed it open despite how the frozen metal made his fingers burn, and led Megan into a graveyard. Here there were neat rows of snow-covered graves, each with a heavily frosted headstone designated with ornate lettering. At the far right end of one row, Aiden stopped and looked to a freshly engraved headstone.

It read, "Charles Geroy Glozzman. May he be remembered for his bravery."

Aiden stared for a moment, taking in the sight, not even realizing that he had shed a tear. Megan and D'Natis were equally somber and silent.

After a few moments, Aiden walked down the row to the left, following it to the end. He stopped before another grave, the headstone much older and weather-worn. Wiping away frost and snow from the engraved lettering, Aiden took a stuttering breath. Megan stopped behind him when she realized what they were looking at, and D'Natis hopped up to her shoulder.

The headstone read, "Lisa May Gailhart. She left us too soon. May she forever rest in peace."

Aiden got to his knees, no longer caring that the cold seemed to be eating at his legs, and stared into the headstone. He no longer cared that his face was red with tears. He had never even seen her grave—though he knew its location—and he had avoided coming to the graveyard when he trained with Jardun. Now, he dared to look at it full on.

"I'm sorry, Mom..." Aiden said, between cold gasps. "I know you wanted me to move on... So I am."

After a minute or so, he wiped his face with his sleeve. A renewed sense of hope began to fill him. There was so much more he needed to know, but he was overcome with the reality that his mother could no longer help him. He could also no longer do it all on his own. He had been running on memories, but now, he needed to take her advice.

Aiden stood up, realizing that Megan was crying as well. He held her hand and began to lead her out of the graveyard. He sniffed, steeling himself against the cold, and D'Natis returned to his shoulder.

"That was-" Megan began, tentatively.

"My mother," Aiden said in a soft voice. "I guess I should have introduced you."

"It's alright."

"I think I need to find the whole story," Aiden said, so lost in thought that he didn't realize he was ignoring Megan's reply.

"About...?"

"Well, about my father. About myself. About Lilit, Vodin, the unKing... Everything," Aiden said, as he closed the iron gate behind them and stepped back into the field where the snow was deep.

He reached underneath his cloak and clutched the familiar shape of the ancient locket hanging from around his neck. He was thankful that Regis had not walked away with it.

Megan smiled. "I thought you said the unKing and Lilit didn't exist..." she said, locking arms with him.

"I said a lot of things," Aiden sighed.

"Tonight, I know a lot of people will breath a little easier, thanks to you," Megan said calmly.

Aiden took little credit for what had happened though. All he could think about was how much time he'd lost, and how much further he could go.

About the Author

A writer, artist, musician, producer, podcast co-host, and owner/ operator of Agnec Press, JA Laflin (Joshua Laflin) admits that his first passion is writing, and music takes a close second. He currently lives in Portland, Oregon, where the people are weird and proud of it. When he's not writing, he might be making music as alias Jahshewa El.

For more information:

http://jalaflin.com

http://jalaflin.com/agnec-press

When you purchase this book (as well as any of the ebook counterparts), a percentage of the proceeds goes to the HCMA (the Hypertrophic Cardiomyopathy Association), an advocate and support group for those who struggle with HCM—a heart disease that affects 1 in 500 people and is the largest killer of young athletes.

www.ingramcontent.com/pod-product-compliance
Lightning Source LLC
Chambersburg PA
CBHW060239030726
47493CB00024B/1353

* 9 7 8 0 6 9 2 3 8 1 0 5 2 *